THE PAPRIKA DIARY
A LONELY SECRET

Monica Shepherd

First Edition Design Publishing
Sarasosta, Florida USA

The Paprika Diary - A Lonely Secret
Copyright ©1993 Monica Shepherd

ISBN 978-1506-906-68-3 PBK
ISBN 978-1506-900-03-2 EBK

LCCN 2018947898

June 2018

Published and Distributed by
First Edition Design Publishing, Inc.
P.O. Box 20217, Sarasota, FL 34276-3217
www.firsteditiondesignpublishing.com

ALL RIGHTS RESERVED. No part of this book publication may be reproduced, stored in a retrieval system, or transmitted in any form or by any means — electronic, mechanical, photo-copy, recording, or any other — except brief quotation in reviews, without the prior permission of the author or publisher.

All rights reserved. Copyright under the Berne Copyright Convention, Universal Copyright Convention, and Pan-American Copyright Convention.

This is a work of fiction. Names, characters, businesses, places, events and incidents are either the products of the author's imagination or used in a fictitious manner. Any resemblance to actual persons, living or dead, or actual events is purely coincidental.

For my son Lee.

I wish to thank the following friends and people for their support and contributions which inspired me during the evolution of this book: Ferrie, Frank, Linda, Lucie, Robin, Sara, Heather N, and Heather S.

Special mention goes to Blythe Leszkay, a criminal lawyer who has a genuine passion for helping writers with her legal expertise at www.criminallawconsulting.com.

A belated thanks to my parents for sharing wartime experiences which may live on in
The Paprika Diary - A Lonely Secret.

CHAPTER 1

No Time Like Now

Thursday, March 20, 1952 at 12:05 p.m.
London, England

Like a thief in the night, a mysterious windstorm sneaked into the Royal Borough of Kensington and Chelsea.

A short distance away, the affluent Kensington High Street was business as usual, bustling with double decker buses, honking cars, bulky black cabs scooting in and out of tight spaces as if they were sporty Aston Martins. Shoppers lined the sidewalk, either in a hurry to go somewhere or taking their time to window shop.

In the midst of the organized chaos, a lunch bell rang at St. Mary Abbots Primary School, prompting students in all-grey wool uniforms to scatter quickly in all directions. One skinny seven year old schoolboy, wearing a belted coat over his trouser shorts, pullover, shirt, and tie, would have looked smart if it weren't for a runny nose and sagging knee high socks.

He stopped to buy a bag of sweets with his ration coupon, a by-product of the war still persisting to this day. Confectionery was just one of the many supplies subjected to rationing. If he lost his sweets, it would be another week before he could replace them.

Nothing about the snotty-nosed schoolboy deserved a second look. But appearances can be as deceiving as a smooth-talking politician. He had an alter ego that was anything but ordinary.

Was it Superman, Captain Marvel, or Dan Dare, the popular comic strip space hero?

"My name is Errol Flynn!" shouted a squeaky voice.

Ever since the schoolboy saw *The Adventures of Robin Hood*, he lived and breathed the famous Australian actor. It didn't matter that Errol had aged because he was forever young in the starstruck boy's eyes.

The schoolboy popped three aniseed balls into his mouth for a hit of licorice, and before anyone could say *Sherwood Forest*, Errol was leaping through the air in Robin of Locksley's tights. The only thing keeping the outlaw from his roast venison and coarse red wine was the Sheriff of Nottingham, a dastardly sort with beady eyes who needed to be taught a lesson — never keep a hungry man from his lunch.

"Take that!" said Robin. He lunged forward, carving the letter R into the sheriff's forehead with his gigantic sword.

Beady eyes ran away, his tail dragging between his legs.

"Run like a bloody farty coward!" yelled the outlaw, as he waved a cheery goodbye.

Errol thought his best ever Robin Hood skit deserved a round of applause. He bowed with a cocky smile.

Several shoppers walking by barely glanced at the grinning schoolboy who jumped over sidewalk cracks, brandishing a coltsfoot rock stick.

Sensing the mood of a less than enthusiastic crowd, a defiant Errol said, "Go ahead, I dare you to throw squishy tomatoes at me!" As much as he was enjoying the moment, he could hear someone whispering into his ear. It was the schoolboy.

"I'm late for lunch." The schoolboy broke his pretend sword in half and dropped the pieces into the paper bag.

Errol took the hint, fading into the background with a parting promise, "I'll be back."

When the schoolboy arrived at the intersection of Kensington High Street and Marloes Road, his slowly melting aniseed balls needed to make like Houdini's vanishing elephant. He wasn't supposed to eat sweets before lunch. If his mother finds out, she would give him a spanking with a wooden spoon, a solid one with the clout of a bobby's truncheon.

The hard little buggers didn't take kindly to chewing. He spat them into the bag where the rock stick and more cherry brown globes were waiting to be demolished. The bag was folded twice and placed on the ledge of a nearby lamp post while he pulled up his socks. His mother always checked his pockets, so he couldn't hide his sweets there.

It didn't really matter where he stashed the sweets. Aniseed on his breath was about as subtle as fresh tar pitch, an encounter with the wooden spoon inevitable.

Without warning, the windstorm sprang to life, roaring down the street, knocking over everything that weighed less than ninety pounds and wasn't bolted to the ground.

The startled schoolboy was tossed into the lamp post. He quickly wrapped his arms around the pole.

"Blimey! My lolly!" he shouted in awe as he watched his bag fly into the air and head southwards to change a stranger's day.

The Target

Broken twigs and branches, bubble gum wrappers, cigarette butts, and dirt blew across the royal borough, creating a maelstrom of debris.

Anna Paprika quickly tucked a clutch purse into the pocket of her brown tweed swing coat, and grabbed her eight month pregnant belly with both hands. When she looked up, she saw a mouse flying into a tree. The wind was that strong it had no trouble pushing her short round body forwards, making it difficult to keep her balance as she waddled like a penguin along deserted Marloes Road. She cast her eyes downwards at the chunky heels and peep toes of her black wedgies, thinking she had to get to St. Mary Abbots Hospital without mishap.

When she stepped off the curb, something smacked the back of her head. Caught off guard, her right ankle turned outwards as she put her foot down, causing her to fall hard on her backside. Momentarily stunned, her eyes followed the assailant as it flew into a bush. She wondered if the brown object was another airborne rodent, a bigger one, like a rat. It took her a few seconds to realize it was a paper bag with something inside.

As if things weren't bad enough, the rapidly moving clouds turned charcoal grey, releasing a torrent of rain. Angry drops splashed down Anna's long narrow nose as she lay in the gutter like a wounded animal. Her wavy wind-tousled black hair began to droop around her face. Hastily pulling out a clear plastic rain bonnet from her coat pocket, she fumbled with the straps, fighting against the wind which tried to snatch the hat from her hands. Finally, the straps were tied securely under her chin.

She moaned, "I like English weather!" That didn't sound quite right. She tried again, "I hate English weather!"

She promised to dunk her enormous naked body in a nice hot bath when she returned home. First, she needed to get to the hospital. It was close by, but her tender right ankle and huge belly made it difficult to get up. As she struggled, a sharp twinge reminded her that she wasn't the only person who felt the jarring impact. Up until that moment, she refused to believe the fall did any harm besides bruise her bottom and twist an ankle.

After what seemed like an eternity but was really only a few minutes, the weather makers lost their interest in Anna and moved down the road.

A broken post-war London strutted once again with confident arrogance, the ambitious project to rebuild crowding out the bombed sites. And although the city was busy re-establishing itself as the greatest in the world, it suffered a dearth of knights on white horses. The same could be said of the rare Phantom Rolls Royce III, but as luck would have it, the stately black beast growled to a stop at the curb. A young lady with brunette hair pinned up in loose romantic curls got out and observed the body lying in the ditch. To get a better look, she lifted the veil of her beige cocktail hat to reveal a face of pearly skin, blush cheeks, and arched eyebrows — a face from a Renoir painting.

Deciding it was safe to provide assistance, the lady reached down to take Anna's hand. Pulling a very pregnant woman to her feet was not an easy task, but as soon as Anna was standing on her own, she pointed at the paper bag, curious to know its contents.

The lady glided over to the bush. Picking up the wet bag, her vivid imagination got the better of her. The contents felt like severed fingers and spiders with firm bulbous abdomens.

Anna took the bag and looked inside. A whiff of sweet licorice suffocated her, and she almost choked on her words, "What is that?"

The lady cautiously peeked into the bag, fully expecting to be mortified. She was very relieved to find the three inch stick things didn't belong on a human hand, and there was no mistaking the other items as bulbous spiders. She really should stop reading horror novels.

With a flutter of her delicate nostrils, she said with disapproval, "Aniseed balls." Two words that should never be uttered by anyone so elegant and lovely.

Anna threw the bag at the bush with a dismissive grunt. Then she allowed herself to be transported in lavish style to St. Mary Abbots Hospital.

The Hospital Waiting Room

The elegant lady produced a white lace handkerchief from the pocket of her red wool swagger coat. Dabbing at the black mascara that had dribbled down Anna's face, she spoke with a posh accent, her sentences running into each other, "Better have a doctor look at you what with your condition you're close to that time God Bless."

Anna admired the lady's designer coat which was well fitted at the waist and flared in perky curves towards the hem. It certainly looked more feminine than hers, and if Anna were several inches taller, a swagger coat would be part of her wardrobe too. She turned towards the nursing station, but it was empty. Was she the only patient with an appointment today? When she looked back, her lovely, elegant good samaritan had disappeared like magic. She limped over to a row of scuffed wooden chairs, took off her soaked outer apparel, and sat down. Since there were no magazines to read, two nineteenth century lifts entertained her with absurd creaking, groaning noises even when stationary, which meant able-bodied staff were encouraged to take the stairs.

She took out a compact mirror and a fine-toothed comb from her purse to fluff her flattened hair. Then she tackled the faint traces of mascara trailing down her cheeks. Rubbing her healthy pink skin with a spitty finger, she remembered her landlady's warning that it was definitely going to rain. Too bad the old woman couldn't predict a hell of a wind.

After her face was cleaned up, Anna carefully tucked strands of damp hair behind each ear. Now what? There was still no sign of the nurses, so she looked around at the hospital decor. Three words came to mind — dull, grey, ugly. The depressing atmosphere spread its gloom over people walking along the corridor until they too became dull, grey, and ugly. She remembered what she saw whenever she walked through the dismal place, watching the ambulatory and the infirm, daring to presume their conditions, sometimes witnessing the rattle of death. Beyond the walls, behind thick curtains or chintzy screens lay all manner of people, yet they were basically the same, stripped right down to their human core by illness.

It was now quarter to one. How much more time did she have to waste while waiting for her prenatal appointment that should have started twenty minutes ago? A squeaking noise caught her attention. It was coming from the rusted wheel of a tea trolley being pushed along by a leprechaun of a lady. As the trolley got closer, the smell of freshly brewed tea wafted towards Anna. She inhaled the comforting aroma, and knew what she needed to warm her chilled bones.

"Yoo hoo, a cup of tea over here!"

The tea lady scowled at the impertinence. "Must be a foreigner," she grumbled to herself. Oh well, even with her failing eyes, she could see the young woman was with child. Tensing her lips, she hobbled over on unsteady legs with a cup held precariously in her little hands. "I had to stretch the tea rations, so don't go expecting anything except what you're used to."

Anna ignored the sour look directed her way, but couldn't help noticing the unmistakable odour of stale whiskey leaching from the tea lady's pores. "Thank you," said Anna.

The English appreciated manners, and the Irish were no exception because the tipsy tea lady nodded curtly before returning to her trolley.

Two nurses dressed in crisp white starch strolled up to their station. Anna watched them with impatience. They were always doing a vanishing act on the day of her appointments. When she complained, they'd look at her as if she had a lot of nerve. They never said it to her face, but she knew what they were thinking. She was a bloody foreigner. Putting down her cup of tea, she walked unsteadily towards them on her painful ankle.

The nurses braced themselves for their least favourite maternity patient.

Before Anna could say a word, pain ripped through her belly as if she were being jabbed with a shish kebab skewer. Having endured the hell of a world war, she wasn't going to act like a scared child now, especially not in front of the British. She said in a calm manner, "My baby's coming."

The nurses looked at each other dumbly, unprepared for the sudden change in routine. Sister Mabel Hardcroft, a solid woman who was almost six feet tall with front teeth that would put a rabbit to shame, replied frostily, "Yes, Mrs. Poop-ree-ka?" She held fast to bitter memories of the London Blitz and took it out on Anna by contorting her surname. "Here for our checkup, are we?"

A second jolting cramp pushed Anna into the panic zone, the grim fact her baby wasn't due for another month. She clutched her belly, as if she could slow down the baby's movements. What she really wanted to do with her hands was slap Sister Hardcroft up the side of her head. But having a hissy fit would make her blood pressure skyrocket, so Anna stayed calm. "Did you hear me? I said the baby is coming."

Sister Hardcroft was doubtful. Anna Paprika seemed too casual to be going into labour, and way too forward. "Your due date is more than four weeks away. Perhaps it's gas pain from eating salami or goo-lash."

Anna didn't need to know perfect English to pick up on the sarcasm. Hungarian food was being denigrated by a shrew who ate blood pudding. Coagulated pig's blood. She replied with the popular colloquial twit, but it came out sounding like, "Tveet!"

"What did she say?" Sister Hardcroft turned briskly towards the other nurse.

Sister Smythe was a blonde lanky-haired female who missed out on puberty. She was rail-thin with no curves whatsoever, and since her colleague was an intimidating giant, she responded meekly with a shrug of her narrow shoulders.

A stronger pain hit Anna, causing her to drop the calm act. "I felt down!" Her English vocabulary was still a work in progress, the one-letter mistake confusing the nurses.

"You were depressed?" asked a dubious Sister Hardcroft.

"My baby wants to be born...NOW!"

Curious onlookers stopped to listen to the expectant foreigner sparring words with an imposing British nurse. Suddenly becoming aware of several pairs of eyes on her, Sister Hardcroft said, "Why didn't you say so? I'll find the doctor who's usually on the bloody floor, but never when you need him. Follow me." She reluctantly led Anna to a consulting room.

Anna lay back on an examination table that was more like a slab of concrete, watching with disgust while Sister Hardcroft straightened the line of her stockings. With rationing easing up, it was nice to wear real hosiery again instead of coating her legs with gravy browning and drawing seams down the middle of her imposing calves. She left the room, retracing her steps along the corridor to the nursing station, white shoes squelching with every step.

Sister Smythe was now joined by Sister Constance, a senior Scottish woman with flaming red hair who wore no makeup except for a blot of clashing pink from a three year old tube of lipstick. She always dressed sensibly, the hems of her frocks lower than the current trend dictated.

Sister Hardcroft walked up to them arching the small of her back which swelled an already massive chest into impossible proportions. "That Poop-ree-ka witch is such a right madam trying to embarrass me, a British nurse."

Sister Constance, who wasn't sure what was going on, looked up from a patient's chart. "Come, Mabel. We've all been subjected to Mrs. Paprika's impertinence, but aren't you being rather harsh because she's Hungarian?"

"You mean an ally of Hitler who absobloodylutely bombed London in the Blitz? Not hard enough, I should think. She and the Fuhrer would have made the perfect couple."

Sister Smythe giggled nervously as Sister Constance rebuked Mabel, "Stop your mincing."

"I'm not talking rubbish!" Sister Hardcroft continued her tirade. "She's uppity and looks at me like I'm a charwoman. I won't have that from a bloody foreigner, and a displaced one at that!"

The wall clock struck one o'clock. The nurses glanced at each other, knowing all too well what it meant. Matron was about to make her rounds.

The Boss
Matron walked purposefully towards the nurses station. She was sixty-four years old with sulphur tinted hair permed into tight curls, standing four feet seven inches with an officious manner to make up for her diminutive stature. Her sensitive nose sniffed the air. Trouble was brewing nearby.

Sister Smythe spotted Matron first. Her voice fell to a conspiratorial whisper, "It's the Medusa," their pet nickname for her.

Having no desire to be confronted by the Medusa, Sister Hardcroft rushed off in the opposite direction. "I better find the doctor for our right madam with the stupid name."

Spotting the quickly retreating Sister, Matron stopped at the station. She demanded, "What's going on here?"

Long and Scrawny
Anna rocked back and forth in excruciating pain. Attempting to ride the cramps took all of her attention until liquid oozed from her womb, the unsettling thought of blood dripping down the sides of the table.

The Lords's prayer chanted inside her head as if she were back in school being lectured by black-clothed nuns with prune faces, or in confession washing away the sins her father insisted his outspoken firstborn must have committed. She would complain that she didn't do anything wrong, and he'd give her the look, a reminder that juvenile thoughts were not excluded from sinning. Huddled in a dark claustrophobic box imitating a vertical coffin, she used to confess about trifling things like painting her big toenails with her mother's red nail polish, and wondered why the priest never said it's okay to do that. Then she'd sit at her favourite pew by the exit to recite the mandatory ten Our Fathers and five Hail Marys.

Sticking her hand into a pot of boiling water was preferable to dealing with the pain of labour. It was so bad that she screamed like she was trying to expel an alien life force, her jet black hair dripping with perspiration.

Matron and the nurses sprang into action when they heard the all too familiar sound of a desperate female trying to push a gigantic object out of an incredibly tiny hole. They flocked like a gaggle of geese into the consulting room where a baby was being born. With large knotty hands, Matron grabbed the protruding head in the nick of time.

The brand new mother suffered a nasty perineal tear before collapsing on the table.

Matron held up the crying baby as if she were announcing to God, "A wee bonny lassie!" She mentally calculated the height and weight of the bundle in her hands. "Oh my, what a long and scrawny thing."

The birthing pain was already forgotten as Anna smiled lovingly at the gooey baby with downy auburn red hair. By the time she reached the second trimester, she was convinced that a baby girl was snuggling inside her. Because she was absolutely certain, she secretly began to call the baby, Marika. It was a pretty Hungarian name which rhymed perfectly with Paprika. Marika Paprika.

The hospital door opened to reveal a privileged man around sixty years old wearing a white coat and holding a pair of coke bottle glasses.

"Late as usual, Mr. Bennett." Knocking the stuffing out of doctors was a Matron's prerogative.

Mr. Bennett slipped on the coke bottle glasses with his customary aloofness. "I was doing rounds."

Not at all impressed, Matron lifted her left eyebrow to irritate the pompous doctor even more.

Anna held out her hands to hold Marika, but the baby was whisked away.

Matron shook her head. "We have to put baby in an incubator." She patted Anna's hand consolingly. "Don't worry, dear, it's routine for babies born before their due date. The incubator will keep baby nice and warm." Matron was as certain as all the other nurses that their Hungarian patient couldn't possibly understand the English vernacular. She boomed, "Do you understand anything I said, Mrs. Paprika?"

Anna didn't appreciate the putdown, and said rudely, "What do you think?"

Matron pursed her lips, but said nothing. If she wasn't already aware of Anna's combative personality, she would have been offended.

Anna looked at the doctor sitting between her legs. She wore sheer nylons rolled down to the knees, the only way her bloated limbs could wear hosiery. She wasn't embarrassed and never had been about her naked body. If anything, it was the doctor who appeared to be on the verge of doing two things, apologizing or bolting from the room.

Matron said, "Baby needs to be monitored for signs of respiratory distress. If this was a few years ago, I'd be very concerned because premies had a poor survival rate. Don't you worry now, your baby has mature enough lungs at thirty-six weeks." Matron pumped her chest and took a deep breath before exhaling a whooshing sound. "Good lungs." Then she left the room.

Anna repeated, "Good lungs." Her baby was going to be all right, the only outcome Anna would accept.

Her newborn could have fallen on the floor if the nurses were any slower. It wasn't her nature to be as insipid as a mouse. But pregnancy made her feel motherly and plain old nice, except when she had to deal with the nurses. How did she feel now? She wanted to stick an apple in Sister Hardcroft's mouth and shove her into a hot oven.

Speaking of roast pig, the nurse appeared at the door and pulled her shoulders back to impress the doctor with her huge rack.

"Carry on," responded Mr. Bennett, without looking up. As he stitched up his patient, his sluggish hormones were vaguely aware that a female, all tits and teeth, was strutting her stuff. In the beginning, he had no problem with the variety and abundance of female body parts. It was titillating, and the subject of many locker room jokes with his equally titillated colleagues. However, the constant exposure jaded him until he felt nothing but total boredom.

"It...was...not...gas...pain," Anna sputtered along like a car running out of petrol.

The Sister's pale cheeks burned bright pink. She had to put up with a dressing down from Matron, but wasn't going to put up with one from a patient who was a foreigner to boot. "I beg your pardon," she said huffily.

Glasses now tucked inside his pocket, Mr. Bennett was on his way out when he stopped to look enquiringly at the Sister. Then he noticed his left shoe staining the linoleum floor with a partial red footprint, and began to scrub the offending sole across the floor to remove the blood. Better make a quick getaway before Matron lectured him again. "I must attend to other matters."

Sister Hardcroft smiled sweetly at the departing doctor. Being a married woman, she would never dream of getting intimate with another man, but it was such fun to flirt with the doctors, especially one who appreciated a well-built woman. After all, she couldn't get her husband interested in her breasts anymore, even when she smeared them with marmalade one anniversary. All she got for her creative effort was a pair of sticky mounds. She continued to smile until the door shut.

The two women were alone in the small room which suddenly felt like a coal mine filled with noxious methane gas and white damp. Toxic mines make people do strange impulsive things. Anna was no exception as she dipped the fingers of her right hand in a nearby pool of blood. She flicked it at the pristine white figure.

Sister Hardcroft stared at the red stains covering her chest. She shrieked, "Buggeration!"

Anna opened her big hazel eyes, reminding the stunned Sister of a baby lamb. "I was trying to get the blood off my fingers," she said insincerely.

The nurse's temper bubbled over like lava from an erupting volcano. She angrily flung her arms into the air as she stormed out of the room, shoving the heavy door all the way open. It squeaked in protest.

Anna didn't have to wait long for Matron to show up with an orderly and a trolley bed. She wagged a crooked finger at the new mother. "You've been a rather naughty patient."

As she was transferred to the trolley bed, Anna gave a firm downward wave. It was her way of saying she didn't care what Matron thought, and she intended to set the record straight. "It was your nurse who was rather naughty."

As far as Matron was concerned, the matter was now closed. "I have already dealt with Sister Hardcroft. End of subject," she said snippily.

Matron marched beside Anna's bed as it was rolled down the corridor and crammed into one of the two lifts that creaked, rattled, and shook during its reluctant ascent. She silently urged the rickety contraption to get to its destination. When it finally reached the maternity floor without stalling, she breathed a sigh of relief. "Let's get you settled."

Six hulking metal beds dominated the putty-coloured ward that was to be Anna's home for the next several days. Wall radiators pinged with the effort of keeping the large room warm while the windows vibrated and crackled ominously from the wind hitting the ill-fitting panes.

Matron said, "The loos are at the other end of the corridor." She pointed at the garish light fixtures. "Out at nine sharp. Do you understand, Mrs. Paprika?"

Here we go again. "Yes, of course I do," Anna said indignantly.

Matron tapped her sharp white cap and walked smartly out of the ward.

Three other beds were occupied with new mothers. A woman with freckles and shoulder length burnt orange hair smiled pertly from the bed opposite Anna. Beside the freckly woman was a plump girl popping a steady stream of Maltesers into her mouth.

There was no mistaking the third woman's nationality. Every inch of her said sassy Irish country lass. She was methodically brushing out her waist long, coal-tar hair as she turned to look at Anna with amazing green eyes. "How'd you do, I'm Colleen. Seventy-six, seventy-seven..." She stopped brushing. "What do you think of the Matron? Quirky, aren't she? Acts like a drill sergeant in a Yank movie throwing all of her fifty pounds around. As a tot, I used to have nightmares about creatures at the foot of my garden who looked just like her." She resumed giving her hair a hundred strokes. "Seventy-eight..."

The plump girl corrected Colleen in a soft girly voice, "I think Matron weighs at least seventy pounds."

Colleen said matter-of-factly, "Never mind, dearie. When you get your first wrinkle, you'll also get the fine art of blarney and learn to appreciate it, not correct it."

The others laughed which brought a double blush to the plump girl's face.

Anna lay against the pillow, feeling a prick in the back of her head from a brittle poultry feather. As she watched the falling rain, the chatty mothers began to compare the cutest doctors. They only stopped when the medicine cart rolled up to offer a tiny paper cup of pills to kill the discomfort of delivery. Anna was the only one who refused medication. The pain will be gone soon enough. Her husband better hurry up and get there because she was yawning herself into a slumber. Stretching her arms over her head to release the kinks in her neck and shoulders, she thought about their baby lying in an incubator, hoping the nurses were taking good care of her.

The windstorm was withering away, leaving behind the pitter patter of rain which drummed softly against the window panes, encouraging Anna into a sleep where time ticked backwards.

CHAPTER 2

Paprika - More Than a Spice

Hungary - 1939 to 1948

The Past
Hungary suffered the loss of significant territory in the first world war, and continued to feel the loss like an amputee without limbs. It was Hungary's Achilles heel and Hitler knew it. Trapping the country into becoming Germany's Axis partner in World War II, he returned some of the lost land to its rightful owner, demanding collaboration with threats of military intervention and economic pressure. Already catapulted by the fear of the Soviet Union taking away its independence, Hungary reluctantly joined Germany in 1940.

The Fuhrer insinuated himself into Hungary's population, planting Nazi officials in high positions. He ridiculed the country's military capabilities, and stole its natural resources. The Jewish population was cruelly targeted with dehumanizing laws, some of which expropriated their homes and businesses, and prohibited marriage to Christians. By 1942, the Final Solution was delivering Hungarian Jews to concentration and extermination camps.

Jews weren't the only targets. Hungarian intellectuals, political dissidents, civil servants, clergymen, gypsies, and homosexuals were calculatingly tortured, murdered, worked or starved to death in camps through a parallel reign of terror.

Random people between the ages of twelve and seventy were pulled off the streets, or dragged from their homes at gunpoint and forced into hard labour digging ditches, building roads, bridges. Others were shanghaied into military service without warning, leaving loved ones to agonize over their sudden disappearance.

Hitler pushed, but the plucky Hungarians finally reacted with anti-Germany demonstrations before turning desperately to the Allies for aid. Secret peace negotiations proved fruitless when Germany learned of the betrayal. To punish Hungary, Hitler decided to occupy the country in March of 1944.

Roll with the Punches

Anna Gonda refused to give up. As long as she was alive, she would carry on like every other Hungarian. Her passion for writing mystery romances blossomed into a career that helped her meet many talented writers supporting each other during dangerous times. It wasn't long before she began to think big with a plan to start a publishing business after the war. Until then, she bided her time by plotting her latest novel, or writing newspaper and magazine articles, the latest piece a tribute to her beloved hometown of Eger.

The best way to describe the place where she grew up was to compare it to an orchestra of lilting flutes, magical harps and laughing trombones. That was before the war. Nowadays, it was mostly clashing cymbals and weeping violins.

Located northeast of the cosmopolitan capital city of Budapest, slower-paced Eger was a historical magnificence. It was one of the most beautiful cities in Europe, famous for its Baroque palaces, Turkish minarets, and thermal baths. It was also famous for wine, like the spicy red in-your-face Egri Bikaver, known as Bull's Blood.

Hungary's pain and glory from centuries of battles could be felt by walking through Eger's hilly cobblestoned alleys and streets, pounding feet releasing the spirits of ancient times. In the sixteenth century, the Turk invasion turned the city into the most important northern outpost of Muslim power for a hundred years. Much of that time could still be felt several hundred years later.

Anna cherished her gentle brother, eighteen year old Horka, a good natured young man with solemn brown eyes who was barely taller than his older sister. He was already a master craftsman creating beautiful objects from raw wood. They were both raised to be self-sufficient with a vegetable plot and a modest vineyard behind their small house. When Anna relocated to Budapest, Horka held the fort until his sister's weekend trips back home.

Because food was scarce, the Gonda's meals consisted mainly of fresh vegetables from the garden and wonderful smelling bread baked in their kitchen stove. Anna occasionally brought home rare treats, her local fame as a literary figure giving her access to black market items such as perfume, cigarettes, meat, chocolates.

Margit, the children's practical mother, turned the meat into hearty soups of goulash seasoned with layers of flavour — sweet paprika, green peppers, onions. A favourite dish was tok, a fusion of vinegar-tanged shredded marrow, sour cream, and generous flecks of dill, transforming the insipid vegetable into a satisfying meal. Bartered flour made the staple dumplings and bread. Pork fat was a popular delicacy, slit lumps sprinkled with paprika and salt, morphing into crackling over an open fire. Homemade wine ended the day on a high note.

Margit often thought of the children's father who died a few years ago from a heart attack. He had been proud of his firstborn even if she was too adventurous. It was a sentiment shared by Margit who refused to give Anna a swelled head, however the occasional compliment had a way of slipping by her.

"If I weren't your mother, I'd wonder if you're really a man dressed in women's clothes," she told Anna. She had no doubt that her daughter was bolder than the average male.

"A woman doesn't need to be a man to be strong," said Anna.

Although Margit looked like the archetypal mother, giving birth and raising kids, she was a walking miracle. Prior to the war, she had been given a death sentence after exploratory surgery revealed tumours throughout her body.

"Take her home, we can do nothing for her," the surgeon said to the heartbroken family.

As Margit grew weaker, she could only tolerate her vineyard's succulent purple grapes which burst inside her mouth with tangy sweetness. To keep her distracted from many painful symptoms, the children played her favourite music on a treasured phonograph player. It was one of the few gadgets her husband put together from bits and pieces that actually worked. Anna and Horka took turns spending the evenings in Margit's bedroom, joining her in the evocative world of classical musicians and gypsy violinists. When day broke, the children would take her to Eger's hot spas, their healing attributes a significant part of her life now that she was dying from cancer.

The unexpected occurred within six months of the terminal diagnosis. Margit was cured. Horka thought God worked His magic through the powerhouse grape and soaring musical notes that took Margit on many rapturous journeys. Anna was convinced that the hot spas dissolved the tumours. Being a mother, Margit had the most common sense. It was all of the above driving her strong will to live for her children.

The Big City
Anna spent most of her time in Budapest.

In the Middle Ages, long before unification into one city, Budapest was two military fortresses known as Buda and Pest, both built on either side of the Danube River. The Mongols, during the thirteenth century, conquered the two settlements. A few hundred years later, the Turks occupied Buda, but were decent enough to introduce paprika, coffee, and Turkish baths, when they weren't busy pillaging and plundering.

After liberation by a Christian army, more battles, revolutions, two world wars, Budapest was drenched in bloody history.

It was no wonder that Magyars were prone to alcoholism and depression. However, there was no denying the city was worth fighting for. The courageous people loved sports and the arts. Family meant everything. Cultivating friendships with great enthusiasm, they often dined in groups at the many charming cafes throughout Budapest. When people wanted to ease their aches or cure an illness, a visit to a healing spa was called for, since the biggest thermal water caves in the world were located below the capital city.

Anna lived in an apartment overlooking the mighty Danube River. Although it was well appointed with tall windows, high ceilings, crystal chandeliers, rich dark wood trim, it was not hers. The apartment belonged to a Jewish doctor and his family who were dragged out of warm beds late one night by German soldiers, and sent to a concentration camp. She was shocked when she saw the cupboards flung open, their contents tossed on the floor in search of treasure. She almost refused the lodgings filled with desperation of the family's forced flight. In the end, she took the apartment because if someone else got it, the remaining possessions would be sold or destroyed. Everything that could be moved was locked up in a backroom waiting for the day she returned the apartment to the Jewish family.

Standing on the apartment balcony, gracefully decorated with curves of black wrought iron, Anna avoided looking at the many bodies frozen in the winter ice, whole or in gruesome parts. Overwhelmed by smoldering fires, endless piles of masonry rubble, shattered glass, broken water mains, and downed telephone lines from wave after wave of Allied air bombings, she switched her focus to the remaining Baroque castles, Gothic churches, and Turkish minarets still standing in defiance. A reminder that Budapest will always be a contender for the most stunning historical city in Europe.

The Maid

Zsuzsi was a short roly poly woman with brutal eyebrows, frizzled brown hair, and a tinny voice which showed no preference. It irritated all ears. Anna first met the bizarre woman banging on her apartment door, proclaiming she will work for the famous author. She bullied her way inside like a strutting rottweiler to make a four-star meal for Anna.

That's how she became the maid.

Zsuzsi was a smoke addict. She did everything with a cigarette dangling from her lips — cooked, cleaned, slept, bathed — the list was endless. Since Anna had no desire to burn down her apartment, it was her duty as a responsible citizen of Hungary to remove the cigarette stuck to her sleeping maid's lips. She pleaded with Zsuzsi, "Go to bed with a man instead." It was all about compromise, knowing the maid hated men, and only had sexual relations once a year on New Year's Eve to satiate the revolting urge, as she liked to put it.

"It's easier for you to throw a cigarette out the window than a man," Zsuzsi retorted before cracking up at her own humour with a phlegmy hacking cough.

February 1945

Broken Dreams

Budapest heard rumours that the long war was now in its final phase, but seeing was believing. The waiting and hoping continued as the city was indiscriminately carpet-bombed by Allied air fortress bombers. Blaring air raid sirens frequently pierced the days and nights to warn of approaching enemy planes, often as many as two hundred flying low in precise formation.

Zsuzsi couldn't get used to the stomach churning sirens and the sinister whistling of dropping bombs followed by the head-pounding noise of collapsing buildings. The tenants in Anna's four storey apartment building would march dutifully down to the marginal safety of the basement, all except Zsuzsi. The strident sirens set off an emotional reaction, evoking visions of a mourning Arab woman dressed in black, her tongue gyrating wildly inside her mouth. The flipped-out maid ran from room to room, tizzily screaming at inanimate objects, "The bombs are coming! The bombs are coming!"

Her strange behaviour didn't end there. She would rush to the balcony and flash a torch at the sky, her free hand rolled into a tight fist which she shook at the droning planes while cursing through cigarette-puffing lips. What with Zsuzsi lighting the way for the bombers, it was a mystery to Anna why her building remained untouched. The immediate area was surrounded by massive piles of ruined structures.

During the latest frenzied episode, a slap from Anna induced an avalanche of tears. The only thing left to do was drag the hysterical maid down to the shelter. They sat solemnly in the dark, Zsuzsi sobbing, sharing a small loaf of bread with the other tenants.

That's when Anna decided she was sick of Zsuzsi's tantrums. "I'm ordering you to go and stay with your family in Szeged." The distant town was located south of Budapest which meant it was not the main focus of Allied forces.

Zsuzsi shook her head defiantly. "I am your faithful servant! I will not leave my duties!"

One week later, she was nowhere to be found. There had been some particularly heavy bombing over Budapest that week, and Anna thought her maid had become a casualty during a shopping trip.

Anna prayed that Budapest won't be destroyed like Dresden, a German city noted for its universities housing innocent students who died by the thousands. A city where women with babies and children were set on fire and burned to a crisp by the massive amount of bombs that dropped on their hiding places as they cowered in fear.

When the war turned against the Germans, they blew up all of Hungary's bridges in their retreat. With its delicious food and exuberant hospitality, a demolished Hungary was no longer the entertainment centre for the more conservative countries along its borders. Budapest was destroyed as the Soviet army and Allied bombers advanced into the capital city.

On May 7, the war ended for Germany. The Red Army took control of a Hungary that lost its regained land and independence. When the Japanese surrendered on August 15, World War II was over.

The Hungarians were in a state of shock when they learned hundreds of thousands of their people were dead, including the Jewish doctor and his family. Property damage was on the scale of a cataclysm with the complete destruction of the Danube fleet, bridges, railways. Half of the industrial plants were gone. Livestock and agricultural machinery went to the same graveyard.

Anna managed to avoid the roving German soldiers harbouring immoral purposes throughout the war, and thought she was safe when the Soviets were welcomed as liberators. But she wasn't prepared for what happened during the liberation.

After the Soviets killed straggling German soldiers and desecrated them by chopping off their legs for their quality boots, it was the average Magyar's turn to be brutalized, killed, or deported to harsh labour camps in the Soviet Union.

One day, Anna decided to visit a male journalist who lived in Budapest. They recently had a brief romance lasting one week before realizing it wasn't going to work. They didn't enjoy sex with each other, but it was no reason to end their friendship.

Anna knocked on the door of his house, a simple two storey dwelling with numerous bullet holes on the exterior walls.

A lean young man, average height, with a generous smile and neatly parted brown hair welcomed his guest with kisses on the cheeks.

"Hello Gyorgy."

"Come see my cellar."

A curious Anna followed Gyorgy downstairs to his cool, dark musty cellar which used to double as an air raid shelter during the war.

Cellars looked the same everywhere. Gyorgy's was no different except, in the back and out of the way, an entire wall of wine bottles nestled inside cubby holes. He had all the materials needed to make wine, including oak barrels.

A tub of large green grapes caught Anna's attention. "Do you want me to squeeze your grapes?" She knew a thing or two about fermenting wine.

"I thought we agreed no more sex."

Anna was confused. "What?" All of a sudden, she realized he was teasing her. She smacked him on the shoulder.

Gyorgy couldn't resist a chuckle. "That's why I still like you. You don't know when you're funny."

Anna was about to say something when she stopped to listen to loud banging at the front door. "What the hell?"

"Quiet!" Gyorgy clapped his hand over Anna's mouth. He whispered in her ear, "Soviet soldiers."

They listened to the door being kicked in with boots and rifle butts, the boisterous shouts of drunken men ransacking the upper floor. After a few minutes, Gyorgy thought the soldiers were leaving, their heavy footsteps retreating. He was wrong. The intruders found the staircase to the cellar and were trudging down the steps.

Gyorgy grabbed Anna and dropped her into an empty barrel. After placing the lid on top, he rushed over to the wine bottles, just as the intruders reached the cellar door.

Four ragged Russian soldiers, their uniforms splashed with food stains and vomit, found the homeowner walking towards them, holding a bottle of golden white wine. They waved their rifles at him, shouting in Russian, "Bring us your women! Your girls!"

Gyorgy put on his game face, trying not to show them he was scared shitless, especially for Anna who was just an arm's length away. He knew Russian, and replied, "There are no girls or women here. I'm alone."

A square bulldog faced Soviet aimed his rifle at Gyorgy's head, his breath reeking of cheap alcohol and puke. "I'm going to shoot you."

Gyorgy thought about begging for mercy, but knew it won't do any good. It would make him dead quicker.

Anna crouched inside the tight barrel not more than five feet from where the Soviets stood, forced to listen to the uncontrollable thumping of her heart. She silently begged God to keep her friend alive, and to get her out safely.

When one of the other soldiers approached Anna's hiding place, Gyorgy had to act fast. In desperation, he offered, "Take all the wine you want." He pointed towards the cubbyholes to lead the soldiers away from the barrel.

The drunken Soviets turned to stare at the gold mine waiting for them. Bulldog face snatched the white wine out of Gyorgy's hand. After shoving him back and forth, the soldiers left with as many bottles as their hands and pockets could carry.

Anna thanked her lucky stars for saving her from being gang raped. One man intent on rape she could handle, but several soldiers was another story.

May 1946

The Intruder

Late one night, twenty-four year old Anna's front door handle jiggled furiously. Someone was trying to break in, and not doing a quiet job of it. Gathering her courage fortified from years of living in a war zone, she stopped typing and put down her cigarette. As far as she was concerned, there were only two choices to make. Neutralize the intruder with a blow to the temple or suffer a revolting fate. Well, there was no way she was going to suffer a revolting fate, not without a fight. She quickly grabbed a heavy crystal vase.

The intruder must have found the spare key hidden under a statue in the hall because Anna could hear it being inserted into the key hole. As the door flung open, an overstuffed, tattered brown suitcase flew across the entrance and into the living room where it fell flat on the floor. It popped open to reveal wrinkled women's clothes.

Zsuzsi walked nonchalantly past her astonished employer who teetered on the brink of crushing the woman's head. Picking up Anna's resting cigarette, she placed it between her nicotine-parched lips. A marathon puff was dragged into her starving lungs as she sauntered towards the small figure struggling with a heavy vase.

Anna brushed off the near calamity with a stern nod of her head. Expecting the obligatory kiss on the cheeks, she leaned forward.

Zsuzsi ignored her boss as she flicked embers into the vase before heading to the kitchen to cook a pot of noodles and cheese curd.

Anna put the vase down and returned to her desk. Not one word passed between the two women as things returned to normal in the apartment.

February 1948

Best Friends
Kati Paprika was twenty-five and a novice actress who split her time between acting jobs and family obligations at her mother's restaurant in Eger. She was also Anna's best friend. Side by side, the two women were remarkable opposites. Petite Anna's raven hair and intellectual nature clashed with passionate Kati's tall fair physique. Despite having an incredibly beautiful woman for a girlfriend, Anna liked her because she was anything but pretentious. Besides, it wasn't Kati's fault she grew up to be a slender five feet nine inches tall with perfect breasts and exquisite bone structure, a vision culminating in deep cobalt eyes and generous golden blonde hair resting in a soft wave on wide shoulders. Anna told Kati to wear a bag over her head when they went out together, or nobody would notice the writer friend. Kati responded by insisting Anna keep her mouth shut, otherwise Kati would sound like an imbecile. From the first day they met inside the Paprika Restaurant, they made each other laugh a lot, the glue that bonded them together.

One day, in Kati's bedroom above the restaurant, the two women puffed on cigarettes while they discussed buying hats to shake away the blahs of a winter day.

Suddenly, Kati jumped up. "I have a brilliant idea. It's time for you to shave," she announced ceremoniously.

"Don't be ridiculous. Hungarian women don't need to shave because hairy legs and armpits belong in our culture. And guess what, the men don't care."

Kati pretended to be horrified. "Anna Gonda, forever the Magyar peasant. I bet you have hair sprouting around your nipples. I don't care if the men don't care. God only knows why we females feel compelled to paint our lips, lengthen our lashes, dye our hair. We totter around on high heels which lengthen our legs and pinch our feet, but we draw the line at shaving." With cigarette in hand,

Kati plunged towards the window, threw it open, and stuck her gorgeous head outside. She berated the startled passersby, "I despise hairy armpits!"

As if that wasn't dramatic enough, she was back in her bedroom, announcing, "I gag at the sight of silk stockings smushing up the leg hairs."

"The communists think that silk stockings, nail polish, and lipstick are petty bourgeoise."

"You forgot hats and ties, but who cares what they think!" Kati scrunched up her fine straight nose as she triumphantly said, "Let me bring you out of the medieval ages!"

Anna chuckled, "When did you come to such a daring decision?"

"Yesterday."

"What happened?"

"I shaved my underarms and legs."

"Who led you out of the medieval ages?"

Without any shame in her voice, Kati said, "Vogue, the American magazine."

"I'm impressed," Anna said, tongue-in-cheek.

Kati ignored her friend as she rolled up her right pant leg and seductively rubbed her bare skin. "Whenever I see a hairy leg or armpit, I'm repulsed."

"Even a man's?"

"Hah, hah. What do you say? Don't tell me that Anna Gonda, the famous writer, is a chicken." Kati began to flap her arms and make demented chicken sounds, "Bwuk, bwuk, bwuk..."

Anna rolled her eyes at the woman's silliness.

Kati stopped bwuking and dashed into the bathroom. She returned with a razor, brandishing it in front of Anna's nose.

Finding it hard to say no to her bothersome but endearing friend, Anna reluctantly took the razor.

"If you don't like shiny smooth legs, the forest will grow back before you know it."

Anna managed a weak smile. After all, she could be a good sport if she wanted to be. Handing her cigarette to Kati, she stripped down to brassiere and panties. She gingerly sat on the edge of the cold porcelain bathtub and lathered her legs with soap, the long handled razor poised over her right ankle. Hairy legs were a big deal. How stupid does that sound? There was no more hesitation as she mowed down the old foliage, ending up with a few nicks on her shin. Running her hands up and down her legs, she enjoyed the silkiness gliding under her fingertips. "I hate to say it, but there's no turning back now."

Kati produced a satisfied look that said, *I told you so.* Then she attempted to creep out Anna with a deep sinister voice, "Welcome to the dark side, A.G."

"Melodramatic as usual, K.P. Why don't you put on a short skirt and show off your legs?"

It was Kati's turn to roll her eyes. "Have gypsies taken your mind? Mama would kill me." She laughed, knowing she was on her way to making Anna crazy. "Let's buy a couple of hats. My treat."

The Hidden Room

Two hours later, they were back in Kati's sitting room depositing their purchases on her coffee table. Before Anna could sit down, Kati promptly took her friend's hand, leading the way along a dimly lit hallway and down dark creaking backstairs into the hot bustling kitchen of the Paprika Restaurant. Salamis, sausages, strings of fresh garlic and onions hung on hooks imbedded in the ceiling. Two short, stocky cooks wearing white aprons splashed with stains scurried around huge pots of food. Fish, meat, and poultry were less scarce these days, but not yet fully adequate to feed a hungry nation. In order to accommodate all the customers who came to the restaurant, the pots were plenty on rich sauce but low on protein.

Kati walked through a secluded alcove off the kitchen, stopping in front of a floor-to-ceiling cupboard. Before Anna knew what was happening, her friend rolled the cupboard away to reveal a door.

Anna was intrigued. What did the Paprikas hide behind the mystery door? Trinkets of gold, a Monet painting, or perhaps a pile of weapons stolen from dead soldiers?

Kati flung open the door.

Anna was more than surprised when a melange of sweet smells billowed towards her. Rich chocolate, freshly ground poppy seeds, and moist vanilla sponge cakes scented with cherry and apricot brandies tantalized her nose.

Standing inside the small room, they were confronted by two black wrought iron baker's racks filled with the most delicious pastries Anna had ever seen.

The two women stood in reverent obedience until Kati finally said, "Rationing is officially over in Hungary!" She proceeded to do a happy little dance with a wiggle of her hips and a jiggle of her breasts.

Anna laughed at the comical sight. "What if food is rationed again?"

"You're not the only one with black market connections. I use mine to trade Mama's jewelry for supplies."

"Why a hidden locked room?"

"It's a perfect place to hide opulent desserts during rationing — north side, no windows, cool temperature. And it keeps meaty, fishy smells from tainting the pastries." Speaking in a whisper, Kati said, "This is our secret. The commies don't need to know this room exists."

"A good place to hide a body," Anna whispered back in jest.

"Such a fertile imagination, my writer friend." Kati smacked Anna on the rump. "You are looking at an order for a big party tonight, but a few pastries won't be missed."

Kati reached for a slice of dobostorta, a multi-layered sponge cake filled with hazelnut cream and topped with crunchy caramel. Then she picked up a black forest cake stuffed with rich chocolate ganache and sour cherries sandwiched between kirsch-soaked chocolate sponge covered in whipped cream and chocolate curls.

"I have to watch my figure." Anna stepped back from the racks. "Go ahead, you're so thin you can eat my share too."

"Stop being a bore. We have a time-honoured tradition to uphold. Food is a Magyar's true religion, so show some respect for your heritage and eat."

Anna reluctantly reached for a low calorie cherry strudel which Kati promptly slapped out of her hand before ending up with two identical pieces of dobostorta and black forest cakes from the second baker's rack. Anna closed the pastry room door and followed her friend to a backroom jammed with boxes of supplies as the latter juggled two plates along her slender left arm and hand.

Kati nudged the door closed with her bottom and tilted her head at a wooden crate. "Sit on that." She was already tucking into the black forest cake. "Yum, yum, yum," she said between big bitefuls, filling her cheeks to overflowing like a squirrel hoarding nuts. She grinned at Anna with cream oozing from her mouth.

Anna laughed at mushy cake decorating the most desirable lips in Eger.

Kati caught her friend in a vulnerable moment by shoving a slab of moist heaven into her open mouth.

Anna groaned and ate up. Once the cream and chocolate French-kissed her tongue, she couldn't resist. "You always have a flat stomach. Not me. By tonight, I'm going to look four months' pregnant."

"What a pity," Kati said sarcastically. They could tease without offending each other. It was like that from the moment they met a few months ago.

"We didn't bring any napkins," Anna reproached her.

"Improvise, as we like to say in the acting business."

"If you insist." Anna reached over and wiped her mouth on the corner of Kati's blue linen jacket, momentarily stunning the blonde.

Kati erupted into laughter. "There's hope for you after all!"

"It's my turn to say hah, hah. What about the two cooks in the kitchen? Won't they complain to your mother?" A commotion of cursing and banging utensils filtered through the backroom door.

"No, they won't. After all, I am the owner's delightful daughter which means I carry some weight around here." Kati bit into sticky caramel and as she crunched heartily, she said, "Baba and Dora are identical twins in eternal competition with each other. The best food in Eger is made right here in the Paprika kitchen." A rare frown brought a dark cloud to her face. "The family has agreed on one thing. We will not become communists to keep the restaurant."

"Try not to think about losing it."

"Easy for you to say. It's not your family business." Kati decided she wasn't going to talk about something she couldn't change. She shook off the sadness by talking about her volatile cooks. "I took two cakes from one rack which belongs to Dora, and two from the other which is Baba's — to keep them both happy."

"But they were in the kitchen."

"The racks are a dead giveaway. If I only take cake from one twin, the other is going to smack her twin with a pot, as if it's her fault. So, I make sure I don't leave either of them out."

Anna directed a disbelieving look at Kati, but the latter didn't budge. "Yes, it's true, they hit each other. And stop looking at me like that." She changed the conversation abruptly. "Do you think we should learn English?"

"Why? There's not much use for it here."

"You never know, it might come in handy one day."

They were interrupted by a voice calling from the kitchen, "Kati, are you here?"

"It's Mama." Kati leaned over and whispered in Anna's ear, "Be quiet."

"This is stupid. I don't know about you, but I'm a grown woman."

"Do I need to point out the obvious? We're acting like children, so with all due respect, shut up." The two women waited as if they were trapped in a portrait of still-life.

Mama Paprika finger-brushed her short curly dark brown hair, a habit which also gave her a nice scalp massage. "Oh yes, feels so good." She swayed her extra-large frame from side to side as she moved around the kitchen, her sixth sense imploring her to check the alcove. She found the cupboard rolled away, and opened the door to the hidden room. Checking the pastries, she noticed two rows on both racks were slightly askew, and there was a cherry strudel which had lost its nice shape. "Getting sloppy, Kati," said Mama Paprika. She turned to look at the closed backroom door. It was supposed to be left open, so fresh air could circulate throughout the kitchen, as well as send delectable messages into the street to snag hungry pedestrians. Her stern look softened. She wished she still had her looks, but also realized God gave her one chance, like he gave everyone else to live through youth. She was glad her daughter was so beautiful.

There in the backroom was where Kati and her little brother hid as small children with their stolen treats. Mama Paprika imagined her daughter's grown face lit up in the old familiar way, waiting for a lumbering big bad mama to catch the sweet-toothed bandit. She decided to keep Kati in suspense a little while longer. She closed the pastry room door, rolled the cupboard back in place, and left the kitchen.

After a few minutes, Kati cracked open the backroom door. She was disappointed to find her mother gone. "My little brother Attila has come home. He's on hiatus from Lyceum University." She suddenly had an interesting idea. "Come to dinner tomorrow night because I won't take no for an answer."

"Okay, since I have a choice."

Romance and the Whole Darn Thing

Anna got the impression that Kati's brother wasn't serious about getting ahead in life. After completing a political economics course and his first term of law, Attila Paprika told his sister he needed a break. He was even thinking of quitting school, the negativity of war reducing his ambition to nothing. Quitters weren't Anna's type. They were the kind of men who sapped a woman's strength, so she arrived at the Paprika home without expectations of anything more than a night of delicious food and friendly conversation.

Kati took Anna's hand, pulling her over to a tall sleek man with broad shoulders in a dark grey suit. He was smoking a cigarette, his back to them as he stood in front of a family portrait on the wall. Sensing someone behind him, he turned around.

It was seldom that a male face and body caused Anna's hormones to bubble like frothing cappuccino. But the bubbling froth thing was happening right now. She stopped listening to her hostess because her undivided attention was taken by the smoke ring escaping from the man's generous, perfect lips. Hard to believe she once thought men who played with cigarettes were adolescent show-offs.

"Did you hear me?" asked Kati. She nudged her best friend in the arm.

Anna barely glanced at Kati. "No."

"You're staring at my kid brother like a horny goat."

Kid brother? Anna's preconceived opinion evaporated into thin air. She walked to the sofa with an extra little wiggle of her hips, hoping Attila will follow her.

Suddenly, Kati laughed. Anna gazed suspiciously in her direction, wondering if the beautiful creature knew what she was thinking. But no, Kati was laughing at something her mother was saying as they stood beside a table of food.

Anna watched Attila sit down beside her. When he started talking, his deep controlled voice and attractive blue eyes mesmerized her. There was no denying he was the most incredible package of male cells she had ever met.

Aware of Anna's attraction to her brother, Kati looked at him to see what the fuss was all about. She saw the same old features. Light blond hair slicked back with not a strand out of place, his long Roman-style nose with a small bump inherited from their father. He carried his tall, way too slim body in a broody sophisticated way. Grudgingly, she admitted that if she weren't his sister, she would be attracted to him.

Kati could stand it no longer. She walked over to the couple who had eyes only for each other. Reaching seductively inside her blouse sleeve, she slowly pulled out an ivory embroidered handkerchief, dropping it with a flourish on Anna's lap. Kati bent down and whispered in her ear, "For the drool which drips down your chin like blood from a pig's slit throat."

Anna was thoroughly engrossed with Attila, and had absolutely no idea what Kati said. She nodded pleasantly before turning to admire the man's lips languishing around his cigarette. She remembered how feminine she felt as his six foot two inch body towered eleven and a half inches over hers. Just like her friends, she watched her weight and looks because favourable things happened to attractive people, and she enjoyed the extra attention an appealing face and body received.

While pleased with her well-proportioned figure, attractive square face, and thick black hair, her moderately bowed legs were a source of discomfort. And short ones made it worse. She wanted horse legs, lovely long gallopers, so that she could race like the wind and be hard to catch. Some of her friends sported the shorter style of dress which showed their knees. Not Anna. However, she was determined to shift the bones by binding her legs tightly with a leather belt at bedtime. The defect was going to be fixed, no matter what it took which meant the self-inflicted bondage was not a problem except during bathroom visits. It was the only weakness she could find in her character. Letting the shape of her legs turn her into a giant rabbit as she hopped from bed to bath and back.

Attila was flattered the author wanted him, knowing men threw themselves at her feet. He was going to be different by playing hard to get at first, spending time at the family restaurant where he drank his buddies under the table with gut rotting Hungarian liquor. Weekends rolled around with a drinking contest to see who could take on the man's formidable talent. Mama Paprika didn't mind because it filled her restaurant to capacity. So far, no one could beat the champion. When the contest was over, Attila played a game of chess with the most sober person and won. There was one exception. He would watch with dread as Mama Paprika nudged Kati with her elbow. "Have a game with your brother. And this time, let him win."

A Courtship

Weeks later, Attila was ready to admit his affection for Anna. The couple's courtship began with hand-holding walks along intimate cobblestoned streets of their town, visiting historical sites such as the stone castle of Eger, integral to the battle against the Turks in the sixteenth century. They once made the mistake of going to the cinema where the movie was overshadowed by communistic propaganda. It was not an enjoyable movie. If Kati was acting in a play, the couple went to see her. Afterwards, they packed a picnic and headed for the nearest park.

During the summer, Attila taught Anna how to swim like a human, graduating her from a dog paddle to an acceptable but lopsided breast stroke. In winter, he taught her the basics of skiing, and how to throw a snowball.

Anna took great pleasure in showing Attila her favourite place in Budapest -- Andrassy Avenue with its elegant cafes, art galleries, and parade of eclectic neo-renaissance palaces and mansions. To maintain the integrity of the architectural treasures, vehicle transportation was absolutely forbidden, making the avenue a pedestrian boardwalk.

She was surprised to discover that she didn't care if Attila was a university drop-out. Grudgingly, she had to admit she shared the same lack of common sense as other women when it came to the opposite sex, especially one as handsome and sophisticated as her guy.

When she got pregnant, the couple decided they weren't ready to have a child. Since birth control and abortions were frowned upon, backstreet abortionists were very busy in Hungary. Ending a pregnancy was painful on so many levels, but all Anna could think about was how to endure the agonizing pain caused by a long metal instrument being shoved inside her by an impersonal woman. When it was over, Anna bled for weeks afterwards, a constant reminder of what she had done.

CHAPTER 3

Saying Goodbye Is Never Easy

April 1949

Eger, Hungary

The Soviet Union continued to dominate Hungary for the last four years. In the beginning, communism was attractive because in theory it propagated salvation, equality, and the breaking down of the class system, as well as opportunities to succeed if people worked hard and played by communist party rules.

Anna was experiencing the reality of a rigid state bureaucracy revealing its true self through severe restrictions and people purges. Hungarians who spoke out against the new rule mysteriously disappeared, never to be seen or heard from again. Only a few dared to be different, fearing retaliation by the omnipotent government taking orders from Moscow.

Hungarians were not allowed to go to church because religion was poison. Businesses were turned over to the communists, crushing entrepreneurs and free enterprise. The wealthy became poor, and young people from privileged backgrounds were barred from university. As if that wasn't enough to kill the Magyar's spirit, the communists forbid people from leaving Hungary because they were Soviet property. Stalin grew strong roots, infecting the entire country with pervasive fear. Life, as Hungarians knew it, was a thing of the past with freedom of choice no longer taken for granted.

Anna's dream of becoming a publisher would come true only if she embraced communism. To be controlled by a state that would force her to print mostly art books and comradely fiction was an unacceptable arrangement. She hated communism. When thousands of countrymen began fleeing the new rule, she planned to follow them.

It was a beautiful day in April when she broke the news of her impending departure during a family supper. Her decision came as no surprise to anyone there. She had always been irrepressible. Her mother and brother couldn't come with her because they were simple hardworking folk who felt the world outside of their familiar boundaries might as well be on another planet. Their souls were indelibly stamped into Eger, so here was where they would live and die. Anna took comfort in the fact that Margit would be lovingly cared for by stalwart Horka, and Uncle Sandor, her mother's brother.

Sitting with Margit on her faded blue sofa draped with handmade ivory lace, Anna made it clear she would never kow tow to communism, her initial reluctance for a confrontation being replaced by the desire to speak out. Because her opponent was vast and powerful, she'd rather leave than see herself and her family imprisoned. Or worse.

"Darling, I understand your creative nature and how you must live by it. You are like your father. Only with him, it was all about inventions. Remember how he spent hours in the basement putting together strange gadgets. Most of them didn't do what he wanted them to do, but he derived much satisfaction from creating." Margit's soft voice wandered off with the memory of happier times.

Anna took her mother's hands, gazing at an older version of herself. "You must pretend you know nothing. I'll write to you when I think it's safe."

"Your Uncle Sandor has become a high ranking party member and given a store to manage. I'll ask him for help."

Horka sat quietly watching his sister's reaction to startling news.

Anna needed to gather her thoughts. Now was the time to think with the mind, not the heart, for her mother's sake.

Margit sensed Anna's turmoil and patted her daughter's hand. "He welcomed communism to Hungary years ago. He's my brother, your uncle, and he loves you very much. You won't get that kind of love anywhere else, no matter how hard you look, so I hope you continue to love him. Even though he's a communist, he still has principles, not like those fat-cat members shouting equality for all from their rickety platforms, but live in luxury we only dream of. Sandor refuses such bourgeoise hypocrisy and continues to maintain a simple life. He believes in setting a good example for the workers." Margit ended her words with a curt nod.

"Hungarians are not stupid. A lot of us realize the world of a high ranking communist is a far cry from that of the mere worker. Tell me, what can one fundamentalist do when there are greedy two-faced men everywhere?"

Margit shrugged. "He has to try."

"If Uncle Sandor is so devoted to communism, how can he protect you?"

"Family is more important than politics and Sandor knows it!"

This is what Anna loved the most about Hungarians. Their unwavering devotion to family. Anna's heart was overflowing with affection. "I will always love my family, and that includes Uncle Sandor." Funny how she didn't put two and two together when she heard him speaking casually about communism. Her uncle was a party member, and she grudgingly accepted his membership will bring some security, fragile though it may be, for her mother and Horka. Anna wanted to laugh. She never thought she'd be glad a relative was a communist.

She said, "I'll smuggle keepsakes out of my apartment and bring them here. Zsuzsi's going to Szeged, and if it's any comfort to you, I hope to be taking Attila with me."

Margit clucked, "What do you see in him? He's egotistical and will only hurt you. Good looking men are nothing but trouble, and big lips are a sign of weakness in a man," she cautioned, knowing it was useless to tell her headstrong daughter what to do.

Anna pulled a long face. It was not the first time that Attila came under scrutiny. She said defensively, "His lips look good to me, and he may not realize he loves me, but one day he will." Looking at Margit's sad face, she tried to find the words to make her feel better. How does one describe a man like Attila to a mother? Should she mention that he enjoys entertaining patrons with drinking contests at his family restaurant, and that no one can beat him because he drinks like a fish. Although she didn't approve, she knew that alcohol temporarily released her boyfriend into a happy place. "He hides his insecurity with drinking contests and sports."

Margit sighed. Her daughter could never be accused of diplomacy. "Obviously, he fills your physical needs." As a devoted mother, she was certain that she knew better, but had to let her children decide for themselves. "I love you, my darling." She hugged Anna. "You will always be welcome back if you want to come home."

Anna was overcome with sadness. "I miss you already."

The Last Supper
Anna and Kati sat inside the Paprika Restaurant eating Hungarian stew, and dumplings that looked like small pinched noodles.

Kati asked, "Do you like the porkolt and csipetke?"

"It's delicious. I wouldn't mind having more than four pieces of meat."

"You'll have to stick around for that day." Kati had already asked Anna to rethink her decision, but asked again. "Are you sure you need to do this? Once you leave, there's no returning."

Anna agreed, "No, there isn't. The communists run the theatre, the ballet, and the opera. They shove their repertoire onto our performers, and ultimately the audience. Writers have been warned to write nothing but praiseworthy words about communism, putting us under such pressure. They want obedience and enthusiasm at the same time, so the more gifted artists prefer to go to prison or labour camps than do their bidding." Anna pressed her right index finger into the table as she continued to make her point. "Who remains? The mediocre artists who become servants of the Soviets. I refuse to be identified as a mediocre servant."

"You think we lost our Hungarian identity?"

"We don't create from the heart anymore."

Kati shook her blonde head. "We will find a way."

Anna leaned forward and whispered, "Be careful. The only thing worse than a Soviet communist is a Hungarian one. For a pat on the head, they'll turn in their own people. Look at the AVO, the secret police. They are torturers and murderers going after anyone who dares to voice a negative opinion. You hear how the party bosses subject our hard workers to lectures on the greatness of Stalin and his philosophy. They cheer and applaud like sheep, as though they love sweating nine hour shifts, six days a week for peanuts."

"Not all of us."

Anna said through clenched teeth, "Enough of us." She took a bite of food and thought of something that would amuse Kati. "The only thing that hasn't changed is what we can eat. Soviet food cannot compare to our gastronomic reputation. And now that food is the topic of discussion, let me say this place does good business."

Kati knew there was more coming, and raised an eyebrow. "Your point?"

"Most of your customers are men."

"So?" Kati flicked her head back, causing her shining hair to sway seductively.

"So?" Anna mimicked Kati in fun, flicking her head the same way, but the desired sultriness eluded her. All she managed to do was pinch a tight nerve in her neck. "Ow!" She smacked the sore spot. "Look at them slopping food all over the tablecloths because their lusting eyes are glued to you, not their food."

Kati didn't miss a beat as she replied, "Too bad you won't be around for me to rub it into your green face anymore." She stuck out her tongue like a bratty child.

The two best friends stopped talking and looked at each other in silence. Both were thinking the same thing. They were going to miss each other very much. When Anna decided to escape from Hungary, she asked Kati to come with her. After much soul searching, Kati declined. She couldn't leave her mother alone. Anna resisted the urge to ask her to change her mind. If Kati wanted to leave, she'd say so. Kati always spoke her mind, just like Anna.

"I'm going to miss you," Kati said, wiping away stinging tears. She felt she was looking at Anna for the last time.

"Same here." It was painful to leave behind family and a best friend who was like a sister. She said, "I haven't heard from Attila. Is he coming or not?"

"I don't know. He's twenty-one, and the war doesn't seem to have matured him. He's more like a starved party animal." Kati put her clenched hand on the table and slid it closer to Anna. "Hold out your hand."

Anna was curious but said nothing. When she did as she was told, Kati briefly placed her hand over Anna's. "A gift from Mama."

A brilliant-cut one carat diamond ring rested on Anna's palm. She quickly closed her hand, so that no one else could see it. "She doesn't know, does she?"

"Mama won't mind. Besides, it's worth a lot and you'll need it one day."

The two women noticed each other's sad expressions. The farewell hurt too much, so Kati got up quickly, smoothing a non-existent wrinkle in her dress. In a loud voice, she said, "See you when you get back from Lake Balaton." The decadent fragrance of Chanel No. 5 wafted seductively around Anna as Kati bent over to kiss her on the cheeks. She whispered, "Keep on shaving."

Custard and Pig Lard

Attila stared at the uninviting vista outside his second floor bedroom window above the restaurant. The sun was setting, casting a reddish-orange glow on the near and distant piles of rubble that still needed to be cleared away.

He made up his mind that he wasn't going with Anna. He cared for her, but wasn't sure it was love. Anyway, he couldn't leave his home and family. Slowly adjusting to the new normal in Hungary, he felt as secure as one could under the communist regime. Trying to escape was a madness because there was a risk of being caught and shot to death.

A pessimistic thought creeped into his brain. *I'm a university drop-out.* He looked at himself in the mirror, and said, "Anna's strong. She'll survive without me." He was trying to absolve himself of any responsibility for disappointing her.

But will you survive without her, especially when your face begins to look like dried up marrow and your sleek body turns to custard? He had tried not to go there, to the place where one inevitably reaches middle age and beyond. Forcing his future image back to where it came from, he got dressed. He wanted to meet up with two cronies from university and hit as many bars as possible to get rid of the unpleasant aftertaste of marrow and custard. Tomorrow, he planned to face Anna just before she left Hungary.

He brushed his hair back slowly, carefully making sure every strand was in its proper place. A dab of pig lard mixed with a drop of cologne ensured his hair remained where he wanted it to, even if there was a tornado. He really didn't have to worry because there were never any tornados in Hungary. After running his long tapered fingers along the fresh crease of his pants, he was ready to party.

Ready, Set...

The next day Anna packed a knapsack with a few personal items. She was setting the scene for a pretend vacation at Balaton, Hungary's popular resort lake. Zsuzsi was gone, but not without a lot of fuss. After days of cajoling, an extra box of cigarettes sent her on the way, the same day her employer gave it to her. A sum of money was withdrawn from the bank, not too much to arouse suspicion, but enough to carry the belief that Anna was embarking on a comfortable holiday. Part of it was hidden inside her sock alongside Mama Paprika's diamond ring which she put on her second right toe and covered with a bandage. The remaining money was put in her purse.

She nostalgically surveyed her living room with a million dollar view of the Danube River. It was time to say goodbye to her apartment. Will she have to say goodbye to Attila too? Since she hadn't heard from him all week, she assumed he wasn't coming.

So much for big lips.

The Surprise

Early afternoon approached as Attila hurriedly packed a small knapsack, threw on a dark brown overcoat, and kissed his sister and mother goodbye. "Look after Mama," Attila said to Kati. He noticed her quizzical look, but didn't offer an explanation.

Even though he spoke casually, Kati detected fear in his deep voice.

"If anyone's looking for me, you don't know where I am."

The two women watched Attila's back until he was gone from their sight. He didn't say he was leaving them, but they knew they were losing a loved one forever.

Kati blew a kiss to send him on his way to Anna.

Attila stopped inside the restaurant to look at the regulars eating their food. He had enjoyed many good times here. There was nothing fancy about the place except for the intricately embroidered cafe-style curtains hanging from large carved wooden rings that were handcrafted by Anna's talented brother. Abruptly, he walked through the front door and into the street before he lost what little nerve he had to leave his precious home.

He sensed his mother watching from a window above the restaurant, and looked up to see her. A tear rolled down his cheek as he trembled with emotion. He brushed it away and waved at his mother, but she closed the curtain. Admonishing himself for last night's stupidity, he hurried along the cobblestoned street hoping he wasn't too late.

Knock, Knock
Who's There?

Anna put her ear up against the front door of her apartment. Someone was on the other side tapping hesitantly at first, then pounding with urgency. Her heart skipped a beat as she opened the door. When she saw it was Attila, she sighed with relief and held out her hand.

Attila took it after what seemed like an eternity.

Anna pulled him towards her, then stood back, holding him at arm's length. She was surprised to see him, and told him so. "I thought you weren't coming." Placing her hands on her hips, she said, "What's wrong? You look strange."

Attila moved to the window, searching the street below. "I've got a headache." He looked briefly at Anna. "I want to be with you."

Anna waited many months to hear commitment from the elusive Attila. When she finally heard it, she melted. "Darling." Walking over to him, she pulled his face down to hers, softly kissing his perspiring forehead. "We will overcome any challenges together."

Attila looked into Anna's eyes fleetingly, unable to hold her bare gaze. He stared out the window at the street below, ignoring the majesty of the Danube River. Listening to the ticking mantle clock, he waited for Anna to tell him they were ready to start their dangerous journey.

Beauty and the Pest

"Where's Attila? I have to talk to him now." The unmistakable scratching voice of Laszlo Furdoo, one of Attila's erstwhile childhood friends, sent uncomfortable chills through Kati as she moved around the restaurant chatting with customers.

Laszlo followed her like a puppy dog until she pulled him away from the tables. She stared at his round baby face and protruding eyes which reminded her of Peter Lorre, an Austro-Hungarian actor who was often typecast as a psychotic murderer or a sinister foreigner. "If you're looking for Attila, he's gone to Balaton with Anna." Kati tested the ruse on Laszlo's ability to smell a red herring.

"Tell him not to come back."

Kati had just spent the last few hours trying to console Mama Paprika, and was in no mood for games with an overweight five foot four inch pest. She grabbed the pest by his sloppy tie, pulling him past amused customers until they were inside the kitchen pantry. "Speak up, Laszlo, or I'll make your worthless life miserable as well."

Laszlo glanced downwards after admiring Kati's beautiful but very cold blue eyes. "You don't like me, do you?"

"Just because I shut doors in your face and serve you cold meals doesn't mean anything except that I like to tease you." But Kati sensed danger as she spoke. Trying to dispel the ominous feeling washing over her now and when her brother was saying goodbye, she touched Laszlo's shoulder. "Sometimes I get carried away because I'm an actress, you know. What's wrong?"

"Attila's in big trouble with the Russian police."

"You mean the Soviet police."

Laszlo shook his meaty finger. "They can change their country's name, but they're still Russian to me."

Kati stared at the stubborn man. "Why is my brother in big trouble?"

"Once they match the face to a name, he's dead." Laszlo waited for the impact of his statement to sink in.

"What?" Kati was confused.

"Last night he was with some of his friends from the Lyceum. They got drunk and high on amphetamines, except for Attila who only got high. So you can imagine..."

"Stop torturing me and get on with it."

"Okay, okay." Laszlo had a peculiar habit of saying okay two times. "Well, they made a ruckus throughout the city before arriving at Stalin's statue. You know, the fifteen foot monstrosity in the Square."

"It's taller." A wave of numbness reduced Kati's normally agile reflexes into a state of paralysis, barely aware she was quibbling about the size of a horrible statue.

"Now that I think about it, it could be forty feet high or..."

"Stop!"

"Okay, okay. Well, you know Bodo, don't you? He was in the square watching the men pull each other's zippers down and..." Laszlo paused to take a breath. He noticed Kati's expression which showed her thoughts turning in the wrong direction.

"No, it's not what you think. They pissed all over Stalin!"

Even for free spirited Kati, this was a shock to her nervous system. She closed her eyes trying to envision such a sight. Sensing more, she looked at Laszlo, waiting for him to deliver the coup de grace.

Laszlo was enjoying himself. Bad news evoked strong emotions, giving him an adrenalin rush. Perhaps if he played his cards right, he might benefit from the Paprika misfortune. He continued in an excited voice which made him sound like a chirping bird. "Bodo saw a Russian officer step out of a nearby building. He was watching Attila and company like a hawk. Desecrating Stalin's person, although a rigid lifeless one, was the last straw. The Russki flashed a light in their eyes and ordered them to get down on the ground. But get this, just as he was reaching for his gun, Attila socked him in the eye. When the Russki fell down, everyone punched and kicked the shit out of him until he was unconscious." Laszlo added, "He's in the hospital and hasn't come around yet."

Kati leaned against the wall for support, her mouth hanging open in shock. She wondered if the odious pesticide Attila sprayed around the basement and baseboards had turned him into a laboratory experiment, something that could happen to her now that the chore of killing critters was passed on to her. It was a crazy idea, but would explain why Attila didn't succumb to the loose behaviour of a drunkard. The only thing he sometimes did after consuming a ridiculous quantity was to have a nice nap.

The amphetamine alcohol combo must have made him feel invincible. In this case, it was a good thing because if the Soviet had his way, the trio of pissers would be dead by now. She wanted to express herself, perhaps throw a fit, but not in front of Laszlo. She regained her composure and turned a cool gaze on his expectant face. "Where are the others?"

Laszlo shrugged his shoulders. "Your guess is as good as mine. Eger has many nooks and crannies that can keep a secret for a very long time."

"Go now, and say nothing to anyone if you value my friendship."

Laszlo decided now was not the right time to inform the beauty in which direction he wanted their friendship to go. Let gorgeously edible Kati sleep on all he had told her. Woman of his dreams.

Kati was now alone. Standing in the pantry with rows of cans and jars, she absentmindedly re-stacked them while thinking about Attila. She spoke out loud, "Anna believes you're escaping with her because of love, but you left to save yourself. That's more like your selfish nature."

Kati dropped a can on the floor, letting it roll towards the door. Memories of growing up together, playing with Attila when they were little, the teasing, the laughter, and the tears. Whatever he was or did, he was still her family.

"I love you, my brother."

The Escape

Anna and Attila sat on a bus that took them to Szombathely, the oldest town in Hungary. It was located a hundred and forty kilometres west of Eger, and just a short distance from the Soviet sector running along the Austrian border.

The couple disembarked from the bus and began to walk. The spring weather was most pleasant, the grass and leaves sprouting with so much energy it looked like they were vibrating. To curious eyes, Anna and Attila appeared to be a young couple hiking through the winding streets, and soon they'll be turning back. But there was no turning back as they passed ordinary buildings and houses studded with bullet holes left by roving German and Soviet soldiers. There was always something to remind them of the war.

The invisible cord connecting Anna and Attila to their homes and families stretched until it could stretch no more. Suddenly, it snapped. Sensing the unfamiliarity of their surroundings, of their future, they silently said goodbye to Hungary and the people in it.

Anna smiled at strangers and they smiled back. "The spring weather is making people less suspicious. Good timing on our part."

On your part, Attila silently corrected her.

The two of them trekked on in their sturdy brown walking boots. Nearing the Soviet patrolled sector bordering Hungary and Austria, their bodies responded to distant watchtowers with a flood of adrenalin, bringing forth a higher awareness of every movement and sound.

It was Attila who first spotted the nondescript cafe on the corner of the derelict street they were traversing. He said, "The Kis-Gundel."

They were greeted by tacky fake red peppers, tattered embroidered tapestries, and a grimy layer of foul European tobacco stains covering the walls. Tough looking characters mixed with the plain peasant folk sitting on bar stools or at the small round tables in the cafe while simmering pots of stuffed green peppers and goulash tried to drown out the smell of aged smoke. Everyone stopped talking to study the two strangers.

Anna was offended by the sordid scene. "Little Gundel indeed. They stole the name, and if the owner of the elegant Gundel Hotel in Budapest could see this place, he'd set fire to it."

Attila stared at her as if she had two heads. "Would you prefer to rendezvous with a lowlife character who has high class tastes? Like Andrassy Avenue with its glut of mansions? We can hike back to Budapest, if you like."

"I don't appreciate the sarcasm."

"Plotting our escape from Hungary brings out the best in me."

Sarcasm upon sarcasm. Anna said, "I give up." She had more important things to contend with, such as keeping the two of them alive.

They stood by the bar waiting for someone to acknowledge their presence, but it was soon apparent one of them had to initiate the introduction. Anna leaned across the bar, beckoning the balding cook by crooking her finger at him. She uttered a password obtained from the friend of a friend who knew about such things. The balding cook relaxed his defensive posture, creating a domino effect which worked its way around the room until lively conversation filled the atmosphere again.

"My name is Zoltan."

Anna and Attila turned around to face a skinny middle aged man with a black strip of a moustache on only one side of his upper lip. The other side appeared pink and puckered as if it suffered the agony of a nasty burn.

Zoltan introduced himself as a guide who will give exceptional service for their money if they wanted to escape to an Austria partitioned into four zones, each controlled by the Soviet Union, America, Great Britain, and France. But first, one had to successfully navigate the Iron Curtain which proved to be an effective deterrent. Europe was now separated by a mammoth border of barbed wire, watchdogs, spring guns, and deadly minefields.

"Hitler and his Nazis tricked us into a war they lost. The Allies dropped so many bombs on Szombathely because of its aerodrome and railway junction. And now, we're prisoners behind the Iron Curtain." Zoltan led the couple to a table where they sat waiting for night to fall.

It gave Attila time to turn his fear into terror while he imagined himself being blown to bits by a mine, even though their guide repeatedly reassured the young couple he had taken many escapees through the area without blowing a single one to smithereens. Zoltan had yet to encounter an exploding spring-loaded gun or a soldier with a killer dog. Witness the fact he was sitting before them in one piece. He lifted his frayed brown corduroy pant cuffs.

"Go on, feel my legs," said Zoltan.

Attila politely declined the man's offer while he fought back the overpowering urge to run all the way back to Eger, far away from the waiting minefield.

Zoltan sized up the patrons and was satisfied. There were no soldiers in civilian clothes to question the presence of strangers. He had a gift for sussing them out. Peering out the window at the dark, he told the young couple to follow him as he left the cafe. Sneaking along back alleys, they reached the minefield marked by six foot high barbed wire. Only a distant watchtower's spotlight and a half moon offered partial visibility of the surrounding area. Zoltan looked furtively around, but they were alone.

Attila glanced at Anna, unable to detect any emotion. If she was nervous, she certainly wasn't showing it. And he was darned if he was going to let her know how petrified he was. He hoped he won't lose a limb or an eye if a bomb blew up in their faces. If it had to happen, let it be total damage. Snuff out his pitiful existence without him knowing it.

Zoltan pulled out his rusty metal cutter, making a small opening in the barbed wire which showed signs of prior damage and repair. "Eventually, they find my holes and seal them up. So far, they haven't caught me. Maybe one day." Zoltan glanced around to reassure them. "But not today." When he smiled at Anna, she could barely make out the golden glint of an unnatural tooth.

Without hesitation, Anna followed the guide through the fence. Then she looked back at Attila who was still standing on the other side.

Zoltan knew his customer was sick with fear. Every time he took his clients across the minefield, he encountered the tell-tale sign of hesitation. Meeting death before a person has made his peace on Earth was a very real possibility. Cool, calm Anna seemed to be the exception. In an encouraging voice, he said, "You are safe with me."

Attila was busy fighting the overwhelming urge to run back to Mama and Kati as he watched his girlfriend reach her arm through the fence. This was the second time that she offered her hand. He took it back at the apartment, so why stop now. He reluctantly placed his hand in hers, and she pulled him over before he could change his mind.

Zoltan turned his flashlight on low beam. "Anna, you will be right beside me. We must walk as one." He wrapped his right arm around the middle of her back, and she placed her left arm around him. "Attila, stay behind me no more and no less than three feet, and walk in my footsteps." He added, "Whistle."

"Why?"

"One note."

Attila decided it wasn't wise to argue with someone who controlled his fate. He pursed his lips and produced a clear strong sound.

Zoltan held up his hand to stop him. "That's enough. Has anyone told you that your lips are made for whistling?"

Attila gave the guide a dirty look.

"If we get separated from each other, whistle for three seconds, just like that. Count to twenty and repeat until I find you."

Losing the guide never occurred to Attila. He decided there was no way he was going to let himself get separated from the man who knew how to get them out of the minefield. Under cover of dark with the flashlight showing the way, he focused intently on placing his feet in the same spots Zoltan had just vacated.

The land was once a vast green forest, but now it was bulldozed and ploughed into a bleak arid brown. Underneath were thousands of live mines waiting to do their job, begging for an errant foot. Although the ground looked deceptively innocent, Anna and Attila stepped as if they were walking on broken shards of glass.

"We're lucky, it's completely deserted here." Anna spoke in a whisper, in case anything louder would trigger an explosion.

"This is a very secluded area," Zoltan commented casually. He decided it wasn't a good idea to tell his paying clients that although this was a short cut, a high concentration of explosives were laid along the path they were taking tonight. The only good thing was that, despite the warning signs posted along the barbed wire fence, large stretches were not patrolled on a regular basis. To perfect their lack of discipline, the soldiers played cards, listened to western radio broadcasts, or shot wild fowl which they sold to local villagers. No soldiers patrolling the perimeters also meant no dogs trained to rip arms off or sever jugulars.

Eerie quiet enveloped the three as if they were navigating a giant moth's cocoon. It was so quiet that Attila thought he heard scary ticking below his feet. He wanted to believe it was his terrified imagination playing tricks on him. Wait just a second. The scary ticking was triggering a good deal of sweat from his armpits. "Stop!" he said in a loud whisper.

Zoltan turned to look at the frightened man. "What is it?" he asked.

That's when Attila realized his heartbeat was pounding in his ears. "Nothing, let's go."

They finally made it safely to the other side of the minefield. The unswerving footsteps of their guide traced a safe passage to Soviet-occupied Austria in less than an hour. For Attila, it felt like an eternity. He wanted to shout with relief, a male thing that said I have conquered death a thousand times over tonight. Instead, he took a cigarette from his pocket. Both hands were still shaking, and he almost stuck rolled-up tobacco in his nostril. Luckily, the guide had turned off his flashlight, so no one saw.

Anna hugged a surprised Zoltan. "That was quite an experience."

Is that all it was? An experience. Attila wanted to retch.

Anna asked Zoltan, "Why do you keep risking your life?"

Zoltan took a cigarette from Attila, and shrugged his shoulders. "If I didn't, I'd be stealing to put food on my plate." He clapped his badly scarred hands together. Should he tell them about his wife and child bombed to death in their own apartment? How he tried to save them and burned his face and hands? How his classic German Shepherd dog, blessed with a profound ability to sniff out mines, pushed a child escapee away from harm, only to be blown to bits for his heroic effort? Or should Zoltan tell them how loneliness drives him to the brink of insanity every time the sun goes down?

Some things were better unsaid. "It's not safe to travel the roads at night, so you will be hiding in my friend's truck. He will take you through the Soviet sector which is the most dangerous part. Then you're on your own in the American sector which also extends into Germany. Don't let your guard down with the Americans until you cross over into British territory. Go straight to the displaced person's camp at Hoher Heckenweg near Munster. And if you make it in time, the Westward Ho plan will resettle you in Britain before it shuts down for good."

Anna held out some money which disappeared quickly under Zoltan's grey cap. In return, he handed her a crudely drawn map of the escape route that continued once his Hungarian milk truck friend dropped them off. Zoltan pointed in the direction of the waiting truck. "Good luck."

The couple passed no one on their way to the vehicle hiding in the dark on a deserted street nearby. The driver, a heavy set man with a ruddy complexion, instructed them to hunker down in the back behind large cold milk cans which rattled when the truck was in motion.

The truck finally stopped beside a cemetery on the opposite side of the driver's modest house. When Anna paid him off, he handed her a salami log and a bottle of milk. "If you feel cold, use that over there." He pointed to a grungy brown wool blanket covered with animal fur lying in the corner. "Relieve yourselves in the ditch outside, and be ready to leave at five in the morning when milk trucks are doing their routes." Then he left the couple alone.

Attila eyed the wool blanket as if it were covered in manure. "I can't sleep." He silently pined for his warm bed back home.

Anna handed him the salami. "Eat."

At six a.m., the milk truck pulled up behind Soviet army barracks at the border separating Soviet-controlled Austria from the American zone.

"Get out! The soldiers will be searching my truck," ordered the driver.

Anna and Attila quickly got out and stretched their cramped limbs, watching the milk truck drive away.

Attila asked nervously, "Shouldn't we be avoiding the army barracks?"

Anna said, "The soldiers will never suspect we're trying to escape if we flaunt ourselves at them."

Not much activity was taking place at such an early hour except for a soldier who appeared at a door, smoking a cigarette with a rifle hung over his shoulder as he gazed at the distant snow-capped Austrian Alps.

"Try to fit in with the surroundings," Anna warned Attila.

He snorted. "What persona should I assume? Let's see, I haven't been a tree in a long time, or how about a jeep like that one over there?" When his stomach began to burn, he put his hand on it, hoping to ease the pain.

It was obvious to Anna that Attila was scared. They were taking a monumental chance walking through soldier-studded territory, but she believed their success depended on presentation. If they pretend to be hikers, they could pull off the deception. She fished inside her black wool jacket pocket, producing a bent cigarette. "We've gotten this far already. Blow some smoke rings and stop touching your stomach."

Attila grabbed the bent cigarette. "You make it sound like I'm playing with my crotch, and it's hard to blow rings when the mouth is quivering." Why didn't he remember to bring a bottle of palinka? He was desperate for a shot of brandy.

Anna picked up her knapsack and hitched it over her shoulder. As she looked over at the barracks, the lone soldier had multiplied into several. Many suspicious eyes watched the couple with keen interest.

Attila puffed quickly as he tried to handle the bent cigarette like a hiker with nothing to hide.

"You're smoking like a chimney. Slow down, don't let them intimidate us." Anna crooked her arm around Attila's. "Act as if we belong here."

Attila cursed his stilted legs. "Act as if we belong in a Soviet army barracks. Oh dear, I forgot to pack my rifle which you told me would be too dangerous if we get caught. Will a toothbrush do?" He didn't tell Anna about the pistol inside his knapsack because she'd make him throw it away if she knew about it. How did she expect him to protect her from the dangers lurking everywhere on their journey to freedom?

"Shut up and laugh at everything I say, even if it's not funny." Anna immediately launched into a Zsuzsi escapade.

In the middle of one of her delusions, the crazy maid thought her employer was not attending an important party. On a whim, she decided to take her place. Elegant guests were appalled by the uncouth woman who was supposed to be a famous author. Her light socket hairdo was completely overshadowed by a pair of eyebrows that looked like tufts of armpit hair. Since she wasn't content to use utensils and a plate, she stuck her finger into the food on the enormous buffet table, smoking two cigarettes simultaneously with a running commentary on how she can cook better than the oaf who prepared the expansive spread.

The violinists erupted into wild gypsy music to distract guests, only to become the back-up band to a wailing weirdo. When Anna arrived unexpectedly, the wailing weirdo was standing in the middle of the cavernous ballroom bursting the seams of one of her employer's favourite evening gowns. She also wore it back to front, so that it displayed too much cleavage. It was inevitable that she would be confronted by Anna and the host, and her backup plan was to do what she knows best. Fudge the facts. She insisted she had introduced herself as the humble maid to the most beautiful and intelligent writer in all of Hungary. As a finale to her performance, her left breast popped out of the gown.

The anecdote got a forced hiccough of a laugh out of Attila and past the intimidating soldiers. He didn't think he could shoot them without being riddled with holes or endangering Anna's life, so he was very relieved nothing happened.

They walked down the road waiting for the right time to disappear. A compass guided them through the densely forested land skirting the road. Eventually, they reached the foot of the Alps, and here the forest trail slipped away, not daring to violate the imposing barrier. Once they made it to the American sector, they boarded a train for Germany. Anna pulled Attila along, staying one car ahead of the train inspectors who were busy checking identification papers. No one bothered the young attractive couple.

Their luck left them as they crossed the Austrian-German border. A German policeman zeroed in on Anna's Hungarian features, stopping the two travelers in the bustling train depot. What was she doing in Germany without identification papers? Their knapsacks were searched, and when the policeman found Attila's gun, he dangled it as if he were holding the tail of a rat.

Anna was shocked to find out that Attila brought a gun despite her warnings. She pretended they were innocent, and in bad high school German, she exclaimed, "How did this go up there?"

The policeman looked at her suspiciously. "You tell me."

Attila interrupted Anna before she could make things worse with more lies. In perfect German, he said, "I brought it along for protection, and my girlfriend didn't know." He silently thanked his parents for hiring a nanny from Berlin when he was a boy.

The truth satisfied the policeman who liked the handsome young man's German. "Say goodbye to the nice pistol because it's the last time you will see it. If you're refugees as you claim, you won't be needing it."

Attila sighed. One of his hobbies was target practice, and he had to resign himself to the fact that he won't be doing it in the foreseeable future. He was going to miss his beloved 9 mm Luger calibre pistol.

Anna and Attila were arrested and escorted into segregated detention cells. Small and reeking of more than one rotten smell, the cells were crowded with people invited to keep the jail guards company because they too were caught without magic papers. Only nefarious people walked the streets with no proof of identity.

The German officer in charge of the jail explained to Attila that if they were genuine refugees they must remain locked up for a minimum of four days before being released. Once they were given the right documents, they could proceed to the displaced person's camp in the British sector.

Four days...who made up this goddamn rule? Being confined in a tiny cold space with stinking strangers was going to make Attila stark raving mad before the first night was over. Under normal circumstances, he would never dream of questioning someone's authority, but the German officer in charge seemed like a fairly decent human being.

Attila tried to negotiate with him. "I demand to be released to the Americans."

The smug German officer laughed heartily as if he were enjoying a private joke. Then he looked at the desperation on Attila's face and decided to give him a piece of advice. "Let me tell you something, my handsome young friend. You're better off with us. They will throw you into a holding camp where you'll spend many months. American Jew soldiers are in charge, so believe me when I say they hate Germans, as well as Hungarians. Without exception, we are all Nazis in their eyes, so you don't want to give yourselves up to them."

Attila spent the rest of the day and night lying on the frigid concrete floor covered by a dirty thin blanket and holding his breath whenever someone released noxious gases. In the morning, he discovered the new sentry fancied himself a chess master who wanted to play with someone of his calibre. A plan was hatched which involved negotiating freedom with a game of chess. Caressing a pawn in his hand, Attila knew he could beat the man with his eyes closed and hands tied behind his back with only his tongue moving the chess pieces, but he was no idiot and not that arrogant. Give the man a good game, and let him win.

Enjoying victory, the guard sat back in his chair as his chest inflated to ape-sized proportions. In return for the cerebral fix, he returned half of Attila's cigarettes, agreeing to produce identification documents once his superior left for lunch.

In exchange for their papers, Attila insisted Anna give the guard a tip for keeping his promise. In return, she gave her boyfriend a look of disapproval. When she got her purse back, most of her money was missing and she was reluctant to reveal the remainder tucked away in her socks. Attila had whetted the man's monetary appetite, that she could see from his expectant face. "Okay, but close your eyes and turn your back, or no money."

When an embarrassed Attila translated the Hungarian order into German, the guard opened his mouth in disbelief. Anna sounded like his sauerkraut of a mother. A woman giving curt orders to two men, one of whom carried a loaded weapon was considered quite out of the realm of normal female behaviour. The guard pondered before grudgingly turning his back, finally deciding the money was more rewarding than staring down a woman with hard eyes.

Anna took out the remaining money from her purse before reaching into her sock for a ten forint banknote.

The guard nodded in appreciation when the currency changed hands. He said, "You can both go now, but a warning. Watch out for the Americans. You are one of us. If they get their hands on you, they will throw you into a worse jail and take everything you have." He stuffed the money into his pants pocket. "During the war, the Americans made German and Hungarian prisoners stand still for three days. If someone fell down from exhaustion, he was shot dead. These sadists know all about schadenfreude."

In Munster, Anna and Attila entered the Hoher Heckenwig camp which was located in an old army barracks. The Allied forces had to improvise housing for the millions of displaced persons in Europe after the war. Hotels, hospitals, private houses, and even partially demolished buildings were turned into emergency shelters. Too many displaced persons and not enough supplies created extremely harsh conditions. Minimal rations and almost non-existent health care caused rampant lice infestation, diseases, and malnutrition. To add to their woes, displaced persons often suffered from depression, being severely traumatized by the war and its aftermath.

Anna was immune to the miserable atmosphere surrounding her. She said elatedly, "The worst is over."

Attila looked horrified at the tired, sickly faces of other refugees dragging their weak bodies, waiting to put their downtrodden lives into the hands of strangers. Wet clothes hung from ropes strung up between rows of long narrow buildings, and mud was everywhere. "This place is just as pleasant as a prisoner of war camp."

Anna gave Attila an annoyed look. "Except that we are free to come and go."

"If you want to ignore the curfew."

A middle-aged man in a moth-eaten black cap and a ragged coat limped towards Attila. The odour of alcohol, tobacco, and outhouse surrounded the man like a thick fog. He grunted in German, "Do you have cigarettes?"

Anna said to Attila, "What's a German doing in a DP camp?"

"Do you want to ask him?" teased Attila.

"You're the one who speaks German," Anna said in a huff.

"That's right, and I'm not asking."

The German grunted again, "I'm a butcher. What are you?" With a menacing smile, he revealed dark yellow and brown stained teeth.

When a disgusted Attila said nothing, the man repeated in a belligerent tone, "I'm a butcher. What are you?"

Anna said sternly in Hungarian, "Go away." She shooed him off with her hands.

The man grumbled something unintelligible as he reluctantly backed off.

"I bet he was a butcher. Poor humans," said Attila.

Anna ignored him. "We can leave for England tomorrow because we arrived at the right time. If you prefer, we could wait a few months for Australia or France." When Attila didn't react, she offered, "What about Chile?"

"Hanging around this overcrowded flea-infested camp with the butcher doesn't appeal to me. I don't want to breathe the air here." Attila knew if they stayed any longer, he was going to look like those tired, sickly refugees. Even Anna would start to show signs of deterioration.

"Then we're going to England. Try to be happy; it's not that hard."

Attila felt like a little kid on the first day of school as he glanced at Anna's profile. She's so eager and confident, not in the least bit worried about the uncertain future waiting for them. Why can't he be like that?

The next day, a train took them to Rotterdam where they boarded the Bearitz, an English passenger ferry that was commissioned as a minelayer by the British Admiralty during World War I. After serving its country again in the second world war, the ferry was refitted to transport passengers across the English Channel, this time a thousand displaced persons.

Everyone was served a full course meal before the six hour journey, however, shortly after leaving dock, gale-strong winds stirred up huge waves that rocked the ship, causing the majority of passengers to become violently sick. The meal had been a British gesture of welcome, but it ended up creating an audio-visual nightmare of retching people which increased the gagging sensation in Attila's throat. The contents of his stomach had long ago traveled back up his throat and over the railing, yet he still wanted to throw up every time he heard someone heaving their guts. Walking amongst mines was a picnic compared to this.

Glued to the railing with his equilibrium askew, he listlessly watched the seagulls swooping down like dive bombers catching vomit in their open beaks. He wondered if fate would have been kinder if he stayed in Hungary to face the consequences of his juvenile actions. Either he'd have been shot on the spot or thrown in jail to endure a beating and removal of his toenails before being placed against a pockmarked wall. Big deal. He looked out at sea hoping to be reassured, but only saw himself drowning in its vast death trap. Of course, Anna was one of a handful of passengers whose body and mind were oblivious to the notion they were supposed to be seasick like the rest of them. Attila missed his mother and sister.

How Not to Ask for a Date

"Kati!" Laszlo rushed into the Paprika Restaurant like a whirling dervish, pushing the double kitchen swing doors open with a flourish.

He interrupted Kati's thoughts about enlisting friends to help out at the restaurant while she acted in a Budapest play. Blonde hair covered in fishnet, she was cutting up chunks of marbled meat because the twins stormed out of the kitchen after a nasty argument involving flying pork appendages. She walked into the kitchen at the wrong moment, and was now sporting a swollen lower lip.

A putrid concoction of strange cologne and je ne sais quoi oozed from Laszlo's pores. Try to smile without gagging, Kati told herself. He wasn't responsible for the way one sperm and egg put him together. Or was he?

"It's unbelievable for Attila and his friends. Such luck would never happen to me." Laszlo picked up a piece of raw meat which Kati smacked out of his hand with the flat of her butcher knife. Unperturbed, he said, "Okay, okay. Guess what?"

Kati gritted her teeth together. No denying it, Laszlo was going to be irritating until the day he took his final breath. After twenty seconds of silence, she realized he needed prompting. "Well, what?"

"The Russki finally woke up from his coma, only he can't remember anything. Not even his own name." Laszlo lifted a pot lid on the stove and stuck his head inside to smell the food. "He's been sent home to Mother Russia. Or was it to his mother in Russia?" He thought about it. "Oh well, same difference. Have you heard from Attila?"

Kati felt the great burden she had been carrying dissolve in a puddle at her feet. For days, she expected the Soviet army at their door and the inevitable trauma for Mama Paprika who was confined to bed with a mysterious malady. She looked coldly at Laszlo. "If you stick your dirty head inside the pot again, I'm going to break all of your fingers."

Laszlo quickly put the pot lid down and backed away from the stove with a smirky grin.

Kati said, "To answer your question, I haven't heard from Attila or Anna. And stop staring at my breasts as if you've never seen a pair before."

"I've never seen yours, Kati," Laszlo said hopefully. He tore his gaze away from her perfect chest, only to be attracted to her unusually succulent lips. Had she been purposely sucking on them to push him into an inferno of passion?

Kati put down the butcher knife and grabbed two oversized oranges from a fruit bowl sitting on the table. The urge to tease won over her disdain for the unattractive man. "See these, Laszlo? They are the only oranges in all of Hungary. Well, my breasts are just like these, only bigger and sweeter."

Laszlo had to live up to the Furdoo name, and wasn't going to be outdone this time. He struggled for a minute, jumping up and down with his right arm extended all the way up in the air as he struggled to grab a two foot long salami hanging from a ceiling hook. Kati watched with amusement until he dragged over a stool and grabbed the salami. As soon as he jumped down, he began to parade around the kitchen as if he were wielding a baton.

"See this, Kati?" Laszlo pumped the salami suggestively in her direction. "My dick is just like this, only bigger and sweeter."

Kati's eyes turned into cubes of blue ice. "You are a pig, Laszlo."

"Oink."

She ignored the porcine grunt by thinking about Attila. If only her brother knew how lucky he was now. But there was no way to pass the critical information to him.

"Kati." Laszlo positioned himself under her nose.

She looked down at the top of his head. "Yes?"

"Would you like to go out with me?"

"You mean on a date? I don't look at you that way. Besides, any man with a salami as big as yours should be dating an elephant."

Laszlo laughed breathlessly, enjoying the beautiful woman's lewd sense of humour. "You're so funny, Kati. Perhaps I can convince you otherwise." Suddenly, he was deadly serious, all traces of fun vanishing from his face. "You don't want Attila to get hurt, do you? You know how far the arm of Russia can reach." Laszlo was desperate for even a crumb of her affection. *Just hug me, Kati. Let me feel your body, your feminine warmth, and I will settle for that.*

"Are you blackmailing me?"

"Uh...no...maybe...yes."

"Shameful boy. I should call you Judas." Kati held up her hand to stop Laszlo from protesting. "Come back tomorrow. I need to think." She picked up the butcher knife and pointed it towards the kitchen doors as blood dripped from the blade.

Five o'clock next morning, Mama Paprika walked with difficulty into the kitchen to make coffee. Being a loving mother, family was everything, and now that her son was gone, she sank into a depression that waited for her when she opened her eyes in the morning. It stayed with her until she had her first cup. After that, it was only a dull ache in her heart.

She found Kati with a cigarette in one hand and a cup of cold black coffee in the other. "You don't smoke unless you're trying to solve something."

Kati had been awake for hours and was very tired. "I'm glad to see you out of bed."

Mama Paprika didn't want to worry her daughter. "One of my better days. So, what's your problem?"

"Laszlo Furdoo."

Mama Paprika sat down at the table brushing her hair with her fingers. "Tell mama everything," she said in her deep voice.

Kati started talking.

Around Mama Paprika's neck was a delicate gold chain displaying a slender cross which she hid underneath her clothes. As she was wont to do with dilemmas, she pulled out the chain and fingered the cross as if it were a rosary. Strength became a character trait when her husband died and she took over the restaurant. The suppliers and patrons expected a man to run the business, so she was going to show them a woman was just as tough. When the communists came into power, she tried to delay state ownership of her restaurant by appeasing the local representatives with free meals and promises that she was not their enemy. All she wanted to do was give them great food, but she would never become a communist, and for this offence, she was going to lose the restaurant soon.

"Kati, you are my daughter. Didn't you think to turn the table on that pipsqueak? Tell him you will inform the communist authorities that he's planning subversive activities against their beloved Stalin." She added, "Who will they believe? A weasel or an angel?"

Kati smiled, knowing the problem was now solved. She showed her appreciation by kissing her mother on the cheek.

Mama Paprika slapped a fleshy thigh. "Good. Now, what do you think? Should I start dabbing Hungary Water on myself?"

"What for?" Kati didn't miss a beat. She was used to her mother's sudden change of topic, and knew she had inherited the trait too.

"What do you mean, what for? I know I'm your old mother, but I'm still a woman. That won't change until I'm reincarnated as a chipmunk." Mama Paprika held up a generous finger to her lips. "Don't let Father Orban know I said that! Anyway, I digress. Hungary Water did wonders for our Queen Elizabeth back in the thirteenth century." Mama Paprika patted various parts of her body. "She put some of the rosemary scent here, there, and everywhere. Seeing the dark side of seventy, she probably drank it too. Anyway, the results were desirable because she snagged a young studly King of Poland into marriage."

"If anyone can get their hands on a studly Polish king, you can. Do you want to marry again?" Kati knew the answer, but liked to banter with her mother.

"Of course not! I just like being a coquette." Mama Paprika smiled tenderly as she reached over and stroked her daughter's soft hair. "Go to the market. We need green peppers and garlic."

Food and Body Parts

Kati was waiting for Laszlo when he returned to the restaurant that evening. She led him to the backroom where he reeked of the same cologne, even stronger now as they stood cloistered in the small space. She sniffed. Her nose detected another strong smell of body odour. It was going to be easy to look at him with revulsion.

The more Laszlo gazed at the beautiful face in front of him, the more he saw crocodile eyes peeking out of a murky African river.

"This is what I will do to you if you ever threaten a Paprika again." She outlined her offensive move.

Laszlo was crestfallen. He never really would have gone to the Russians. All he ever wanted was for Kati to lust after him. Maybe she doesn't like him because he's too short. Hell no, the woman's a giraffe. "Okay, okay. You win."

Kati smiled with satisfaction. "Checkmate."

As Laszlo turned to leave, he noticed the two oranges sitting proudly on top of all the other fruit in the bowl. "I'd really like to suck on those oranges, Kati." He looked hopefully at her breasts.

Kati looked up at the salami once again hanging from the ceiling. "And I'd really like to stick that salami into my..." she opened her mouth, making Laszlo's hormones bounce like Mexican jumping beans, "...meat grinder." Kati patted the well-used machine attached to the countertop. She looked hopefully at his crotch.

CHAPTER 4

Hello England

Friday, April 29, 1949
Southampton, England

The Bearitz berthed at the seaport of Southampton. Mist shrouded the coastline producing an epic aura which projected the land to another worldly dimension normally inhabited by ghosts and goblins. Not quite the inviting scenery for a boatload of anxious refugees.

An optimistic Anna was happy to be in the country of British royalty, tea, and crumpets. On the ship, other Hungarian refugees told her of the stories they heard about England. Although rationing of food, petrol, and clothing remained after World War II was over, they kept telling her the next decade promised to be a prosperous one. Skilled labour was being recruited from other commonwealth countries to repair London as well as staffing up new hospitals and schools. Manufacturing firms were doing brisk business making consumer items like televisions, radios, refrigerators, washing machines. Overall employment in the business sector was on the rise with women working in increasing numbers. If they kept it up, they could surpass the number of men in London offices.

Disembarking with the other refugees, she and Attila were processed as displaced persons. An interpreter told them that England will take couples as single people only. To enforce the no-marriage policy, they were assigned to different locations, the British government's protocol for controlling the thousands of homeless people pouring into Great Britain.

Anna planted a parting kiss on Attila's mouth. "We'll do what they say, for the time being." Not knowing English was holding her back, and she wished she had taken Kati up on her suggestion to learn the language.

Anna was put to work at a women's hostel in Glasgow, Scotland while Attila stayed in Southampton making bricks as part of the initiative to rebuild Britain with the help of boatloads of Jamaicans, Africans, and Asians arriving after the war.

Within a week, he developed enlarged wrists, his swollen hands red and peeling from piling the newly formed clay blocks one on top of the other. The piles had to be briskly grabbed in batches from the speedy conveyor belt and placed in kilns to be cured. Just as he got used to the physically demanding job, he was relocated to a busy hospital. Someone took the time to translate his papers and thought a dropout law student shouldn't be a brick maker. He should be an orderly pushing a mop and pail, or whatever else the ladies in white told him to do.

Anna missed Attila.

By the month of July, it was time to take control of her life again. She picked up her knapsack and collected her boyfriend from Southampton. Together they headed for London where the green oasis of Hyde Park drew them to a Victorian mansion owned by Miss Gertrude Partridge.

The Landlady

Miss Partridge was called many things. Sweet and dignified were none of them. Being of an average height at five feet five inches, she would blend in with the rest of the population if it weren't for her turnip torso straining at drab size twenty frocks. Her resemblance to the root vegetable made her instantly recognizable, along with a steel grey hair bun, a pair of day gloves, and fifteen year old blood red Oxford shoes polished daily with a sheared wool scrap.

During the war, she lost three dress sizes and felt remarkably skinny, but when bread was de-rationed last year, she gained back every pound she lost. Miss Partridge loved all things bread, especially if they were crumpets.

Being a feisty woman, she often left people speechless with snippy jabs. Therefore, it was indeed a dubious honour when she chose to like someone, but she wasn't entirely without redeeming qualities. Along with thousands of other women, school children, and even the Royal family, she helped her country during the war by knitting navy or pukey olive green socks, scarves, and sweaters for British soldiers. She also knitted blankets and fingerless mitts to keep the soldiers' hands warm while they were shooting weapons during the winter. It was amazing to her that the humble knitting needle was so crucial to the war effort it was on the scrap metal exemption list. The same could not be said for London's decorative iron railings, most of them removed from people's properties and public places. A wasted effort because hundreds of tons could not be recycled into tanks or guns, and ended up clogging the Thames River.

Miss Partridge lived in one of many detached Victorian mansions on the periphery of Kensington Palace and Hyde Park, having inherited the 1880's architectural dream house from her dearly departed parents. As a headstrong child, she was impervious to the drafty sash windows and cold damp from poor insulation because there was so much to admire -- the patterned brick work, high ceilings, huge rooms, bay windows, decorative cornices, and ostentatious fireplaces in every room. To show his fierce patriotism, her father commissioned a mosaic of the Union Jack's red, white, and blue for the front door's stained glass panel. As tacky as Miss Partridge thought it was, it maintained a place of honour for being the British flag.

The house really was too big for her, and the older she got, the harder it was to maintain. She recently decided to rent out a couple of rooms at a bargain price if the tenants helped her with the chores. It was a sound financial plan which would earn her money and clean her house for free. Sharing her private space was a difficult decision, and when she made up her mind to go ahead, a homeless Anna Gonda and her boyfriend Attila Paprika were standing on her doorstep the very next day.

The Hungarian couple pretended to be married as they pointed at the handmade 'Two Rooms for Rent' sign in the drawing room bay window, one of Miss Partridge's favourite spots to read books or watch the rain. Before the war, she would also watch for the daily horse-drawn wagons bringing milk, and when she needed fruits and vegetables that didn't grow in her back garden, she would wait by the bay window for the produce cart calling along her street once a week. Nowadays, the only wagons in her neighbourhood belonged to the street cleaner, or the coal and ice man.

Miss Partridge delegated her retired school teacher ego the task of teaching the foreigners English with a mobile chalk board and old school books. To speed up the learning process, she placed a hefty Oxford dictionary in Anna's left hand and the key to a home library of English classics in her right.

She took it personally whenever Anna mixed up gender-specific pronouns. Breaking her pupil's annoying habit of using 'she' for the male species and 'he' for females was proving to be a difficult task.

It was not Anna's fault that the Hungarian language didn't recognize differences between men and women. Her landlady would have none of it. "What's the difference, you say? How about a handful of private parts?" Miss Partridge was about to point at her nether region when she decided it would be too vulgar. "If you can speak Hungarian which has to be the most difficult language in the world, you can certainly master English!"

Anna was not at all intimidated by the bellowing Miss Partridge, and since she didn't understand every word, she shrugged her shoulders. "What's in a name?" she said with a sly smile.

Miss Partridge hated being challenged. And was she being ridiculed with a quote from Shakespeare's Romeo and Juliet? She shouted, "What's in a name, indeed!" Her shoe stomped on the bare wood floor, the persnickety pounding causing Anna to laugh out loud.

The elderly woman was shocked by her pupil's reaction. A foreigner was laughing at her in the sanctity of her own home, and that's when she had her very first epiphany. She was a self-centred old harridan, and if anyone should be laughing it was her. At first it was difficult to let go, but it wasn't long before the Victorian mansion thirstily soaked up her pealing notes, for it seldom had the pleasure to do so.

February 1950

Diamonds are a Girl's Best Friend

Attila was hired as a mailroom clerk at Hammersmith Hospital right after he and Anna arrived in London. There were no more worries about running into blood and guck as an orderly. As for Anna, she made herself useful by cleaning and cooking meals for their landlady.

One night during bedtime, Anna said, "If Miss Partridge finds out we're not legally man and wife, she'll make us leave. Why don't we get married?" She wasn't in the least bit concerned about an outraged landlady. It was just an excuse to bring up the subject of marriage to a skittish Attila. Funny how she now played games with the man she loved.

"What about the conditions imposed on us when we were granted immigrant status? I already feel like a felon for walking away from our assigned jobs."

"We are none of the government's business. Besides, we're not stuck behind the Iron Curtain."

"They can deport us."

"No, they won't," scoffed Anna. "You worry too much."

"That's because you don't worry at all, so I have to do it for both of us."

"Very funny." Anna said impatiently, "Well, what about getting married?"

"I can't afford to buy you a real diamond."

Anna looked down at the cheap zircon ring on her left hand. She used to wear the imitation diamond on her right ring finger, but switched to her left before meeting Miss Partridge for the first time.

Just like that, the opportunity was here to reveal Kati's parting gift. She couldn't say anything earlier because she didn't want Attila to misunderstand. Who could blame him if he thought his girlfriend had stolen his mother's diamond ring.

She went to the wardrobe closet and returned with Mama Paprika's ring.

"I may not be an expert on diamonds, but it looks expensive. I don't remember you having something like that." Attila didn't like what he was thinking. "Did you steal it?"

"That's why I didn't tell you sooner," said Anna indignantly. "Your sister gave it to me as a goodbye gift. She said I'll need it one day."

Attila believed Anna. It was an act of kindness very typical of generous Kati. "That's my sis," he said fondly.

"It belongs to your mother."

Feelings of sadness and familial love tugged at Attila's heart. Mama Paprika and Kati had unintentionally given Anna her wedding ring. "Okay, let's get married."

Monday, April 17, 1950

A Celebration

Anna and Attila's wedding took place at the local registrar's office.

The groom admired his mother's ring on the bride's finger. He then looked at her radiant face, but there was no fairytale emotion bursting from him.

A happy bride said, "I love you."

"Me too."

Anna laughed at her husband. "Other women would feel cheated. One day, you'll confess your undying love, but not today because I won't believe you."

Back at the house, Attila opened the door wondering if his bride expected him to carry her across the threshold. Before he could make up his mind, their landlady barricaded the foyer with her turnip torso, arms crossed under her heavy bosom.

In an accusing tone, she said, "Finally decided to get married." She pointed at Anna's diamond ring which replaced the zircon that was supposed to fool her. "Follow me," she said severely. Then she marched into her drawing room which was furnished with antiques -- a Queen Anne ivory brocade chesterfield, a large round mahogany table with matching chairs, a solid oak roll top desk, and an upright Broadwood piano. But the most eye-catching item in the room was a grand marble fireplace which took up one half of a wall.

The newlyweds were overwhelmed in a most unpleasant way by wallpaper decorated with millions of tiny pink flowers and dark green leaves circling the room. Miss Partridge ceremoniously pulled back the bay window's ivory curtains covered in large red and orange flowers. Sunshine streamed through delicate sheers, turning the room's clashing floral patterns into a wild donnybrook.

She said briskly, "Surprise! I prepared food for a Victorian Tea in my neighbour's kitchen." When she saw the couple's blank look, she pointed at the mahogany table in the corner.

Anna and Attila turned in the direction of their landlady's pointing arm. Since they were expecting to be evicted, they were stunned to see an elegant tea service spread out on the lace covered table.

"I will talk to both of you as if you understand perfect English, although I must say you are quick learners and will assimilate the language in no time at all." Miss Partridge motioned to the newlyweds to sit down on the chesterfield.

She walked up to a portrait of a dour middle-aged couple hanging above the fireplace. "These severe old fogies are my parents. Can you see the resemblance?" She hollowed her cheeks and put on a haughty face. Then she clapped her hands together, complimenting herself in the third person, "Well done, Gertrude. You should have been an actress."

Her behaviour was a tad disrespectful. She glanced at her parents, as if to apologize. "I should be grateful I inherited a big old dusty mansion and a dwindling pile of money to pay for the repairs and renovations." The old lady pointed at a Victorian six-light chandelier and wall fixtures made of brass and opalescent glass. "The gasoliers are just showpieces now. I converted to electric heat, so no more nasty smell or black soot on the ceilings." She pinched her nose and looked upwards as if it would bring clarity to the clueless couple.

"New plumbing was a godsend. Did you know that before London built a proper sewer system in the late 1800's, raw sewage gushed into the Thames? People were so ignorant that they drank water from the very same river. Cholera epidemics were rife and most children didn't live beyond their fifth birthday."

Can you imagine? In the poorer parts of London, chamber pots were emptied willy-nilly out of windows, and a vile outhouse was shared by an entire street of families." Miss Partridge rolled her eyes with a shudder. "Thank the good Lord my parents were upper middle class, so they could afford a flushing toilet."

The newlyweds tried to follow what Miss Partridge was saying, but not having much luck.

"I knew you were getting married today because the registrar's clerk is my neighbour down the street. I must say it was an absolute shock to learn you weren't really man and wife, but I forgive you because you did the right thing." Miss Partridge paused, then said doubtfully, "I guess I'm not such a stiff broom after all."

She pulled out a chair, prompting the couple to sit at the elegantly laid table.

Three red floral china cups, saucers, and matching bread plates edged in gold were complemented by spotless silver cutlery. The centre piece was a matching china teapot surrounded by silver trays of scones, trimmed cucumber sandwiches, and a Victorian sandwich sponge cake tinged with lemon peel, layered with strawberry jam and dusted with sugar sifted through a pretty doily. Silver-footed crystal pots of clotted cream, orange marmalade, and butter completed the table.

Food rationing of sugar, butter, lard, cheese, eggs, meat, bacon, porridge, shredded wheat, and tea was still enforced, but Miss Partridge had ways of finding what she needed, when she needed it. Her next door neighbour's cousin was a farmer who provided most of the staples that he kept from the government. He made more money doing business with black marketeers who would re-sell his food at higher prices to people who could afford them. During the war, blackouts were an opportune time for the marketeers to break into warehouses and steal supplies. Nowadays, they continued their break and enter habits when it suited them.

Even though Miss Partridge was an unlikable woman, she was elderly and a former teacher, thus commanding respect in the neighbourhood. Her neighbour drove into the rural countryside to get extra eggs, butter, milk, and cream directly from her farmer cousin for today's wedding, all without coupons. No wonder Miss Partridge was irked by the unfairness of rationing. She thought it was even more unconscionable that West Germany ended rationing in January, all except for sugar. Germans enjoyed a glut of food, including meat, at moderate prices. Every opportunity she got, she would complain that it was positively disgusting.

As for flour, it came off the ration list in 1948, along with bread, which made it easier to bake the cake and scones, and prepare the cucumber sandwiches for today's Victorian Tea.

Miss Partridge said proudly, "Before rationing began in January of 1940, I had the impeccable foresight to stockpile staples in my cellar — mostly tins of spam, fish and beans, tea, marmite, marmalade, biscuits, and dried fruit. And porridge, of course, but it didn't last long. Neither did the tea and biscuits.

I must show you my cellar soon. It has a cold storage room lined with lead sheets to keep out the mice, and let me tell you, descending into that dark vaulted cellar isn't easy for me. It possesses the charm of a medieval torture chamber with mold creeping along the walls in patches." She shook her head with a sour face. "I absolutely refused to enter it when I was a young girl because I would have nightmares from seeing dead animals hanging from hooks." Those days were long gone, but the old woman still avoided the built-in brick shelves where the animals dangled, and she always skirted trepidly around the stained stone-flag table where the carcasses were prepared for supper.

Out of the blue, Miss Partridge revealed, "I have a twin sister." She had no idea why she blurted out her little secret. Maybe because she hadn't talked about her estranged sibling in fifty-five years. And maybe because her tenants didn't understand her. "Abigail and I were in love with the same dashing man." She sighed. Going down memory lane was still a painful walk. "We were eighteen, lovely young fillies with honey blonde hair. I never forgave either of them for eloping behind my back, making an utter fool out of me. Never spoke to Abigail again."

Miss Partridge was exhausted. It took all her reserve energy to dig up the past. She decided there was nothing else to say. Picking up the empty teapot, she disappeared into the kitchen. She was hardly gone when she was back, this time with the teapot full of brewing tea. "I used to have a beautiful silver tea service, but it tainted the flavour." She frowned with the disagreeable memory.

"I never use cozies because they stew the tea and destroy its perkiness. If one is not on time, one should drink it lukewarm and not insult the tea with a wretched cover that looks like a chicken or rabbit." Her right eye had a habit of glaring with intense anger even on neutral occasions, and today was no exception.

Attila spoke quietly in Hungarian, "Anna, she does this strange thing with her eye. Do you know what she's saying?"

"She said something about a rabbit. We cooked a lot of it at the hostel."

Miss Partridge held up her free hand. "I do believe my ears are burning which means you were talking about me. I prefer the far more interesting subject of tea,

England's most popular beverage since the seventeenth century. It happens to be the second most popular drink in the world, next to water."

She picked up the teapot, and with a strainer in her other hand, she filled the cups containing a smidgen of milk. "The tea scalds and froths, producing infinitely more flavour if you add the milk first. And with much appreciation to black marketeers everywhere, I am offering you Darjeeling, the champagne of tea. Quite appropriate for celebrating a marriage." She raised her cup to the couple who took the hint and raised theirs too. "Wishing you happiness and good health. Cheers." After she took a sip, she said, "I always think more clearly with a cuppa."

There was no stopping Miss Partridge on her favourite subject. "Victorian and High Teas are for very special occasions. On an average day at four o'clock sharp, I take afternoon tea and crumpets, or scones. However, once a month, I take the time to enjoy Irish and Scottish teas. When I'm honouring the Irish, I wear my greens and serve on green linen and Irish lace the likes of barm brack, a yeast tea bread with dried fruits and spices. The Irish are a very superstitious lot, but out of respect for their belief that the civilization of one's life depends on tea, I stir the tea clockwise to appease specters, and cross baked goods with a slash of the knife to release the devil." Miss Partridge paused to take a deep breath of satisfaction while her right eye threw deadly rays at Attila.

"I wear a red tartan sash that goes over my right shoulder and down under my left arm for Scottish tea." She leaned in towards the couple as if she were whispering another secret. "Between you and me, oatcakes are blander than pasty glue. Not that I ever tasted pasty glue. I much prefer delightful shortbread, such a simple biscuit that I bake myself."

She was enjoying her one sided conversation so much that she didn't notice the bride's preoccupation with the groom. When she turned to offer cucumber sandwiches, she realized she was an intruder in her own house. Hastily, she stood up and waved the couple out the door. "I'm going for my daily after-tea walk through the park." She was certain they couldn't understand her, but told a white lie anyway. She always took a walk before tea. It was obvious, even to a spinster like herself, that the newlyweds wanted to be alone.

It must have been the Darjeeling tea. She heard stories about it being an aphrodisiac, but pooh-poohed the notion for years. She never felt any stirrings within her loins whenever she drank it. Maybe it only worked when one had tea with a remotely interesting partner. The stodgy old arthritic women and men who occasionally joined her for tea were hardly worthy of a sex romp.

Miss Partridge didn't think the couple's passion would last. Men. Bunch of Peter Pans who don't know how to appreciate a woman.

Tuesday, January 2, 1951

Attila walked into the drawing room and found Anna knitting a winter scarf in pale blue wool. He showed her the evening newspaper in his hand. "Listen to this article," he said.

Without missing a stitch Anna replied, "I'm listening."

Attila began to read in English, "Hungary has once again rationed sugar, flour, and starch products under a decree to be issued today. Rationing ended in Hungary in 1948, the first country to lift it in post-war Europe. The decree said that rationing was necessary because of last summer's drought, and storing was needed for an eventual national emergency."

Anna was not surprised. She remembered the warning she gave Kati after she did her jiggly dance to celebrate the end of rationing. "Our families will be fine. They know how to survive."

Summer

The Perfect Porkolt

As the couple continued to advance in English, Attila was promoted to assistant accountant where he found his niche in numbers. Anna accepted a part-time position as a typist and Hungarian translator for the BBC while continuing to clean and share kitchen duties with Miss Partridge. The two women were both strong and opinionated, yet the gap in their ages was the reason they got along so well. Anna thought of the older lady as a motherly figure, and Miss Partridge saw Anna as the daughter she always wanted.

Attila did not share his wife's affection for their landlady. Her wrathful eye disagreed with him like a bad case of heartburn, even though she grudgingly appreciated his culinary expertise, for it was he who prepared the best Hungarian meals. Growing up with his sister Kati in the home of a restaurateur father and chef mother meant they were taught from an early age how to cook. Attila enjoyed cooking, especially if he wanted good rich food. He wasn't impressed with Anna's slapdash style of throwing stuff into a pot.

One day, Miss Partridge came home with a pound of fatty beef valued at more than the maximum allotment of one shilling and twopence. She was fortunate that the butcher was a favourite former pupil who slipped her the extra meat in the back alley behind his shop.

Attila insisted on giving Miss Partridge a lesson on cooking an authentic porkolt, his favourite Hungarian dish. "You are about to witness a master chef," he said, making Miss Partridge wish she had never taught him English. He tucked a small towel into the waistband of his pants, and with the dexterity of a Chopin, his hands began to cut the slab of fatty beef into perfect cubes followed by a huge mound of ultra-thin sliced green peppers which would help create a rich sauce for the stew. Next was an equally huge mound of onions prepared with his mouth open and his tongue hanging out. It was a trick he learned to avoid oniony tears. As for his battle axe of a landlady, it would do her good to cry, so he didn't turn around and share his tip. Besides, he couldn't let her see him looking like an enormous fool.

Miss Partridge was not impressed with the arrogant culinary display, her eyes welling up from the spray of microscopic onion cells. *Miminy piminy show-off. It's just a stew, for heaven's sake.* She'll show the Europeans, especially a fuss pot like Attila, a thing or two about keeping a stiff upper lip. She folded her arms under her bosom.

Attila tossed the onions and half the green peppers into the hot lard to begin a ritual of alternately stirring and adding drops of water to keep the ingredients from browning. "This is a very important first step that takes twenty minutes."

Twenty minutes! First step! How many steps were there? Miss Partridge was horrified at the thought of spending even five minutes with the annoying man. She quietly left the kitchen.

When the onions and green peppers were ready, Attila dropped the beef into the pot which sizzled as it seared, the delicious meaty aroma filling the kitchen and adjacent scullery. "You have to keep turning and stirring to stop the meat from burning." After three minutes, he removed the pot from the heat and coated the contents with a generous scoop of paprika from a one pound supply his mother had sent him. Then he added salt, the remaining green peppers, and enough water to make plenty of sauce before putting the pot back on the range.

The rich red colour of the porkolt was assessed with a keen eye. "When you think you've added enough paprika..." He paused to turn around and face Miss Partridge with a handful of the sweet spice. Surprised to find he was alone, Attila finished his sentence anyway, "...add some more."

He went ahead and tossed the paprika over his shoulder, having no doubt whatsoever that it would all land in the pot behind him. He turned around to find his aim was perfect.

With or without Miss Partridge, Attila was going to make the best damned porkolt of his life, the way his mother taught him. And now he couldn't stop thinking about Mama Paprika and Kati. It was time to take a chance, so he and Anna mailed a letter to Uncle Sandor, hoping the comrades left their own alone.

News from Home

Anna waited two months for the flimsy blue airmail envelope that lay on the side table by the front door. She smiled at her mother's delicate handwriting as she began silently reading in Hungarian. 'My darling daughter, Sandor brought your letter to me. You can send letters to him because he has a trusted friend in the post office. People think you ended your Balaton vacation by trekking remote villages in search of a story, and this is what I told the communists who came to the house to question your whereabouts. But don't worry, being blessed with the blood of a Magyar, I learned how to deal with the lower echelons. Good old-fashioned bribery. I gave them a crate of wine that turned into vinegar, so sure the lofty comrades couldn't tell the difference.

Sandor was very angry when they threatened me. He sees something he didn't see before, that while communist doctrine is the right way to live, on paper and in one's dream, in the hands of imperfect men it is a tool to enslave people. He had congratulated them when they built new homes for the gypsies, but soon realized it was politically motivated. Their real intention was to ensure a faithful following of third class citizens to keep them in power, only it backfired. The communists ended up with rat-infested pigsties that became a health hazard to the surrounding area. They had to be demolished.

I'm sorry to say the Paprika Restaurant and home were finally confiscated. Tell Attila not to worry because his mother is living with Kati now, so she's all right. And believe it or not, Bela Becsi, the actor, has fallen in love with Kati. I know, you're thinking he is too old. As for your brother, he continues to gain recognition for his woodwork. Please don't worry about me, I'm doing well. That is all the news I have for you. Remember, we love and miss you very much. Write again soon, your loving mother.'

September 1951

A Woman's Breasts are Sacred

Anna learned she was pregnant. Now she had two priorities -- raise a child and work her way up to respectable author in the west.

September kept getting better when a letter arrived from Kati. Anna was just as excited to hear from her best friend as Attila was to hear from his sister. Kati had a tough decision to make. In the end, she decided to say absolutely nothing about the stained statue incident because the last thing she wanted to do was destroy the couple's new life. She would spare Anna the truth and spare Attila the painful fact he left his home too hastily.

Instead, she wrote proudly about the growing passive resistance in Hungary. It was the workers' way of sabotaging the economic stability of the communist state by stealing from employers and falsifying facts and figures to create confusion while at the same time personally benefiting from their illegal acts.

She then spent two long paragraphs fawning over her older handsome boyfriend, introducing him as the famous actor who was utterly devoted to her.

Sounds like a canine, Anna thought, and realized she was slipping back into the insulting banter she used to enjoy with Kati. However, it wasn't the same anymore, not without her flesh and blood best friend.

Attila dropped the letter on the nightstand. Kati had lulled him into a false sense of security before breaking bad news. An aggressive cancer took both of their mother's breasts. Horror filled his head as he thought of her being butchered by the simplest of country peasants rounded up by the communists and brought to the cities to become doctors and lawyers after only two years of inept training.

Thursday, March 20, 1952 at 11:55 a.m.

Prenatal Appointment

Four weeks before the baby was due, Anna was going to nearby St. Mary Abbots Hospital. Miss Partridge said emphatically, "Weather forecasts are always wrong. These old bones say it's going to rain, so take a brolly!" She held up a long skinny umbrella with a six inch spike tip, a handy weapon for women traveling alone at night.

Anna refused, deciding her baggy tweed swing coat and plastic bonnet were enough to protect her from the elements, if indeed Miss Partridge was right. As she waddled south along Marloes Road towards the hospital, a very strong wind threatened to knock her over as the cloudy day took on a disturbing atmosphere.

She tucked her clutch purse inside her coat pocket and braced herself...

CHAPTER 5

Life Goes On

Thursday, March 20, 1952 at 5:20 p.m.

Back to the Present

Anna woke up to find her husband standing beside her hospital bed. It felt like it was only a few minutes ago that she had given birth and laid her head on the prickly pillow for a snooze.

"Sorry, I'm late," said Attila. "My supervisor has no compassion for new fathers."

Anna didn't care about the mean boss. "We have a daughter."

Attila helped her out of bed, and as they walked along the corridor leading to the nursery, he noticed her limping. "What happened to you?"

"Aniseed balls hit me in the head which made me fall down and twist my ankle, so a Rolls Royce took me to the hospital."

Attila gave his wife a sideways glance. *Humour her. She just gave birth.* "That's nice."

"I need a cigarette." Anna could once again have a forbidden smoke after going without for the last five months of pregnancy.

Attila reached into his coat pocket, pulled out a flat tin, and lit a cigarette before handing it to his wife.

As soon as Anna inhaled a puff, she was overcome by a nauseous feeling. She handed the cigarette back with a grimace. "It tastes awful."

They stood at the glass partition searching rows of newborns who were all miraculously asleep. A cheery Sister with a big smile appeared on the other side, motioning them to come inside. She happily led the parents to a glass incubator.

Anna gazed at Marika's tiny pink body lying peacefully inside the incubator. She said softly, "My kislany."

"Is that the name of your baby?" asked the Sister.

"No, it means child in Hungarian."

Attila's eyes melted into pools as he gazed upon his daughter for the first time. He hadn't realized how much joy he would feel until he saw his little girl. "I can't wait to hold her," he said.

Anna was pleased. It was great to share a tender moment with the man she loved.

Attila looked behind him with curiosity.

"What's the matter?"

"I thought someone was behind me."

"The nurse?"

"No, she's standing over by the corner." He not only felt someone hovering behind him, but was sure he detected the unmistakable scent of Hungary Water which sadly reminded him of his mother.

Anna asked, "Are my baby's lungs okay?"

The Sister produced another warm smile. "It looks like your kislany was meant to be a blessing in your life."

When the wailing cry of another baby told them it was time to leave, Anna reluctantly turned away from the incubator. She said to Attila, "I like the name Marika."

"Marika Paprika? She'll get teased at school."

"She'd be teased even if her name was Mary. Besides, should we let cruel little children tell us what to do?"

"Not if you put it that way."

Anna kissed Attila goodbye and returned to her hospital bed. Too excited to sleep, she finally drifted off several hours later.

The Next Morning

"Wake up!"

Anna opened her startled eyes to find Miss Partridge holding a cylindrical tin labelled English Toffee. She grabbed her brush on the side table and ran it through her hair, wondering how the landlady managed to sneak in before visiting hours.

"Hello, my dear." Miss Partridge bussed Anna on the cheek. Looking around cautiously, she said, "I have no doubt the hospital food is still as vile as it was when I had my gall bladder removed many years ago. Must be even worse now with all the restrictions on food." She wrinkled her nose at the ghastly fact. "Eat this while I find my way to the nursery to see my little princess." It was an order. She put the tin down on the nightstand, took off her navy blue day gloves and handed them to Anna. "Gloves are my only extravagance. I have a pair for every day of the month, and these ones are made from nylon, the new wonder material which dries fast and doesn't wrinkle."

"Why are you giving me your wonder gloves?"

"Not so many questions. I'm going to move the screen around your bed."

Anna was going to point out that she only asked one question, but when she touched the tin, she became distracted by a surge of heat on her bare fingertips. A small gasp escaped from her lips.

Miss Partridge arched her eyebrows as if to say, I told you so, and made her exit.

Anna's loose fillings buzzed apprehensively at the thought of gooey toffee. She gingerly opened the lid, not quite sure what to expect, but certainly not what was inside the tin. Porkolt. She realized the reason for the gloves, and put them on before picking up the hot spoon dipped in the stew.

When Miss Partridge returned a short while later, she was beaming with pleasure. "I have introduced myself to an angelic newborn who is going to grow up into a beautiful, special lady." A perfectly satisfactory idea popped into her head. "I want to be the godmother."

Anna found herself nodding in agreement. "I think you'd make a wonderful godmother for Marika." She teased, "And I'm enjoying the toffee."

"Yes, dear, very amusing," replied Miss Partridge in her usual stern voice. "Your husband made the stew with rabbit, which is not on the ration list, but they're hard to come by. I have a resourceful neighbour who knows a farmer, and he just happens to be her cousin. He sells pork, rabbit, and pigeon meat."

Anna grimaced, "Pigeon? Isn't that a dirty bird?"

"Not if you're starved from rationing."

Two weeks later, Marika was ready to go home. The Paprikas' second room was transformed into a soft pink nursery, a colour that did not inspire Anna, but she decided to accept it without protest. Cuddling Marika in a soft white shawl, she said, "I was a tiger. Now, I'm a pussycat because of you." She kissed her baby's warm pudgy nose.

THE PAPRIKA DIARY, A LONELY SECRET

Tuesday, July 15, 1952

Goo Goo Ga Ga
Miss Partridge handed Attila an envelope from his sister.

When he opened it, he found a letter and folded white tissue paper. His eyes filled with tears the more he read. He said sadly, "My mother is gone." Inside the tissue was Mama Paprika's favourite necklace which he picked up to show Anna. "This is for Marika."

As he stared at the delicate gold cross and chain, the tragic news hit him with full force. He cried angrily, "Mama's been dead all these months, and I knew nothing!"

Anna put her arms around him, but he pushed her away. He left the house and didn't come back that night.

The next morning, Miss Partridge found Anna sitting in the kitchen. "What a selfish way of grieving. Alone and angry."

"Both his parents are dead."

"You must have been worried sick all night. I must say, Anna, you have a tolerance I do not share. Not for bloodsucking men. They lord it over women. Do anything and go anywhere -- restaurants, hotels, pubs, and cricket matches. If a woman walks into any if those places by herself, she'll be called a tart. And if we work, we're expected to hand our salary to the husband. On top of that, we still do all the housework and shopping."

"There are decent men if you search hard enough. Hungarian men respect women, but you're right. Many of them expect the working woman to raise the children and do the housework. If the mother is clever, she will raise her son to share family duties. I must say that Attila's mom was both clever and strong, but it's mostly because he's a clean freak that he helps with the housework. As for cooking, he thinks he's a chef."

Attila's veneer of European sophistication still irked Miss Partridge. She reluctantly agreed. "I really shouldn't have said such an awful thing about your husband."

It was the very next day that she witnessed an astonishing sight.

"Goo goo ga ga!"

The strange high pitched incantation was coming from the nursery. Miss Partridge peeked her head around the slightly open door expecting to see Anna. Instead, she found Attila down on all fours making hideous faces and noises to induce Marika into fits of laughter. The little girl was enthralled by her daddy's silliness.

Miss Partridge was beside herself as she tried to stifle the guffaws that wanted to erupt like a geyser. She returned to the kitchen to make a cup of tea. If Attila knew his detested landlady watched him, he would never do it again, and who could deprive Marika of any future goofiness?

Miss Partridge tittered away at what she had just witnessed.

"What's so funny?"

Attila startled the old lady with his sudden appearance, but she recovered quickly. "Nothing at all." *With the dumpling of his eye, he's a side order of mushy peas.*

Friday, March 20, 1953

First Words

On Marika's first birthday, Anna cut a lock of the tot's soft auburn hair and tied a white ribbon around it for Miss Partridge.

"I'm going to put it in my jewelry box where I keep all my precious things." The elder lady leaned behind the sidearm of her Queen Anne chesterfield, lifting a box with pretty primrose ribbons. "I shall open it for you, Marika," she said cheerfully, as she took off the lid and pulled out an object with golden fur. "This is a teddy bear!"

Marika stopped playing with the coloured wood beads on her playpen to look at the bear wearing a red bow tie. She gurgled with delight and grabbed it with her long slender fingers.

"Do you like the teddy bear?" Attila asked his baby daughter, not at all expecting a response.

"Teddeeee!" said Marika.

Attila looked at Anna. "Did she just say her first word?"

"I think so." Anna didn't exactly jump up and down for joy. She would have liked "mummy" to be her daughter's first word.

Miss Partridge clapped her hands with delight. "Let's enjoy a cuppa."

Anna glanced at the mantle clock as it chimed four times. As usual, Miss Partridge was right on the dot.

Fashion, Dreams, and Raw Steak

The British had grown very tired of clothing restrictions and the 'make do and mend' policy. And although fashion still had a place in society during the war, it was with great relief that the people welcomed the end of clothes rationing back in 1949.

Anna now had a wider selection of clothes to choose from. To show off her figure, she wore clingy jersey frocks and modified box suits with padded shoulders, avoiding the surplus of severe military clothing that was designed to promote patriotism throughout the war, and still circulating as women's wear.

In recent months, the tea-length full circle dress made from yards of extra material was the new fashion statement, now that the utilitarian wartime look was over. Women wanted to wear prettier clothes in brighter colours, and so did Anna. She bought two dresses which emphasized her bust by pinching her waist before flowing in symmetrical folds down to her calves. But she refused to wear flouncy nylon petticoats which poofed the voluminous dresses to ridiculous proportions on women of her short stature. For evening wear, she changed her sensible wedgies to stiletto heels and suffered the uncomfortable garter belt girdle to slim her hips and hold up her nylons.

She had a weakness for large earrings which were the only jewelry she wore, aside from her wedding ring and the occasional necklace. She made sure her earrings were properly displayed by keeping her thick wavy hair short and simple. More often than not, Marika pulled them off as soon as her mother's ears were within grabbing distance.

Attila's wardrobe reflected the current men's fashion of looser trousers which were often hemmed with cuffs. Single or double-breasted jackets and overcoats favoured the broad shoulder look, although he didn't need help in that area. Colours remained sombre with charcoal grey being the most popular. The tartan plaid sports coat was in vogue for leisure times, but Attila thought it should only be worn by old men in the privacy of their homes, sparing the rest of the population. When he wanted to dress down, he donned a pullover paired with trousers. He did like the wet-look hairstyle which was similar to his own, so the bathroom cabinet was adequately supplied with Brylcreem, replacing the pig lard he used back in Hungary.

He put on a few pounds after they got married, but it only made his lean, taut muscular frame look stronger. His regular hundred laps at a nearby public swimming pool kept him perfectly toned. Being such a strong swimmer, he once yearned to be a member of Hungary's national swim team. His youthful dream was to enter the Olympics and win a gold medal for his country. Part of his training involved bicycle riding up and down every mountain he and his supportive buddies could find, testing each other's fortitude and never stopping until they reached impossible destinations. Afterwards, they flaked out on a soft patch of grass and bounced razor sharp pocket knives off their rock hard thighs.

By then, it was a competition for the winning thigh. The men would goad each other, "Mine is harder than yours!"

No matter how good Attila was at sports, his father didn't think he was good enough. Being a lawyer or a doctor was more noble and befitting a son of his. Attila found an ally in his strong sister and decided to disobey his father, but tragedy struck when he died. Attila never realized how much he loved his father until he was gone. Overwhelmed with guilt, he made a promise to the headstone in the cemetery that he will study law, but he hated every minute of it. As time separated him from the first day of his father's death, he neglected his promise. He finally walked away from university. There were so many distractions -- the war, the Soviets. And of course Anna.

Attila's self-deprecating humour became more pronounced. He mocked himself, but Anna didn't get it. He began to mock her with venom. "What's the matter? Afraid you can't convince the British that Hungarians are as wonderful as the characters you create? To them we're just 'Hungary' Nazi lovers." He gnashed his teeth as if he were a wild animal tearing into a juicy raw steak.

"Oh, shut up, you can be so negative. Writing in English isn't easy for me. I would use Hungarian if..." Anna produced a sweeping bow, "...your Highness translated what I write into your perfect English. But I don't want to hear a single unkind word from you, so you're not hired!" The new mother's waning ambition didn't bother her too much except when Attila made her the target. "Go comb your hair."

Attila was relieved about not being given the job of translator. A two-people war would break out in the Paprika household. He walked out of the room to find a mirror.

Wednesday, May 27, 1953

The Prediction

Marika started walking a couple of weeks ago, and toddled into the kitchen to explore hidden treasures in the cupboards. She picked up a small pot, banging it enthusiastically on the floor, prompting Miss Partridge to dash into the kitchen.

She asked, "How was the doctor's appointment?"

"Marika's fine. But I met a strange, tiny old woman in the waiting room."

When Anna stopped, Miss Partridge encouraged her to say more. "Go on, don't keep me in suspense."

"I was sitting in a chair holding Marika on my lap. The old woman sits down beside me, although there were many empty chairs. She put her bony wrinkled hand on Marika's head, and says, 'You're going to have such sadness with this one'. That's it, nothing more, even when I asked her what she means. It's like we stopped living."

"Tish tosh! Tiny old woman with grizzled hands have nothing better to do than upset others with ludicrous prognostications."

"What do you mean?"

"Prog-nos-ti-ca-tions has to do with predicting the future. Crystal ball nonsense. Anyway, how can that precious child ever cause sadness for anyone?"

They looked at Marika who was clutching Teddy.

Sensing Mommy and Grammy watching her, Marika glanced back at them, shining a cherubic smile before becoming engrossed in Teddy again.

"See. Ignore the old hag and I don't mean me."

Anna decided to take Marika for a long walk in her stroller. When they reached Hyde Park, the little girl was placed in a sandbox beside a set of swings and slides. Anna sat down on a nearby bench watching a tall young woman walking towards her. She wore brown capri pants with a loosely tailored white shirt, and held the hand of a boy with dark brown hair and jade green eyes. As soon as she let go, the boy raced to the sandbox.

The young woman sat beside Anna. "Lovely day, isn't it?" Weather had the most remarkable effect on people. It brought out the impulse to speak to a stranger.

Anna looked at the woman whose pleasant strong-jawed face was smattered lightly with freckles and enhanced by a gamin-style cut of straight strawberry blonde hair. "I'm glad winter is over."

"Are you Hungarian?"

Anna raised her eyebrows. "How did you know?"

The woman chuckled politely. "I have a friend from Hungary, so I recognize the accent. She moved to Sydney, Australia, and often writes to me about how much she loves it down there. The summers are hot and sunny, and the winters are more like a cool spring which suits me just fine. But the best thing I ever heard are all the jobs waiting for immigrants."

Anna said, "Sounds like a nice place."

"Nice enough to live in, I'd say." The two mothers realized they weren't paying attention to their children and simultaneously glanced at them playing in the sand.

"Do you know we haven't introduced ourselves? My name is Marjorie Cooper."

"Glad to meet you, I'm Anna Paprika. How old is your son?"

"Edward is five. Is that lovely little girl your daughter?"

"That's my Marika. She's fourteen months old."

The air came alive with the gleeful noises the children were making. Marika watched Edward fill a tin bucket with dry sand and pat it down with a spade. When he turned it over, she giggled as the bucket-shaped sand collapsed.

The two women talked about trifling things until it was time for Marjorie to say goodbye. They agreed to meet again in the park every week, same time, same bench.

A reluctant Edward had to be dragged by the hand, much to the amusement of both mothers. "Starting young, aren't they?" Marjorie said jokingly. As she looked down at her son, she brushed specks of sand out of his hair. Then she turned towards Anna. "Your daughter must be very special because Edward doesn't usually play with little girls."

Wednesday, July 21, 1954

Don't Try This at Home
Two year old Marika ran over to a gigantic bed of multi-hued pansies, squatted down and snapped off a purple one with a yellow centre. The velvety smooth petals had her full attention as she stroked each one gently.

Anna came over, pulling her back to the sandbox. "You're not supposed to pick the flowers in the park, sweetheart."

"Why not, Mommy?"

"Never mind. Go and play with Edward."

Anna sat down beside Marjorie who had just arrived and was brimming with joy. "I've got some jolly good news."

"Rationing is finally over. Can you top that?"

"You tell me. Richard and I are moving to Australia."

Although Anna wasn't surprised, she was disappointed to lose the companionship of her English friend. "We've just become good friends. Will you write to me?"

"Of course."

"I wonder if Australia can make Attila happy. He likes the sun and heat which means here in England he's a miserable sod most of the time. I don't know if it's me or what? Maybe I don't please him anymore." Anna spoke wistfully. "Marriage changes men. When you get to know them, that's it. The cute..." Anna tried to find the right word.

"Quirks?"

"The cute quirks are now..." Anna paused again.

"Irritations?"

Anna agreed, "Yes, irritations."

"Yours or his?"

Anna glanced at her friend. "His." The two women broke out laughing.

"I'm chuffed about all the exciting places we'll explore in Australia. It reminds me of my days in the WAAF, going from one new military installation to another. Wherever I was needed. You name it, I did it. I packed parachutes, cooked food for the pilots, chauffeured them in jeeps, learned how to do aircraft maintenance. The list goes on."

"You are a woman with many talents."

"I like to think so. I bet you were tough during the war."

"Hungarian women are born tough. So, what does WAAF mean?"

"Women's Auxiliary Air Force." Marjorie took a pen from her purse and wrote an address on the cover of her magazine. "We'll be visiting my other Hungarian friend in Sydney and then going to try our luck in Melbourne, Victoria. I'll write to you when I get there."

They parted with a hug and a promise to keep in touch.

Anna flipped through the magazine feeling a little despondent. She stopped to read an article titled *Create Your Own Cowlick*. She groaned at the absurdity. Apparently, cowlicks on little girls were the current fad. All a mother had to do was spend the next several months twisting a section of hair at the roots until it was permanently kinked.

Anna shook her head until she saw pictures of cute kids with wayward follicles. No doubt about it, a sweet enough face could carry it off, a sweet enough face like Marika's.

The strange ritual began every day after bath time. A squeaky clean child sat on Anna's lap along with Teddy while she twisted a section of hair on the right side of her daughter's forehead.

Marika said eagerly, "Do Teddy!"

"Teddy barely has fuzz to cover his body."

"Do Teddy!" screeched Marika.

Anna had an idea. She disappeared with the bear. When she returned, Teddy had strands of brown knitting wool sewn to the top of his head between his ears.

Marika watched in delight as her mother wrapped Teddy's strings around her finger.

"What on God's green Earth are you doing?" bellowed Miss Partridge. She was dressed in her red tartan sash as she stood in the doorway with a tray of milk and leftover shortbread from the afternoon's Scottish tea.

"Making a cowlick."

"You say it with absolutely no shame in your voice. A cowlick on a teddy bear. What the bloody hell for?"

"Marika's getting one and so is Teddy. And that's the first time I heard you swear."

"Oh pooh, I'm British." Miss Partridge placed the tray on the nightstand, and planted herself in front of Anna. "Now listen carefully, my misinformed young lady. When one is unfortunately afflicted with such an offending piece of hair, one usually goes to great lengths to hide it. Don't forget, this little girl will be a big girl one day." Her mouth pursed into a slit of disapproval. "So, why are you doing it?"

Anna tucked Marika and Teddy into bed before replying. "Why not? When I was younger, a widow's peak was the rage. We drew them in with eyebrow pencils if nature wasn't so kind."

Miss Partridge's eyes opened wide at the appalling wonder of what some women do to alter what God had given them. "Anna, I admire your lack of greed when it comes to material objects, but this obsession about changing yourself with beauty tricks disturbs me. It's all because of men, isn't it?"

"What do you mean by obsession?"

"Filling your mind with utter rot about the way you look."

"Grammy Porridge, you won't get any argument from me, no matter how much you're in the mood for one. And it's not obsession."

"Suit yourself, my dear." Miss Partridge actually smiled, not flinching anymore at the unflattering nickname Anna picked up from Marika. As hard as she tried, the little girl could only pronounce Miss Partridge's name as if she were a bowl of gummy breakfast cereal. It was still an endearment, and Lord knows she was finally ready to include affection in her life.

Something else needed to be said. "By the by, what is that strange thumping late at night? It appears to be moving from the area of your bedroom, down the corridor, and after a couple of minutes, it starts up again. I haven't dared to investigate in case I witness an awful mating ritual." Miss Partridge's wrathful eye narrowed with suspicion.

Anna grinned as if she was hiding a secret. "It's one of those beauty tricks." She said nothing else because going to the lavatory with legs tied up by a leather belt wasn't something to boast about.

Miss Partridge looked skeptical. "What I said about your obsession is correct, and if you're telling me a white lie, then poppycock to you!"

Feeling a strong wave of affection, Anna gave her landlady a tender hug.

"Mommy! Grammy Porridge! Me and Teddy too!" Marika yelled from the bed.

THE PAPRIKA DIARY, A LONELY SECRET

The two women grabbed Marika and Teddy in a smothering hold, making the little girl squeal with delight. Afterwards, the two women ended up in the kitchen.

"Do you want a cup of tea and a crumpet drizzled with scads of butter? Now that rationing is over, I intend to bathe in the glorious yellow stuff, and not feel guilty about it!" A small yawn escaped from Miss Partridge's lips. That settles it. She was tired and it was time to go to sleep. "Tomorrow, I will be visiting my next door neighbour who bought one of those new contraptions called a refrigerator. She absolutely swears by it. Perishables stay cold longer, although I dare say it will put the ice man out of business."

Anna studied the elderly woman's pale face and the way she was rubbing her left arm. "Are you all right?"

"Of course. Nothing a good night's sleep won't take care of."

The next day, Miss Partridge made up for her less than robust demeanor by bounding into the kitchen as if her Oxfords were fitted with springs.

Anna had just finished making breakfast for Marika.

"Now that your charming husband has gone to work, would you like to help me clean up the attic?"

"Feeling better?"

"But of course, dear child. All I needed was a good night's sleep, and I got that, thank you very much. Did you know we used to drink ale with our breakfast until Queen Victoria introduced tea as a morning beverage?"

"In Hungary, all we drink is coffee and hard liquor. Oh, and bodza. I never used to have tea until I came here, but I must say I like it."

"All respectable people like tea. What's bodza? It sounds frightful."

"Bodza is a drink made of lemons, sugar, and elderflowers."

"Maybe not so frightful."

"It's delicious, and Attila prefers coffee."

"As I was saying before, respectable people like tea."

"You don't get along with her, do you?"

"Him."

"I haven't made that mistake in a long time." Having slipped up many times in the past, Anna knew Miss Partridge was correcting her choice of pronoun. "Why don't you like Attila?"

"I don't suffer fools lightly."

"What do you mean?"

"I can't stand stupid people."

"He's not stupid and I love him." Anna stressed the last word to show Miss Partridge she remembered her lesson.

"Does he love you?"

Anna was surprised at the question. "Of course he does. He chose to leave his home, his country, and a family he loved, to be with me. He risked his life in a minefield for me, but most importantly, we have a child together."

Miss Partridge looked at Anna's strong face. "What you say sounds like the basis for love, I think." She felt maternal towards the younger woman. In a softer voice, she said, "I'm sure he loves you." She put down her cup. "Let's go up to the attic and bring the playpen for Marika and Teddy."

The ceiling sloped down on either side of the attic creating a pyramid shaped room. Years of dust lay over crates and shelves of cluttered items. Some were broken and useless, but Anna's eye for antiques picked out a few valuable pieces. The two women prepared a space for Marika's playpen, and started throwing the broken things into a box.

The landlady pointed at a large round stain on the wood floor. "Before proper plumbing was installed, there used to be a huge wooden water tank connected to the roof gutters with downspouts. The rain would flow into the receptacle and down through a pipe to fill the toilet tank and provide water for the kitchen tap."

"Receptacle?"

"A fancy word for tank."

"I know it rains a lot in England, but what about those days when it didn't?" asked Anna.

"The house maid would haul water from a neighbour's pump."

Anna was distracted by what she found when she lifted a grimy, yellowed cloth sheet. She sounded like she had found a pot of gold, "Oh, look, an old Remington typewriter!"

Miss Partridge offered, "You can have the typewriter since you seem so pleased to discover it."

Anna stroked the keys, holding back the desire to tap on them. She never wrote well using pen and paper, preferring to churn out the words through a rackety typewriter.

That evening, Attila entered the kitchen while his landlady was cooking. "Hello, Grammy Porridge," he said without thinking. He heard Marika say it so often that it rubbed off on him.

"I beg your pardon?" Miss Partridge was offended. She drew the line at Attila using such familiarity at her expense.

Her wrathful right eye tried to stare him down, but he had a few drinks at the local pub and felt pretty darn good. "I'm waiting for you to squeeze my ear until it hurts as you drag me up the stairs to the bathroom to wash my mouth out with soap. Or you can give me a swift kick up my arse with your sexy Oxford shoe." Attila grinned like a foppish clown.

Miss Partridge harrumphed, "Enough of your impertinence, young man. It simply won't do."

Attila walked out, muttering in Hungarian, "Old witch." He wanted to move out months ago, but the arrangement with Miss Partridge was worth keeping, and the house's proximity to the park was ideal for Marika. He would just have to do his best to stay out of the old witch's way while saving money for a place of their own. It was harder to do now that his wife no longer worked at the BBC.

It wasn't long before Anna started using the typewriter. The keys were hesitant at first, but after a rubdown with an oily rag, they moved fluidly except for the 'e' which needed an extra push to go all the way down. When it did, it clacked instead of pecked, ruining the rhythm her nimble fingers had built up. No matter, she felt a sense of satisfaction until she thought of Attila who was going to dig at her with his barbs once he finds out. He certainly had a way of turning her into her own worst enemy.

When Attila arrived home one afternoon, he thought he heard a familiar sound from the past floating down the stairs. He followed it up to the bedroom to find Anna hunched over an old typewriter, her fingers pounding the keys. Peck, peck, clack, peck, clack.

"Do it when I'm not around which is what I assume you've been doing," Attila snapped. "The noise gives me a headache. And the room looks like a pigsty."

Anna stopped typing, startled at the sudden intrusion. He was digging with the barbs again. She looked around to find two dresses lying on the bed and a pair of her shoes in the middle of the floor. This is a pigsty? She held back the urge to shout at him, knowing it was a wasted action. It would mean she's out of control. Then it became too easy to whip out a simple insult followed by a litany of horrible heart-tearing words. It happened to other couples, and she didn't want it to happen to them. Besides, it would spoil the enjoyment of the day. She squeezed her lips together as she usually did when she felt like snapping back.

Attila went downstairs to the quiet drawing room to wait for Marika. She and Miss Partridge were taking their daily walk. He realized he was harsh with Anna, but if he didn't say anything, she'd eventually be typing into the early hours of the morning. It was like an addiction with her, and her stamina was incredible. A bad combination. Besides, he really couldn't stand the noise. He walked over to the bay window. It was a lovely warm English day. An old oak tree planted off to the side of the small front garden didn't care about the weather, its branches drooping forlornly.

He wondered if his wife could ever make it again in the literary field, but seriously doubted it. There was quite a dramatic change in her over the last two years. The ambitious attitude had weakened after they escaped Hungary; even more so when Anna became a mother. Now that he was a father, he understood the change in her. He had changed too, knowing he had an important responsibility to take care of his family. All he wanted to do was settle down into a comfortable life, and hoped his wife didn't expect anything more from him.

September 1954

Drink to One's Health
On the last Sunday of the month, Anna and Attila watched Marika playing with a toy set of cups, saucers, and a teapot filled with pretend tea of warm barley water.

"Look at the time," Anna said.

"It's quarter after four. So what?"

"Miss Partridge hasn't come down yet." Anna got up. "She's late for afternoon tea."

At that moment, Miss Partridge appeared at the top of the stairs making her way gingerly to the bottom, her hand gripping the banister. Grey hair straggled out of her usually tight bun.

Anna met her half way up the stairwell. "You look tired."

"Tish tosh, it's nothing. Retired teachers like myself get their comeuppance for the misery they inflicted on their pupils."

"I didn't quite get all that."

"I'm being punished for my wicked teacher ways."

"That's ridiculous. You missed tea time. Will you go see your doctor?"

"Yes, I missed tea time, and no, I will not see my doctor."

"I mean it. If you don't call the doctor, I'll take you there myself."

Miss Partridge sat down in the drawing room as Attila got up and vanished into the kitchen. A few minutes later he wheeled out a trolley with a pot of tea and all the fixings.

Miss Partridge was surprised. "That was nice of you, Attila." Expecting a rather inferior cuppa, she cautiously took a sip, but enjoyed an exhilarating one instead. She was even more surprised. "To my knowledge, this is the first time you made tea."

Attila was certain about one thing and it was this, "Everything I make in the kitchen turns out good."

Anna rolled her eyes at the man's lack of culinary modesty while Miss Partridge appeared to be sucking on a lemon. She was absolutely right to dislike the man, even though he made a decent cup of tea.

"Well," the old school teacher corrected Attila.

"Well what?" said Attila.

"Never mind, I feel better already." Miss Partridge must mind her manners, for Anna's sake. "Your concern warms my old heart."

"Marika adores you," said Anna. "You see how she follows you around the house. She called you porridge first…before she said mommy."

Attila interjected, "You mean daddy."

"No, I don't."

"Yes, you do."

"All right Attila, you win." Anna picked up a small cushion and threw it at him.

A chuffed Miss Partridge didn't want to act like a pleased fool in front of the bickering parents. She continued to maintain her grumpy facade.

"Promise me you'll see your doctor. Do it for Marika."

Up to that point, Miss Partridge had no intention of going to the place where her clothes ended up hanging from a peg. Her first doctor saw her through fifty of her years before dying and being replaced by a fiftyish white coat. She felt she knew more than he did, but the way Anna put it, she really should go, for her goddaughter's sake. Anna was such a cheeky one.

"I promise."

Monday Morning

Sherry is Good Medicine
Dr. Abel was the most popular physician in his area. He had a way of making his patients feel comfortable even if they were receiving bad news.

He was surprised to see his most reclusive patient, the only person that refused to bend to his charm. "It's been a very long time since you last paid me a visit." His eyes danced with humour. "I hardly recognize you."

Miss Partridge gave him the once-over, starting with the top of his greying hair, down to an unremarkable face except for his extremely large nose, his white coat, his nicely polished shoes, and back up to his face. She stared him in the eyes. "No need to amuse me with chit chat, doctor. Get on with the check up, and warm the stethoscope before it touches my person, thank you very much."

Dr. Abel shook his head and chuckled. "As feisty as ever, and probably just as stubborn." After the examination, he returned to his office to wait for Miss

Partridge. When his fully clothed patient reluctantly sat down in front of him, he said, "We have a long standing doctor-patient relationship, but you've never let me call you by your first name, Gertrude."

Miss Partridge didn't see why she should change the order of things now, especially because she wasn't terribly fond of her first name. "You may call me Gertrude if I may call you by your first name, Archibald."

"Fair enough," conceded Dr. Abel. "Let's discuss your health, shall we? I detected an irregularity in your heartbeat which could be of concern. Therefore, I want you to see a cardiac specialist and reduce your activities. Perhaps it's time to think of getting a smaller house or a flat."

Miss Partridge looked at him as if he had asked her to carry his love child. "I'm not an invalid, doctor. What I am, is at least twenty-five years older than you, and will do as I please."

Dr. Abel sighed, ruffling the top of his hair with his hands. His patient was still the same curmudgeon. "Suit yourself."

Miss Partridge hated it when Dr. Abel obliged her. Now, she felt as if she had to apologize for asserting herself in no uncertain terms. "I appreciate your concern, but everything in this old body is in working order, so I will carry on until I'm beckoned to the hereafter."

"My secretary will arrange for you to see a specialist." Dr. Abel stood up and walked Miss Partridge to the door. "I want to see you again in four weeks. In the meantime, it'll do you good to have a modest glass of sherry before bedtime. It relaxes your heart and slightly dilates the arteries."

As soon as he disappeared, Miss Partridge left before the secretary could pick up the phone.

Back at home, she made a cup of tea and a fried crumpet soaking in butter. Just what she needed after enduring the indignity of getting undressed and having a man poking at her private anatomy. She didn't buy the story that male doctors were doctors first, and men second.

What a load of utter rot.

She'll just tell Anna that she got a prescription to imbibe sherry which was a half-truth.

March 1955

A Touchy Subject

There was much to like about exciting London which was steeped in culture and history. If Anna needed a change of pace, a trip into the countryside would find quaint villages and towns with quirky traditions such as cheese rolling in the

Cotswolds and wife-carrying races in Surrey. But England didn't feel like her final home, and it took a friend to show her the way. Marjorie's latest letter made her realize she wanted to live in Australia, and she had to convince Attila of the same. Maybe it won't be so difficult. After all, she convinced him to escape from Hungary with her.

The evening came when she was ready to bring up the subject. She flopped down beside Attila on their bed, remembering visions of a younger woman who always said what was on her mind. Now that she no longer enjoyed the perks of a popular author, she was sure she had lost her leverage. "Marjorie says there's no shortage of jobs, and her husband found a job in a couple of days." She said a teeny lie because it took him five days. That was because he had to choose from several offers.

"What are you trying to say?" Attila really didn't have to ask. He knew.

Anna spoke without any emotion to give the impression she was offering a perfectly sensible suggestion. "Why don't we think about moving to Australia?" The more she watched Attila's poker face, the more she saw him succumbing to irritation.

Attila gave a non-committal reply, "I'll think about it." His wife was ready for another major upheaval and confronted him in her usual abrupt fashion.

This was more than Anna expected after tossing the lure. She decided to wait for other opportunities to reel in her husband.

Wednesday, May 11, 1955

An Emergency

Anna studied her three year old daughter's hazel eyes rimmed with thick lashes. They were perfect. She stroked Marika's long, straight auburn hair which accentuated her delicate oval face. Did black and blond make auburn? Then there was the cowlick which was even more perfect. "Except for the colour of your eyes and hair, you look like Kati when she was a little girl." *If she grows up looking like her auntie, she'll be a knock-out.* "I love you, darling."

"Me too, Mommy."

As Anna admired her daughter's shining face, she noticed a tiny black mole under her left eye. *Was it possible for a tot to look exotic and angelic at the same time?*

"Why are you touching my face, Mommy?" asked Marika.

"You have a beauty spot under your eye."

"Is it all right to have one?"

"Yes, of course. I shall give myself one." Anna picked up a black eyebrow pencil and pecked a spot under her left eye to match Marika's mole. "The only problem is the bathwater will rinse mine away."

"Mommy, I want mine to come off too."

Anna smiled as she touched the tip of her daughter's nose. "So you can put it right here, silly goose?"

"Let's play chasies!" The little girl was off and running.

"Remember, no running on the stairs!" Anna chased a squealing child down the stairwell, taking two steps at a time.

Marika looked up and yelled, "No fair, Mommy!"

Suddenly, Anna felt sharp pain in her abdomen and clutched the banister to keep from tripping on the step.

"Mommy, what's wrong?"

Anna was bleeding. She tucked her hand between her legs as she rushed to the bathroom toilet, blood flowing far too quickly into the bowl. Doubled over by a nasty cramp, she made the effort to talk calmly to her daughter. "Get Grammy from the back garden."

Marika became frightened when she saw blood splashing down on the carpet her mommy was running over on the way to the bathroom. For the first time ever, she ran down the stairs instead of walking. She had broken a strict rule, but she needed to get to Grammy Porridge fast.

Miss Partridge was down on both knees puttering in her vegetable and herb patch when she looked up to see Marika running past her beloved red roses and lavender bushes like a bumblebee was chasing her. "Hello, precious, look at this culprit." She held up a slender, greenish yellow bug. "The carcass of a diabrotica howardi undecimpunctata, the dratted spotted cucumber beetle. It has the audacity to invade my garden. By itself, this insect is one of God's creatures, but when it destroys my English cucumber, it is the enemy!"

"Grammy! Grammy! Mommy's sick!"

"Oh, heavens! Let's go, dear." Miss Partridge struggled to get up with her creaking knees locked in a bent position. Marika grabbed her hand, futilely trying to pull the heavy woman up. Finally, the two were hurrying across the lawn and into the house.

While an ambulance rushed Anna to Attila's hospital, Marika sat on Miss Partridge's lap, too frightened to cry. "I don't ever want to go to the hostipal, Grammy. What's wrong with Mommy? Will she be all right?"

Miss Partridge smiled briefly at the mispronunciation while thinking Marika was quite mature for one so young. "Don't worry, dear. Your mommy is in good hands, and your father's waiting for her at the hospital."

"Grammy Porridge, was blood coming out of mommy? Whenever she cuts vegebals, blood comes out of her finger. She says I have to be careful when I eat with my fork because I might cut my mouth."

Miss Partridge sighed. Anna did have a tendency to cut a finger every time there was a knife in her hand. "Hush now, child. Let us pray good things for your mother, and she'll be fine." Worried sick about Anna, she stroked Marika's hair with an agitated hand.

The Fix

The first thing Attila saw was Anna covered with a bloody sheet. Trying desperately to fight back rising panic, he called her name, but his deep voice trailed far behind her drifting senses. There was nothing he could do, so he had a cigarette while the doctors examined his wife. He had his last puff of smoke when Mr. Callum, one of Hammersmith's surgeons, strided towards Attila with gangly legs knocking at the knees. The doctor wore a constant frown of concern which meant Attila couldn't tell whether it was because of Anna or not.

"Your wife had a miscarriage." Mr. Callum paused for a moment, then asked, "Is this the first time?"

Abortion was on the tip of Attila's tongue, but he couldn't bring himself to mention the crude operation many years ago. There were many other Catholics working in the hospital who would be sure to let him know how they felt if they ever learned of it. He hoped his wife kept it a secret. "I don't think Anna had any idea she was pregnant." Now that he had bonded with his daughter, the loss of an unborn child was hitting him like a ton of bricks.

"We need to stabilize the bleeding."

Attila cringed at the b-word. "Anna bleeds heavily every month," he offered.

"Is there a medical reason?"

"Not sure."

"Why don't you wait here, and I'll see you when it's over." Mr. Callum clapped Attila on the back to reassure him before he left.

For the next two hours, Attila paced the corridor, chain smoking, until Mr. Callum left the operating theatre.

"We performed a dilation and curettage, D & C for short. It's a procedure to clean out the lining of your wife's uterus. Now we wait to see if it was successful."

"Has the bleeding stopped?"

"Not yet." Mr. Callum paused as if he wasn't sure he should say anything else. He finally said, "Complications could arise if she continues to lose too much blood, and she may have to be transfused. Worst case scenario, we're looking at a hysterectomy."

Complications like death? Attila said fearfully, "If you take her uterus, she won't be able to have any more children."

"Your wife's ovaries will be removed too."

"Why?"

"It's routine procedure for a hysterectomy."

The possibility of no more children weighed heavily on Attila's mind as he walked into Anna's room to find her in a deep narcotic sleep, her face so ashen it scared him. Sitting down beside her, he picked up her cold hand, wondering if things were ever going to be okay again.

It was an hour before Anna opened her eyes. "What happened?" she asked groggily.

"You had a miscarriage and needed surgery to stop the bleeding."

Still under the influence of the anaesthetic, Anna's full moon eyes grew impossibly larger. "Pregnant?" She looked as though she was on the verge of tears, but instead a strange look came over her. Staring at a dirty spot on the bare wall in front of her, she said, "They didn't stop it."

A commotion ensued with doctors and nurses barging into the room, and ordering Attila to leave. He was resigned to hanging around the corridor, listening to Anna's voice overwhelming the doctor's hushed tones. Not during the traumas of war or their escape from Hungary had Attila ever heard his wife panic. Now he got his chance and it made him physically ill.

Mr. Callum opened the door and said to him, "Maybe she'll listen to you."

Attila hurried to his wife's side to plead with her, "You're making the bleeding worse."

Lying in bed probably bleeding to death, Anna was helpless. "He wants to take out my uterus, so I can't have any more babies."

Attila's hand squeezed hers tightly as a distraction.

"You're hurting me."

Attila loosened his grip. "The doctor says you need the operation."

"I want Marika to have a brother or a sister."

"So do I." Attila's voice trailed away, gripped by the pain of a parent who won't be having another child.

Strange lights that only Anna could see began to fill the room until she realized she had to make a decision. "Do the surgery. I'm not ready to die yet."

An Early Christmas

Anna returned home three weeks later. It took the same amount of time to recover half of her physical strength, but she didn't feel the same. She was irritable and fell into a state of lethargy. Could it be the transfused blood from an anonymous donor flowing in her veins that made her feel so peculiar, or was it her missing organs? Or was it because she won't ever get pregnant again?

Her landlady continued to worry like a surrogate mother until the postman delivered a letter. "Good things do come in small packages."

Marjorie's ongoing discovery of Australia's sunburnt life brightened Anna's day. Every word was again stirring up her desire to experience another new adventure. When Marjorie invited her to visit, she thought of nothing else. There was something mysterious and promising about Australia, a growing country on the other side of the world, and she wanted to be a part of what it had to offer.

That night, she handed Marjorie's letter to Attila without saying a word.

He could see hope flickering across his wife's solemn face.

Catching his wistful look, Anna jumped out of bed. "Let's visit Australia."

Attila decided to give his wife an early Christmas present. "No, let's go live there."

Anna leaped into her husband's arms as if someone had released a room full of scorpions. They toppled onto the floor in a knotted heap.

Attila bounced up and pulled Anna to her feet.

She tucked a loose blond hair falling over his forehead. "When can we go?" Her voice was already stronger.

Her husband held up a protesting hand. "Hold on, there's a few things we have to take care of. It's not like escaping from Hungary when it was just you and me, and nothing else." Anna's brush with death frightened him, and he couldn't bear the thought of trying to raise Marika without her. He knew why he blurted out the decision to move to Australia.

It would return his warhorse of a wife to him.

Once he sorted out the details to make the move happen, the more he settled into the idea of living in Australia, virgin territory with great potential for immigrants. London was never boring, but it was old, dirty, and quite dangerous. The emissions from diesel buses and coal burning chimneys caused thousands of Londoners to die from a massive smog back in the winter of 1952. The deadly weather caused an increase in crime with thieves using the smog to break into shops and houses. Even worse, they physically attacked Londoners who couldn't see more than a couple of feet ahead as they tried to make their way home.

Then there were the Teddy Boys, an oxymoron of rebellious, bigoted white working class youths dressing up as refined Edwardian dandies in their long jackets, elegant waistcoats, and tapered pants, threatening to incite violence in the streets of London. How does a father explain to his daughter that not all teddies are cute and fuzzy.

Saying goodbye to the witch was a bonus. Attila psyched himself up for the next big change in their lives. The following day, he signed his family up for the Assisted Passage Migration Scheme seeking subsidized fares to Australia.

Within three months, he had his answer. The government of Australia wanted Attila with his brick making, hospital orderly, and accounting skills. Being Caucasian and living in Great Britain sealed the deal quickly. He and Anna each paid ten pounds sterling for passage on the S.S. Orsova. Marika was going to travel for free.

On the day they learned the good news, Anna stayed behind at the supper table with her landlady.

"All right, what's going on?" Miss Partridge had the uncanny ability of knowing when she was going to hear unpleasant news.

Anna reached across the table to touch the papery-skinned hands in front of her. "We're moving to Australia."

Miss Partridge said nothing. Anna had knocked the whammy out of her, and it took her a full thirty seconds to collect her senses. She finally said, "I've seen you snap out of your sadness, and I was so relieved because an unhappy Anna is an unhappy Grammy Porridge. If going to Australia to start a new life has lifted your spirits, then go with my blessing, but I shall miss you terribly." Her eyes filled with tears. "I shall spend every possible moment with Marika."

She had lived a solitary life, and didn't know what she was missing until the colourful Paprikas landed on her doorstep. Now she was going to be alone again.

October 1955

Once a Teacher, Always a Teacher
"Come here, children!" Miss Partridge ordered Anna and Attila into the drawing room. "I'm going to give you a brief lesson on Australia's history."

In Hungarian, Attila said to Anna, "The battle axe thinks I'm an ignoramus."

"Make her happy and listen to what she says because it's upsetting her to lose Marika."

Attila moaned, "Okay."

As soon as the couple sat down, their landlady said sternly, "Australia's immigration policy needed to address an acute shortage of labour after the war was over. The country planned to achieve this goal by boosting its population of eight million with immigrants from other parts of the world. Plenty of skilled labour would improve the economic situation and escalate Australia's status as a worldwide nation."

When she paused, Attila got up to leave.

"Sit down! I'm not finished!"

Attila opened his mouth to say something, but Anna patted the chesterfield. "Let her finish."

Reluctantly, Attila sat down again. He was going to enjoy saying goodbye to his bossy landlady.

Satisfied she had their full attention, Miss Partridge continued, "A more dangerous reason lurking in the average Australian's life is the threat of communism. This real possibility requires a show of people-strength to defend the country against any future war." She stopped when she noticed Attila looking out the bay window. "Eyes straight ahead!"

Attila couldn't believe his ears. The deluded woman thinks she's back in the classroom teaching little boys and girls.

"As I was about to say, preferential treatment has always been given to British migrants, but it was becoming difficult to attract enough of us. We Brits don't want to leave a United Kingdom enjoying a high employment rate for a country that will pay lower salaries. Australia had no alternative but to relax its white policy and permit other races to enter as immigrants. To make the lofty plan happen, the country began to accept non-British European immigrants after decades of trying to keep Australia predominantly white and British in nature, and it coincided with the World War II refugee crisis. Within a couple of years, the country allowed Asians to settle permanently for business reasons, a promising change to the discrimination which forced many Chinese settlers to return to China in the nineteenth and early twentieth centuries." Miss Partridge crossed her arms under her bosom. "As it so happens, Australia has indeed become a leading nation."

Attila waited, but his landlady said nothing more. She kept looking at him with that angry eye of hers. He said, "I'm sitting and looking at you like an obedient student. What's wrong now?"

"I'm finished."

A True Friend

It was Marjorie's turn to finish the lesson in a much more pleasant manner. Her airmail envelope arrived before the Paprikas left London.

'Dear Anna and Attila, I hope this letter finds you in good spirits and good health. Moving to another country can be quite an ordeal, but don't forget that Richard and I are delighted to have you as our guests for as long as you need us. I can hardly wait to meet you in Melbourne. In the meantime, from a practical point of view, here's a few things you might like to know about your new home. Australia is enjoying a very prosperous decade. A post-war immigration boom has paved the way for full employment, a decent standard of living, and new detached housing on large blocks of land in brand new suburbs. Dare I say America has influenced our way of life here? Black and white television and modern music have begun to pop up everywhere, adding quite an exciting dimension to the culture. Television programs consist mostly of musical variety and quiz shows, and many programs are being imported from America and Britain...'

Anna continued reading with keen interest. From the wonderful things Marjorie wrote, the newcomers were going to have no problem falling for quirky emerging Australia.

Saturday, November 26, 1955 at 10:00 a.m.

Hungry Mice

Miss Partridge watched Attila place two brown suitcases in the booth and a navy blue steamer trunk on the bench seat of the black cab waiting outside her house. Speaking with a sadness that had built up over the last few months, she said, "My dears, you are so young and alive, having experienced misfortune here, but it's all part of life, isn't it? Put the bad behind as you begin a new life far away from England. Please write and send pictures of Marika because I want to see her growing up into a fine young lady." She bent down and held out her arms. "Come here, princess. I need the biggest hug you can give me."

Marika let the old woman embrace her tightly.

Miss Partridge showered a bunch of kisses on the goddaughter who was more like her grandchild. "I love you, princess."

"I love you too, Grammy Porridge."

Miss Partridge released the little girl with great reluctance and disappeared inside her house. She returned with a book and handed it to Anna. "I want you to have my Oxford dictionary." The landlady struggled with her emotions, choking back the tears. "You will always be welcome in my home."

An echo from the past reminded Anna of the day she said goodbye to her own mother. She took the book with a final hug for Miss Partridge.

It was Attila's turn as he decided to be magnanimous by offering his hand. The former landlady hesitated before clutching it, and they both ended up having an awkward moment.

The old woman waved goodbye until the cab disappeared down the street. With a heavy heart, she closed her front door. She said forlornly, "Now it's just me and some hungry mice scuttling behind the walls."

Twenty-Eight Days with Malik

The Paprikas were embarking on an important journey, and this time Attila was caught up in all the excitement. He was born to prefer a routine life over chaos and uncertainty, but the occasional adventure did have a way of adding spice to one's life. With his family in tow, they boarded a bus at Victoria Coach Station headed for Southampton where another cab drove them to the busy cruise terminal. As they walked along the dock, hundreds of hardy seagulls flapped and squealed high above, undeterred by the rain that began to fall.

"Mommy, what's that?" Marika asked, pointing to a huge ship. Its unusual corn-colour hull trimmed in rich red commanded attention as it drew admiring glances from passersby.

"The S.S. Orsova is taking us to our new home in Australia. Do you remember the pictures I showed you of kangaroos and koala bears?"

"I like the kola bears because they sort of look like Teddy." Marika smoothed down the crinkly plastic bonnet she wore to keep the rain off her hair.

Anna smiled at the way her daughter pronounced koala bear.

Marika's eyes opened wide as they approached the choppy, muddy water. Seven hundred and twenty-two feet long, the S.S. Orsova loomed over the dock, the largest object she had ever seen in her short life. "Is our new home far away?"

"Thousands of miles away."

"Will we get there tomorrow?" asked Marika.

Her daughter's naivety made Anna smile again. "In a few weeks, just before Christmas."

Attila stared at the restless water which made him queasy as he remembered the six hour voyage on the Bearitz. This trip was a hell of a lot longer, and having to endure another bad storm could permanently screw up his DNA.

The rain dropped steadily on the water while dark-faced stewards wearing white jackets directed the Paprikas to their tourist cabin in the bowels of the ship. Two sets of neatly made bunk beds and a nightstand in between left very little wiggle room inside the cabin. Beside the door was a tiny bathroom.

While they were unpacking, a short, thin young Indian steward with very dark skin, pitch black hair and goggly eyes, appeared at their half open door.

"Begging your pardon, Malik at your service."

The roller coaster accent intrigued Marika. She wondered why the steward's words sounded strange and funny at the same time.

Attila thought he was a little too pushy and shut the door.

Picking up a folder from the nightstand, Anna said, "The trip to Australia will take twenty-eight days."

Her husband shuddered as the horror of the Bearitz crossing reared its ugly head again.

Bad Timing

The Paprikas stood at the deck railing, the ship dwarfed by the intimidating size of the ocean with nothing but wave after wave and blue sky. It was a haunting image that was almost frightening to behold. Ancient people raised their hands and bowed their heads in supplication to inanimate objects, receiving the same kind of revelation Anna was experiencing as she soaked in the captivating energy of the sea. As the ship sailed past the southern tip of Portugal, she said, "It looks so green and peaceful."

"I see a piece of flat land with some trees poking out of it," muttered Attila. He was not impressed.

Anna gave him a dirty look. "Do you have to be so clinical?"

Attila lit a cigarette, inhaling deeply as he scanned the distant horizon before blowing out a thin stream of smoke. "Talk about food and I become a poet."

During the day, the recreation staff kept Marika and the other children busy with play activities, giving her parents a chance to be alone together. Locked in an intimate interlude inside their cabin, they discovered sex was rather awkward in a skinny bunk bed.

Knock, knock. "It is Malik here." The annoying voice on the other side of the door was like a sledgehammer bashing a thumb.

Attila groaned.

"Don't answer," Anna said breathlessly.

The knocking persisted. "Hello, hello! Begging your pardon, I can hear you!"

Malik succeeded in making Attila's blood boil. Stark naked, he jumped up, grabbing a white towel to cover his package as he swung the door open. Anna was shocked. Her husband wasn't an exhibitionist by nature.

The steward was not in the least bit phased by a half-naked passenger. "You must see Rock of Gibraltar." He waved happily at Anna lying in the bunk bed discreetly covered with a blanket.

Miss Partridge intruded into Attila's unpleasant thoughts — mind your manners or no rice pudding with supper. He counted to three before slamming the door shut. The poor kid must be a half-wit who doesn't understand anything about sex because if he did, he'd have left them alone. After calming down, he decided to give Malik a break and not complain to his boss.

Anna patted the bunk bed, and said with longing in her voice, "Attila..."

Her husband gave her a look that spoke of deflated anatomy.

"Darling?"

"Let's go see a big rock."

If At First You Don't Succeed

The ship was headed back to open sea, bringing them closer to weather that was hotter and far too humid. Offering a bit of respite were the morning breezes which turned into moderate winds by midday. Attila remained hopeful that the voyage over the blue-green water would continue to be a smooth crossing. And although he wasn't blown away by Malta's strategic Rock of Gibraltar which guarded the entrance to the Mediterranean Sea, or by sewage smelling Naples, Italy, he actually enjoyed visiting the historic lava-covered city of Pompeii and the emerald green Aegean Islands. In between ports of call, he spent much of his time leaning against the railing smoking cigarettes. It was easy to forget his worries here. No beds to make, no meals to cook, no boss to satisfy. If only this trip, just like it is right now, could last forever.

For some unknown reason, Malik took a special interest in the Paprikas. It wasn't surprising that he hurried them out to the deck when they reached the Suez Canal of Egypt. He took Marika's hand, running ahead with her to become two children escaping their parents. Taking a personal interest in the passengers was not part of his duties, but he didn't seem to care about any consequences.

The man-made structure was an awesome sight to behold as the Orsova sailed along, a searchlight built into the ship's bow to help it navigate the narrow traffic lane without incident.

Malik put his hands together as if in prayer. "I am master of disguise." Before the Paprikas knew what was happening, he began to mimic German, British, and Australian passengers against the backdrop of the mighty Suez Canal and the boring flat terrain of desert on either side of it.

Anna and Attila were speechless, held hostage by the most peculiar, unexpected performance from an Asian half-man, half-boy. It was entertaining though, and they politely clapped.

Returning to his sing-song accent, Malik said, "I pick it up, just like this." He snapped his brown fingers for emphasis.

"How old are you?" asked Anna.

Malik was happy because passengers never asked him to talk about himself. "I look like child, but I am nineteen. I am from India. My parents have hard life. I send them money, so they can eat and buy good shoes for my little sister, Prabha."

Anna looked at Attila, silently telling him that Malik was a nice kid.

The next day, Marika was having fun with the other children while her parents were gyrating in a tepid bath.

Knock, knock.

"Did you hear that?" Anna whispered into Attila's ear.

"No."

A thick Hungarian accent penetrated the cabin door. "Hello, Mr. Paprika! Hello, hello, are you there?"

A frustrated Attila groaned, "Damn it! Malik is imitating us now!"

He jumped out of the bathtub, stubbing his big toe against the hard porcelain. "Shit, shit, damn it!" Angry, dripping, and totally naked...all that, and more, charged the door like a rampaging rhinoceros, and swung it open to total strangers.

A portly middle aged man accompanied by a woman of duplicate appearance had friendly smiles on their faces which rapidly turned into gaping expressions of shock. The woman turned around to look at the suddenly very interesting light fixture on the opposite wall.

The unexpected strangers stunned Attila into a morass of idiocy. Luckily, his brain was programmed to act swiftly in situations of this nature, sending urgent signals to his hands to cover up. While cupping his intimate parts, Attila decided honesty was the best policy, "Pardon me, I thought you were someone else." The end of his sentence was punctuated by a rolled up towel flying out of the bathroom. He grabbed it with one hand to preserve his modesty, and wrapped it around his waist.

The portly man raised his bushy eyebrows which brought Attila's attention to a single hair that was so freaky long it sprouted out of his right eyebrow and down over his eye. He wondered what the portly man would do if he reached over and plucked out the alien hair.

"Mr. Paprika, I assume. My name is Karoly Kovacs." He pointed to his wife who was still staring at the light fixture. "This is the back of my wife Piroska."

Attila mumbled, "Nice to meet you."

The woman burped up an unfriendly hello.

Mr. Kovacs said, "We are from Budapest. Malik told us there was another Hungarian couple, so we wanted to introduce ourselves." He switched to

Hungarian. "If your wife threw the towel, then who were you expecting that you would open the door so naked?"

Attila wasn't enjoying talking to a nosy stranger from Budapest while minimally wrapped in a towel with water trickling down his body, and a throbbing big toe. He was irritated, but felt the need to be polite, thanks to a handful of well-placed cuffs on the ear during his formative years. He replied in Hungarian, "I thought you were Malik."

Suddenly, Attila realized the implications of what he said. He had just condemned himself as a pervert, and Malik too. Oh God, and Anna. "No, it's not what you think."

But it was too late. The portly man's wife balked with revulsion as she pulled her husband away from their cabin neighbour who was a degenerate destined to receive God's wrath.

Mr. Kovacs said, "We'll meet Mrs. Paprika some other time. Don't worry, your secret is safe with us because we don't want to cause any trouble." As he hurried away with his wife, he said to her, "Magyars like that give us all a bad name."

Attila slammed the door shut. That's what he should have done right after he opened it. Better yet, he should have stayed in the bathtub with Anna.

"Attila…" Anna said longingly from the bathroom.

"Not in the mood anymore."

Are Swiss Watches Waterproof?

The ship docked at Aden, a Yemen city built inside an old volcano where noon temperatures reached an impossible one hundred and forty degrees fahrenheit. Passengers who didn't have the luxury of air conditioned cabins, filled the scorching air with plenty of moans and groans.

Having grown up in a country where summer was just as hot, Malik looked comfortable as he glided over to the Paprikas reclining in a row of deck chairs. "You must buy Swiss watches here. Vedy, vedy cheap."

Attila was never too hot and bothered to correct someone's pronunciation. "Say…very, very cheap."

"Vedy, vedy cheap."

"Very…very…cheap." Attila rolled his r's for emphasis.

"Vedy, vedy cheap."

Attila decided this exercise could go on forever. He lied, "Much better."

Malik smiled happily. "Thank you, thank you."

The Paprikas watched impassively as merchants came to the passengers who stayed on the ship. Like giant mice, they climbed swiftly up the boarding ladders screeching in a jumble of broken English. "Swiss watches! Swiss watches for sale! Bulova watches, cheap, good watches!" yelled a merchant displaying his wares up and down the entire length of two thick chocolate brown arms.

Attila wanted a watch, so he called the man over to his chair.

The merchant eyed the hot tourist, deciding he had an easy mark. He tried to sell a watch for four English pounds, but Anna interrupted the Arab's staccato chatter, bargaining the watch down to half the original price, much to Attila's acute embarrassment.

"As salam alaykom, you have Arab blood in you?" the merchant asked Anna, noting her black hair and healthy face.

When Anna didn't return his greeting, he cornered his next customer.

Attila turned to his wife and admonished her, "Don't embarrass me like that again."

It was hard to remain composed in the sweltering heat with an unappreciative husband. "You were willing to buy the watch for double the price to avoid any haggling by your dear wife?" Anna took the newly acquired Swiss watch from Attila's hand. Without warning, she threw it high in an arc over passengers standing at the railing. A cluster of people watched the timepiece sail over the railing and into the ocean, then turned to see what the face of a cuckoo looked like. Anna pointed at Attila.

She said to her husband, "Did that embarrass you too?"

Attila stared at her with a poker face, hiding the angry humiliation he was feeling. He loved watches and really wanted that one.

Germs and Gems

By the time the ship docked at Colombo, Ceylon, everyone wanted to see if the rumours about it being another paradise were true. To the disappointment of all, Colombo turned out to be a dirty third world city inhabited by hordes of noisy, excitable, brown skinned people desperate for money from the well-dressed tourists who had to fight off the pushing beggars.

Anna and Attila stepped ashore with Marika, only to be dismayed by the squalor. There were going to be no visits to the eateries to taste the local food which must be harbouring parasites mutating aggressively from the unsanitary conditions. Instead, the family planned a quick run-through of the main street, so they can say they saw Ceylon.

The Paprikas stepped into a rickshaw waiting in a long line of carriages beside the dock. With the strength of a racehorse, the dark sinewy foot driver ran past dilapidated shops and throngs of ragged beggars who followed them in angry desperation, screeching and begging at the top of their lungs. Once the rabid crowd was left behind, the Paprikas entered a tiny, inconspicuous jewelry store where a huge smoky topaz caught Anna's eye. She was thrilled with its rectangular clean-cut beauty, and bought it for the same price as Attila's watch. Did everything of value carry a price tag of two English pounds?

Sharks Breed Like Rabbits

The Orsova was going to reach the west coast of Australia in a couple of days. During the voyage, the Paprikas didn't think about their new home. The heat, food, and new sights kept them busy with the present. Nights under the stars and evening sea breezes saturated with salt water molecules were soul-rejuvenating, but the trip would soon be over. Back to making beds, cooking meals, pleasing the boss. The reality of starting afresh replaced Attila's initial excitement with the same old rotten feeling of apprehension, giving him a stomach ache.

New adventures suddenly seemed highly overrated.

On the morning of the second last day, they stood on deck as the Orsova sailed into Fremantle, Perth's port city.

"Look at the sharks! There must be a hundred of them!" exclaimed Anna to Marika. From the railing, she pointed at the grey triangles slowly circling the ship as if they were giving a choreographed dance, hypnotic to watch, and belying the deadly menace under the surface.

"I see maybe forty sharks," said Attila. He was in a ruttish mood.

"What's the difference when you're talking about sharks?"

"A difference of sixty."

Anna said nothing. Her husband's sarcasm could be so annoying.

As the Orsova entered the Great Australian Bight at the bottom of the continent, the ship encountered a storm which Attila and the majority of passengers would remember for the rest of their lives. The storm was so ferocious it caused terrible bouts of nausea and vomiting which kept the stewards very busy cleaning up the messes.

Attila stumbled out of the cabin leaving Anna to worry about him. She was grateful she possessed a constitution that didn't succumb to seasickness because at least one member of the family had to take charge. Luckily, Marika had fallen asleep before the storm started, and was still sleeping.

Anna asked Malik to find her husband and bring him back.

The young man knew where to go. Attila was lying outside the bar, nauseous as hell, loaded with alcohol and dramamine. With the help of two other stewards, Malik struggled all the way back to Anna with a load of dead weight.

Attila flopped down on the bunk bed with a handkerchief stuffed in his mouth. Mercifully, the water was calm the following day, and he vowed there won't be any more ocean voyages for him.

Red Satin Ribbons
Before disembarking at the port of Melbourne, Anna handed Malik a sealed white envelope containing a modest sum of money. "We want you to have this."

The young man bowed his head respectfully as he produced a handful of red satin ribbons. Placing them in Anna's hand, he said shyly, "For Marika's pretty hair." He turned to the little girl and bowed again. "You remind me of Prabha. Goodbye."

"Bye Malik," said Marika.

As the Paprikas headed down the ramp, their names floated through the hubbub noises of chattering people. They looked up to find Malik standing against the ship's railing, waving a large hankie as white as his teeth.

CHAPTER 6

Evil Down Under

Friday, December 23, 1955 at 1:07 p.m.
Port of Melbourne, Victoria

The Paprikas waited in a gigantic terminal filled with customs officials at long wooden tables processing the throngs of disembarked passengers. Friends and relatives were overjoyed at reuniting with loved ones, the crying and laughter filtering around the Paprikas as they scanned the sea of strange faces.

"To your right, Anna!" Marjorie maneuvered gracefully around people hovering around their stamped trunks and suitcases. She sported longer strawberry blonde hair with side bangs sweeping down to soften her square jaw in a flattering pageboy, and had even more freckles on her face and arms, courtesy of the Australian sun.

Edward was holding the hand of a man who was not much taller than him and had the same facial features and dark brown hair.

When Anna saw Marjorie, she waved enthusiastically until they grabbed each other in a big old-fashioned hug.

Marjorie stepped back to admire her Hungarian friend's sleeveless red and white floral frock cinched at the waist with a narrow white belt. She smiled at the scarlet toenails peeking out of white cork wedge sandals and the tanned face framed by short wavy black hair tucked behind each ear to display two oversized pearl white button earrings. "Thank goodness you didn't step off the boat in a siren suit or a kangaroo coat. They served their purpose during the war, but no more!" She gave Anna another squeeze and said, "You look as cool as a cucumber. Don't you know it's ninety-five in the shade?"

Anna laughed. "Hah! That's cold compared to what we went through on our trip. You missed it all by flying over here."

Marjorie's husband, Richard, a slight jovial man with a pronounced Cockney accent heartily shook hands with Attila. It was hard not to notice he was at least eight inches shorter than his wife, but he didn't seem to mind, and neither did she. Without any encouragement, he helped Attila take their baggage out of the terminal.

While the men were busy loading up the Cooper's car, the women and children formed a close circle as they got reacquainted with each other. Edward was now seven years old with healthy golden brown skin which made his green eyes pop. He was tall and lanky for his age, having inherited his mother's height, but in every other way he was his father.

Marjorie prompted her shy son who was tenaciously holding a bunch of wilting daisies. "Go on, say hello to Marika and her mom, Mrs. Paprika."

"Hello," said Edward as he handed the daisies to Marika. "For you."

Marjorie smiled broadly at the little girl. "You arrived during a hot summer. Down here, the weather is opposite to the weather in England, and do you know you'll be celebrating your first Australian Christmas in two days?"

"What does opposite mean?" Marika looked up enquiringly at her mother.

Anna said, "When we enjoy summer here, Grammy Porridge will be having winter."

"How come?"

Marjorie chuckled, knowing it will be a few more years before the little girl understood all about Earth's relationship with the sun.

"Not now." Anna distracted Marika by taking her hand and leading her out of the terminal.

Richard's grey Morris Minor was trussed up like a Thanksgiving turkey with ropes and belts securing the blue steamer trunk on the roof. A thick rope held down the booth threatening to pop open and dislodge the suitcases and bags of souvenirs collected during ports of call stopovers.

As they drove through Melbourne, Marjorie said, "When I first arrived, I went to the local library and did some research on the history of this city. Apparently, most of the migrants from Britain in the 1850's chose Melbourne as their new home, all because of the lure of gold. And gold there was. Diggers who hit the motherlode drank champagne from buckets, and if a maid caught their fancy, they draped her in silk and jewels. By the 1860's, the sleepy little port town became a major world centre with civic buildings like parliament and the post office. Fast forward to this decade, and a lot of old buildings with hideous gargoyle statues are being replaced by these brand new tall glass and steel buildings." Everyone in the car looked up at the skyscrapers lining the street. Marjorie reached over and patted Anna's hand. "You'll be pleased to know that immigrants from continental Europe have established many fine European cafes here. After you settle down, I'll take you to Pellegrini's. Richard loves the Italian food and I can't get enough of the espresso coffee."

Men in shorts and short-sleeve shirts, and women in summer frocks and sandals ambled along the sidewalks, their metabolisms slowed down from the heat. The odd person shuffled across the busy roads in front of traffic, oblivious to the squealing of rubber. Trams ran along streamers of metal tracks imbedded in the asphalt, and automobiles driven by impatient foreigners not used to a slower pace tried to outmaneuver the imposing public transportation with sporadic success.

"Unfortunately, the economic progress has created traffic jams," remarked Marjorie.

They stopped at Myer's to enjoy the big department store's delicious minty green, chocolate chip ice cream in a square cone. At the same time, they were treated to a celebration of next year's Melbourne Olympics with the first-time introduction of Christmas window displays. The most popular window was Father Christmas in his sleigh giving a ride to two of his reindeer while another got a ride from an athlete on a bike. And the most famous reindeer with the red nose looked like he was racing the torch runner.

Next stop was the Cooper's home in Bacchus Marsh, a small town located thirty-five miles west of Melbourne. It was situated in a fertile valley with two rivers running through it, an ideal place for a close-knit community. The drive was a pleasant one through refreshing landscapes of parks and gorges along the highway with not a hint of the huge arid desert covering most of central Australia.

When Richard's car pulled up to their street, the Paprikas admired the Coopers' attractive two storey red brick house sitting majestically on top of a gentle hill with meticulously pruned English lavender bushes gracing the path leading up to the front door.

"Welcome to Bacchus Marsh," said Marjorie. She stretched her arms out as if she were preparing to embrace a loved one.

Attila leaned forward to inspect the front wall of the house, remembering the physically challenging work that went into making a brick.

Being gracious hosts, the Coopers watched with curiosity, but said nothing.

The first thing Marjorie did was make Marika feel at home with a chocolate wrapped in dark blue and white paper. "Do you remember Fry's chocolate cream bar?" said Marjorie. "You can buy many English goodies here."

Marika happily took the chocolate which was one of her favourites.

The children were given carte blanche to decorate the majestic pine tree waiting for them in the living room. As soon as they hung up the last of the ornaments, there was a lot of running and squealing because Edward chased Marika with his pet frog. On Christmas Day, Anna helped Marjorie make a special lunch of stuffed goose, roast potatoes, gravy, and garden peas. For dessert, threepences and sixpences hidden inside homemade spiced Christmas pudding were the main attraction for the children's prying fingers.

Tuesday, January 3, 1956
Mid-Morning

Red Back Spiders Love Shoes
Richard took Attila for a drive along the Princes Highway, cutting through bush country on their way to Geelong, a small but growing city located thirty-five miles south of Bacchus Marsh. It was home to the industrial giants of Shell Refinery, Ford, Corio Distillery, and Pivot Phosphate Works. In the suburb of North Shore along Corio Bay, the Shell Refinery opened for business back in 1954 with state of the art docking facilities for the enormous oil tankers.

After waiting patiently in the shade of a tree beside Shell's parking lot, Richard was soon heartily shaking the hand of the newest accounting clerk. "Congratulations, Attila."

"Thank you for bringing me here. Now Anna and I will have to move to Geelong to be closer to work."

"I'll help you find a car."

Not used to acts of kindness from a virtual stranger, Attila was again touched by Richard's generosity. "You've made the unnerving experience of moving to a new country almost enjoyable."

Richard smiled sheepishly, "My pleasure, old man. Can't take all the credit though. I was a rather wound-up bloke until the Aussie hospitality rubbed off on me."

Geelong's public housing registry was stuck at zero vacancy, delaying the Paprikas' plan to move there. They decided to rent a home in Bacchus Marsh, and Attila bought a second hand Morris Oxford for the daily commute to the Shell refinery.

Marjorie offered them some parting advice. "An Australian's best friend is the life guard. When you're at the beach, listen to him. He spots the sharks first and it's everybody out of the water. Give the highly poisonous red back spider plenty of space and they will leave you alone. Just make sure you check the insides of your shoes with a stick before you slip them on."

Richard interrupted his wife, "You'll give them nightmares."

Marjorie scoffed, "We have yet to see a red back spider. The only thing that should give them nightmares are the Aussie flies, the little buzzers."

Richard offered, "You have to put up fly wire on all your windows, otherwise you'll be practising the Aussie salute all day long. And get a fly swatter for every room. They'll come in handy."

Marjorie continued her conversation, "You must go north and spend a day at Lerderderg Gorge. We think it's spectacularly wild and rugged, and you will also enjoy the huge park surrounding it."

"I've never understood why it's also called Lerderberg Gorge," Richard interrupted his wife again.

"Yes, dear, it's something to wonder about," she said to placate him. "Anyway, as I was saying, there's something for everyone — greenery, creeks, wildlife galore. And make sure you take a gander at the You Yangs Mountains that lie between Melbourne and Geelong. It's all about eucalyptus trees, koala bears, and great big granite rocks made for climbing. Edward absolutely adores the place, so I'm sure Marika will love it too."

Quick, Hide the Car

The Paprikas arrived at a narrow street lined with nondescript single storey wood frame houses built on tight lots. Houses were located on the north side of the street. Due south was a large open field belonging to a rundown farm.

Unfortunately for Attila, their new home looked the same as the first time they saw it. "Such a delightful shack."

"It's temporary," Anna dismissed his cynicism. "I want to sprinkle salt on the door step to cleanse the home and bring good fortune."

Attila was heaving baggage up to the front door when he balked at Anna's foolishness. "What?"

"It's a Hungarian tradition, and my mother did it."

"Didn't your family have more than its fair share of bad luck?"

"It could have been worse."

"It could have been better." Attila pretended to check his pants pockets. "No, I'm not carrying any salt with me. How about you?"

"You're not funny."

"Really? I think I'm so hilarious, I might piss my trousers from laughing."

Anna refused to get sidetracked by her husband's nonsense. "I can ask the neighbours for salt."

Attila was horrified. "Are you crazy? What will the neighbours think of their new neighbours, namely us? Besides, what's gotten into you? I don't remember you being superstitious."

"Thank yourself for the way I am now." Anna gave her husband a cold look. "I won't tell them what it's for. They'll think I want to cook something."

"You give me far too much credit. As for cooking something, asking for a half cup of salt might arouse suspicions about your ability to cook. Even though you're not a good cook, you're not terrible."

"Gee, thank you very much, kind sir. You're such a sweetheart." It was a futile exchange, so Anna waved her hands dismissively in the air. "I give up. But if bad things happen to us, I'll be glaring in your direction."

"Shades of Miss Porridge. Our luck has been better than we expected, and all without salt. Don't blame me for the fact you believe in foolish notions."

Anna switched to Hungarian, "Do you want Marika to hear you? And stop with all the compliments, I can't take anymore. Anyway, I said it was tradition. You're the one who calls it superstition, trying to make me feel like I'm an idiot. Did you hear me? Tra-dish-on." She painstakingly broke the word down into syllables as if she were talking to a child.

Mildly curious people relaxing on their porches and swatting at flies, watched the new family move in to their neighbourhood. Cornelia and Henrick Van Anderson, a Dutch couple who immigrated to Australia six years ago, lived next door with their seven year old son Pim and five year old daughter Luna, a moppet with short raggedy white hair. That evening, they introduced themselves with dishes of meat loaf, mashed potatoes, and peas. Dessert was a tray of pepermoten biscuits made with several spices — cinnamon, nutmeg, cloves, pepper.

In just a few weeks, the Paprikas had financial security, a reliable mode of transportation, a roof over their heads, and a next door playmate for Marika. It was easier to settle down in Australia than Attila thought. He decided to think big by dedicating his nights to earning a chartered accountant's degree. While he was busy working and studying, Anna set up Miss Partridge's typewriter, its clacking racket feeding her creative streak. When she wasn't typing or doing chores, she was mending long distance connections with letters to her family and Miss Partridge.

Anna thought things couldn't get any better when she found a Hungarian butcher on the outskirts of Geelong. He sold authentic Hungarian salamis and English blood pudding which Anna grew to enjoy in England, even though it reminded her of the despicable Sister Hardcroft. Every Saturday, Attila drove his family to Mr. Csaba's store which was more like a meat factory. The knotted pine floor was always covered in clean pine sawdust, and the store's back wall was outfitted with a long conveyor belt originating from a hidden room. Laden with orders, it hummed in motion through a hole in the wall after Mr. Csaba called out to an invisible assistant. The rich meaty smells of smoked sausages and salamis were mouthwatering, and Marika looked forward to those smells every time they headed to the butcher.

Mr. Csaba was a corpulent man with a face almost as red and meaty as his salamis. He liked Marika. "Such a pretty girl. Here's a piece of salami." He cut a small slice for her every time she visited his store. "She doesn't speak Hungarian? Why not?" He wanted to be offended, but whenever he looked at her sweet face, he couldn't feel anything but affection.

Sometimes Anna spoke to Mr. Csaba in English, and sometimes in Hungarian. This time she spoke Hungarian, not wanting her daughter to listen to a conversation far too sophisticated for her little ears. "We want her to know flawless English, so we only speak to her in that language, and ourselves for that matter. Because we look and talk different, the western world is prejudiced against European immigrants." Anna paused to make sure the butcher was still listening to her. "That's why we don't want our daughter to have an accent."

"I know Hungarian, Mr. Csaba! Budos paraszt!" chirped Marika.

Two things happened. Mr. Csaba's mouth fell open and Anna was rendered speechless. Suddenly, Mr. Csaba began to laugh great big laughs which made his cheeks turn fire engine red. He said to Marika in English, "That's good Hungarian, kis madar. But I hope you don't think I'm a stinking peasant!"

"No, Mr. Csaba. What is kis madar?"

"It means you are a sweet little bird." Reverting to Hungarian, the butcher said to Anna, "Say hello to Attila for me. You should learn to drive, then you can come by yourself and he can stay home instead of waiting outside like he always does."

Anna said nothing because she didn't want the butcher to know Attila had tried to give her driving lessons. There were some people who weren't meant to get behind a steering wheel, and it didn't take long for Attila to discover Anna was one of those. He lost track of how many times his wife drove the car into ditches. When she drove up onto curbs, he had serious doubts. When she almost backed the car over the edge of a canyon, he had enough. The close call with death also stamped its lasting effect on Anna, especially since Marika sat innocently in the back with Teddy. She vividly remembered how she limped for days after Attila slammed his unforgiving shoe over her frozen sandaled foot to apply pressure on the brakes. He saved their lives that day. So, she accepted the fact that as long as he drove her to places she needed to go, it was fine with her. If he was at work, her good friend Marjorie took her shopping.

Outside Mr. Csaba's store, Anna lectured Marika, "Don't say those words anymore. They are not nice."

"Mr. Csaba said they were good."

"He meant you spoke perfect Hungarian."

"Why do you and Daddy say them if they're not nice?"

Not only was Anna surprised by her daughter's Hungarian vocabulary, she was taken aback by her mature question. "We shouldn't say them either."

Wednesday, October 24, 1956

A Revolution

Holding a cup of coffee in one hand and a newspaper in the other, Attila rushed into his office at Shell. Instead of taking his usual first sip, he sat down and hurriedly read the cover story. He grabbed the phone on his desk and called Anna. "The Hungarian Freedom Fighters are opposing the People's Republic and its Soviet policies. A revolution started yesterday when the youth were demonstrating in Budapest."

The Paprikas waited anxiously as Soviet Union forces stepped in and began to crush the uprising that spread throughout Hungary. Their beloved homeland fought a furious battle against one of history's greatest enslavers of humanity. Even though the revolution was over in a matter of days with a predictable ending, the rest of the world reacted with shock upon learning such a tiny country possessed the courage to make a stand against the powerful Soviet Union.

Anna was philosophical about the outcome. "Hungarians succeeded even though they were defeated. They revealed the truth about communism, and now everyone will see the Soviet Union as a fiend that holds onto its satellite countries through intimidation and torture."

"You forgot murder," added Attila.

It was a difficult time for relatives in other parts of the world. The couple were no exception as they worried about their families and friends back home.

"The uprising began with something as simple as not letting us sing our National Anthem. Maybe this will be the beginning of the end of communism," said Attila wistfully.

Eventually, they received the welcome news that their loved ones lived safely through the revolution.

Thursday, November 22, 1956

And the Winner is...
Melbourne opened the Summer Olympics. Out of respect for Hungary's fight against tyranny, Australia raised that country's flag instead of its own, a decision which touched the hearts of all Hungarians.

In the previous two Olympics, the Soviets watched the Hungarian water polo team win the gold medals. Since the Soviet Union owned Hungary, it had to do something to stop the humiliating defeats. The Soviets learned how to play like the Magyars.

The Hungarian water polo players heading for Melbourne had been unaware that while they were training on an isolated mountain outside Budapest, a revolution was taking place and their countrymen were being brutalized by Soviet forces. It was when the only English-speaking member of the water polo team bought a Melbourne newspaper that they learned of the Hungarian Revolution.

Days later, the team was stoked with contempt towards the Soviets as they fought one of the most vicious matches in Olympic history.

Attila and Anna sat in the crowd rooting for the Magyars who were leading in the second half of the semi-finals. A roaring chant rumbled throughout the stadium causing the seats to shake. "Go Hungary! Go Hungary! Go Hungary!" The Australians were clearly supporting the Soviet Union's opponents.

An excited Attila said, "Can you hear our players? They're swearing at the Soviets! It must be a psychological tactic to make them so angry they won't play well."

"There's too much kicking and punching from both sides. Everyone is getting angry." Anna looked around at the crowd shouting and shaking their fists. "Maybe we should leave before something bad happens."

Attila turned towards Anna to make sure she understood the importance of supporting their country against the Soviet Union. "I'm not going to miss this game. The star of our team is Ervin Zador, and he's already scored two goals."

Suddenly, the crowd went berserk and began rushing towards the pool.

Attila shouted at Anna, "What happened? People are going nuts!"

Anna said in a disgusted tone, "A Soviet player punched Zador in the face."

The wounded prodigy was bleeding profusely as he left the pool, his spilled blood enraging his team as well as the spectators.

Attila said angrily, "I was right here and I missed it because of you."

"This is not my kind of entertainment. Take me home."

"Not until the match is over." Attila dug in his heels.

"Fine. Let's watch a bunch of men behaving like spoiled children."

The couple remained in their seats quietly watching a riot take place in front of their eyes. It was over once the Melbourne police, who were on stand-by around the stadium, brought the chaos under control. The match resumed without the twenty-one year old star player, but Hungary was still the better team and won without Zador. They continued on to the finals and won gold.

On New Year's Eve, Attila ruminated over a cigarette and a cup of coffee. What malicious deity had looked down on Earth and decided too much time elapsed since the last worldly upheaval? Let's test the stuff of humans starting with a Suez Canal crisis, a Hungarian Revolution, a violent Summer Olympics, and defection to the West by half the Hungarian water polo team.

Throw in the Paprikas' move to Australia and 1956 was a pivotal year.

Last Week of January 1957

Everybody Loves Gifts

A letter and a late Christmas parcel from Miss Partridge arrived on the same day the Coopers left for England to visit family on an extended vacation.

"Miss Partridge says she's doing fine and has a new addition to the house — a refrigerator. She makes it sound like she adopted a baby." Anna carefully separated brown parcel paper from a cardboard box, so that she could re-use both items later. She then removed layers of packing material before lifting out a small furry object. "A Teddy Jr. for you, Marika."

The little girl shrieked with delight as she took the adorable golden baby bear and ran off to introduce her bears to each other. Next were jars of marmalade and marmite, followed by Darjeeling tea leaves stored in a compact wooden box. The cardboard box was not yet empty.

"Cigarettes for you." Anna tossed the package to Attila. She opened a jewelry box and found a gold filigree brooch that was lovely with its stunning simplicity. As she pinned it to her blouse, Marika came back, snuggling the teddy bears in her folded arms. Anna said, "Whenever I wear this brooch, I will think of Grammy Porridge."

Marika parroted, "Whenever I hold my teddies, I will think of Grammy Porridge too." She skipped out of the house to show Luna her new teddy bear.

"Whenever I smoke a cigarette, so will I think of Grammy Porridge," Attila joked, although he was aware it might receive a lukewarm response.

Anna ignored him. "I'm still worried about her."

"Uh-huh." Attila was back to reading the newspaper.

"Let's get a refrigerator to replace the icebox."

"Uh-huh."

"Attila!"

"What?"

"Never mind," snapped Anna. She should know better than to compete with a newspaper.

Saturday, February 2, 1957 at 6:58 a.m.

Big Shots Like Putt-Putt Scooters

The Paprikas were woken up by the sound of distant hammering. Attila stumbled over to the living room window, and peered blearily at the field across the street. Brown-backed workers were moving in and out of a shearing shed with a corrugated iron roof that had shorn its last sheep a decade ago. Large signs were hammered into the ground at the four main compass locations hoping to attract all the folks who lived on the periphery of the field.

Attila read the sign facing their house:

> *Come One, Come All to Riley Gibson's Farm*
> *Threepence Admission to:*
> *KJ's ANNUAL FUN LAND CARNIVAL*
> *Punch & Judy Puppet Show*
> *Dart Games*
> *Sheep Shearers Contest*
> *Pet the Moreno*
> *Chiko Rolls Candy Floss Coca Cola Fanta*

"Marika was talking about this the other day," remarked Anna.

"You'll have to take her because I'm going to work." Attila crawled back into bed.

"Why?" Anna got up, too awake to fall back asleep. She was surprised by her husband's comment because he didn't go to Shell on Saturdays.

"Because we're busy, and I was just promoted to head cashier and paymaster, that's why. And don't say anything about me not going. You're not the one who has to work to make a living for this family."

"Are you belittling the work I do at home because I don't get a salary?" Anna grabbed her hairbrush.

"Housework is not a real job."

Anna angrily brushed her hair. "Now that you're responsible for millions of pounds of the company's payroll, it must be nice to drive around the refinery in a putt-putt scooter, Mr. Big Shot." Her words dripped with hostility.

"You're not thinking logically, and I don't want to talk about it anymore." Anna was driving Attila crazy with the brush. "For God's sake, it makes my hair hurt watching you yank yours around. You're going to lose most of your hair one day."

"Shut up."

Without another word, Attila rolled onto his stomach and placed a pillow strategically over his head.

Anna continued to fume at him for being unreasonable about a day that was supposed to be shared together as a family.

Twenty-four Minutes Earlier

Across the Street

Igor Raznatovic woke to the crowing rooster. He and the bird had a relationship. He tried to kill the bird every day, but the bird wouldn't let him. Picking up a manure soiled boot, Igor threw it out the window at the fowl sitting on a wooden fence. The crafty fowl ducked, and the boot missed its mark.

Igor scratched the stubble on his face as piercing black eyes stared at him from the cracked mirror hanging on a wall in his dingy one room shack, a veritable grub hole. His toilet was an outhouse in the back. At least his lodging was free while he worked as an itinerant farmhand on Riley Gibson's farm. He had just finished eating bread slicked with vegemite when the hammering noises started. The commotion irritated him last year, and it was irritating him again this year. He glared at the shearing shed as if he were a magician trying to make it disappear. Once the workers finish setting up the stalls inside, the trucks will be delivering the animals.

Five years ago, he didn't know it was his last year in Yugoslavia. His parents died in a car accident leaving him a thirty-five year old orphan. He didn't have much luck with jobs, having gone from one menial posting to another. People ignored him, but he knew he was special because the Voice of God spoke to him.

At first, Igor was suspicious of the intruder that hijacked his mind shortly after he lost his parents. He would swear at it which made people think he was swearing at himself. Things changed dramatically when he discovered the truth. He bought the Bible and kept it under his pillow, so his head could absorb its goodness while he slept. He listened when the Voice told him to find his new home in Australia where labourers were in short supply. He knew enough English to get by, and it wasn't as if he had anything holding him back in Belgrade.

He slipped on a pair of dirty blue coveralls over a brown-stained white singlet which stretched tightly across his growing pot belly. Walking over to a chest of drawers, he flicked a speck of dust from a black fedora sitting on top. The hat was never worn during farm chores, but he felt compelled to wear it today. As he put it on, he remembered the day he first saw it. He was walking along a street back home on his thirty-fifth birthday. Stopping in front of a tailor's shop, his eyes spotted the handsome black felt hat with its perfect teardrop crown displayed in the corner of the window. The Voice told him to buy the hat because it will make his five feet eleven inch frame look taller and more distinguished. Let the people who never gave him any respect see that he was just as good as them, even better.

He put on his work boot and walked unevenly out the front door to retrieve the other one. He hated his farm job, so he always looked forward to outings with Niel Smithy, his only Aussie mate. Smithy's first name was pronounced like the Nile River in Egypt, and he made sure to tell everyone he met for the first time. They would walk along the streets of Bacchus Marsh while Igor glared at women with their condescending faces.

The whoredom of a woman may be known in her haughty looks and eyelids. Ecclesiastes Chapter 26, Verse 9.

That's what the Voice told Igor, and he could only agree with its wisdom. "What do you want me to do?" he asked in his thick east European accent. He felt an urge that could not be ignored, telling him the Voice needed him to do something important.

Kill her children with death.

Igor knew what he had to do. "Revelation Chapter 2, Verse 23."

Aussie Flies Love Perfume

Anna opened her front door to find Cornelia Van Anderson, her next door neighbour. She was a pear shaped woman, her hips significantly out of proportion to her upper torso. She was not much taller than Anna, and always wore a pink gingham apron around her waist, just like today. She liked chatting with Anna over the back fence while the two women hung wet laundry on identical clothes lines.

Cornelia said enviously, "You are lucky to have such a good child. Marika ish happy, and not shnotty nosed like the bratsh who run around here trying to make trouble. I wish my daughter wash polite and quiet." Cornelia spoke as if she wore loose dentures, but it was just her heavy Dutch accent. "Luna and Pim have been fighting all morning. Can you take Luna to the fair with Marika? I will take Pim."

"Okay. I'll leave the door open."

Marika looked through the living room window at the shearing shed with the glinting roof. A gloomy aura filled the air. The last thing she wanted to do was visit the fair, a stark contrast to yesterday when she couldn't wait to go. "I want to stay home with my teddies."

Marika's sullen mood surprised Anna. She thought of something to cheer her daughter up. Marika liked to wear pretty clothes, especially can-can petticoats and frocks with sashes that tied into floppy bows at the back. Anna took out a red cotton pleated skirt, short-sleeved white blouse, and pretty pink undies with three rows of lace adorning the derriere. Marika put the panties on with the lace facing the front.

"The lace is worn on the back."

"I want them in the front, so I can see them, mommy."

Anna shrugged her shoulders. "All right." She combed her solemn daughter's long straight hair up into a ponytail. "You're not sick, are you?" Her hand on Marika's forehead could not detect a fever.

"I feel strange. I don't want to go!" The little girl turned to give her mother a petulant look.

Anna wasn't used to any opposition from her daughter, and she didn't like it. "It will be fun, and I promised Luna's mother I'll bring her to the fair. She's waiting for you in the living room, so enough." Anna picked up Malik's red ribbons and tied a bow around the girl's ponytail.

"If Daddy was here, he wouldn't make me go."

Anna's patience snapped. Attila annoyed her earlier, and now Marika picked up where he left off. "Give me your hand," Anna said curtly. The pair walked out of the house and crossed the street as if they were going to a funeral with Luna skipping ahead, singing *Old MacDonald* in a squealing voice.

They were the only people in the field while the faint buzzing of clipping shears and bleeting sheep floated towards them through the shearing shed's open windows.

Marika tried desperately to pull her mother back home. In a whiny tone, she said, "I don't want to go."

"Stop saying that!" Anna held the little hand tighter as she began to march through the field. The sun was merciless as it shone down on the baking ground, causing long cracks to open up the earth. Ants scurried in and out of the chasms, busy with whatever ants do.

When they arrived at the shearing shed, they noticed three empty trucks parked nearby. Two men were tossing buckets of dirty water over the ground in front of a barn located a short distance away. When the buckets were empty, the men refilled them with clean water from a well outside the shed.

Luna hopped on one foot outside the shed door where an elderly white-haired lady sat on a bench crocheting a table cloth. She was minding a two year old boy who made siren noises as he pushed a red fire truck over the dirt.

Marika kicked up a fuss when she and her mother caught up with Luna. "I want to go home! I want to go home!"

Flies attracted to the scent of Anna's Je Reviens perfume buzzed aggressively around her face. She batted at them, but they regrouped and attacked her again, raising her annoyance another notch. She checked her watch. It was five minutes past eleven o'clock, and far too hot to argue anymore. Walking Marika to the well, she said, "Stay right here. I'm going to make sure Luna finds her mother, and then I'll take you home." Anna pointed her arm at the shed door. "Luna, wait inside for me."

The girl disappeared inside the shed.

Anna was not happy with her daughter. She said sternly, "I don't want Luna to see how disappointed I am in you."

Marika was nearly in tears. Her mother was mad at her because she wanted to go home.

"Just this morning, Luna's mother was saying how good you are. Now look at you." Anna turned to the elderly lady. She said, "Can you watch my daughter?"

The elderly lady nodded pleasantly as she waved a friendly hand.

After Anna went inside, a young woman emerged from the shed. "Let's go, mum," she said.

Suffering from memory loss, the elderly lady forgot what Anna asked her to do. She dutifully followed her daughter and grandson back home.

Marika was now alone. She could still feel the pounding sensation in her chest because Anna had walked too fast for her little legs. She balanced herself on a cement block pushed up against the well and looked inside.

It was spooky down there.

Stay or Go

Igor leaned against the entrance to the greying brown ramshackle barn which had seen better days. He had just mucked out the stalls for a couple of old horses and the farm's lone cow. A new mare was expected to arrive tomorrow, so the rest of the barn got a light cleaning. Hot and sweaty, he had removed his fedora for the chores. Now he put it back on, pushing it down to secure it firmly to his head. In his dirty blue coveralls, he looked strange with the pristine hat perched over his face. He glanced at the shearing shed turned carnival fiesta violating his peaceful space. There were all sorts of stupid people in there amusing themselves. He wished he could amuse himself because pitching hay and shoveling manure was a thankless job.

Suddenly, his eyes became riveted to a little girl leaning over the well.

The Voice commanded him to listen. *If she looks at you Igor, that is the sign you are waiting for.*

Igor scoured the area, his jet black eyes narrowed into slits. If he gets the sign, he must act fast. "Look at me, look at me, look at me," Igor chanted softly to the little girl in monotone waves.

Marika glanced to the left at the barn where a figure leaned against the barn door. She turned away to look at the shearing shed, hoping her mommy would hurry up and take her home. Then she glanced down into the well again, wondering what lay beyond the water.

She looked at me! Igor could hardly believe it. But it happened. He saw her look at him with his very own eyes. The sign his Voice told him to watch for. He sprang into action like a crouching tiger stalking its prey, stealing steps towards the little girl, afraid someone was going to walk out of the shed and blow his mission to kingdom come. A thought occurred to him. How will he know if she works for the devil?

Look at her, Igor. She's so very pretty that she has to be the devil's helper.

The man from the barn was walking purposefully towards Marika with a scowl that scared her. She took a step towards the shearing shed just as his face softened into a friendly smile, instantly eradicating the menacing undertones.

Marika stopped, her tender years confusing her.

The well was the only obstacle separating Igor from the little girl. As he smiled, he spoke with an accent, "Would you like to see horses in the barn?" He glanced at the shed door to make sure they were still alone. "I've got lolly for you."

Marika looked shyly at the man who sounded kind of like her daddy, but said nothing.

Igor produced a shiny copper twopence from his pocket. "This is for you." He looked at the shearing shed again. So far, no one had come out yet. *Hurry up!* He held out his hand and turned on the smile. "Let's see the horses." He wanted her to come willingly, however time was not on his side. His tone took on a sense of urgency, "There's a baby horse just born. And don't forget the lolly."

A baby horse! Marika wanted to see it. She politely took the twopence the man held out to her.

Igor grabbed her outstretched hand as it clutched the coin, the baby softness making him quiver. He walked her towards the barn, his strides getting longer the farther away they got from the shed. "Do you go to church every Sunday?" he asked.

Marika shook her head. She knew Luna and her family went to church, but she didn't know why.

Igor growled under his breath, "She definitely works for the devil." When Marika attempted to pull back, he dragged her the rest of the way into the barn.

Marika didn't see any horses from where she was standing, and tried to free her hand. Igor did not let go. Confused by the man's change in behaviour, she wanted to get away from him.

Igor pushed her roughly into the centre of the floor and slammed the barn door shut. He slid a thick horizontal bar across to lock it from the inside. The rank enclosure made things worse, so that Marika's tiny heart started to pound again. She didn't know what to do except whimper from fear.

An open window high up on the barn wall overlooked the shearing shed. It let in a patch of sunshine, the rays hitting the hay-strewn floor while streaks filtered in between cracks of ailing wood planks.

"I want to go to my mommy," Marika's tiny voice trembled uncontrollably as she began to walk towards the locked barn door.

They weren't alone. A skinny man with black matted hair and suspicious darting eyes, a few inches shorter than Igor, emerged from behind a stall holding a pitchfork. He paced nervously back and forth in front of the closed barn door while Igor looked out the window.

"What ya goin' to do to her?" The skinny man grinned, displaying a perfect set of rotting black teeth.

Marika couldn't understand why the men scared her, and began to cry.

"Shut up!" said Igor in a threatening tone.

Marika was so terrified she stopped sobbing.

The skinny man kept pacing. "Pretty one, ain't she?" He said to Marika, "My name's Niel, just like the Nile River in Egypt. Have ya heard of Richard Straffen?

He's an English bloke who did things to little children. What about the Woodcock bloke in Canada?"

Igor yelled at his idiot mate, "Shut up, you doofart!" He went to the window and looked out. Suddenly, his body stiffened. "Get over here quick," he ordered Niel.

Niel hurried over and peered out of the window.

Igor whispered into his ear, "The mother."

Anna stood outside the shearing shed looking for Marika. She couldn't have been gone more than five minutes, so where did her daughter go? Anna turned a complete circle, glancing at the barn just as Igor and Niel hid from her. Then she looked at her house. Marika must have gone back home instead of waiting for her.

Anna was angry with her daughter as she hurried home.

With the mother out of the way, Igor was home free. He growled, "Come here, little girl."

Marika was glued to the floor. She didn't want to go anywhere near the terrifying man.

"I said come here!" yelled Igor. He picked up an eight foot long pole lying on the floor and smashed it on the child's head, the impact knocking her down.

Marika was still conscious but unable to get up, her head throbbing from electric shocks zapping her brain. She whimpered, "Mommy!"

"Do as I say or I'll hit you again." Igor threw down the pole, so that it hit the floor with a bang.

Niel recoiled from the sudden attack, "Ya duffed her up. Are ya doin' it?"

"Not if you don't shut up!" Igor was going to fulfill his mission today. Pure zeal enveloped him as he absorbed the soft little form lying helplessly on the ground, imagining what lay underneath the pleated red skirt. The devil's colour. "I'm going to introduce you to my ruler." Igor said sternly, "Be a good girl and do as I say."

Marika heaved with wracking sobs as she watched Igor pull down his coveralls. He held out a strange long thing to show her how proud he was of it.

The little girl's throbbing head made her sick and she cried louder. "Don't hurt me anymore!"

Igor bent over and clapped his hand over her mouth, squeezing hard to silence her before letting go. "You want me to hit you again?"

Marika didn't like the smelly hand that stunk like poo.

Igor lifted her skirt and pulled off her underpants, throwing it into the corner of the barn.

Marika urinated on the floor while the two men watched the spreading puddle. She was very embarrassed and begged forgiveness, "I'm sorry, I didn't mean to do it."

But her begging made no difference. The bad man began to do horrible things to her. She tried to scream, but her voice was trapped inside her throat, her frantic mind racing with the words she couldn't get out.

Help me, Mommy! Help me!

Afterwards

Igor buttoned up one of his coverall straps and pranced around the barn, hands raised in triumph as if he had won a boxing match.

Niel didn't dare cross the invisible wall Igor built around himself and the girl. From the way he was acting, Niel knew his mate wouldn't hesitate to kill him if he even breathed on her. He welcomed the diversion, but now he wanted to hightail it to the Outback. "Igor..."

"Shut up!"

Niel hurried over to the window scanning the area outside for impending trouble. What he saw alarmed him. "The mother's back! She ran into the shed!"

Igor ignored the warning. He glared with hatred at the girl who lay in a fetal position on the floor. "Dirty little girl wearing lacy underpants and ribbons in your hair, enticing men to do wicked things. God is going to finish his punishment."

He slipped into his pocket the twopence Marika had dropped when she fell to the floor. Then he walked with purpose to a rusted metal bracket on the wall beside the barn door where three whips hung on large hooks, their frayed cracker tips resting on top of a large cedar storage box. Unlocking the box with a key inserted in the keyhole, he opened the lid and removed a coiled whip. Looping the wrist band around his hand, he caressed the brown stiffness before flicking the whip into the air to make it uncoil with a sonic crack.

"The whip's turn," Igor said coldly.

He pushed Marika over onto her stomach with his boot, giving him unfettered access to her back. The whip struck four times.

Marika tried to scream with each painful lash, but nothing came out.

Niel could hear distant voices outside, and racked his meagre brains trying to find a way to reason with his mate, to encourage him to make a run for it.

Igor threw the whip down and pushed Marika onto her back again, making her sob from the wicked pain. She cried weakly, "Mommy."

He felt a surge of power as blood seeped through her blouse and between her legs. He smirked at the pathetic attempt to call her mommy for help. Such a mewling voice. "You must die." Igor was ready for the final act. He grabbed Niel's pitchfork and positioned it above the tiny heaving chest.

Out of half closed eyes, Marika watched the giant fork. She drifted in and out of a black blanket trying to wrap itself around her, but she refused to close her eyes completely until her mommy came. The four tines of the giant fork were so big compared to the forks that her parents stuck into their food. If the man pushed the giant fork into her chest, she will die, just like he said. She was afraid of that word, remembering her nursery teacher explaining what it meant to a boy whose grandfather died. She will die like the boy's grandfather if the man sticks the huge fork into her.

Niel finally summoned the courage to speak up, "I didn't reckon on bein' a wowser, but it's life in gaol for killin' her." He stuck his head out of the window and searched the area for signs of trouble. When he turned towards the trucks, he locked eyes with a rugged looking man with a round face and a blond crewcut who was leading a group of men and a woman, all of them calling Marika's name. He jumped backwards in surprise. "There's a bunch of blokes headed this way!"

Igor was getting ready to raise the pitchfork and plunge it into Marika when his idiot mate interrupted him again. Furious, he grunted, "Butt out!"

The rugged man peered through a crack between two planks in the barn door to see a man pointing a pitchfork at a little girl. There was something very wrong with what he saw. He ordered the woman who tagged along to find a phone and call the police.

"Open the bloody door!" shouted the rugged man. He and his men began to heave against the barn door.

As Igor listened to the commotion, he heard the Voice telling him he wasn't going to kill the little girl today. It was time to open the door. He placed the pitchfork against the wall to remove the bar, and cracked open the door. Then he grabbed the pitchfork again with a smile.

Niel's jaw dropped open with disbelief. He wasn't the brightest spark in Bacchus Marsh, but he knew Igor should not be opening the bleedin' barn door.

The rugged man rushed into the barn with four of his men, his fists in fighting position. He was ready for a fight as he reached for the pitchfork, but Igor released it without a struggle.

"Get out of my way!" Anna shouted desperately, pushing aside the human barrier to walk right into a nightmare. Already disoriented by escalating panic, her eyes flipped cartwheels at the sight of her daughter's skirt pulled up over her thighs, her bloodied, battered body curled into a fetal position. It was such a shocking, horrible scene that all she could say was, "This can't be happening."

Marika was beginning to lose consciousness, but as soon as she heard her mother's voice, she felt a wave of hope. Her eyes fluttered open. "Mommy," she cried out in a barely audible voice.

No one heard her because they were listening to the distraught mother.

"This can't be happening." Anna kept mumbling the same thing, rooted to the floor like a mannequin in a dress shop.

Marika was falling again. She sobbed louder, "Mommy." She was desperate to be protected from the bad man before she closed her eyes.

The rugged man tapped Anna gently on the shoulder which caused her stiff legs to move falteringly towards Marika as if she was in a trance. When she knelt down, she became part of the show, stripped bare by the group who performed the same indignity on her wounded baby.

"Mommy, don't touch me," moaned the little girl.

Anna stared at the small tear-stained face, thinking this was no longer the daughter she used to know.

"Mommy, where were you? Why did you let him...hurt me?"

The instrument of evil descended upon Anna in the form of a ravenous beast with giant talons, poking her repeatedly through the heart, shredding and ripping until the organ was barely beating. The beast mocked her. *It's all your fault, you lousy mother.*

Marika struggled against the sleep that wanted to come, but she had to be sure her mother would protect her before she let go. "Mommy, don't let the bad man in the hat...hurt me...anymore." She attempted to lift her arm to point at Igor, but it fell back down by her side. Mommy has to save her from the bad man who caused her so much pain. The bad man who called her a dirty little girl and wanted her to die. Her eyes flickered over to the strangers pressing against each other to get a closer look. "Mommy, make them go away...pull my skirt down."

Anna tugged at her daughter's red skirt.

"I won't die, will I, Mommy?" Those were Marika's last words before she finally let the black blanket wrap itself around her.

As soon as her daughter closed her eyes, Anna released a bloodcurdling scream which galvanized the men into surrounding Igor and Niel. Up until now, they had unwittingly become a captive audience watching the most shocking thing in their lives. It was hard to believe that the passive man in the black fedora had heinously attacked a child. At first, they weren't sure if the perpetrator fled the scene or was hiding in the barn. It soon became obvious he was Marika's attacker with his urine-smelling coveralls and undone strap hanging down his chest.

Anna jumped up and lunged at the unkempt man with the hat. She wanted to kill him by wrapping her short strong fingers around his neck. But the men from the search party held her back, telling her to stay with her daughter. She slumped down by Marika's side again, asking pathetically, "Is someone getting an ambulance?" Her heart was broken and still she couldn't cry. "I shouldn't have left her alone. Why didn't I go to the barn first?" Taking a deep breath, she shouted angrily at the being who was supposed to protect the innocent, "I hate you, God!"

Igor scowled at the tormented mother's blasphemy.

The sunshine moved away, dragging Anna's memory with it as she crouched beside her unconscious daughter. No one watching her could guess what she was thinking because she wasn't thinking anything, the only way to stop the unbearable pain of guilt without killing herself.

The rugged man had been holding the pitchfork close to the tines with his work glove, and now he put it down. Lifting the tail of his white shirt, he ripped it with his sharp canine tooth, tearing off the rest with his hands. Speaking in a pronounced German accent, he approached Anna cautiously, as if she were a mother bear protecting her baby cub. "Remember me? Helmut Jung, the owner of *Fun Land Carnival*." He offered the piece of shirt. When Anna didn't move, he said gently, "Take it."

Anna grabbed the cloth, but instead of using it as a compress, she draped it over Marika's legs to hide them from the crowd.

Helmut turned his attention to Igor and Niel. "Get them out of here," he ordered his men.

Igor wasn't going to go quietly. He shouted at Anna, "Your precious daughter is a dirty little girl! She pulled her underpants down for lolly!" He wanted to punish the woman for her blasphemous words.

The group was dumbfounded at the sudden outburst. Up until now, Igor didn't say a word. Could a little child lure a man into raping her? They turned to look at Marika lying unconscious in her own blood.

Helmut eyed the smelly, slovenly man with contempt. Blaming the child for her misfortune was the lowest of the low, quite typical for a child molester. He positioned himself in front of the barn door keeping a watchful eye on mother and child.

Anna was the only one in the barn besides Marika who didn't react to Igor. She refused to listen anymore as her mind tasked itself with burying the horrific attack. Caressing her daughter's hair, she sang softly to her, "Baa, baa, black sheep...have you any...wool? Yes sir, yes sir, three bags full. One for the master, one for the dame...and one for...and one for...and one for..."

Distant emergency sirens drowned the shaky soprano voice floating around the barn like a broken record.

Twin Cars

Attila was almost a third of the way to Shell when he stopped at a red light. A grey Morris Oxford pulled up beside him, and now two identical cars chugged in unison waiting for the light to change. As it was already a blistery hot day, the family in the second car had rolled their windows all the way down.

Attila listened to the laughter and chatter of children excited about going to the beach. He looked over to see two young girls in their bathing suits playing catch with a big red and white striped ball in the back seat. Sitting in the front, the mother cooled herself with a handmade accordian fan which she occasionally flicked at her husband in the driver's seat.

Attila guiltily watched the paper fan flip back and forth. The work he was supposed to do today could wait. Suddenly, he made a u-turn and headed for home. The Shell refinery's storage bins of oil sat on the horizon like jutting monoliths that began to shrink as he drove away. The refinery was constructed of various appendages branching out to encompass miles of land; a mammoth complex reminding him of a hungry mass of pulsating steel as he drove towards it during the work week, and then as he drove into its mouth, he was swallowed, to be regurgitated when he left at the end of the day.

He imagined the hungry mass moaning with disappointment, and chuckled at his silliness. Anna had the creative imagination, not him.

Hello, Kind Sir

A ten year old Buick ambulance with chipped white paint and bad brakes entered the farm using a private dirt road on Riley Gibson's farm. It screeched to a stop behind police cruisers parked beside the barn. Two white-coated attendants carried a folding stretcher into the barn while police approached the human gaol surrounding Igor and Niel. A couple of constables attempted to push back curious people who spilled out of the fair and nearby houses, drawn towards the blaring cacophony of sirens. It was impossible to ignore the magnetic lure of a possible tragedy.

A young constable with a hollow chest and receding brown hair stood in front of the two captives trying to figure out why they were so calm. Perpetrators are usually agitated and looking for a way to make a run for it.

Igor smiled pleasantly at the constable, his voice sticky like honey, "Hello, kind sir."

Helmut listened with disdain at the man's obvious attempt to suck up to the police. He turned his attention to the search party giving statements to another constable about Marika pulling her underpants down for lolly. They made it sound as if the man had the right to punish the naughty little girl.

When Helmut woke up that morning, he was expecting a regular day filled with noisy kids and excitable animals. Not in his wildest imagination could he have known what was waiting for *Fun Land Carnival*.

A Spelling Bee
An unmarked police car pulled up, dislodging three men in street clothes, one of them carrying a large black case. They all disappeared into the barn.

Minutes later, everyone stopped what they were doing to watch Marika and Anna being bundled into the tall box-shaped ambulance, the wonky siren blaring as it took a short cut through the field.

Igor grinned like a seedy church pastor at one of the three new men approaching him. Although the man looked out of place wearing a trench coat on such a hot summer's day, Igor knew he was facing a high ranking officer with his hulking presence and authoritative composure.

"Hello, sir. How are you this fine day? My name is Igor Raznatovic, spelled R-a-z-n-a-t-o-v-i-c." He spoke respectfully as if he was waiting to be thanked for a job well done.

As lead detective inspector, Matthew Worlock preferred to interrogate suspects in a more intimidating environment. He ignored the attempt to engage him in casual conversation, but he learned something. From the way the suspect meticulously spelled out his foreign name, Worlock surmised he had quite the ego.

A nervous Niel piped up, "The name's Niel Smithy. N-i-e-l. Mummy named me after the Nile River in Egypt, but she spelled it wrong on the birth certificate."

"Your mummy is an idiot who doesn't know how to spell Neil. N-e-i-l. So you made up a stupid story." Igor sneered at his mate.

Niel grumbled under his breath, "S'not true."

Worlock quietly watched the two suspects interacting with each other. The subservient beaten look on the Nile River character told him the man took orders from the foreigner.

"Take them away," Worlock said to his men.

Adam Reed, one of the inspector's best detectives, was a young man of average height and weight with short black hair, ruddy cheeks, and thick black eyebrows that looked almost like a unibrow. As he approached the inspector, he said, "Witnesses heard the victim implicate the foreign perp."

Worlock listened patiently while Detective Reed recounted the witness statements. He wasn't disappointed. Multa Paucis, Latin for *Say Much in Few Words* was his second favourite motto after, In Omnia Paratus, or *Ready for Anything*. He believed in complimenting someone when they deserved it. "Well done, Adam."

The top of the detective's ears blushed a bright red. "Thank you, sir."

Any other time, Worlock would have ribbed the man about his ears, but not today. With hands in his pockets, he returned to the barn and searched the stalls in the back, but they were empty. The occupants, two old horses and a cow, were lazing under some trees by a muddy watering hole in the field.

Fifteen years of police know-how showed as he scrutinized the blood on the floor, the urine stain, the lacy undies lying in a corner, the whip, and the pole. He stopped in front of the pitchfork leaning against the wall and knew it would have killed the little girl if fate hadn't intervened. Shaking his head slightly, he went back to the blood. This was going to have all the drama of a notorious crime. The public is going to teeter between sympathy and revulsion, vilifying the victim more than the rapist. Even the ones who feel sympathy wouldn't want the child living in their neighbourhood or playing with their kids, as if she had a bad case of the cooties.

Rape is an offence, but human beings are a strange lot. He recently watched Elvis Presley singing and chatting with Ed Sullivan on television, from the waist up only because the camera was forbidden to show his swivel hips. The virtuous people of America indignant about flexible hips. What a hoot. If only he could move like that when he danced.

The mob mentality was not going to be unique in this case. A psychiatrist once explained to the inspector it was human nature to think like that. How anyone could form a malicious, callous opinion about child rape victims and still call themselves a human being was beyond his scope of intelligence.

Billy Goats Eat Cardboard Boxes

Attila made a left turn onto his pebbled driveway when he saw the raised hand of a constable directing a police car followed by an ambulance cutting a fast path through the field opposite his house.

There was a crowd of people, police cars, and policemen. Whatever it was, it was big. He watched the ambulance drive past him, trying to see through the small back window, but it was too high from his vantage point. He got out of his car and stretched his long legs. The Morris Oxford got him places quickly, just not comfortably. Now that his curiosity was aroused, he walked over to a constable directing vehicles to move along with one hand while his other tried to stop people from entering the field.

"What happened, officer?"

Constable Sutherland gave Attila the stock answer he had already repeated too many times. In a monotone, he said, "There's been a bit of an incident, but it's none of your concern. Move along now."

"There's Marika's dad!" A neighbourhood youngster rode past on his scooter blowing huge pink bubbles out of his mouth.

Attila's heart had the audacity to skip a beat, and he admonished himself for making a connection between his daughter, an incident at the farm, and the words of a pint-sized troublemaker. He searched the sea of unfriendly faces, hoping to find Marika safe and sound, but she was nowhere to be seen.

Constable Sutherland dropped his blunt manner. "Are you Marika's father?"

Attila could only nod dumbly.

The constable motioned to the other officer on traffic duty that he was on his own for a few minutes. He spoke to Attila again, "Please come with me. Inspector Worlock is in charge of the investigation." The two men walked through the parched field towards what Attila surmised was stark terror, and it was waiting for him.

Half way across the field, he finally got the words out which fought with his thumping heart to be heard. "What happened to my daughter?"

"Inspector Worlock is waiting for you, sir." The constable was thinking there's no bloody way that he was going to tell a father his young daughter had been brutally raped and beaten up by two men. He wouldn't be able to cope with the father falling apart on him. Let Inspector Worlock do it.

As Attila approached the cordoned off area, a police car was leaving with two scruffy men sitting in the back. The rat faced one needed a bath with Dettol and a steel brush. The other had eyes to match his black hat, and also needed a good scrubbing. When the black darting eyes looked at him, Attila was sucker punched by the truth. The lowlifes had some horrid connection to Marika; his sweet little angel who was teaching him the world of an innocent child, something he couldn't see when he was a youngster.

The inspector watched Constable Sutherland walk towards him with a tall distraught blond haired man who was obviously the father. Worlock knew he wasn't officially told yet, but also knew he harboured a suspicion about what happened to his daughter. This was going to be bloody hard.

Attila faced the inspector who was a couple of inches taller than his six feet two inch frame. He looked like a U.S. army captain with his light brown crewcut, solid build, muscular jaw, and worldly steel blue eyes. Miss Partridge would have admired his posture which reinforced the character of a soldier, and would have clucked appreciatively over the *Made in Britain* grey trench coat hanging from his sturdy shoulders, a clashing contrast to everything else about him that said American. In the stifling heat, it also sent the message he was different.

Attila didn't see a drop of sweat on his face, so maybe he didn't perspire. He kept glancing at the strong jawline, unable to look into the inspector's eyes. As long as he didn't look directly into them, he hoped the man would stay silent because anything he had to say would destroy him.

Worlock said gently, "Hello, Mr. Paprika. My name is Inspector Worlock." He motioned towards the shearing shed. "Let's go in here."

The policeman's Australian accent surprised Attila who was expecting an American twang or Queen's English. He followed Worlock into the shearing shed empty of the people who went outside to see the commotion of the sirens. The floor was liberally covered with sawdust and yellow hay, and the stalls were occupied by bleeting sheep. Three billy goats munched on a cardboard box filled with chiko rolls of spicy cabbage while a crowd of flies buzzed over piles of fresh manure.

The inspector didn't want to keep the poor father in suspense any longer, allowing his imagination to run amok. Although, he had to admit to himself an imagination run amok was close to the truth in this case.

"I'm very sorry, Mr. Paprika. Your daughter is the victim of a serious assault."

"You mean she was raped, don't you?" said a fearful Attila, his face ready to crumple up and bellow out gut-wrenching sounds.

It was hard to watch the father contorting with pain. "She's alive, Mr. Paprika. Hold on to that."

Attila rubbed his pounding temples. Since Inspector Worlock didn't try to deny his daughter was raped, the obscene word filled his aching head with horrible visions. The chomping goats, bleeting sheep, and buzzing flies made Attila cover his ears from the deafening noises. "Oh my God!" Tears ran down his face and onto his stiff white collar before he realized what he was doing. He couldn't believe he had broken down in front of another man, and struggled to compose what little was left of his dignity by wiping away the wetness from his cheeks. He had never cried in front of another man before, not even his father. Especially not his father.

Worlock knew there was nothing he could say or do to make the wretched man feel better. Breaking bad news to a victim's family was always the hardest part of his duties as a policeman. He patted Attila's shoulder to let him know he was not alone. "You've got to be strong for your daughter, and your wife needs you."

"Was she hurt too?" Attila's voice was tinged with confusion.

"I believe your wife's suffering from shock, otherwise she's physically all right." Worlock knew what he was thinking. How could his wife let this happen to their precious daughter? "I'll take you to the hospital."

They emerged into a swelling crowd of Bacchus Marsh folk inching closer to the barn while the men in blue were distracted.

Engulfed in absolute misery, Attila felt no sympathy from the gawkers who looked like they were having fun with the best piece of gossip to befall their town. Everyone quietly moved out of the way as he headed for the police car. "What are you bastards looking at?" he shouted angrily.

The crowd said nothing because their main objective was to get a peek at the dirty little girl and the sinister interior of the barn. They heard there was a lot of blood, and the mention of rape had ears flapping from all the shocking tidbits, real and imagined. Rumours said she asked for it.

Attila thought he noticed a couple of faces emanating sympathy like beacons of light, but they flickered away all too quickly. The sea of condemnation consumed what little solace he could find.

The Black Hole

Anna lost pieces of her mind as the ambulance raced towards Royal Melbourne Hospital. The siren gave her a splitting headache, and she had to press her temples to ease the throbbing.

When the ambulance brought her to the hospital, she was ready to jump into a black hole that waited for her. Heavily sedated in a private bed, time stood still as she tried to jump into the hole. But something was holding her back.

The Damage

Professor Todd Laramy was the attending chief surgeon at Royal Melbourne Hospital. Respected by patients, staff and colleagues alike, he remained a humble figure despite his superior medical skills. He pulled off his mask and surgical gloves as he watched the unconscious little girl being wheeled out of the operating theatre.

One of Worlock's men, Detective Leonard Davis, waited outside the theatre admiring the pretty nurses. The younger ones giggled shyly at the cute policeman with the bedroom eyes and dimpled cheeks. Professor Laramy almost collided with the detective who had parked himself in front of the theatre doors, his attention diverted to the more pleasant aspects of his job. Detective Davis thought surgeons of Professor Laramy's stature were supposed to be bent old men with little or no hair. He found himself wondering about the age of the doctor with the youthful body, full head of curly blond hair, and wrinkle-free face.

Professor Laramy said, "The child endured one of the worst rapes I've ever seen. She suffered severe internal trauma and will bleed from multiple tears for several days, if not weeks. And if I'm not mistaken, she was beaten with a whip." The doctor paused when he noticed the detective nodding his head in agreement. "Luckily, her blouse cushioned the blows otherwise it would have been worse. The material fused to the open wounds due to the blood and heat of the day, so we had to soak portions off her back. But there's still enough blood on the blouse that it can be salvaged as evidence. She also has a scalp wound and a closed head injury which we're treating as a depressed fracture of the cerebral hemisphere. However, there doesn't appear to be any swelling of the brain itself." Professor Laramy paused several times to give the detective time to make notes. "She remains in a coma, so we wait and see, as duration might be an indicator of brain damage." The doctor wondered if Marika was going to wake up. All he could do for the tot was stitch her up and hope for the best.

If only his ex-wife could hear what he was thinking. Throughout their marriage, she reminded him that, like all doctors, he did not possess the godly powers the community bestowed upon them. Maybe that's why humility was one of his stronger traits.

Marika's torn body was uppermost in his mind, and he ended up inside her private room where she lay naked on her stomach, covered by a white sheet. He had seen patients mutilated and scarred for various reasons, but still had trouble accepting disfigured flesh and bone. A collage of comatose patients filled his vision. Some recovered and some didn't. And what about the child's mother suffering from shock? Who knows how she was going to cope with her daughter's rape once the shock wore off.

Professor Laramy went in search of an ice cold coca cola to quench his parched throat.

Can't You Do Something?

Attila felt so alone by the time he arrived at the hospital. The violation against his daughter placed him in a world apart from the one everyone else inhabited, the one he used to live in. He looked at the rearview mirror reflection of the driver's eyes. Detective Reed wasn't with him. He looked at Worlock sitting stolidly beside him. The good inspector wasn't with him either. The only persons on the planet who shared the agonizing hell of today were his daughter and wife.

He shook his head sadly before half-heartedly trying to distract himself. "What part of Australia are you from, inspector?"

Worlock's emotions were visibly in check, but he felt awful for the Paprika family. The little girl will have to live with the depraved assault for the rest of her life, and so will her parents. He was no doctor, but the nature of his job gave him an idea of what awaited them. He said, "Don't let my Aussie accent fool you. I hail from England."

The man's British, looks like a yank, and talks like an Aussie. Another time, another place, Attila would have enjoyed a conversation with the interesting inspector.

Worlock scanned the hospital entrance as the car headed up a wide path leading through manicured grounds. He stepped out of the car, then stuck his head inside the rolled down window. "Adam, watch out for the press."

"Yes, sir."

"I heard that. I don't want the whole bloody world to know what happened to Marika." Attila's voice cracked as he pleaded with the inspector, "Can't you do something?"

"I'll do what I can to protect your daughter from the media. There are gag orders, but not for unethical blokes. And I'm sorry to say word of mouth has a way of spreading like wildfire amongst the general population." Worlock wanted to toss a life preserver to keep the father from drowning. "It's not much of a consolation right now, so I'm sure the wound you're suffering is big enough to swallow Ayers Rock. And let me tell you, that's one gigantic monolith. But the good news is that we detained two suspects who, by all witness accounts, are responsible for your daughter's injuries. They'll pay for what they did to her."

The Ugly Truth

Professor Laramy sat at his desk facing Attila and Worlock. The father's face told him he knows what happened to his daughter. The doctor picked up his second coke of the day. "Can I offer you a drink?"

Attila shook his head.

Professor Laramy took a sip. "Are you ready to hear what I have to say, Mr. Paprika?"

Attila stared at him with a broken heart. He wanted to say he wasn't ready, that he'll never be ready. But he gave a slight nod instead.

No matter what Professor Laramy said, it was going to destroy the father. Might as well get to the point. "Your daughter was raped and assaulted." He paused to give Attila a moment to deal with the devastating news.

Attila dropped his chin to the floor and beyond, the same direction where hell was supposed to be, but it was really all around him, squeezing him until he could hardly breathe. He already guessed his little Marika was raped, but to have the doctor confirm it was agony. His emotional pain shot through the roof, escalating the two other men's sympathy for him.

"She was beaten with a whip, and has a depressed fracture of the skull which will heal on its own, although she'll always have a slight dent in her head. I'm afraid she's unconscious, and we won't know the state of her mental condition until she wakes up." Professor Laramy said enough to kill any father's spirit. He couldn't bring himself to say he wasn't sure if Marika would regain consciousness.

Attila said angrily, "What do you mean you won't know the state of her mental condition? I'm no doctor, but I can tell you."

Professor Laramy nodded sympathetically, concerned the father will go berserk right in front of him. "You're right, Mr. Paprika. I have to consider the fact that your daughter lapsed into a coma which isn't a usual symptom for this type of fracture. It happens, but very seldom. At this stage, all we can do is monitor her vital signs."

"She will wake up, won't she?"

The father was not stupid. Professor Laramy hoped he wouldn't be asked that perfectly sensible question, and he tried to be as ambiguous as possible, for the father's sake. "It's just a matter of waiting. We have fine doctors assisting in Marika's case, including Dr. Bowker who is a psychiatrist. He's also monitoring your wife." Professor Laramy looked at the inspector.

Worlock offered, "Mrs. Paprika found your daughter in the barn with the two suspects." He asked the doctor, "How is she?"

"In shock, but no injuries." Professor Laramy added, "A sedative is helping her rest comfortably."

"I don't understand how this could have happened," said a confused Attila.

"We don't know all the pertinent details yet, Mr. Paprika," said Worlock.

"I suggest you go see your wife, and then your daughter." Professor Laramy stood up. "Your wife is exhibiting signs of detachment, so please avoid talking about the rape for now."

Worlock reached over and patted Attila's shoulder. "Go with the doctor, there's a good chap."

Attila's eyes blazed with fury as he balled his right hand into a fist. "If I ever get my hands on those two degenerates, I'll kill them."

At thirty-five years old, Worlock guessed he was only a few years older, but at that moment he felt like the man's father. He said sympathetically, "I understand, Attila."

The inspector's steel blue eyes turned a deep sapphire before returning to their original cool colour. The change was over in a blink, and Attila thought he must have imagined it. Oh God, now he was hallucinating. But it was the first time Worlock called him by his given name. The personal touch reassured him. He believed the inspector would do everything in his power to help Marika.

Attila moved along the corridor as if he were on death row taking the final walk. "Where's Marika?"

The doctor pointed to a door beside the nursing station.

Attila was almost afraid to look in case there was a large sign telling everyone that here lies the four year old rape victim everybody's gossiping about. But there was nothing out of the ordinary. Doctors and nurses went about their business without paying any attention to the door.

His view was suddenly blocked by a middle-aged man about five feet six inches tall with salt and pepper hair and a stomach that could only be that big if it were stuffed with a pillow.

Professor Laramy said to Attila, "This is Dr. Bowker, the psychiatrist I told you about."

Dr. Bowker was a nervous sort of person who frequently adjusted a pair of round wire-rimmed glasses on his nose. "I'm very sorry about what happened to your daughter, Mr. Paprika," he said in a consoling manner.

Attila nodded abruptly, annoyed by the interruption.

"Her physical injuries will heal, although in cases like this, the mind has a difficult time coping. Since your daughter is very young, she won't understand the nature of the attack — a blessing in disguise. As for Mrs. Paprika, the shock to her system has placed her in a fragile state of mind." The psychiatrist scanned Attila's face for signs of trouble. "May I ask how you're feeling?"

Attila hated psychiatrists, and this one loved the sound of his own voice. He thought they were a worthless lot invading the minds of people who just needed a swift kick in the seat of their pants, just like he got from his father. He wasn't going to let this windbag make Marika live through the attack again, not as long as he was in possession of his faculties. If he has to lie to her, at least it was better than the truth.

"Mr. Paprika?"

Attila wanted to rip into the psychiatrist and tell him that his feelings were none of the man's business. But he merely said, "Yes, you may ask." He turned and went into Anna's room.

The sun shone through the window onto his wife. Her black hair was stuck to her forehead, beads of perspiration settling above her upper lip. A white sheet lay in a heap on the floor.

Attila whispered to the sleeping form, "I should have let you sprinkle the doorstep with salt, and maybe this would never have happened." Then he realized how fucking stupid that sounded. He didn't believe in superstition masquerading as tradition.

He picked up the sheet, and when he covered his wife with it, she struggled to open her eyes. He wanted her to get up and be the woman who carried him away from the war in Hungary to peace in England, and now to the nightmare in Australia, the country she convinced him to live in, for Christ's sake. He needed her strength to help him through the worst day of his life.

"Anna, we need to talk." Attila wanted his wife to reassure him that Marika had not been raped and tortured. All Anna had to do was tell him it never happened, and he could make himself believe everyone was lying to him, even the doctor, that it was all an elaborate hoax to make him go mental.

"What happened to Marika?" Attila looked behind him to make sure they were alone because he had just ignored the doctors.

Anna started crying.

This was not good. She never cried, at least not in front of him. He didn't know how to make her stop, so he shook her.

The shaking rattled Anna's brain, setting free the horror she was trying to hide from herself. Her vacant eyes turned away, unable to look at Attila for more than a second. "She's just a baby. How can anyone hurt her like that?" A weird expression formed on her face. "What's going to happen when she gets married? Her husband will think she's a slut." She whined repeatedly, "What will happen...what will happen..."

Attila balked in surprise. Like all parents of daughters, he was going to reach the point in Marika's life when he hoped she would be a virgin on her wedding day. But it was supposed to have been a milestone of the future, not something he considered since she was still so very young. The shock of what his wife said angered him, and yet brought home the awful truth. Marika could very well be ostracized or worse. For Anna to say it here and now, when she should be helping him understand why their daughter was violated with such cruelty, made him reach out and slap her.

The sting on Anna's cheek stopped her hysterical ranting, and she stumbled over to the window. With the sun shining down on her, she started to block out the awful memory again.

In a pleading tone, Attila said, "We have to help each other, so we can help our daughter. Say it. Marika was raped."

Anna covered her ears with her hands. "No! It did not happen!"

Attila walked over and stood beside her, staring silently out the window. Please don't leave me alone with this horrible nightmare, he silently begged the unblinking profile. It was no use. He left the room, leaving Anna gazing into the sun, and didn't care if it blinded her.

When he arrived at Marika's door, a nurse appeared by his side telling him to wait until the doctor was finished. So, he waited while gnawing creatures perforated the lining of his stomach.

Finally, Professor Laramy exited from Marika's room. "You can see your daughter for a few minutes."

Attila shored up what little courage he had left and went inside. A nurse's aide sitting in the corner smiled at him with compassion. His water-filled eyes caused the room to swim as he looked down at the still form lying in bed. Here was the proof this was no nightmare that would go away. It was real. He couldn't deny it now, not like Anna. Not as he gazed with a broken heart at his tiny daughter. She appeared to be moving, but it was only his drowning eyes. He blinked several times to clear his vision. Marika looked so peaceful lying on her stomach except for a white sheet covering the bottom half of her back. Attila grimaced at spots of blood staining a large gauze bandage covering his daughter's back.

"I'm going to faint." When his knees buckled, the aide rushed over and helped him recover his balance. He kept muttering, "I'm fine, I'm fine," until the aide returned to her chair.

It was a hot bright day outside, but not in that room. It felt like the cellars below Eger Castle, the cold darkness pervading Attila's nostrils. The putrid atmosphere surrounded him as he leaned over and planted a kiss on his daughter's white cheek. He held her lifeless hand until Professor Laramy touched his shoulder. "Why?" the father asked in a broken voice.

"I've asked myself that very question many times since I became a doctor, and the feeble answer I come up with is that we're only human. We bleed. We hurt." Professor Laramy didn't want the father to give up hope. "We do recover." He decided Attila needed to go home and gather his strength for whatever waited for his family. "Doctor's orders, take a break and come back tomorrow. The nurse at the front desk will give you something to help you sleep."

"Call me if anything changes."

"Of course."

Attila took one more look at his battered daughter lying in a coma, then grudgingly allowed himself to be led away. With a bottle of pills in his hand, he walked unsteadily towards the exit door, depleted of energy and rational thoughts.

Detective Reed was waiting for Attila before he reached the exit. "Come with me, sir. We'll use a back door to avoid the reporters at the front entrance."

"Marika…"

"Inspector Worlock is posting a man by her room."

"He was right about this spreading by word of mouth."

"It's a bloody mess, sir." Detective Reed tried to think of something to say to comfort Attila, but his consoling words sounded dreadfully lame. The inspector was so much better at it.

When the police car reached his street, Attila forced himself to peer at the distant barn standing in the field, decrepit and decaying from many years of unforgiving sun. People were moving around the perimeter, but he wasn't watching them. He looked into the barn as if he had x-ray vision, imagining what Marika must have endured, and could imagine only too vividly. His body ached with pain as he tried to block out the revolting picture.

When they stopped in front of his house, he was shocked to find eggs splattered against the walls and door.

"Looks like the work of bloody stupid ankle biters. Cruel little nippers." Detective Reed promised to caution the neighbours with children.

Escaping into his house, Attila ignored the stares of callous people sitting on their porches discussing over a chug of lager the most scandalous crime that ever occurred in their town. A few of them felt sorry for the family, but most had already passed judgment on Marika, blaming her for being a dirty little girl. After all, isn't that what the rumours were saying? She pulled her underpants down for lolly. Even the people who were sorry for the Paprikas knew they won't be able to look at Marika without feeling uncomfortable. A thing like this hardly ever happened in peaceful civilized countries, and when it did, no one quite knew how to deal with a little girl barely out of diapers who wasn't a virgin anymore.

Attila locked the doors and closed all the windows and curtains, plunging the stifling house into semi-darkness. What should he do? He couldn't sit down. His nervous legs kept him walking back and forth in his small living room until he found himself in Marika's bedroom. It was furnished with a narrow bed covered by a soft pink chenille blanket with thread tufts missing where his daughter pulled them out to make her special thread ball. A wardrobe closet stood to one side, and a large cardboard box of toys sat in the middle of the room. Teddy and Teddy Jr. lay side by side tucked into the blanket on the bed because Marika would never leave without making sure they kept each other company. Tears filled his eyes until he couldn't see the bedroom anymore. He wiped them with a handkerchief and looked down at the brown bottle of pills in his hand.

"They must be kidding. A goddamn pill to make me feel better."

He angrily threw the bottle against the wall beside the kitchen, casting glass shards and round yellow pills in all directions. His eyes followed the last pill as it rolled under the stove. Why did he do that? He was going to have to clean up the broken pieces, locate every pill, and toss them into the garbage. But not now.

His grief was too much to bear, so he started drinking, and wasn't going to stop anytime soon. Alcohol tasted so much better than bitter drugs. If he drank enough, he might get lucky and reach a state of paralysis. Even if it was just for a few hours, the distraction will buy time to pull himself together and be strong for Marika.

The worst of emotions from grief to anger to fear needed to be brought under control. He was due for a long hard cry. Not the quiet sob of a small child, but a belly aching, eye swelling torrent. The tears flowed until he couldn't cry anymore, his wracked body lying in a stupor on the chesterfield. He had never endured such physical pain, not even when he rode non-stop up and down mountains trying to keep up with his mates who were trying to keep up with him.

Wasn't it only last week the Paprikas felt like they finally fit in the neighbourhood? Now they were plunged again into the role of outsiders. Branded lepers. Attila struggled to get to his feet, but he didn't think he had any. They disappeared from the bottom of his legs which made him stumble back on the chesterfield. "Fine! Be that way with me!" He shouted at his neighbours from inside the house. "I don't give a shit! Most people are scum, and the lot of you are no different! But you have no right to treat my little daughter like that!" The enormous shock of the day caused his brain cells to shut down until he mercifully blacked out.

Why Am I Here?

As the strong sedative lost its hold, Anna paced the hospital room in confusion. When she noticed the door, she opened it and called out to a passing nurse, "Where am I?" She stumbled back to the bed and sat down, trying to keep her heavy eyelids open.

Within a few minutes, Dr. Bowker was smiling benevolently at Anna like a Buddha wanna be. "How are you feeling, Mrs. Paprika?"

"Sleepy. Where am I?"

"Royal Melbourne Hospital. You're sleepy because you were sedated, but the effects will wear off soon."

Anna was perplexed. "Why am I here?"

While allowing for the shock she had sustained, it wasn't what the psychiatrist expected to hear. Perhaps Mrs. Paprika needed a moment to gather her thoughts. "Do you remember what happened to your daughter?"

"I think so."

"Yes?" Dr. Bowker waited patiently. Let her tell him what happened.

"I remember lots of hay. There's a farm close to our home." Unexpectedly, she said, "I think she fell down and hurt herself over there."

Dr. Bowker fidgeted with his glasses before nibbling on the end of his pen, deep in thought. This was a sad case, but an interesting one from a professional perspective. The mother's reaction was clearly one of denial. Did she remember what happened to her daughter, but refuses to accept or admit it?

Suddenly, he had a foreboding thought. He had prescribed an extra strong dose of phenobarbital when he found her in a highly agitated state after Attila's visit. Although temporary loss of memory is a known side effect, he hoped Anna's forgetfulness wasn't caused by the drug.

"I need to go to her."

"I'll take you."

The corridor was coated in a dewy haze as Anna followed Dr. Bowker with faltering steps. It was like maneuvering a fun house with its tipping floors and maze of deceptive mirrors. She rubbed her eyes, but the haze persisted. When the doctor stopped, he was standing outside a door guarded by a policeman.

A dreadful feeling coursed through Anna as she entered the room. She was momentarily distracted by a light fixture casting a harsh glow around Marika. As she slowly approached, she tried to remember what happened to her daughter. A vision of hay was stuck in her mind. Marika must have fallen out of a wagon hayride, or was it from a hayloft?

She wanted to throw up, but there was nothing in her stomach. She touched Marika's hand and sat down beside her. "Why does she have a bandage on her head?"

"She has a skull fracture and a gash. As for her other injuries..."

Anna interrupted him, "Leave us alone."

When the nurse's aide stood up, Dr. Bowker waved at her to sit back down.

Anna was relieved when the doctor left the room. If she didn't stop him, he would keep on talking, and all she wanted to do right now was focus on Marika. The aide sat unobtrusively in the corner, so she could concentrate on her child's face.

A fractured skull. Thank goodness they didn't put a person's head in a cast. She didn't dare look at the stained gauze poking out of the sheet. Instead, she watched her daughter's nostrils flare and collapse ever so slightly as she breathed in and out.

Everyone Should Have a Worlock

Worlock hung up the trench coat he wore everywhere, except on his daily runs. He even wore it occasionally inside the police station when he felt like it. Today was not that kind of a day. As he headed for his office, he called out to four of his men to follow him. They were a bunch of good coppers, and he was proud to lead them.

"We're going to put these mongrels behind bars. The Igor character nailed himself to the wall. He didn't even try to escape. The other one seems to be a lackey." Worlock pointed his finger at each man. "It's up to you and me to hand the Crown prosecutor a big box of evidence with a pretty bow on top. To put it bluntly, their guilt has to stand out like a dog's balls to send them to gaol, or they could be out sooner than you know to attack another innocent little child, and get away with murder this time. There's no doubt in my mind, if they had a few more seconds at their disposal, they would have done away with the Paprika girl." He paused to make sure they knew what he wanted. Satisfied with the vibes he was getting, he asked, "Any questions?"

The men shook their heads.

"Right, let's get started."

Worlock knew Igor was waiting for him. Let the child rapist wait. He sat down and dialed a number to connect him to his favourite Crown prosecutor. "Hey, Angelo."

"G'day, Worlock." Angelo Murano was a native of Naples, Italy who had immigrated to Australia about ten years ago at the age of twenty-four. "I hear you got a case for me."

"Only been a couple of hours, mate. If you keep on top of this one, I might give you a pansy from my garden. A purple and yellow one."

"It's the yellow and purple ones that tickle my fancy." Angelo chuckled. Sometimes their sense of humour was just too weird. And sometimes they had to remind each other they were manly men, and only manly men would dare joke the way they do. "When this is over, I'll join you on one of your stoked-up runs if you and your scurvy men play a game of soccer against me and the other layabout prosecutors." He admired Worlock's ability to run three miles every sunrise, increasing his endurance with the added bonus of pounding out the unsavoury elements of his job.

Criminals Watch Perry Mason

Igor sat handcuffed to a chair bolted into the dark green tiled floor. He looked around with his piercing black eyes taking in the grey walls and the barred window. It was worth it, what he did to that little girl. He had never felt such ecstasy before in his life, and his only regret was that he didn't finish his mission.

He felt the top of his head with his free hand, sorely missing his black hat which needed to be back on his head where it belonged. He flinched as he remembered how the stains on his skin were callously scraped, and after all the indignities, he was shackled to the chair in itchy prison clothes. He was pleasant enough, yet he was treated like a criminal. The officers didn't seem to understand it was Marika's fault for parading around in her red pleated skirt and frilly underpants.

When Worlock and Detective Davis entered the interrogation room, they were repulsed by the prisoner's skunky body odour.

Igor knew it was only a matter of time before he again faced the officer in command, the one at the farm who didn't say a word to him. He almost didn't recognize the inspector without his trench coat. Surely, a man who loved his coat so much that he wore it in the blazing heat will understand how a man like himself also had the same kind of attachment to his hat. Igor smiled serenely. "Hello, Inspector Worlock. Can you return my hat to me?"

Worlock was momentarily taken aback when Igor called him by his name, but no one knew it. He looked calmly at his prisoner. "You won't be seeing your hat for a while." As soon as the words were out of his mouth, he realized he should be mollifying the skunk, not alienating him. Obviously, the man was fixated on his hat. "I'll see what I can do. In the meantime, let's remove those cuffs."

The detective stepped up and released Igor's restrained hand.

Igor clasped his hands together and put them on the table.

"Ready to make a confession? Then I advise you to wait for your solicitor," said Worlock. The last thing he needed was a confession thrown out of court on a technicality.

"I want my hat."

An admission of guilt would have been the whipped cream on a vanilla cherry sundae, but with the evidence already stacking up against Igor, it was a moot point. Worlock said, "It will be better for you if you co-operate with the investigation."

Igor had no intention of making it easy for the police, not after the strip search. No point in being nice to the inspector, even though he got those handcuffs removed. It was a ploy to butter him up and make him spill the beans. "I watch Perry Mason on Gibson's telly and you're not going to trick me. I have my rights."

On the way out, Detective Davis said, "Strewth, the man smells worse than a piss pot. Just say the word and I'll give him the third degree."

Worlock smiled. "With a rubber hose, no doubt."

"Those were the good old days, sir."

Sunday, February 3, 1957 at 8:00 a.m.

The Sweet Scent of Camay
Attila woke with a start. He stared at the ticking alarm clock trying to figure out what day it was. While he was trying to figure it out, he forgot about Marika. As soon as he remembered, he felt his stomach lurch. It was odd though. He didn't feel so helpless anymore. During his boozed-up sleep, he must have adjusted to the catastrophe, just as he hoped. To survive the next fifty anticipated years of his life, he must promise to get Marika through a living nightmare.

And he was going to stop drinking for her sake.

Attila scrambled on all fours looking for broken bits of the pill bottle. By the time he found the label with the hospital's phone number, he had a nasty bleeder on the middle finger of his right hand. He held the cut under the cold water tap in the bathroom, then wrapped a face towel tightly around it until he could find a box of bandages. Grabbing the phone, he started dialling with his left hand, but his index finger kept slipping out of the holes. "Pull yourself together and dial the damn number!" he yelled at himself.

Finally, he reached the hospital switchboard. "This is Attila Paprika. I want to know how my daughter is doing," he said apprehensively.

The telephone operator said curtly, "I can't give out any information."

Attila exploded, "Is that the best you can do? I'm her father!"

"You would be father number seven."

Attila slammed down the phone, cursing all reporters. "Bloody vultures!"

His head throbbed from the previous night's booze binge, and his hands shook, making it difficult to bathe and dress. Without any doubt, a colossal amount of alcohol combined with acute stress was a recipe for a nasty headache and palsy. He taped up his cut and made a cup of coffee he couldn't swallow. He lit a cigarette, dragging each hot puff into his grateful body. "Yes, you miserable bastard, you're going to help Marika, no matter what you have to do or say."

He went to her bedroom and picked up the two teddy bears. The smell of his daughter's Camay soap lingered on their fake fur, reminding him how she loved to hug her bears and talk to them as if they were human babies. He pictured her snuggling up to them when he kissed her goodnight. The sweet vision was rudely interrupted by the truth crashing down on him like a guillotine blade.

Attila yelled out in frustration, "Marika!" He desperately needed to be physical with a pair of hands that couldn't choke the living daylights out of the depraved soul-less men who hurt his sweet daughter. Stepping into the narrow corridor, he stood in front of his bedroom door and punched it. His right hand went through the cheap wood which scraped his knuckles and hurt like blazes, but he didn't care.

He left the house with his head down, knowing he was being watched even at this early hour on a Sunday morning. Neighbours who shared push mowers and sat on each other's porches enjoying a drink and loose talk about the football pools or the Irish Sweepstakes. Now, he and Marika were the subject of their loose talk.

Monday, February 4, 1957 at 4:40 p.m.
London, England

News Travels Fast
Miss Partridge walked briskly along the street carrying a string bag stretched with groceries. It was a damp cold winter day, and she was in a hurry to return home before it got dark. When she reached her street, she stopped to read the news headlines at the corner news stand.

"What is today's titillating story?" A word caught her eye as she glanced at the black metal stand on the pavement. She walked over to get a better look, her eyes not being what they used to be. The Daily Mail banner promised something luridly sensational with 'London Tot's Horror Down Under'. As soon as Miss Partridge finished reading it, a foreboding feeling grabbed her heart. Against her better judgment, she decided to buy the Daily Mail.

"What's this, Miss Partridge? The Times not up to snuff today?"

Miss Partridge looked up and down, and up and down again at the tiny cockney vendor. He was a permanent fixture on the corner, and every time she saw him, he reminded her of a craggle-faced jockey. She couldn't begin to count how many times she was tempted to ask him if he won any good races lately.

"I decided to do something different today, Reggie."

The vendor laughed. "Good on ya, Miss Partridge. It wouldn't be the story of the tot, would it now? This is the last copy. The Daily Mail scooped all the other linen drapers 'cause everyone wants to read about the Brit girl bein' raped and tortured. Pardon me ma'am for usin' them words in front of you. Crikey, only four years old. What's this world..."

"With all due respect, Reginald, belt up! I'll read it for myself." Miss Partridge was totally discombobulated by Reggie's verbal diarrhea. She barely remembered to pay the speechless vendor before hurrying back to her house, breaking the routine rhythm of the brisk walk she employed for decades. She shut the front door with a bang, and dropped her bag on the floor which caused her eggs to crack. Pulling off her gloves, she picked up a pair of glasses, searching the article for a clue that would tell her she was worrying for nothing. There were no names, but the Paprikas fit the description to a tee. They were Hungarian parents with a four year old London-born daughter who immigrated to Australia, and yet she refused to believe it was her goddaughter. She shook her head in defiance.

When Miss Partridge got to the part about red ribbons, she dropped the paper on the rug. A vice-like tightness crushed her chest as she struggled up the stairs to her bedroom, knowing with all her heart it was her goddaughter. She stumbled over to her cherished photograph of a happy little girl wearing red ribbons in her hair. Struggling to open her jewelry box with shaky fingers, the elderly woman grasped the lock of baby hair still delicately held together by the pure white ribbon. Bursting into tears, the unrelenting pain was merciless as it shot through her upper back.

"Filthy buggers!" she cried out at Marika's violators, as if they could hear her and feel ashamed.

Overcome by dizziness, Miss Partridge lost her balance beside the bed. She reached out a free hand in a desperate attempt to steady herself, but was powerless as she fell on the floor. Clutching Marika's lock of hair in her other hand, she lay perfectly still while a brilliant light flooded her with peace.

Tuesday, February 5, 1957 at 9:03 a.m.
Melbourne, Australia

Italian Pig Latin
Worlock paused before picking up the phone on his desk. He wanted to speak to Angelo Murano about the Paprika case, and found himself remembering their developing friendship. He glanced at a bronze plaque on his desk which was engraved with his favourite motto, In Omnia Paratus, a birthday present from his Italian best friend.

Twenty years ago at the age of fifteen, Worlock moved with his father from London to Melbourne. Worlock Sr. was worried about the rise of the German

Nazis, and had a premonition of a second world war coming to Britain. Although his son might be conscripted into the Citizens Military Forces, he would be assigned within Australia or its territories, lessening the young Worlock's chances of dying in battle.

When World War II entered its second year, Worlock was stationed in the remote city of Darwin. With only a few months of military training, he patrolled the Northern Territory for Japanese invaders. Nothing happened until the following year when he was in the wrong place at the wrong time. One of his soldier buddies discharged his rifle in a drunken rage which left Worlock with serious leg wounds. He had to be sent home. To strengthen his damaged leg muscles, he took up running, and when he was ready, he joined the Victoria police force. He wanted to be a policeman, just like his father. Worlock Sr. lived to see his son turn into a fine young detective before dying of cancer.

Worlock thought of Angelo who joined the war after Italy surrendered and sided with the Allies. Petrified for her twenty-one year old son, Angelo's widowed mother prayed every day in church for his safety until the war was over the next year. Angelo realized the risk of becoming a mama's boy, so he left behind his anguished mother and four siblings when Australia encouraged the Italians, Greeks, and Dutch to immigrate by paying their passage. Being a brainy, ambitious sort, he enrolled in law school. He paid his way with several part-time manual jobs and upon graduating with honours, he was hired as an assistant Crown prosecutor for the state of Victoria. The brash, young barrister was promoted to Crown prosecutor sixteen months later. In his official capacity, he kept crossing paths with a tenacious English constable who had a knack for catching the bad blokes he was chasing, and solving crimes unerringly as a detective before rising to the rank of youthful detective inspector.

The policeman's refined accent was always ripe for a quid bet. Angelo wagered his new mate would eventually sound like a bona fide Aussie. After all, the accent was cockney with a twang. Any Englishman can imitate that. Maybe it will take several more years, but he assured him it was inevitable, just like kids drink kool aid. Worlock retorted that Angelo's Italian accent would be the first to crack. Three years later, both were crowing like native Aussies, producing even more fodder for a ripping good tease.

Worlock smiled as he remembered one amusing boys' night. Angelo had just returned from a trip to Naples, and both were banging down cold lagers at their favourite bar.

"Angelo, you go back every year to rejuvenate your sagging Italianio accent. When you get off the plane in Melbourne, every word you utter ends with an 'a'. But it isn't long before you revert to the charms of the laconic drawl."

Angelo grinned mischievously. "Hey, paesano, youa woulda prefera I talka likea thisa alla the timea?"

The not-too-swift bartender was dropping off more lagers, and asked, "What's that mate? Pig Latin?"

Both men guffawed with laughter, enjoying the silliness that only one too many amber fluids could produce.

Worlock let the memory go, and called Angelo. Wasting no time, he said, "Silboy is defence barrister."

"Give the pommy a cupie doll." Angelo was impressed. "Raznatovic and Smithy waived conflict of interest. Olly Silboy, barrister-at-large, is going pro bono for the perv and his sidekick."

"It didn't take long for the Public Solicitor's Office to retain Silboy's services. He practically tripped up the steps in a rush to meet his new clients."

"A twinkle toes, Silboy is not." Angelo then said, "The issue of insanity was raised, therefore Raznatovic has been remanded for psychiatric observation."

"Is he fit to stand trial?"

"Competency hinges on his mental state at the time of the trial, not when he committed criminal acts against the Paprika girl. All he has to show is a low level of understanding of the proceedings, the roles of the judge, prosecutor and defence barrister, and be able to assist Silboy in his defence. From what we've seen so far, he's going to pass the competency test with flying colours."

"What about his state of mind at the time he brutalized Marika?"

"The evidence says he likes raping and torturing little girls, and was too methodical to have been insane at the time. Even if his reason for attacking Marika was motivated by distorted perceptions, he formed an intention and has some knowledge of what he was doing."

"How about the committal hearing?"

"There's more than enough evidence to proceed to trial."

"Who's your psychiatric expert?"

"Elias Creighton. He's got a solid reputation in forensic psychiatry and the study of criminal behaviour." Angelo added, "Raznatovic screwed himself, proving he's a danger to society, and the degree to which he violated a helpless child should earn him over twenty years in gaol. More, if I convince a jury he attempted to murder the girl."

"Judges are a joke. They never throw the book at criminals like Raznatovic, and thanks to the Crimes Act of 1928 being amended in 1949, rapists can no longer be put to death."

"There tends to be an abhorrence towards taking a life in the name of justice. Raznatovic deserves the death penalty, but it more than likely would have been commuted to a gaol sentence. Also, the fact that he transported the girl to the barn to do his dirty deed will go unpunished. Like the other Aussie states, we still don't have a kidnapping provision."

Worlock agreed. "The law only protects females abducted for marriage or carnal knowledge." He knew Angelo had a high conviction rate, but in this case, a stroke of luck could come in handy. "Raznatovic is a violent pedophile who deserves to rot in gaol. As for Smithy, I don't think he touched the girl, but he didn't help her either."

Angelo said matter-of-factly, "Smithy goes down with the sinking S.S. Raznatovic."

Worlock could think better when he was by himself. He wasn't worried about Igor or Niel being released on bail. The men had no assets, and no relatives or friends who could put up any kind of serious money. Besides, it was improbable that even the most lenient judge would free a child rapist claiming to be insane.

Usually he enjoyed setting in motion the events leading to a conviction, but right now he couldn't stop the images of the unconscious little girl lying in her own blood. He remembered the mother being led into the ambulance as if she were the walking dead, and the father's tears cutting through him like a knife. The zoo of spectators reminded him of the Coliseum during its heyday. Romans gathered inside the circular amphitheatre, turning into total degenerates thirsting for blood, pain, and death to befall their fellow human beings.

Worlock shook his head slowly, finding it hard to believe how little human evolution had progressed in eliminating cruelty.

Let the Healing Begin

It was the third day that Attila tried to walk past the reporters without being seen. There was no way to avoid them. They were now camped at every hospital door. A cigar-chomping reporter spotted him carrying two teddy bears. He matched the father stride for stride, trying to push the latter up against the nearest tree with his barrel chest to force him to stop. It was a good thing Attila already diffused his anger by punching his bedroom door a couple of days ago, and was now nursing an injured hand, otherwise the reporter would be looking at him from the ground. He raised his hand to push the man away, just as a constable rushed over and hustled him into the hospital.

The nurses and doctors silently watched the solitary figure with a teddy bear tucked under each arm head straight for Marika's room.

"Mr. Paprika."

Attila turned around and saw Professor Laramy.

The doctor noticed a faint stubble on Attila's face. Puffy eyes, the sign of a long hard cry must have done some good because the father was composed as he stood there holding a couple of stuffed animals. It was a touching moment. "You're coping well today, a positive sign." The two men walked together down the corridor. "I've been here all night, but there's been no significant change in your daughter's condition. If you need to speak to me afterwards, I'll be in my office."

"I tried to get information over the phone..." Attila didn't finish his sentence, his mind returning to a severely injured daughter.

Professor Laramy finished it for him, "...and the person at the other end was not co-operative. I'm sorry, people were jamming the lines claiming to be a relative." He ripped a piece of paper from the clipboard in his hand and jotted down some figures. "Here's my private number."

Attila nodded his thanks before he entered his daughter's room. He found Anna holding Marika's hand.

After gently placing the two teddy bears on either side of Marika, Attila looked at his wife. Was she back to normal? "Anything I need to know?"

Anna refused to tell him that she couldn't remember much of anything. "Marika's in a coma because of a fall...at the farm." She began stroking her child's hair.

Marika was still positioned on her stomach, but the bandage on her back was gone. Instead, a makeshift metal platform held a crisp white sheet a few inches above her body to avoid contact with her shredded back.

Attila resisted the urge to peek under the sheet because he felt more in control. The sight of his daughter's torn flesh could send him spinning into a frenzy again. As for Anna, flip-flopping emotions plagued him without respite. He blamed her for Marika's misfortune and wanted her to suffer like him. Then he could see she was punishing herself, even if she didn't know it. With every stroke of their little girl's hair, she was trying to erase her guilt. There was nothing else to do but carry on the charade to avoid reopening wounds that were slowly beginning to heal.

Doctors Don't Know Everything

Miss Partridge entered the hospital room on a molecule of air, floating gently to her goddaughter's side. She saw the little girl's spirit floating along the ceiling, and knew that Marika didn't want to return to her damaged flesh.

Princess, it's me, your Grammy Porridge. I want you to come back to your mommy and daddy, and live your life.

Marika looked sadly at Grammy, wanting to go with her, but then she looked down at her parents and two teddy bears.

I love you. Miss Partridge blew a kiss and evaporated.

Anna watched Marika jerk her limbs. "She's moving! Get the doctor!"

Attila jumped up and rushed out the door.

Marika returned to the conscious world in a cloud of pain. When she opened her eyes, she saw her mommy. It took a great deal of effort to speak, her slurred words disjointed, making it hard to understand her. "My bottom hurts...so does my...back." She tried to get up, but was too weak. "My head hurts too."

Anna cautioned her, "Stay still until the doctor gets here."

"I saw Grammy Porridge and she...told me..."

"What, dear?"

"She...she said I have to come back."

Attila returned with Professor Laramy and a group of medical staff.

"Has she said anything?" Professor Laramy glanced into his patient's eyes with a light.

Anna said, "She's in pain. I think she's...what's the word where you see things that aren't there?"

"Hallucinating," replied Attila.

"That's it. She was hallucinating because she says she saw Miss Partridge who lives in England."

The doctor said, "She might be having disruptive memory flashbacks while she tries to regain consciousness." He smiled kindly at his young patient. "Hello, Marika. My name is Professor Laramy. I'm a doctor, and so are these two people in white coats. The lady with the cap is a nurse and she will give you something to take the hurt away." He looked briefly at the nurse who stood by with a syringe.

The door opened and Dr. Bowker walked into the room. He didn't waste any time getting Attila's attention. "There's a concern Marika may lapse back into a coma if we don't help her deal with what happened. We need to ask her some questions."

Anna turned to Attila, speaking in Hungarian, "What does he mean?"

Attila ignored her. His main concern was to prevent people from talking to Marika because he desperately wanted to hide the truth from her. She was his little girl. He ached with indecision, but needed to give an answer because the doctors were waiting for him to say something. He had to admit there was an infinitesimal part of him wanting to know what his daughter was thinking. A cruel thing was urging him to say yes. He never thought he'd hear himself saying it, not after promising he would do whatever he can to keep the truth from her.

God knows he didn't want her to fall back into a coma. He said reluctantly, "All right."

Professor Laramy asked very gently, "Marika, do you know why you're here?"

Jesus Christ. Attila ground his teeth together, the ensuing pain from a sensitive nerve shooting through the roof of his mouth. How was a little girl going to perceive an act of rape?

With a look of confusion, Marika grabbed her teddy bears. "No."

The doctors moved to the other side of the room, whispering to each other.

Dr. Bowker returned to the bed. "What's the last thing you remember doing?"

They could see the little girl thinking hard, a slight crease in her baby soft forehead showing the strain. "I don't know." Suddenly, the room began spinning and she cried, "I feel sick!"

Professor Laramy nodded at the nurse who injected the needle into Marika's backside, causing her to yelp from the piercing pain. Within seconds, she was fast asleep.

Outside in the corridor, the doctors regrouped in a huddle, leaving the patient's parents waiting nearby. When the group glanced at Anna, it made Attila look at her too. Her ignorance was his albatross, but he couldn't help feeling sorry for her again. The strong vivacious woman was gone.

Anna touched the bandages on her husband's finger and the scrape on his knuckles. She asked meekly, "What happened?"

"Later," Attila said abruptly.

Dr. Bowker cleared this throat. "Mrs. Paprika, why don't you go to your room and lie down?"

Anna felt as stupid as she must look. "Is there something I don't know?"

"You can help your daughter by getting some rest." Dr. Bowker knew Anna couldn't handle the truth, not while she was suffering from an amnesia that was self or drug induced.

Anna gave a mortified look as if she was begging them to end her misery, and left.

Dr. Bowker said, "It appears Marika doesn't remember the incident."

"Is it permanent?" Attila asked cautiously. He was afraid to let elation take over, just in case they were wrong, but what if they weren't? A loss of memory would help him to forget someday.

Dr. Bowker knew what Attila wanted to hear. "Your daughter suffered a terrible attack. Her youthful way of dealing with it was to go into a coma and block out the horror, so her mind removed any trace of it from her consciousness." The psychiatrist noticed the look of hope spreading over Attila's face, and hurried on, trying to present the full picture.

"She's suffering from psychogenic amnesia, making the rape a memory in her subconscious. In all likelihood that's where it will remain. However, maybe tomorrow, maybe five years from now, the horror may resurface."

Attila went from despair to hope in less than two minutes. "What is psychogenic amnesia?"

"It's a memory disorder caused by psychological stress. There's an inability to recall recent past events leading up to the amnesia, but usually no problem with long term memory. In Marika's case, hers is a situation-specific amnesia caused by a shocking event. The brain instinctively knew it had to protect itself by repressing the traumatic incident. We can't tell you if there'll ever be a full recovery of memory. Gaps often persist, but the presence of a familiar face, object, or even a place relating to the incident may trigger the memory."

Professor Laramy offered, "Amnesia is connected to the body's internal defence mechanism. A self-induced coma usually precedes the amnesia which is exactly what happened to Marika. We just have to wait and see if she regains the memory she chose to forget."

"Okay, we wait and see. What about Anna? She's denying what happened to Marika. I can't say I blame her. If it were my fault that my daughter became an easy target for pedophiles, I'd do my best to wipe out any memory of it because I'd rather kill myself than live with the knowledge I caused it."

Dr. Bowker said, "Your wife may eventually acknowledge the facts, or she may not. I suggest she may be suffering from a mutated form of psychogenic amnesia. Her..."

"What?" Attila interrupted him. This was unbelievable. First his daughter and now his wife.

The psychiatrist continued, "Her memory disorder appears to be self-punishment from feelings of enormous guilt. She blames herself for what happened to Marika." It was best to say nothing about a drug-induced memory loss if he wanted to keep his reputation intact. "I'd like to follow your wife's progress on a regular basis."

When Attila remained silent, the psychiatrist said, "If Marika is still a young child and remembers, it will likely be a distortion of the truth. She will have no idea what it all means. You should not attempt to handle the matter by yourself. Call me or Professor Laramy." Dr. Bowker began to slide his glasses up and down his nose until they were back at the very same spot. As if he had found a more comfortable position, he said to himself, "That's better."

"Anything else, Dr. Bowker?" asked Professor Laramy.

"Oh yes. Should your daughter remember when she's old enough to understand, the same advice applies. Call us. A shocking attack buried for so long could cause a significant mental disturbance."

Attila had other plans. *If Marika ever remembers, I will deny it until I'm dead.*

He stood in front of the two doctors, eyes glued to his daughter's closed door. He remembered the fear he felt when they asked their questions, waiting nervously for Marika to respond. What a bastard of a father he was. On the one hand, he made pious promises he would do or say anything to keep the horror from her, but when the doctors wanted to test her reaction to the assault, his curiosity won him over. He sure as hell wanted to know what she was thinking, and convinced himself he could help her if he knew. But the devil perched on his shoulder whispered into his ear that he was like everyone else, like those people who need to satiate their ghoulish thirst with the sufferings of strangers.

After thinking about it, he shook his head. He wasn't like those people. The pain he felt for his daughter was real because it was personal. He was going to try his hardest to keep the truth from her, but he had an uphill battle because Marika might have to face similar probing questions again.

The Law and Nudist Colonies

Worlock walked into Angelo's office located conveniently near the Melbourne Law Courts. Somewhere underneath stacks of case law binders was a handsome desk made of dark brown Australian walnut. Piled up against one entire wall were numerous file folders, the overflow from a cramped cabinet. There was no lack of light as a relentless sun bored through narrow slats of the window's white venetian blinds.

Worlock said, "Marika doesn't remember the rape."

Angelo leaned back in his chair, his white shirt sleeves giving off a bluish hue which told Worlock that his good mate also uses *Dolly Blue* in the wash to counteract the dingy yellow of aging shirts. When the lawyer tossed his pen on the desk and threw his arms back to clasp the nape of his neck, his biceps flexed a good bit of muscle, the pleasing result of weekend soccer games.

He noticed Worlock's favourite apparel falling around his solid frame and onto the floor as he sat in a chair. *Poor bloke's got to be sweltering.* When he began wearing it all the time during his detective days, Angelo thought the man was peculiar, but after getting to know him, he discovered an honest down-to-earth guy who just happened to like wearing a trench coat. Surely one little obsession can be overlooked, especially if it doesn't hurt anyone.

Angelo wanted to reassure his friend. "On the contrary, it enhances the case. A crime so vicious, so repugnant, the victim developed amnesia to block out the memory." He paused for a moment, then said, "Smithy took an IQ test which shows borderline intellectual function."

"Can it kibosh a guilty verdict?"

"Not on my watch. If Smithy had an IQ well below 50, there might have been cause for concern."

"You're going to have trouble with the mother."

"I only need Marika. The photos of her back don't do her justice, so she has to take the stand."

"Tough luck they turned out grainy."

"Look on the bright side, the other photos were spared." Angelo blessed himself with the sign of the cross. "Razzy's fit to stand trial which you probably already know."

"It's Razzy now, is it?" said Worlock.

"The perv's got a mouthful of a name. Try saying Raznatovic three times after a few lagers." This was one case he didn't want to lose. "Razzy pleaded not guilty by reason of insanity to rape, assault, and wounding with attempt to commit murder. A pathetic last-ditch attempt to avoid gaol."

"Not guilty by reason of insanity may be seen as an admission of criminal acts. Isn't Raznatovic claiming he had no intention of hurting or killing Marika?"

"He's covering all bases. Insane, he's home clear. Sane but lack of intent, he's home clear if the jury buys it." Angelo winked at Worlock. "The evidence is weak and circumstantial for attempted murder, but I like a challenge."

"What's going to happen to the passionate, stubborn do-gooder after a few more seasons under the belt?"

"I'll have an arsenal of tricks that should impress even a limey like you."

"Fine by me. I view some aspects of the law like I view nudist colonies."

"How so?"

"I can tell you, but then I'd have to kill you."

Angelo chuckled. "Listen, no worries. I'm going to do my best to shove attempted murder down Silboy's croaking throat, and remove any doubt in the jury's mind about insanity being a live issue." Angelo got up and walked over to a narrow table beside the window. He poured a pitcher of lemonade into two glasses, handing one to his visitor. "Just between you and me, do you think Razzy's starkers?"

Worlock waged an internal tug of war. He had no doubt whatsoever that Igor was mentally unbalanced, but how much of an imbalance? He thought of Marika and her ruined life. If Igor was found not guilty by reason of insanity, he could end up in a mental institution at the Governor's pleasure, and soon afterwards be walking the streets again, free to molest and murder. He wanted Igor in gaol for a very long time. "He may be twisted as a pretzel, but knew right from wrong when he attacked the Paprika girl."

Angelo offered a lemonade toast, "The pedophile rapist will soon be a convict."

Evil is Always Attracted to its Opposite

Attila stubbed out his cigarette and reluctantly followed the inspector into Marika's room on the day of her discharge. Although Worlock was there for an unofficial visit, Attila fought back the urge to tell him to sod off. After all, he was a decent bloke who was just doing his job.

A nurse was reading one of Marika's favourite stories, Puss 'n Boots, as the little girl lay on her left side hugging a plump pillow to avoid rolling onto her back. She listened intently while looking at the pretty colour pictures.

Worlock put his hands inside his coat pockets and walked to the middle of the room. The distraction caused Marika to look up and glance shyly at the huge sombre man standing in front of her.

The nurse stopped reading and waited.

"Hello, Marika. Do you mind if I talk to you?" asked Worlock.

She looked at her father who nodded reassuringly. "Okay."

Marika's voice was so tiny that Worlock had to lean forward to catch the word. He looked at her fragile face and big eyes, understanding now why Igor was attracted to her sweetness. Evil is always attracted to its opposite. "My name is Matt Worlock. I'm a policeman and I like to help people." He smiled kindly to show he meant what he said. "How are you feeling?"

"I hurt."

"I'll let the doctor know." Her soft childish voice moved Worlock. Maybe some good news will ease the pain. "You're going home today."

Marika managed a tiny smile, relieved to be leaving the unlikable sterility of the room that was her bedroom for the last three weeks.

"Can you tell me what you were doing before you came to the hospital?" Worlock glanced at Attila, both of them waiting silently for a response. It was a foregone conclusion that the little girl would give the same answer as before, but time had passed. Perhaps she had more to say this time. Anxious seconds ticked by.

Marika had no idea what the big man wanted to hear from her. Usually she remembered what she did the day before, and the day before that, but she couldn't remember anything in particular, especially if it meant thinking back more than two days. She said, "At home with my teddy bears." It was the best answer she could think of, and hoped it was the right one because she didn't want the big man to get upset. She looked at her daddy for support.

"Do you remember a fun fair that was located on a farm near your home?"

"No." Marika was confused. How could she forget about a fun fair?

"Do you remember a barn?"

Attila began to grind his teeth, dreading what his daughter might say.

"What barn?"

It was all over for now. Worlock patted Marika's hand and said goodbye.

The Discharge

The dark became Attila's friend, the reduced visibility protecting his daughter from reporters as he prepared to take her home.

Tobacco-fumigated bodies of previously bored men with cameras and notepads jostled each other as they surged around the hospital trying to reach the back exit before it was too late. Once they got there, a contingency of constables pushed them over to the trees along the driveway behind the hospital.

Worlock peered through the exit door window. Night had settled in, making it difficult to dispatch the press from the hospital grounds. They could easily have hidden behind the trees and scared Marika by jumping at the car that was driving her home. He decided to let them remain as long as they kept a discreet distance, and although they were allowed to take photos, they weren't allowed to publish them or reveal her identity in the newspapers. The reporters had waited a long time to see the infamous little girl who caught the fancy of a man who was sick, evil, or enticed. And he knew they would obey him for the privilege of seeing Igor's unholy desire.

Worlock shielded Marika and Attila, his solid frame made bulkier with his trench coat ballooning out from the breeze that whipped up out of nowhere.

Marika noticed many strange men watching her intently as she walked towards the waiting car. "Daddy, why are they looking at me?"

"They're waiting for someone else."

She said nothing as she got into the car. Although this was the first day she walked more than a few steps, the jagged pain in her lower abdomen didn't make her wince. She was too distracted by the sight of men with faces blurred by the dark, some carrying cameras which looked like metal boxes. They stood in small clusters under the lights of lamp posts; sordid shadows hoping to lure her into their world. Her daddy said they were not waiting for her, but she was sure they took pictures of her as flashes popped like smothered firecrackers.

The Mind is a Sneaky Thing

Marika was glad to be back home, its comforting familiarity overshadowing the egg stains revealed by the porch light above the front door. The only other things out of place were the drapes drawn on all the windows and a hole in her parents' bedroom door.

Anna became adept at burying oddities in the deep recess of her mind, like the bright red scars snaking across the small of her daughter's back. And how strange that the barn in the field brought such a sick feeling in the pit of her stomach, she stopped looking at it. But she did ask Attila about the egg stains. "They're stuck like glue. What if I use sandpaper? Would you mind if the paint comes off too?"

"Leave them alone."

"Can you give me some sandpaper?"

"I said leave them alone."

"They look horrible. What will the neighbours think?"

Attila grabbed the scrubbing brush from his wife's hand and flung it across the room. "Fuck the neighbours! And fuck the eggs!"

Anna never brought up the subject again.

Ouija Boards

Attila no longer enjoyed the same relationship with his Shell mates. Back at work after a month's absence, he found himself fleeing the office at lunchtime. He preferred the cold shoulder treatment, but more often than not, he received stammering condolences offered with averted eyes. At first, he felt annoyance which soon turned to anger. When the anger threatened to make him do something to be regretted later, his pen guided his hand across ledger paper as if it were a pointer on a ouija board.

Marika is an innocent little child whose world is teddy bears, snakes and ladders, hopscotch, fried bread with vegemite. She is a victim of an evil bastard of a man who preyed on her and he will pay for it. Anyone who blames Marika...

He tossed the pen on his desk. Crumpling up the paper, he threw it into the trash basket. "Wasted on the bastards."

A Constant Reminder

The barn stood as it always did for the last several decades. Only now it was the object of loathing as if it were to blame for what happened to an innocent young girl. For it was Attila who hated the barn and what it stood for. He scorned the decaying building, feeling the combined sensation of ice and searing heat coursing upwards from the middle of his chest until it flooded his face with an uncomfortable burn. With or without the barn as a sore reminder, he could think of nothing else but various ways in which to annihilate Igor. Because if he wasn't thinking that, his mind would be going over in detail the torture his daughter suffered at the pervert's hands.

Marika was still enduring torture by being confined to the house like a prisoner, the closed curtains creating a gothic atmosphere. When she opened them, brown parcel paper taped to the living room window hid the barn from her.

To complete the isolation process, she was withdrawn from nursery school to avoid the tactless tots who might know too much. Punished by so many people, she was also cursed by their next door neighbours who forbid Luna to play with her anymore. Luna wasn't even allowed to look at her former playmate, in case Marika invoked the curse of the evil eye and contaminated her with filth.

As soon as Attila discovered the Van Andersons were shunning Marika, he marched to the back garden and shouted at them, "What if it happened to your daughter?"

News from England

Marika peeked behind the living room curtains again although she was forbidden to do so. It had taken days to summon up the nerve to pull back the heavy dark red material, but the brown paper covering the windows continued to thwart her. She said in a confused voice, "Mommy, why can't I go outside or look out the window? I want to play with Luna."

"The sun will hurt your eyes. Do as your father told you, and come away from the window." Anna shooed Marika with her flicking hands before closing the curtains, plunging the room into the all too familiar deeper shade of dark.

"Mommy, my head still hurts, and so does my bottom."

"The pain will go away soon."

That night the phone rang, interrupting Attila on his way to the fridge. He wanted to ignore it as he did with other calls from reporters or people with nasty things to say. On a whim, he decided to answer the phone, a perfect opportunity to vent. He removed the pillow muffling the irritating noise. "Hello!" he barked defensively into the black mouthpiece.

"Hello, Attila."

A familiar voice soothed Attila's ears like a Brahm's lullaby. "Marjorie."

"Richard and I are so very sorry about what happened to Marika. While we were in England traveling the countryside, we didn't see a newspaper until we got back to London. As a matter of fact, if we didn't buy fish and chips wrapped up in old newspaper, we still wouldn't have known. We remembered the red ribbons, so we knew it was Marika. We took the first plane home and called you many times. Then we drove over to your place, but it looked as though you closed up the house and went into hiding. We left a note in your mailbox."

Attila almost cried with the discovery that two of their closest friends didn't desert them. Consumed with Marika's pain and his own, he had forgotten about the Coopers. "There was no note. Bloody neighbourhood kids must have stolen it. They bang on our door and pelt the house with eggs. People keep calling, so we stopped answering the door or the phone."

"You must be absolutely devastated. May I ask how Marika is doing?"

"She doesn't remember what happened. Incredibly, neither does Anna, so the subject is taboo."

"Perhaps it's the best thing for Marika. Although I'm a mother, I can't imagine how absolutely horrible it must have been for Anna. Can I speak to her?"

"She refuses to speak to anyone, but I'll let her know you called. Right now, she prefers to hide out in her own little world."

"What is she doing during the day?"

"Besides looking after Marika, she does most of the cooking and housework. It's when she's sitting alone in the bedroom staring at her typewriter, that's when you know something is very wrong. Usually, she's making an awful racket."

"Anna needs time to accept what happened."

"I'll let you know when she's ready for company."

"Please call me or Richard if you need anything."

"Thanks, I will."

"You already have so much to contend with, however, you ought to know we have sad news from London. Anna wanted us to bring gifts to Miss Partridge. Unfortunately, the poor dear died of a heart attack before we got there. A kind neighbour helped us contact her solicitor, and he'll be sending a letter to you about her estate."

Attila didn't say a word. Two tragedies linked to the Paprikas. Marika lost her virginity and Miss Partridge lost her life.

"Attila, are you still there?"

"Sorry, my mind wandered. I hope Anna can handle more bad news because I can't keep it from her."

He needed to confess his darkest thoughts, but not to Marjorie or Richard. It had to be someone who would fall into his hell hole without hesitation and pull him out. His mind went home to Hungary to the last remaining member of his family. Picking up a pen, he wondered how he should explain something so ugly and deplorable that it destroyed his sweet child forever.

When Attila dropped the letter into a mailbox, the anvil sitting on top of his head eased its pressure. Kati will know what to do.

Wart Hog Crashes a Shopping Day
Shopping was a task that Attila took over when Anna refused to leave the house. He couldn't really blame her for wanting to avoid the artificial smiles greeting him, or the hushed conversations behind his back as he shopped for food. They were thinking, there goes the father of the dirty little girl.

When Marika succumbed to crying jags because of her confinement, Attila couldn't bear to listen to her sadness anymore, knowing he was treating his own daughter like a freak. Well, no more of that. "It's time to go shopping, Marika."

She smiled happily, unaware that her daddy was protecting her from the barn on their way to the car.

"Wait."

Attila turned around and saw Anna standing at the front door with her purse. Looking down, he noticed that she was wearing two different coloured shoes, brown on the right and black on the left. He said nothing.

"I'm coming with you."

"If you want to come shopping with us, you better get in the car," Attila said reluctantly. He watched Anna sit down beside Marika in the back seat, thinking he was now babysitting two children.

During the drive, Attila remembered how his wife reacted to Miss Partridge's death. Silence punctuated the tragic news, making him wonder if she had plunged farther into her own private abyss. The reading of the former landlady's Last Will and Testament was a strange event. If Attila had inherited one thousand pounds instead of Anna, he would have been visibly overjoyed with such generosity. All she did was nod her head. The head nodding didn't skip a beat when Marika was bequeathed the princely sum of five thousand pounds to be held in trust until her twenty-fifth birthday. As for the big old dusty mansion, Miss Partridge left it to Abigail, her estranged twin sister. Miss Partridge couldn't mend their relationship while she was still alive. This was her way of making peace.

When the car pulled up to their local store, Anna bravely said, "Wait here. I'll go inside with Marika."

Attila stayed behind the wheel watching mother and daughter walk inside Pitch's General Store. He glanced through the shop window, but all he could see was a pile of boxes.

Mrs. Pitch, the proprietor's wife, was a middle-aged jovial woman with a huge round body and a flushed face with rashy skin. She was friendly to every customer.

Anna and Marika stood in front of the glass counter display of penny sweets located beside an antique cash register. "Hello, Mrs. Pitch, I'd like to buy some lolly for Marika," said Anna.

Mrs. Pitch pointed at the little girl with a fat arm covered in a dusting of white flour. Her red face turned purple with anger as she opened her mouth to reveal a missing upper front tooth. "Get out, she's not welcome here," she said in a very cold voice.

Marika grabbed onto her mother's skirt as Anna jumped back in surprise. "Excuse me?"

Mrs. Pitch raised her cold voice to an octave that could shatter delicate eardrums. She screamed, "Get out! Don't you understand even the simplest English?"

"How dare you!"

"She's dirty, and all because she wanted lolly." Her tone dripped with icicles of hostility as she enunciated the last word.

"You're very rude, and I will never shop in your store again."

"Suits me fine, you...you foreigner! You don't know how to bring up children!"

Marika tugged nervously on Anna's skirt, "Mommy, is my mouth dirty? Did I get some food on it?"

Bristling with fury, Anna grabbed Marika's hand and stormed out of the shop, barging her way past three women who were filing in one by one.

Watching Anna marching towards him like a storm trooper, Attila leaped out of the car. "What happened?"

Anna snapped in Hungarian, "If you bothered to come inside, you would know why!"

"You told me to wait in the car."

"Never mind! If you were there, you could have heard for yourself!"

"Mommy, Daddy, doesn't she like me anymore? Is my face dirty?" Marika asked her questions in a soft bewildered voice.

The last sentence was all Attila needed to hear. "Both of you get in the car."

Mrs. Pitch was scooping out flour from a huge vat sitting up against the wall behind her counter when Attila approached her like a gunslinger in a western showdown. The fat woman's face was still purple from her vulgar behaviour. He had only slapped a woman once, and it was Anna because she was hysterical on the day Marika was raped.

As for Mrs. Pitch, he didn't want to slap her. He wanted to slug her, but he knew a man must never punch a member of the opposite sex. Instead, he imagined his right fist dislocating the fat woman's jaw. He said loudly, "I couldn't find your swastika flags." He didn't care anymore about being branded a Nazi sympathizer. People believed that about Hungarians, so let them go on thinking it. But what would the fine people of Bacchus Marsh feel about one of their own?

The accusation bewildered Mrs. Pitch, and she could only sputter over the oddest thing she had ever heard. The three women who were waiting for their flour orders looked utterly shocked. They didn't know whether to rescue the proprietor or go home and spread the rumour that she was pro-Nazi.

Attila eyed the shopkeeper with disgust. In a tone dripping with sulphuric acid, he said, "What kind of person blames a tiny child for a monster's criminal act? I'll tell you. A person who is the result of inbreeding. You're a total disgrace, and so is the dress you're wearing. It makes you look like a desert wart hog. The only thing missing is an oxpecker perched on your shoulder." Having retained every subject he learned in school, the first thing that came to mind was a lesson on African desert animals. If he had to compare humans to their animal counterparts, Mrs. Pitch bore a striking resemblance to the desert wart hog. Why he mentioned her dress he couldn't be sure. It made him sound like a nancy, but he hoped it would bother Mrs. Pitch just as much as being accused of unpatriotic behaviour or looking like an ugly animal. When her skin turned a deeper purple, Attila knew it bothered her the most.

"Goodbye, Mrs. Bitch." Attila emphasized the 'B' to confirm he had indeed turned her name into an insult.

The confrontation was enough to make his sensitive tooth throb like it was being stabbed with multiple needles.

Mrs. Pitch opened her mouth to shout her best obscenity, but Attila didn't wait for her response. He disappeared out the shop door, slamming it so hard the glass pane shattered all over the floor and onto the sidewalk outside. Good. He'll know just what to say to the police if they come calling at his house.

Anna held Marika in the back seat of the car. "She's a nasty woman who deserves to be dipped in her flour and fried to a crisp."

Attila closed his eyes. For a fleeting moment, he heard the old Anna.

Mrs. Pitch was the beginning of the end of life in Bacchus Marsh. When he got home, Attila doused his sick tooth with clove oil, so he could think clearly without pain clouding his senses. During his confrontation with the nasty woman, he made the decision to move his family away, but to where and how? He didn't have enough money to buy a house, and didn't want to ask Anna for her inheritance, not unless there was no other way. The last time he checked there still weren't any vacant council homes in Geelong, but the longer the Paprikas stayed in Bacchus Marsh, the more likely Marika will be accosted by another insensitive lout who would take pleasure in telling her about her past.

Dear God, his five year old daughter has a past.

CHAPTER 7

In Sympathy

Eger, Hungary

Kati Becsi arrived at her second floor flat in an old three storey building overlooking a central courtyard of dormant Hungarian lilac bushes. She carried a letter from Attila which previously waited for her in the communal mailbox. Weighing the feather light blue envelope in her hand, she jokingly said, "It feels as though my dear brother wrote more than two sentences this time." Her husband Bela was not home, so she made a cup of espresso and sat down to read the letter.

Tiredness which plagued her relentlessly had escalated during the last couple of weeks. It was with her when she arrived home today, but finding the letter dampened its hold. There must be something newsworthy for Attila to make the special effort to write to her. It didn't take long for her forehead to crease when she started reading. Something was wrong. When Attila finally told her what happened to Marika, she was just as shocked as the time she learned of her mother's cancer diagnosis. She was still grieving the loss of a mother. Now, she had to grieve the loss of a niece's innocence.

She closed her eyes, trying to push away the stubborn fatigue enveloping her with its tenacious grip as a new sensation begged her attention — the overwhelming need to take away the pain crippling her brother and his family.

The front door opened and big, strong Bela breezed in, lighting up the staid sitting room with his love for Kati. Although he had the stature of an ox, his curly brown hair made him look like a school boy with a pleasant wrinkled face.

"How is my darling who sits so solemnly in the dark?" Bela flicked on the light switch.

"I need to speak to you."

"Yes, my sweet, I always have time for you." On his insistence, Kati took a leave of absence from the theatre which coincided with Bela cutting back on his tours.

"The espresso smells divine." Bela sniffed the air and moaned with satisfaction. "Guess what I bought? Dobostorta!" He held out a square pastry box in front of Kati, balancing it delicately on the flat of his palm as if he were presenting the Koh-I-Noor diamond on a swath of red velvet. "How about a big slice?"

Kati shook her shimmering blonde hair. "The last thing I want right now is food. I have a letter from Attila..." She paused to choose her next words carefully.

"And?" Bela noticed his wife's dejected look. She was getting ready to deliver bad news.

"Marika was raped." The revolting word left a horrid taste in her mouth. She said, "The poor child doesn't remember anything, and Anna refuses to admit it happened."

Bela was horrified. "This is terrible! Poor little girl." It wasn't the type of bad news he expected to hear. "Have they caught the man?"

Kati held up two fingers.

"Oh no!" Bela's booming voice bounced around the room. He suddenly feared Kati will do something to affect her already delicate condition. "What are you thinking?"

Kati made up her mind. She was going to find the elusive energy to go to Australia. "I'm going to be with my brother. Anna has all this strength and good advice for strangers, but can't deal with a personal crisis. She blames herself and it became too much to bear. So, now she carries on as if the bad will disappear all by itself."

Bela could feel the bitter taste of acid swishing up to his throat, eating away at the enamel of his teeth. He couldn't let her go because he would never see her again. Placing his hands on Kati's shoulders to stop her from leaving the room, he pleaded, "You can't go."

Kati frowned at him. "Attila needs me. Use your influence to get me a tour in Vienna. Then I can slip away to Australia."

"What you ask is impossible. Besides, you need more rest."

To be protective was a good thing, but Bela was smothering her. "It's nothing. My medical tests were normal." Kati pushed his hands away and headed for the bedroom.

"No, they were not."

Kati spun around, glaring at Bela as if she didn't know him at all when only a few moments ago she thought she knew him well. "Why don't you give up? Nothing you say will stop me." She walked over to the mantelpiece and picked up a photograph of Marika. "Remind you of someone? It could be a picture of me when I was four."

Bela made one last effort to stop Kati by telling her the truth. "You have leukemia."

Kati couldn't believe her ears. Surely, Bela was reading the part of a play where the husband betrays his wife's trust by revealing a deep dark secret. But there was no dog-eared script in his hand. The truth hit Kati like a punch on the nose, and she screamed at her husband, "You rotten shit! Who are you, and who is my doctor to hide such a thing?"

Tears trickled down Bela's face. To see Kati suffering was unbearable. "He wanted to tell you, but I told him I will do it."

"And when were you going to say something? When I was lying in my coffin draped in white lilies?" Kati motioned wildly with her arms.

"I wanted your last days to be free of fear."

"You wanted, you wanted! What about what I want..." Kati's voice trailed away into nothingness. The enormity of her condition sank to the bottom of her soul. "You shouldn't have told me now. I feel even worse. Better to have told me in the beginning."

"I love you so much. You are my life. I told the doctor I'll do it, but I couldn't. I didn't want your light, your fire, your love for life to die."

"You're a coward who denied me the chance to fight."

"Stop it, Kati. Cancer means death. Remember your mother?"

"How dare you inflict your fear on me! Yes, I remember her! I also remember Anna's mother. She fought it and won." Kati knew she was too far gone to have the energy to leave the city, let alone the country. The frustration burst from her. She lashed out at Bela, but he ducked her violent swings, and she ended up hitting the air. Missing her target made her angrier. She began to yell, throwing pillows and plates, and kicked over the coffee table. She fell down on the floor sobbing, feeling her life being taken away from her.

The old woman who lived below couldn't tolerate the commotion above her head. She banged on the exposed metal pipes snaking along her kitchen wall.

The clanking noise brought some energy back into Kati's spent body. She got up and rushed to the window. Flinging it open, she leaned over the narrow ledge, shouting, "Shut up, you shriveled old hag! I'm having the crisis of my life!"

Kati looked so sad and helpless that Bela could safely take her into his arms. As he held her, stroking her face, her glorious hair, he begged her forgiveness while he whispered love poems in her ear. He knew he would lose her soon, but was grateful to be blessed with the time he did have with such an incredible woman. "I don't want you to die," Bela sobbed like a child.

"Who am I? Your mother or your wife?" Kati teased him in a tired voice.

"I will fight this cancer by hating it."

"It wants me, not you."

Kati finished her goodbye letter to Attila before dying.

Grief

Attila couldn't believe his beautiful young sister was dead. "My family is gone."

"I'm here," Anna said, trying her best to console herself and her husband.

"You're not helping."

"What do you want me to say?"

"That Kati is alive."

"I can't do that."

Attila left the house and drove to the You Yangs Mountains where he sat on a gigantic rock and had a good cry.

CHAPTER 8

I Finch Street

Saturday, April 13, 1957

Geelong, Australia

Attila took one last look at the barn. It was easy to imagine burning it to the ground as he held a lit match to his cigarettes. Standing on his front doorstep, he stared at the thing that dared him to start a fire. The putrid air holding both Marika's innocence and destruction belched out between the cracks in the rotting wood planks, laughing with confidence at the gutless blusterer. He burned his fingers many times before he dropped the match, startled by the sudden searing sensation. Now, he had to think about the trial which must come first. He said brusquely, "Barn, your days are numbered." Then he cursed himself, "Stupid bastard, you just threatened an inanimate object with death."

As he drove his family away from Bacchus Marsh, Attila remembered how desperate he was to protect his family. He decided to ask Anna for her inheritance when, clear as the outline of a B17 bomber, Worlock filled his vision. It was thanks to the inspector that the Paprikas were heading to a council home in Geelong.

Due to a brisk demand for cheap housing for the workers at Shell, Ford, and Pivot Phosphates, Geelong's extensive paddocks were transformed into the new subdivision of Norlane, named after Norman Lane, a fine and respectable young soldier who was the first Geelong resident to die as a prisoner of war during World War II.

Worlock waited for the Paprikas outside a simple yellow stucco bungalow at 1 Finch Street, a prefabricated structure from the Netherlands. "There's a good mix of neighbours here -- Aussies, Hungarians, Germans, British, Dutch. I heartily recommend your decision to leave Bacchus Marsh."

Attila shook the man's hand. "Thank you, Matt." He could now call the inspector by his first name, after all he had done for them.

"All my friends call me Worlock."

"Into black magic?" teased Attila.

Worlock chuckled. "The only casting I do is with a fishing pole. Besides, you're thinking of Warlock spelled with an 'a'."

Attila gave an embarrassed grin. "I feel somewhat foolish." He pointed to the bungalow. "How did you do it?"

"I know the Geelong Housing Commission…a bunch of good blokes. Just be sure to pay your rent on time, or they'll send a hairy walloper after me." What he didn't say was that he used his influence to bump the Paprikas to the top of the waiting list.

Attila laughed. It felt good to let go. He surveyed the street feeling no unspoken barbs of hostility emanating from the neighbours. No barn to curse with death threats.

Worlock said, "The trial is scheduled for late August or early September." He put his hand on Attila's shoulder. "Angelo is going to file a motion to proceed by pseudonym which should keep Marika's identity a secret during the trial."

"How does that work?"

"Although the media has a social responsibility to report assaults on children, the justice system has a responsibility to ensure the child is not further victimized. I must admit it's not common practice to protect an identity during a trial, but we have to start somewhere."

"What about the bloody reporters?"

"The editors have gag orders, and once the trial records are closed, they'll be sealed for ninety-nine years. The people who know about the case will die long before the records are available to the public."

A little girl's excited voice was coming from the back of the house.

"I left a present on the back porch." Worlock looked at his watch. He had to be somewhere else, so he got into his car and drove a short distance to the top of the street where he turned onto Melbourne Road and disappeared.

"Daddy!"

Attila found his daughter admiring a shiny red tricycle with white wall tires. He read the handwritten note tied to the handlebar, "To Marika, from your friend, Worlock."

"Who's that?"

"Remember the big man who visited you in the hospital?"

"He wore a long coat." Marika sat on the hard white seat and squirmed. "It hurts!"

A folded up kitchen towel was placed on the seat, and from that day on, the little girl couldn't be separated from her red tricycle.

Much to Marika's delight, their yellow stucco house was located on a grid of streets named after a variety of birds. Galvanized chain link fences and the occasional wooden fence divided the neighbourhood into neat rectangular lots. To soften the stark environment, sapling trees protected by wire fencing were planted along the strip of grass bordering the curb on either side of the street.

The interior of the house was furnished with box beds, spindle-legged tables, and chairs. Cheap checkerboard black and white squares of linoleum tiles covered the kitchen floor, and a black potbellied stove used for heating the house was inappropriately placed beside an icebox. Creaky wood boards were laid throughout the rest of the home, including three bedrooms, a bathroom, and a living room. The toilet was segregated in a gloomy laundry room only accessible from the back porch.

To Attila's chagrin, a crawlspace underneath the house was a hangout for a family of feral cats. Less vocal species of ants, butterflies, grasshoppers, spiders, and the odd garter snake lived in the front and back gardens.

It was important to keep his daughter's identity a secret in Geelong. One way of doing that was to plant budding green bushes guaranteed to grow quickly into imposing barriers along the perimeter of the fence. Although no one showed signs of recognition, and the intrusive reporters moved on to other news, their last name was easy to remember. The Paprikas would maintain a low profile by avoiding the new neighbours until time dulled people's memories.

Monday, August 12, 1957

Don't Accept Coffee from a Lawyer
Attila and Anna waited outside the Crown Prosecutor's office.

"Why is a prosecutor concerned about Marika falling from a hayloft?" asked Anna.

Attila taunted her, "Do you want to know?" *Just say the word, Anna, and I'll tell you.*

Before she could reply, Angelo came out of his office, greeting the couple with a handshake, "Glad you could make it. How's Marika?"

"Okay, except for bad headaches," said Attila.

"I hope she feels better soon." Angelo had a busy day ahead of him, so he directed them to a pair of chairs inside his office. He wasted no time. "Mrs. Paprika, do you remember what happened to Marika last February 2nd?"

Anna sat on the other side of the prosecutor's cluttered desk gazing at him with confusion. Struggling for words, she sounded like she was trying to speak in an unfamiliar language. "I was...looking for her. When I found her, she was lying...in a barn...badly hurt."

"Why were you looking for her?"

"I don't remember."

"How was Marika badly hurt?"

"She fell down from the...hayloft."

"Do you remember seeing other people in the barn?"

"No."

Angelo watched Anna's body language, ready to find a crack in her facade, but he couldn't detect anything to discredit her. She seemed to believe what she said. Either that, or she was a very good liar. He said, "Would you mind if I have a private chat with Attila?"

Anna left the room, relieved to avoid any further questions.

Angelo said, "The trial will start September 9. Are you ready?"

Attila's face was a grim mask. "I'm not looking forward to being in the same room with my daughter's rapist. But I'll be there. Everyday."

"Good man."

"Does Anna have to testify?"

"She's no good to us in her condition. Besides, her testimony won't make a difference to the Crown's case. And the defence has nothing to gain because there's enough evidence to prove Raznatovic raped and beat your daughter. The bone of contention is whether he tried to kill her and if he was in his right mind." Angelo poured a cup of hot coffee from a thermos. He offered it to Attila who declined with a shake of his head. "Your wife has put herself in a delicate situation."

Attila shrugged his shoulders. "She doesn't act like the woman I married."

"As you already know, Dr. Bowker thinks her amnesia is a form of self-punishment. She had to block out the rape, or she'd lose her sanity if she tried to come to terms with it." Angelo paused to take a sip from his cup, and grimaced. The coffee was awful. "Maybe with time on her side, she'll accept what happened."

"Does Marika have to testify?"

"Unfortunately, the photographs of her back injuries didn't turn out the way I hoped. The jury needs to get the full impact of her wounds."

"How do I show up at the trial every day without telling Anna?"

"Act as if you're going to work."

"What if she calls me and I'm not there?"

"You were in a meeting."

Attila asked, "And when Marika has to go to court?"

"I have an idea — send Anna on a vacation. That way she won't know any better."

"Easier said than done."

"Not if you persuade her to go with a friend."

"She's changed so much."

"The woman you knew died on February 2nd."

Angelo was blunt, but right. Attila said, "There was no one like her."

"Can you arrange for babysitting once Anna leaves?"

"The only friends I trust to look after Marika won't be available. Richard will be working, and I imagine his wife Marjorie is going to take that vacation with Anna."

Angelo knew of someone. "You can trust Sofia, my wife. She's wonderful with kids and expecting our first child. We also happen to live in the seaside town of Portarlington which is close to Geelong."

"I couldn't impose."

"A vacation for Anna was my suggestion. Drop Marika off at our house before you head to the courthouse."

Before Attila could respond, there was a light tap on the door.

Angelo called out, "Come in."

A tall young woman with a movie starlet face, sexy brown eyes and high cheekbones, walked in carrying a Myers shopping bag in each hand. She wore a straight black skirt and a loose white cotton blouse hiding a barely noticeable baby bump. Her ebony coloured hair was long and wild, so different from the hairstyles that women wore these days. As Angelo got up to greet her, she dropped the shopping bags on the floor. With a pouty red-lipped smile, she reached up and raked her red fingernails through his hair. Just because she was pregnant didn't mean she should stop wearing makeup and nail polish.

Angelo pecked her glowing cheek. "Attila, as you may have guessed, this is my lovely wife, Sofia."

Attila had been busy admiring her muscular calves. He said politely, "How do you do?"

"Nice to meet you, Attila." Sofia spoke flawless English with a charming Italian accent. "I'm sorry to intrude but I couldn't stay away from my handsome marito." She pinched Angelo's chin.

Angelo said unashamedly, "She's paying me back for all the times I pinched her, and not on the chin."

Although Sofia was a welcome distraction, Attila couldn't forget the conversation that took place before she showed up.

The prosecutor knew what Attila was thinking. "No worries, I'll protect your daughter when she testifies."

Attila couldn't tell Angelo how petrified he was of Marika being a bullseye for a pedophile and a bunch of strangers. All of them privy to details so intimate, so gruesome, that made him want to puke. He wanted to take his daughter far away where no one knew who she was and what had happened to her.

CHAPTER 9

The Reckoning

Friday, September 6, 1957
Melbourne Law Courts - Courtroom 2

Justice John 'Birdman' Cobb
The twelve men sat in their seats listening intently to Justice Cobb. He had just finished shifting them around the jury box. All the taller ones sat in the back row, giving the shorter men in the front a clear view of the courtroom.

The judge was a slight figure with grey centipede eyebrows that often took on a life of their own. His beak nose earned him the nickname of Birdman amongst the younger barristers who were not yet impressed by his legal stature. Perched on the beak nose was a pair of black framed glasses.

There was nothing more exciting to him than the law. It was an intellectual stimulant, challenging, evolving. He had worked hard to gain the respect of his peers, and kept such meticulous trial notes that other judges envied his writing skills. As a dedicated purist of English law, the foundation of the Australian legal system, he had the utmost respect for British Parliament which accomplished the remarkable feat of transferring the law to each state of Australia back in the colonial days.

Born right here in Melbourne to early English immigrants, he was proud to be an Australian with an English heritage. Nothing could take his pride away, not even the unkind souls referring to him as the judge who was past his prime. But no one doubted his intentions to prevail in the quest for truth and justice.

Even if he lived to be a hundred, he would never understand how a homely bloke like himself was lucky enough to find a woman as lovely, patient, and gracious as his wife. She was statuesque with a figure that always excited him even though it was a little more plump these days. When she refused to dye her grey hair anymore, he loved her more for it. During their intimate moments, he liked to call her Mrs. Miniver, the English character played by Greer Garson. The two women had much in common.

Besides relying on his wife's figure and charming personality, he took up hobbies to distract him from the stresses of his career. After Saturday supper, he couldn't wait to retire to the study to passionately search books for obscure words. There was something immensely enjoyable about ambushing the barristers with a strange word and watching the lack of comprehension cloud their faces. So far, not one barrister rose to the challenge by giving him the right definition, not even smart-aleck Angelo Murano. When he didn't have his beak buried in a musty book, he grew prize winning tomatoes which he shared with friends and colleagues.

To the amusement of guests in his home, he doted on Panther, a slinky black cat that he loved like other people loved their dogs and children. At first, he refused to have anything to do with the hungry thing his wife found in the garden. The clever kitty waited every night for the surly judge to fall asleep before sneaking into his bed and wrapping her purring warmth around the man's mostly hairless head, her long bushy tail resting on Mrs. Cobb's throat like a fur choker. Purring into the sleeping judge's ear did the trick, and without realizing it, he allowed the blue-eyed puss into his private space.

The four-legged addition to the household provided many opportunities for Mrs. Cobb to use her expensive Hassalbad camera from Sweden. She would hide in corners or behind the chesterfield to capture hilarious touching moments between judge and cat. An album was devoted to her husband shooing the feline from his comfy overstuffed leather chair, the kitchen counter, the bed, the bathroom basin, the bathtub. When Panther began to turn the judge into a gibbering idiot, the photos changed to scenes of kitty sleeping on the judge's chest and lap. But his wife's favourites were of her husband kissing the top of Panther's furry head, and the look he gave when he saw her madly clicking her camera. His expression reminded Mrs. Cobb of a robber caught with his hand in a cashier's till. It was priceless.

Judge and cat soon completed the bonding process with a nightly game of crumpled paper ball catch.

Pre-Trial Instructions
Justice Cobb was ready for the new jury.

"Please listen carefully to the Do Not List. Do not communicate with anyone about the case, and that includes another juror, at least not until the trial is over and you are sequestered for deliberations. Do not speak to an accused, witness, barrister or his associates. Do not listen to anyone who wants to talk about the case. Should anyone attempt to engage you in such conversation, your stock answer will be, I cannot discuss the matter."

The judge instructed the jurors, "Repeat after me, *I cannot discuss the matter.*"

"*I cannot discuss the matter,*" said the twelve men in near perfect harmony.

"If they persist, walk away with your fingers in your ears, singing Waltzing Matilda. If they try to influence you, inform the tipstaff immediately. Do not read, listen to, or watch any news reports about the case. Do not use a dictionary to check the meaning of words relating to the trial. Do not investigate the facts or the law, and do not conduct any tests, experiments, or visit the scene of the crime.

Please continue to pay attention because the basic principle you must adhere to, as jurors, is presumption of innocence. Australian law requires that an accused be presumed innocent until proven guilty by the Crown. Your role is to act as judges of the facts based on the evidence you hear, however, I will be the judge of the law. So, when I tell you what the law is, what I say prevails. You will then apply the law, that I give to you, to the evidence. It matters not if you happen to agree or disagree with the law.

An opening statement provides an overview of what the barristers expect the evidence will show. At the beginning of the trial, the Crown may present an opening statement, and although the defence is not required to do so, it may choose to give a statement after the Crown, or at the start of the defence's case.

The Crown will try to prove the charges against the accused and present evidence by way of witnesses and exhibits. In defending the accused, the defence may present evidence although not required to do so, unless the issue of insanity is raised. And in cases where multiple accused are being tried together, you must give them separate consideration by determining which evidence applies to each one.

An accused has the right not to testify, and no presumption of guilt may be raised or inferred for not doing so. If the accused testifies, you must treat the testimony like any other witness testimony.

When a witness testifies to what he saw, heard, or did, it is called direct evidence. Circumstantial evidence relies on inference to connect it to a conclusion of fact. A perfect example is a fingerprint found at a crime scene.

You can choose to believe the entire testimony of a witness, a part of it, or none at all. When making your decision, you should take into consideration the witness's memory of what he saw, heard, or did, his manner on the stand, his prejudices, his interest in the outcome, the reasonableness of his testimony, and whether other evidence was contradictory.

If you hear testimony that a witness lied under oath on a previous occasion, you may consider it in deciding whether or not to believe the witness and how much weight to give his testimony.

And what about the barristers? They are an impressive breed, aren't they? They help you to interpret the evidence, but every single word uttered by them is...not evidence. Not a one. Only the witness's testimony is evidence, along with exhibits that are admitted into evidence.

As sure as night follows day, the barristers will put forth objections to questions and witness testimony. I will rule accordingly. If I sustain, either the witness is not allowed to answer and you will disregard the question and its possible answer, or testimony is disallowed. If I overrule, the witness answers. If I order testimony stricken from the record, you must not consider it in your deliberations.

At the end of the trial, the barristers will give their closing arguments. Then I will give my summation at which time I will discuss the relevant laws and charges in depth. Then off you go into deliberations where you should select one member as your foreman. He will preside over deliberations and speak for you in the courtroom.

You may ask for a copy of the court reporter's record, only if absolutely necessary, and you may use the notepads that will be provided to you during the trial. Whatever notes you make may be brought into deliberations. When it's all over, they will be destroyed. But a word of caution. Do not allow yourself to be distracted with note-taking while a witness is giving testimony, and do not be unduly influenced by your notes. Rely on your memory. I take notes, but I've been doing it for a very long time. Nothing gets by me."

Justice Cobb was satisfied he didn't forget anything. "You will be given a transcript of these instructions that you may refer to during deliberations. Enjoy your weekend, gentlemen."

THE PAPRIKA DIARY, A LONELY SECRET

Monday, September 9, 1957 at 8:45 a.m.
Melbourne Law Courts

The Trial

Attila didn't think today would ever arrive. When it did, it was faster than he thought. He drove to the Melbourne Law Courts on a warm cloudy day. The only way he could force himself to attend the trial was to reward himself with a bottle of Jamaican rum afterwards, his promise shot to hell.

He stood outside the two storey Supreme Court on John Street marveling at its renaissance revival architecture. The statue of Lady Justice sat on top of the entrance creating controversy for not being blindfolded, even though she was representing the old saying, Justice is not Blind. Behind her loomed a magnificent towering dome supported by twenty-four ionic columns. Without a doubt, the Supreme Court was an imposing sight that made Attila forget why he was there. For all of ten seconds.

The Defence Barrister

Olly Silboy walked towards Courtroom 2 in his junior barrister's black wool robe. He liked wearing the formless robe because it detracted from his pigeon-toed walk. Years of having to wear clod hopping boots and leg braces as a boy had only mildly tamed the deformity. His ivory tie-wig, with its elaborate side curls and two dangling ties at the back, completed the formal attire, as well as hiding a premature bald spot at the back of his head.

Approaching from the opposite direction, Angelo met his short stuffy adversary outside the courtroom doors. He thought Olly wasn't half bad looking in a Spencer Tracy meets Red Skelton sort of way, but he was never going to admit it to anyone. He teased Olly, "How does it feel to defend a child rapist?"

Olly had a hoarse voice as if his vocal cords suffered from chronic laryngitis, the downside of many years spent crying and screaming about how he hated his ugly orthopedic devices. "If it isn't my learned colleague trying to annoy me before the trial starts. Well, it won't work." Caught in a fib, the annoying twitch above his left eye pulsated in jabs. He was glad Murano couldn't see it.

The Crown prosecutor's robe, black jacket, and white jabot were missing a tie-wig. Olly lectured him, "Still can't follow decorum."

"Beg yours, Silly-boy." Angelo avoided saying the obvious, that it was his quest to stretch the boundaries of outdated pomposity. Besides, the robe and wig made him feel like a pale-faced sheikh wearing roadkill. Today, no wig. He'd much prefer to walk into the courtroom in a dark tailored suit and white shirt. "You need to lighten up, mate. And you really should practice preventive maintenance for your speaking voice. Instead of those ice cold drinks you like, switch to warm tea with lemon, or better yet, do a sin--atra." Angelo split the last word in two to keep Olly guessing.

"Silboy." Olly hated it when people made fun of his name ever since grammar school. And he hated Angelo Murano, smug bully bastard with a glib tongue. Curiosity got the better of him. "Okay, I'll bite. What's a sin--atra?"

"Don't tell me you never heard of Frank Sinatra, the American crooner? He sucks on lemon drops before he sings."

"Up yours, Murano." Olly didn't appreciate being made to look like a dimwit. "And I'm not your mate."

Angelo reached out to straighten Olly's crooked jabot which hung like a bib around his neck and down the front in two long rectangular strips of white cotton.

Olly brushed the prosecutor's hands away. "Don't touch," he said brusquely.

"Just trying to help."

"As in a thumbtack-on-the-chair kind of help?"

"Crikey, we were law students at Queensland University." Angelo said with a wink, "I don't pull silly pranks anymore."

Courtroom 2

Worlock stood outside a pair of ornate cedar doors watching people enter the courtroom. As first witness for the Crown, he was required to wait outside until he was called.

Attila sat down on a hard bench in the second row, ignoring the stares of strangers overcome by the scent of cologne splashed liberally under his armpits to mask the nervous sweat. He wondered if there were any people in Victoria who didn't know about his little girl being raped inside a barn. Maybe the ones who were not yet born or disintegrating into skeletal dust six feet below the ground.

Angelo and his associate were seated at the prosecution table in front of the court bench and to the left of the jury box. Olly and the legal aid solicitor were at the far left side of the courtroom, closest to the door that their clients will walk through, but the furthest away from the jury.

The twelve male jurors filed into the courtroom, taking their seats in solemn silence. They all wore dark suits, clean white shirts, new ties. Attila looked into each juror's face trying to determine if they were capable of making it right for Marika. These are the men who will decide Igor's fate. He wasn't sure if he had faith in the Australian judicial system. Just because the jurors were property holders or respected members of the community didn't mean they would make the right decision. It must be obvious to everyone connected to the case that Igor was guilty. Insane or not, the man should face the same fate all innocent people encountered during the war.

To know they were going to die, and be killed.

The men in the jury box weren't trained to make an impartial judgment on another human being, let alone Igor who was evil incarnate. Attila would have preferred to see some females on the jury, since they would show more sympathy for Marika. But he was surprised to learn that women weren't allowed to be jurors. There was no choice but to put his faith in Angelo Murano and twelve ordinary, flawed males.

The courtroom, with its dark stained wall panels and wood canopied justice's bench, closed in on Attila. He had never felt so claustrophobic in his life. Cologne-pungent sweat trickled from his armpits, making their way down to the waistband of his pants as the door closest to Olly's table opened up.

Everyone stopped talking.

From the dungeon-like basement holding cells, two bailiffs escorted the accused into the courtroom. Olly tried to make Igor look like a respectable citizen in a navy blue suit and tie, his neck bent forward like a carrion, his face a picture of smugness. Niel wore dark brown, fidgeting with the starched collar of his white shirt, teeth as black as ever, his eyes darting around the courtroom with suspicion.

Attila's identity spread rapidly throughout the room, and he could feel the spectators watching for his reaction. They were hoping he'd jump up and make a trashy scene. He stiffened his spine. No way was he going to satisfy the bastards. He watched Niel sit next to the legal aid solicitor, followed by Igor settling into a chair beside Olly. The distance between himself and them was too close for comfort. Not only was he a crack shot with a rifle, strong swimmer, ping pong champion and marathon cyclist, he was also a decent hurdler. He could easily leap over the railing and land on top of Igor.

The burly tipstaff, who looked like a bouncer in a bar, was stationed in the well before the bench. He suddenly bellowed, "Order in the Court! All rise!"

Everyone stood up and watched Justice Cobb enter the courtroom. As he climbed the podium, he stepped on the hem of his new black silk judge's robe which caused him to barrel into his seat. It was hardly the imposing, dignified figure he wanted to present to the courtroom. He adjusted his bench wig and glasses, his centipede eyebrows hovering above the rims.

Being one of the first to embrace a less formal style of legalese, he also wanted to ditch the uncomfortable greying horsehair bench wig that he wore today. The aging wig was reflective of his legal ranking and it covered the top of his head and part way down the sides with tiny tight prim curls. Mercifully, it wasn't half as bad as the full bottom wig he wore for special ceremonies. Wigs were supposed to identify the key players in the courtroom and be an emblem of dignity, although he suspected it intimidated rather than earned respect. If he gets his way, the traditional hairy accessory would go the way of the dodo bird.

He glanced at the two reporters from the Melbourne and Sydney Morning Herald sitting on the back bench. The two men were chosen to attend the trial because of their reputations. As for the rest of the reporters waiting outside the courtroom, they could mill around like randy sheep for all he cared.

Back in the well, the tipstaff shouted, "Supreme Courtroom 2 is now in session! The Honourable Justice John Cobb presiding!"

"Be seated," said the judge.

Everyone sat down except the tipstaff.

"What is today's case?" It was only a formality. Justice Cobb knew all about today's highly sensitive trial.

"Her Majesty the Queen versus Igor Raznatovic and Neil Kelvin Smithy, your Honour."

Niel silently cursed the tipstaff. *Not Neil, you drongo. It's Niel, like the Nile River in Egypt.*

Justice Cobb eyed the wig-free Crown prosecutor with a combination of admiration and annoyance. With a curt backward wave, he beckoned the prosecutor. "Approach the bench."

Angelo got up and walked over to Justice Cobb.

"Mr. Murano, has there been a change in the dress code for wigs?"

"No, your Honour."

"Every day that you attend this trial without a wig, you will be found in contempt and fined five pounds. Is that clear?"

"Yes, your Honour." *Even if you fine me ten pounds a day, I'm not going to wear the blasted wig,* thought Angelo.

"Bromopnea," said Justice Cobb, his voice barely above a whisper.

The bloody word game. Angelo gritted his teeth as he said, "I don't know, your Honour."

"Bad breath."

Angelo stared at Justice Cobb. Was the man implying he had a stinky mouth? Angelo cupped a hand as if to cough, but was really sniffing his breath. All he smelled was his morning coffee.

"Return to your seat, Mr. Murano."

When the prosecutor sat down at his table, Justice Cobb asked, "Are all parties present and accounted for?" Another formality. He was well acquainted with both lawyers before him, and he expected above average shenanigans from the impulsive prosecutor as the trial ran its course.

Angelo stood up again. "Yes, your Honour, I'm Angelo Murano." He glanced at the prosecution table occupied by his associate, a young puffy-faced man with locks of dark brown hair peeking out from under his white wig, a symbol of his junior barrister status. His narrow set eyes were framed with lashes so dense that the blokes teased him about wearing mascara. He insisted he was a red-blooded male who inherited thick eyelashes from his Greek mother. His flamboyant style of clothing did nothing to support his claim that he was all man. Today, hiding underneath his black robe, he outdid himself with a grey jacket that was so shiny it made him look like he had been dipped in silver sparkles.

Angelo was willing to overlook his associate's Liberace-style wardrobe because he was a very hard worker, and fiercely loyal. "This is Thomas Bartlett, my associate." It was all for the record because Angelo and Thomas spent many a day in Justice Cobb's courtroom. "We are acting on behalf of the Crown in this matter." When he was finished, he sat down in his seat, prompting Olly to stand up.

"Yes, your Honour, I'm Oliver Silboy." It was his turn to introduce the legal aid solicitor sitting at the opposite end of the table. "This is Paul Collins, a solicitor from the Public Solicitor's Office, and we're acting on behalf of the defence in this matter." The solicitor, who was barely older than Thomas, looked like he needed a shave, when in fact he used his razor that morning. It was hard not to notice the way he sat on the end, his long left leg jutting out from under the table, like one half of a chicken wishbone waiting to be snapped in two.

Justice Cobb couldn't help thinking that Olly, with that rough voice of his, sounded more like a petty crook with a long criminal record than an esteemed barrister. He said, "Thank you, gentlemen. Will the accused, Mr. Raznatovic, please rise?"

Olly motioned to Igor to stand up with him.

Although Igor and Niel already entered pleas at their arraignment, formality required the tipstaff to announce, "Igor Raznatovic, you have been charged with three offences, all of which took place on or about the 2nd day of February 1957. The first offence pursuant to the Crimes Act of 1928, Section 33, that you did assault complainant X. How do you plead?"

Olly said, "Not guilty by reason of insanity."

"You are also charged with a second offence pursuant to the amended Crimes Act of 1949, Section 40, Sub-section 1, that you did rape complainant X. How do you plead?"

"Not guilty by reason of insanity."

"You are also charged with a third offence pursuant to the Crimes Act of 1928, Section 8, Sub-section 1, that you did wound complainant X with attempt to commit murder. How do you plead?"

"Not guilty by reason of insanity."

The tipstaff said to Justice Cobb, "The accused pleads not guilty by reason of insanity on all three counts, your Honour."

Justice Cobb said, "Will the second accused, Mr. Smithy, please rise?"

Niel stood up and waited nervously.

"Neil Kelvin Smithy, you have been charged with three offences pursuant to Section 309 of the Crimes Act of 1928, all of which took place on or about the 2nd day of February 1957. The first offence, that you did act as a principal in the second degree to the assault of complainant X. How do you plead?"

Niel was angry the tipstaff mispronounced his name again. He said petulantly, "Not guilty."

"You are also charged with a second offence, that you did act as a principal in the second degree to the rape of complainant X. How do you plead?"

"Not guilty."

"You are also charged with a third offence, that you did act as a principal in the second degree to wounding with attempt to commit murder against complainant X. How do you plead?"

"Not guilty."

"The accused pleads not guilty on all three counts, your Honour."

"Tipstaff, please swear in the jury."

"Will the jury stand and raise your right hand?"

The twelve men dutifully obeyed.

"Do each of you swear you will try the case before the court fairly, and that you will return a true verdict according to the evidence and instructions of the court, so help you, God? Please say 'I swear'."

"I swear."

"You may be seated."

Justice Cobb acknowledged the jury. "Good morning, gentlemen." Then he turned his attention to the Crown prosecutor. "Mr. Murano, you may proceed with your opening statement."

Blessed with an excellent memory, Angelo preferred to work without his notes during opening and closing statements. That way he could persuasively influence the jurors with his natural ability to reel off words as if they were unrehearsed, allowing him to use the power of the eyes to connect on a more profound level. Like his gorgeous Italian spitfire of a wife often said when she stared into his baby blues, 'eyes are the windows to your soul'.

His tall stylish build, muscular biceps, and rock hard stomach were hidden by the voluminous black robe, but everyone could see his handsome face which looked younger than his thirty-four years. His thick black hair sported a few rebellious locks, making the ladies swoon and follicle-challenged men envious. When he tilted his head ever so slightly, raising an eyebrow in an enquiring sort of way, he bore an uncanny resemblance to the debonair English actor Dirk Bogarde.

Angelo reminded himself that jurors had no legal experience, making it crucial to meet them halfway. This was done by converting the legal jargon into easier language they were sure to understand. At the same time, he had to be careful not to sound like he was talking down to them.

"Your Honour, gentlemen of the jury, I represent the Crown." He nodded at the jurors as a way of getting acquainted. "What is the role of the Crown? We must prove the offence an accused is charged with. To be guilty of an offence, the physical act and the psychological aspect or the intention behind the physical act, must be proved beyond a reasonable doubt. I stress the word intention because the physical act alone does not make an accused guilty unless the mind is also guilty. The accused must have been intending to do harm in order for a conviction.

The opening statement is like giving directions to someone who's going on a trip they've never taken before. As they take the trip, they will have a better understanding of what may lie ahead. My job, as a prosecutor representing the Australian government, is to give you a preview of what the Crown expects the evidence will show."

An effective method of grabbing attention was to apply the 'pause'. Angelo mentally counted to ten before he resumed talking. "The Crown's evidence is expected to show that Igor Raznatovic, hereinafter also styled the accused, did unlawfully, intentionally, and knowingly cause the rape, assault, and the attempted murder of complainant X."

Angelo paused again. The high was beginning, and it was all pure and natural, his body creating a buzz from a couple of hormones thriving on what he did for a living. "The Crown's evidence will show Mr. Raznatovic lured the four year old complainant into a dank dirty barn where he intentionally inflicted grievous injuries upon her tiny body." The prosecutor decided it was as good a time as any to remind Silboy that all the hoopla and drama basically boiled down to a contest between prosecutors and defence lawyers. "Here's the twist. Defence claims Mr. Raznatovic was insane for the sole purpose of avoiding a gaol sentence."

Olly was outraged. It was a little too soon for Murano to behave like a king fuckin' dick. "Ob...jection! Argumentative! The Crown is attempting to improperly influence the jury."

"Sustained." Justice Cobb checked his watch. Angelo provoked an objection less than three minutes into opening remarks. Must be a new record for him. He looked at the jurors to make sure they understood. "The jury will disregard it."

"The Crown hopes you will see the evidence for what it is, that Mr. Raznatovic wilfully committed criminal acts against the complainant. We expect the evidence will prove beyond any shadow of a doubt that he is guilty of all charges."

Angelo switched his attention to the second accused. It was time to placate him by pronouncing his first name correctly. A simple thing like that could play to the prosecution's advantage sooner or later. "The aiding and abetting charges against the second accused, Niel Smithy, are serious offences not to be taken lightly. If a person reaches an agreement with another person to commit a crime or was aware that a crime is being committed, he becomes an aider and abettor by helping or encouraging the principal offender in some fashion, or simply by failing to report the crime to the proper authority.

The Crown expects the evidence will prove Niel Smithy, hereinafter also styled the accused, did unlawfully, intentionally, and knowingly become an aider and abettor to the rape, assault, and attempted murder of complainant X, as if he caused them himself. His guilt in aiding Mr. Raznatovic will become evident when you learn he is a capable individual possessing the free will to stop the accused from committing criminal acts, either by physically overpowering him, or by getting help from a fair camped nearby.

He did not seek help because he was an accomplice who encouraged Mr. Raznatovic to commit unlawful acts by making sure the latter wouldn't be interrupted while he used the complainant for his sadistic pleasure. It is the Crown's hope that you will find Niel Smithy guilty of all charges, to ensure he's punished for the part he played in the despicable crimes against complainant X."

Angelo once had a habit of trailing the end of his sentences, but now he made sure the last word was the clearest. This tactic ensured the jury listened right up to the end. None of the spectators would ever guess that he used to speak in a monotone that could put the courtroom to sleep. It took several trials of oratory practice to turn his voice into a vibrant performance. Satisfied he was on top of his game, he sat down.

Olly got up, quickly reviewing his legal notepad. Unlike Angelo, he relied heavily on his notes. "Charges are not facts. What the prosecutor just said are nothing more than claims of what the Crown hopes to prove against Mr.

Raznatovic and Mr. Smithy. With all due respect, don't believe a word of it until you have heard all the evidence.

Normally, an accused is under no legal obligation to prove he's not guilty or to explain the evidence presented by the Crown. However, Mr. Raznatovic has raised the issue of insanity as his defence. The law presumes an accused is sane which places a legal burden on the defence to prove insanity within a reasonable doubt, or on a balance of probabilities." The barrister broke it down for any juror who was still not comprehending. "In other words, prove the accused was more likely to be insane than not."

He looked briefly at Igor. "As Mr. Raznatovic pleaded not guilty by reason of insanity, the evidence probative of his mental disorder will be placed before you, and the Crown's witnesses may be cross-examined to raise reasonable doubt. Even if he committed the physical acts of rape and assault, he did not intend to harm the complainant. We expect the evidence will prove insanity which nullifies the state of mind element of these charges.

Mr. Raznatovic pleaded not guilty by reason of insanity to the charge of wounding with attempt to commit murder because he had no intention of killing the complainant. Therefore, the defence expects you to throw out the charge."

At this point, Olly took a radical departure from his usual dry opening statement. If it works for Murano, it can work for him. "I'm the Crown's opponent, the stitch in his side, the crick in his neck, and like any good lawyer, I will defend my clients' right to a fair trial whether they be poor, aboriginal, retarded, or insane." He reached for a glass of iced water on his table to ease a tickle irritating his throat.

Angelo stifled a smile. Silly-boy, you are more like the pain in my ass, he thought smugly. And you might as well crunch ice cubes for all the good that cold drink is doing for you.

Olly took a sip and put the glass down. "Sorry for the interruption, your Honour." He turned to the jury again. "If, at the end of the day, you don't remember anything I said up to now, I ask you to remember the following. Mr. Raznatovic pleaded not guilty by reason of insanity because he was labouring under such a defect of reason as to not know that what he was doing was wrong, and according to Australian law, he cannot be held accountable for his crimes. When it's all over, we expect you to find him not guilty of all charges."

Olly was not so confident about Niel's outcome. He looked at the accused who was trying to loosen the knot on his tie. Should Igor be found not guilty by reason of insanity, Niel could still be found guilty. "A person is not normally convicted solely for their presence at a crime scene, or not knowing what to do, or not providing appropriate help. Niel Smithy was present while the complainant was attacked, but the defence evidence will show he labours under a cognitive handicap which prevents him from doing the right thing. After hearing all the evidence, we expect you will dismiss all charges against Mr. Smithy."

Olly was finished with opening remarks.

Angelo wasted no time announcing his evidence-in-chief. "The Crown calls its first witness, Inspector Worlock."

The policeman walked through the courtroom doors and towards the witness box looking oddly out of place in a dark grey wool suit and solid navy blue tie, his trench coat waiting for him outside. When he placed his left hand on the Bible and raised his right hand, the tipstaff said, "Do you swear to tell the truth, the whole truth and nothing but the truth, so help you God? Say 'I swear'."

"I swear."

Angelo took over. "Please state your full name and profession."

"Matthew Oscar Worlock, detective inspector and member of Her Majesty's Victoria Police for the last fifteen years."

Angelo made a mental note to rib Worlock about his middle name. "Thank you, inspector. Please sit down." He was going to make sure their friendship won't become an issue during testimony. Although no one knew how close they really were, it was better to be safe than sorry, especially with Olly all over the case like a split personality. "Please describe your role in this case."

"I was in charge of the police investigation."

"What happened on the morning of Saturday, February 2nd, 1957?"

"At thirty-six minutes past eleven a.m., the police responded to an emergency call at Riley Gibson's farm in Bacchus Marsh where a crime scene was located."

"Where is Mr. Gibson's farm in proximity to the complainant's home?"

"The farm is on the other side of the street, directly opposite the house where the complainant lived at the time."

"Please describe what you saw at the crime scene."

"The complainant was lying unconscious in pools of blood inside a barn. She had urinated on herself and was suffering from obvious signs of a brutal attack, requiring her to be transported by ambulance to the hospital."

"Did you find anyone else in the barn?"

"The complainant's mother."

"What was her condition?"

"She was unharmed as she was not present during her daughter's attack."

"Where were the two accused?"

"They were being held outside the barn by a search party from a traveling fair known as *Fun Land Carnival*."

"Why were the accused being held?"

"The search party found them in the barn with the complainant, and Mr. Raznatovic had suspicious stains on his clothes."

"Let's stop there and take a brief history of the complainant and her family. Where is she from?"

"Objection. Irrelevant."

Justice Cobb said, "I will allow it."

Angelo repeated the question, "Where is she from?"

"London, England."

"What about her parents?"

"They originate from Hungary."

"What does her father do for a living?"

"He's employed at Shell Refinery."

"Do they have any other children?"

"No."

Angelo wanted to draw compassion for Marika by stressing she was all about family, a little kid, an only child with decent hardworking immigrant parents hoping for the good life in Australia. He picked up a large cork board displaying photographs and a scale map of Riley Gibson's farm, placing it on an easel beside Worlock.

"Inspector, I'm showing you Crown exhibit C-1 for identification. Do you recognize the photographs?"

"Yes, these are photographs of Mr. Gibson's barn, shearing shed, and well."

"Please point to the structures in the photographs and identify them. If you wish, you may use the pointer on the easel."

Worlock picked up the pointer and touched the photograph closest to him. "Shearing shed." He tapped the photograph towards the middle of the cork board. "The well." The one to the far left. "The barn."

"Did you measure the distance between these structures?"

"I did."

"What is the distance between the shearing shed and the well?"

"Nineteen feet."

"How far is the well from the barn?"

"Fifty-four feet."

"On the scale map, please identify the three squares below the well and the barn."

"They represent the trucks which transported animals to the fun fair."

"Do the photographs and scale map represent a fair and accurate description of the crime scene on February 2nd?"

"Yes, they do."

"Your Honour, we offer Crown exhibit C-1 into evidence."

"Any objections, Mr. Silboy?"

"No, your Honour."

"Let the record show Crown exhibit C-1 admitted into evidence."

"That's all for now, inspector." Angelo said to Justice Cobb, "Your Honour, the Crown reserves the right to call the witness at a later time."

"Very well. As lead investigator, Inspector Worlock may be seated at the prosecution table."

Angelo said, "Crown calls Luna Van Anderson to the stand."

Luna was dressed in a pale blue Sunday frock, white bobby socks, and glossy black shoes. Not at all frightened by the courtroom, she skipped down the aisle, her mother right behind her.

Angelo escorted the child to the witness box while Cornelia sat down in a front seat staring at her daughter with a tight worried look on her face.

When the tipstaff got up with the Bible, Justice Cobb ordered him to sit down again. A witness as young as Luna wouldn't understand the meaning of an oath. But he had to make sure she possessed sufficient intelligence and understanding of the duty to tell the truth.

"Young lady, do you know what telling the truth means?"

Luna said, "Yes, sir."

Justice Cobb didn't want to sound like a prig berating a child, so he overlooked the witness downgrading his authority. "Do you know what a lie is?"

"Yes, sir."

"Well, what is it?"

"Saying things that didn't happen."

"That's right. You must tell the truth only. No lies. Is that understood?"

"Yes, sir."

"Proceed, Mr. Murano."

Angelo asked, "Why was complainant X at Mr. Gibson's farm?"

Confusion spread across Luna's face until she remembered the no-name game she and her mother played to help her follow the strange rules today. Complainant X meant Marika. "She was going with me to the fun fair."

"Did anyone else go with you?"

"Her mommy."

"What time did all of you arrive at the fair?"

"Five past eleven." Luna held up a wrist to show her Mickey Mouse watch. "I got it for my birthday."

Angelo admired the watch with an appreciative nod. Then he asked, "What happened when you got to the fair?"

"The comp..." Luna struggled with the word that was too long for her immature vocabulary. "Can I call her my friend?"

Justice Cobb was impressed with the girl's resourcefulness. "Yes, you may. For the record, the complainant will be referred to as *friend* during this witness's testimony."

Angelo asked again, "What happened when you got to the fair?"

"My friend wanted to go home. So, her mommy told me to wait inside the shearing shed."

"Did your friend say why she wanted to go home?"

"No, but she kept saying it."

"Did you see anyone else outside?"

"There was a boy with a fire truck."

"Was he by himself?"

"An old woman was there. Does she count?"

Angelo wondered if any elderly women in the courtroom would be offended. "Yes, she does. Anyone else?"

"No."

"What happened after that?"

"I could hear my friend's mommy telling her to stand by the well, and then she came and took me to my mommy."

"Thank you, I'm finished."

Luna called out to her mother, "Can I go home now? I don't like it here."

A few sympathetic chuckles from the courtroom were quickly silenced with a severe look from Justice Cobb. "Just a minute, young lady. Mr. Silboy, do you wish to cross-examine?"

"No, your Honour."

"Young lady, you may now go to your mother."

Luna hurried over to Cornelia who was already headed for the door.

When they were no longer in the courtroom, Angelo said, "The Crown calls Dr. Allen Trip."

A mature man in a milk chocolate brown suit and a skinny tie with diagonal brown and beige stripes walked up to the witness box. He sported flat-top hair better suited to a younger face, and except for the occasional sunburn, a hazard of his job as a criminalist, he had the chalky pallor of a person who spent most of his time under fluorescent bulbs.

After the witness was sworn in, Angelo said, "Please state your full name and profession."

"Dr. Allen David Trip, Victoria State criminalist with a Phd in chemistry and a background in science, biology, and forensic science."

Angelo believed a jury was impressed by scientific evidence, even from a man who had poor taste in suits, trying to hide his age behind skinny striped ties and youthful haircuts. "Did you attend the crime scene on February 2nd?"

"Yes, I did."

Angelo handed photographs, Crown exhibits C-2 to C-8, to the witness. "Do you recognize what are in the photographs?"

"Yes, I obtained two sets of shoe prints; one set matching Mr. Raznatovic's size 11 work boots, and the other a match to the complainant's child size 8 sandals."

"How did you obtain the prints?"

"The area around the barn and well sits on podosol soil which is of a highly sandy composition. When it gets wet, it makes a good medium for shoe prints. On the day of the crimes, the ground outside the barn was damp from buckets of water from the animal trucks. The soil around the well was also damp with water."

"Using the cork board, please show the route that Mr. Raznatovic took with the complainant as you describe the pattern made by their shoe prints."

"I picked up the prints belonging to Mr. Raznatovic and the complainant at the well. They were headed towards the barn in an uneventful walking gait, side by side, before their tracks disappeared. I again picked up the prints along the side of the barn. At this point, Mr. Raznatovic's stride was longer and the complainant's prints turned into drag marks, suggesting she was dragged to the barn door the rest of the way." Dr. Trip ran the pointer along the ground and stopped at the barn door.

In the last photo, the prints were unrecognizable. "What is in this photograph?"

"They are several pairs of shoe prints made by the search party in front of the barn door."

"Dr. Trip, would you say these are fair and accurate photographs of what you saw that day?"

"Yes, I would."

"Your Honour, we offer Crown exhibits C-2 to C-8 into evidence."

Justice Cobb said, "Mr. Silboy, any objection?"

"None, your Honour."

"Crown exhibits C-2 to C-8 are admitted into evidence."

"Request permission to approach the jurors."

"You may proceed, Mr. Murano."

Angelo walked to the middle of the jury box holding up the photographs that the witness had just identified. He didn't have to say a word because Marika's child-size feet were doing the talking. They were telling the jurors that a petrified little girl was being forced into the barn by her assailant.

Next up were exhibits C-9 to C-13, identified as photographs of Marika's head injury, blood, tissue, and fingerprints found on the varnished pole that broke her skull. Angelo went to the exhibit table and grabbed the pole, strutting towards the jury as if he was getting ready to vault across the courtroom. But all he did was turn around and stand beside his table.

"Do you recognize this pole, exhibit C-14?"

"It's the pole that was found at the crime scene."

"How long is it?"

"Eight feet."

"Did you test it for fingerprints?"

"Yes, I identified two sets of fingerprints at one end of the pole which are a match to Mr. Raznatovic."

"Did you find anything else?"

"Type A positive blood and tissue were found on the pole at the opposite end of Mr. Raznatovic's fingerprints."

"What is the complainant's blood type?"

"Type A positive."

Angelo didn't need to say anything more. Let the jury draw its own conclusion. He held exhibit C-14 high in the air to give everyone a clear and unobstructed view of the weapon. He wanted it to make a bold statement, and the only way to do that was to create a moment Justice Cobb wasn't going to like. But it was more important to give the jury an idea of how much it hurts to have a big pole bash them on the head for the purpose of ending a life. The Crown prosecutor smacked the pole on the prosecution table where Angelo's associate sat oblivious to his intentions.

BANG.

Thomas shrieked like a referee's whistle and tossed his pen in the air which Angelo caught with his free left hand. Playing soccer had its fringe benefits. People gasped in shock before erupting into animated conversation.

Justice Cobb, who was making notes, practically flew out of his chair. He was surprised he didn't have a cardiac arrest right on the spot. Once he recovered, he shouted at the spectators, "Order in the court!" It was at times like this that he wished he had a gavel used in American and Chinese courts. He turned towards the Crown prosecutor. "Table bashing. That's a new low for you, Mr. Murano.

Your ad hoc performances bruise the dignity of this court and will not be tolerated. Is that understood?"

"Yes, your Honour." Angelo cast his eyes to the floor which made him look like a repentant school boy. The all-important element of surprise would be lost if everyone was prepared, unlike Marika who never knew what hit her. Angelo was satisfied he had rattled everyone's bones. After relinquishing the pole, he picked up exhibits C-15 to C-19. "Dr. Trip, do you recognize these photographs?"

"They are blood and semen samples obtained from Mr. Raznatovic after he was taken into custody on February 2nd."

"What is Mr. Raznatovic's blood and semen type?"

"Type B negative."

"What did you find on his genitals?"

"Type A positive blood."

By now, the jury knew it was the complainant's blood.

Once the exhibits were officially part of the trial record, Angelo picked up a pair of coveralls by one of its shoulder straps. "Dr. Trip, do you recognize exhibit C-20?"

"Those are the coveralls worn by Mr. Raznatovic on February 2nd."

"Did you find anything on them?"

"Five type A positive blood stains."

For the benefit of the jury, Angelo made sniffing noises as he waved the coveralls in front of him like a flag. He was exaggerating because the odour was barely detectable after all these months. "Did you find anything else?"

"Urine stains."

A reminder of Worlock's earlier testimony that the helpless victim was so frightened during the attack, she had peed on herself and the barn floor.

Angelo pushed through exhibits C-21 to C-24, photographs of the coverall stains. Once they were entered into evidence, he picked up another photograph, exhibit C-25, which was given to Dr. Trip. "Do you recognize the object in this photograph?"

"It's a vaginal swab test performed on the complainant."

"Who performed the swab test?"

"That would be Professor Todd Laramy, the chief surgeon at Royal Melbourne Hospital."

"Who tested the swab?"

"I did."

"And what are the results?"

"The swab tested positive for semen."

"What is the semen's blood type?"

"Type B negative."

"Please remind the jury of the semen blood type belonging to Mr. Raznatovic."

"Type B negative."

Angelo felt like he just scored a hole in one, and wanted to boast. But the only person who would tolerate his bragging was his wife Sofia. With barely a downward tilt of the head, his eyes to the floor, no one the wiser, he took a few seconds to praise the Lord. Dr. Trip's statement deserved the utmost deference by everyone in the courtroom.

While Angelo was having a religious moment, Attila was suffering acute embarrassment for his daughter. How many little girls suffer the indignity of having vaginal swabs put on public display? Creaking benches caused by uncomfortable people adjusting their seated positions barely registered on him. As much as it was an attention grabber, it was also very disturbing to hear taboo material in public. Two women got up and walked out of the courtroom. Attila wanted to follow them.

Angelo moved on to exhibits C-26 to C-31 which were Marika's blouse, skirt, and the grainy photographs of her back injuries. He pointed at the blouse's multiple dried blood stains. "Why is there blood on the blouse?"

"The complainant was wearing it when she suffered wounds to her back."

Angelo picked up the whip from the exhibit table, and knew he was being watched with suspicion. Was he going to crack it across the room and give elderly, pedantic Justice Cobb another scare? Maybe when the courtroom was empty, he would have a fling as John Wayne. Right now, he settled for a question. "Do you recognize this whip, exhibit C-32?"

"That is the whip which caused the wounds to the complainant's back."

"Where was it found?"

"Inside the barn near the complainant."

"Was it tested for fingerprints?"

"Bloody fingerprints belonging to Mr. Raznatovic were found on the handle."

"What type is the blood?"

"Type A positive which was also found at the tail end of the whip."

Angelo thought, that's right jurors, the little girl's spilled blood.

The jury next reviewed exhibits C-33 to C-37, photographs of the whip and the blood staining the barn floor. More of the little girl's spilled blood.

Angelo was satisfied. So far, all of the Crown's exhibits had been admitted into evidence. He picked up exhibit C-38. "Do you recognize this pitchfork?"

"It was found at the crime scene inside the barn."

After the exhibit was admitted into evidence, Angelo asked, "Did you test the pitchfork?"

"Yes, I did. There were bloody fingerprints deposited on the handle and two sets of fingerprints on the stick."

"Did you identify the bloody fingerprints on the handle?"

"They belong to Mr. Raznatovic. The two sets of fingerprints on the stick belong to Mr. Raznatovic and Mr. Smithy."

"What type is the blood?"

"Type A positive."

Angelo gripped the pitchfork as if he were Igor preparing to plunge it into his tiny victim. Locking eyes with the jury, he wondered what they were thinking before he let go of the pitchfork. He finished up with the witness after exhibits C-39 to C-42, photographs of the pitchfork, were entered into evidence.

Justice Cobb said, "Mr. Silboy, cross-examine?"

"If it pleases the court." Olly asked, "Dr. Trip, can the miracle of science determine if Mr. Smithy deposited his fingerprints during the commission of the crimes?"

"No."

"Could they have been deposited at some other time?"

"Yes."

"What is Mr. Smithy's blood type?"

"Type O negative."

"Did you find O negative blood type fluids on the complainant or at the crime scene?"

"No."

"Was any type A positive blood found on Mr. Smithy?"

"No."

"Could he have used a condom?"

"No condom was found at the scene, or on his person."

"That is all."

The line of questioning by the defence was inevitable, and although it was looking good for Niel right now, Angelo knew there was still plenty of time to cook his goose.

Angelo recalled Worlock to the stand, aware that having testified at many trials, the inspector didn't need to be reminded he was still under oath. It was time to throw another spanner in the works. He asked, "Did Mr. Raznatovic try to kill the complainant with the pole?"

"Objection! Speculation. Leading his own witness."

Angelo persisted, "Your Honour, Inspector Worlock is an exemplary police officer…"

"With all due respect, the Crown's witness is not a mind reader," interrupted Olly. "As for my client, he has repeatedly stated he had no intention…"

"Stop right there, Mr. Silboy," reprimanded Justice Cobb. "I don't see your name on the witness list."

"Yes, your Honour." Olly silently cursed himself for getting sucked into Murano's games and making a stupid legal blunder.

Angelo wasn't ready to let it go. "Your Honour, credibility is an issue where Mr. Raznatovic is concerned."

"Objection!"

"Sustained!" When Justice Cobb became angry, he sometimes spoke in single words rather than sentences. "Chambers. Now."

The judge's chambers was a gloomy office, the four walls made of dark Australian walnut. A scowling Justice Cobb sat down at a large matching desk in front of the window.

Olly stood out of the way, staring at a wall portrait of the stern-faced judge.

Shaking his head with disappointment, Justice Cobb said, "Mr. Murano, you're quarreling like an aggressive rookie which has subjected the court to acrimonious behaviour. Not only that, the legitimacy of the legal system is compromised if a barrister, like yourself, feels free to display incivility in the courtroom." He didn't take his eyes off the Crown prosecutor, but was fully aware that Olly kept shifting around the room. "Be ashamed."

It was Angelo's cue to grovel. "I apologize, your Honour."

Justice Cobb knew the young barrister was challenging the traditional old school values of pomp and decorum. "Undermining your primary duty to the court disrupts the administration of justice which, in turn, harms the complainant's interests. However, I'm giving you another chance because I understand your strong desire to be a fearless advocate in this case."

Angelo went back to the courtroom, knowing full well he deserved the lecture.

When Olly tried to follow the prosecutor, Justice Cobb said, "Not so fast, Mr. Silboy. Do you have the temerity to practise your dance moves in my chambers? Or do you find my portrait so interesting that you want to stare at it all day?"

"No, your Honour." Then Olly realized the judge might think he didn't like the portrait. He quickly offered, "It's a good likeness." He really wanted to say it was an eerie portrait that followed him everywhere he went with inscrutable eyes. Definitely in good company with the Mona Lisa.

"Xenobombulate, Mr. Silboy."

"I don't understand, your Honour," said the barrister apologetically.

"To malinger, as in shirking one's duty."

Olly wondered if he should remind Justice Cobb why he was there. He decided it was a bad idea to tell a judge he was forgetful. Olly hurried back to the courtroom.

As soon as Justice Cobb returned to the bench, Angelo asked the inspector, "Did you interrogate Mr. Raznatovic?"

"Yes."

"Your Honour, the Crown wishes to submit exhibit C-43, Mr. Raznatovic's statement."

"Mr. Silboy, any objections?"

"No, your Honour."

"Exhibit C-43 is admitted into evidence."

"Inspector, did Mr. Raznatovic tell you why he used the pole to attack the complainant?" asked Angelo.

"He said he wanted to stun her."

"Did you find the complainant stunned at the crime scene?"

"No."

"Please remind the court how you found her."

"Unconscious."

"What did the accused say about the pitchfork being in his possession?"

"He said he picked it up because he was afraid of the search party trying to break down the barn door."

"What else did Mr. Raznatovic say?"

"He said he opened the barn door for the search party."

Angelo hoped the jury would see the disconnect between Igor's purported fear of the search party and pretty much inviting all and sundry into the barn. "Let's talk about pitchforks, in general. Are they capable of causing death?"

Olly stood up. "Objection! Misleading the jury."

"Overruled. The witness will answer."

"Yes, they can cause death."

Angelo said pleasantly, "Thank you." He had found a way to appease Justice Cobb and convince the jury that pitchforks were deadly weapons. If the jurors were smart, they have to believe Igor was really planning to use exhibit C-38 as a killing instrument. This should lead them back to the pole and the Crown's contention that Igor attempted to kill Marika with it.

When Olly didn't begin his cross-examination fast enough, an impatient Justice Cobb methodically tapped the bench with his forefinger. "We are waiting, Mr. Silboy." He hated the frittering of time in his courtroom.

"If it pleases the court." Olly stood up quickly. "Inspector, did you see any other exit in the barn besides the barn door?"

"There was an exit in the hayloft and a side door."

"Did the accused use either exit to try and escape?"

"No."

"Did Mr. Raznatovic tell you why he opened the barn door for the search party?"

"He said it was time."

"Did he explain what he meant by that?"

"He just kept saying, it was time."

"In your police investigations, have you ever come across a victim killed by a pole as long and unwieldy as the eight foot pole that was used to strike the complainant?"

"No."

"Can a whip cause death?"

"If it's used in a strangulation hold."

"Did Mr. Raznatovic use the whip in a strangulation hold?"

"No, he did not."

"How quickly could a person commit murder with a pitchfork?"

"Objection."

"Overruled. The witness will answer."

"Perhaps a couple of seconds."

"Then why is the complainant still alive if the pitchfork was meant for her?"

Angelo stood up, "Objection. Calls for a conclusion."

"Overruled."

"It takes time to execute a course of action."

"Mr. Raznatovic said he was using the pitchfork to defend himself against the search party. Isn't that right?"

"That's what he said."

"Did he admit that he was trying to kill the complainant with the pitchfork?"

"No."

"With the pole?"

"No."

"I'm finished with the witness."

Igor sat like a stiff corpse listening intently to the testimony. Of course he wasn't trying to kill Marika with the pole. He wanted her alive while he punished her, but the pitchfork was another story. He glanced at Niel, his piercing black eyes warning the doofart to keep his mouth shut.

Justice Cobb checked the courtroom clock. It was almost noon. "Court will recess for lunch. Trial resumes at one p.m."

Courtroom 2 at 1:00 p.m.

The tipstaff stood up. "All rise!"

Justice Cobb entered the packed courtroom with a cautious stride, his robe skimming the floor. He pulled his robe away from his feet, climbed the podium without tripping, and sat down. "Call your witness, Mr. Murano."

Angelo waited until his next expert witness was sworn in. "Please state your full name and profession."

"Professor Todd William Laramy, chief surgeon and medical instructor at Royal Melbourne and Alfred Hospitals."

Even without his white coat, Professor Laramy looked like a doctor in his well-cut navy blue suit. He had just pulled an all-nighter at the hospital, two emergency operations back to back, lasting well into the morning. After three hours of sleep and several cups of strong coffee, he was in court, ready to testify.

Angelo asked, "How long have you been employed at these hospitals?"

"Twenty-one years."

"Were you the attending doctor at Royal Melbourne Hospital on February 2nd?"

"Yes, I was in charge of the complainant's case."

"Please describe her injuries."

Igor primed himself to catch every word so that he could play them over and over again. He had been waiting a long time, the anticipation of this day turning into a voracious hunger that kept him awake many a night as he lay in his cell.

Professor Laramy said, "The complainant suffered extensive internal and external wounds from the rape, as well as bruises and contusions to her torso and legs. She also sustained four severe lacerations across her lower back, and a depressed skull fracture which did not require surgical intervention. After being in a coma for three days, she regained consciousness without any recollection of what happened to her."

Attila heard it all before, but here in the courtroom full of strangers, it was like he was hearing Marika's injuries for the first time. The words stabbed him gleefully as if they were dancing sabre swords. *Someone stop me before I start screaming,* he silently begged. He got up to leave the courtroom, but froze.

"Do you need to leave the courtroom?" asked Justice Cobb.

Right then and there, Attila knew he was going nowhere. He gave a terse shake of his head and sat down again.

Justice Cobb wanted to believe the poor man regained control of himself. He motioned to Angelo to resume questioning.

"Professor Laramy, does the complainant still have memory loss?"

"Yes, she's suffering from psychogenic amnesia."

Spectators began to chatter away at the shocking testimony as if no one could hear them. Justice Cobb demanded, "Silence! Do I hear magpies in the courtroom?" He focused his glare on two middle-aged women seated together who suddenly looked down at their shoes. "Magpies. Interesting creatures that mimic thirty-five species of birds, even dogs and horses. Oh yes, humans too. If I hear one more peep, the magpies will find themselves ejected from the courtroom."

The two women continued to gaze at their shoes to avoid making eye contact with Justice Cobb.

Although Angelo didn't like being interrupted, he thought the judge was absolutely hilarious. He'd never heard of anyone being compared to the black and white feathered bird. Anyway, who was he to complain? He was the master of interruptions.

Uncomfortable silence descended on the courtroom in a matter of seconds.

The Crown prosecutor had everyone's undivided attention as he said to the witness, "When Mr. Raznatovic bashed the complainant over the head with the pole, could he have killed her?"

"Objection. Speculation."

"Overruled."

"Yes, if the pole hit the complainant a little harder or landed two inches farther down the side of her head, it would have likely been a fatal blow."

"Please summarize the violent injuries that were inflicted against the complainant."

"The bruises and internal lacerations are consistent with a small child being raped by a large adult male. It would be the skull fracture, coma, and whip wounds that suggest over-the-top violence."

"No further questions."

Olly stood up to cross-examine. "Does a person usually die from a depressed skull fracture?"

"Not usually."

"Is being in a coma a common symptom of a mildly depressed skull fracture?"

"Although rare, it cannot be ruled out."

"As the complainant suffered a depressed fracture that did not require surgery, and is still alive, can you say with medical certainty that Mr. Raznatovic tried to murder her with the pole?"

"Objection. Calls for speculation."

"Sustained."

"No further questions."

Angelo stood up. "Redirect, your Honour." He couldn't let Olly have the final word. "Professor Laramy, you stated it is unusual for a patient to die from a depressed skull fracture. But have you ever had a patient that did die?"

"Objection. Irrelevant."

"You introduced this line of questioning, Mr. Silboy. Overruled."

"Yes, one of my patients developed a subdural hematoma which didn't respond to treatment. It resulted in a fatal stroke."

"Subdural hematoma?"

"It refers to a collection of blood in the space between the outer and middle layers of the covering of the brain."

"Thank you, that is all." Angelo sat down. *That's right, jurors. A depressed skull fracture can kill.*

The testimony was wearing Attila down, and he began to compile a mental list of gruesome tortures that would make the pedophile scream in agony.

Worlock suddenly glanced backwards as if he knew what Attila was thinking. He was ready to jump up and halt a disturbance should the father want to create one. He couldn't blame the poor man for trying, but the Italian hot-head and the two magpies had already provoked the judge into a testy mood.

Angelo called Dr. Bowker, his last expert witness for the day.

"Doctor, what is psychogenic amnesia, and how does it relate to the complainant?"

The psychiatrist's white shirt and grey jacket fit far too snugly, and when he took his next breath, a loose button holding his jacket together popped right off. He was flustered as the jacket fell open to display his huge round stomach, and tried to cover the expansive spread with his hands. When he looked at the barrister, he couldn't remember the question. His face began to perspire.

Angelo raised his eyebrows quizzically. "Psychogenic amnesia, Dr. Bowker?"

It was enough to prompt the witness. With a relieved expression, he hurried along to make up for lost time. "Psychogenic amnesia is a self-induced loss of memory caused by an extremely stressful incident or trauma. In the complainant's case, it is a trauma she can't cope with, so her mind blocked it out of her consciousness. However, somewhere in her subconscious, the trauma still exists." The witness paused to catch his breath.

"Go on, Dr. Bowker."

"What has happened here is that a portion of the complainant's mind took over the role of protector and buried the thing which would destroy her. We can only hope it never resurfaces."

"Could her memory return?"

"Yes, it could."

"Thank you, that is all."

Eager to cross-examine the psychiatrist, Olly was already speaking as he stood up. "Did you see the complainant's injuries?"

"Yes, the head and back wounds."

"How did you react?"

Dr. Bowker paused to remember the moment he first saw Marika lying unconscious on her stomach. "I was quite disturbed."

"Did you say anything to Professor Laramy or the other hospital staff?"

"I said I was glad the sick individual is behind bars."

"Nothing further, your Honour." Olly was right to make Dr. Bowker revisit his reaction to Marika's wounds. Sweating in the jury box was the sign of a sensitive man who felt strong emotions.

Not so fast, Silly-boy. Angelo stood up. "Redirect, your Honour."

"Proceed."

"Dr. Bowker, did you examine Mr. Raznatovic or review his medical file?"

"No."

"How much weight should the jury give to the comment you made about him?"

"It was a knee-jerk reaction, not a psychiatric diagnosis."

"No further questions."

The trial was adjourned to the next day.

Attila rushed to the exit knowing Inspector Worlock wanted to speak to him, but he couldn't handle anyone right now. He needed to go home and have several drinks to settle a vein pulsating visibly across the right side of his forehead. With his long muscular legs, he had no trouble evading reporters who tried to keep up with him. He thought with disdain, try bike riding up steep mountain roads until every molecule of oxygen becomes more precious than gold. Breathe slowly to conserve what little there is of the precious substance, but don't stop moving because you're not finished by a long shot. Keep plodding on, even though your heart is ready to burst. Then dodge exploding bombs and Soviet soldiers, and maybe you can catch me.

Tuesday, September 10 at 9:00 a.m.
Courtroom 2

Angelo wanted everyone to realize the Paprikas were just like them, a normal happy family torn asunder by an unspeakable crime against their daughter. And all every decent person should want was to live in a community free of lowlifes like Raznatovic and Smithy. But decency was an irrational concept when it came to little girls and rape. Marika was a moral dilemma dividing Bacchus Marsh into two groups, the sympathizers and the hostiles. They did agree on one thing. A soiled child was an embarrassment and needed to disappear from their lives.

As a purveyor of justice, Angelo was concerned about the public sitting in the jury box. The jurors were witnessing important testimony, and soon they will see the victim which must make them feel sorry for her, no matter what else they think.

The prosecutor was ready for his first expert witness of the day. "The Crown calls Dr. Elias Creighton."

A tall slim man walked through the courtroom doors in an expensive Italian charcoal suit which accentuated his height and grey temples. He was a dashing sort of character with a masculine nose, thin lips, and a cleft chin.

After he was sworn in and seated, Angelo said, "Please state your full name and profession."

"Dr. Elias Creighton. Forensics psychiatrist with a PhD in criminal justice."

"How long have you been a psychiatrist?"

"Twenty-eight years."

"Did you perform an evaluation of Mr. Raznatovic?"

"Yes, I did."

"Did you ask him about the crimes that occurred on February 2nd?"

"I asked him to tell me what happened that day."

"What was the accused's reply?"

"He said he punished the complainant because she pulled her underpants down for lolly."

Angelo glanced at the jury. Even a slow-minded juror could see that a manipulator was trying to pass blame to his little victim. "What did you ask the accused next?"

"I asked him to explain what he meant by punished."

"What did he say?"

"Nothing. So, I told him the complainant was raped and beaten."

"What was his reply?"

"He said, you call it rape, I call it punishment."

"Did Mr. Raznatovic admit to raping the complainant?"
Olly stood up. "Objection. Asked and answered."
"Overruled."
"Yes, he was admitting to rape."
"What is wrong with Mr. Raznatovic?"
"The study of criminal behaviour has seen a major shift from a biomedical to a socio-psychological perspective. When I applied the new framework to Mr. Raznatovic, one trait became very clear. He is a clever manipulator fitting the profile of a psychopath or sociopath, an individual who misbehaves socially and is incapable of forming lasting affectionate bonds with other human beings. This type of individual is extremely insensitive to the feelings of others."
"Go on, Dr. Creighton."
"When Mr. Raznatovic exercises his deviant nature, he treats people like objects to be used for his gratification."
"What does deviancy mean?"
"The term refers to behaviour and ideas which most people find offensive. It extends to sexual behaviour where the deviant departs from acceptable standards of proper sexual conduct."
"How does it apply to Mr. Raznatovic?"
"He prefers to rape and inflict mental and physical pain on his victim as a means of sexual gratification."
"Has he expressed remorse for what he did to the complainant?"
"No."
Angelo picked up a document. "Your Honour, the Yugoslavian government did not permit Dr. Janos Wagner, Mr. Raznatovic's former physician, to testify in person. Instead, the Crown and the defence submitted questions for him to answer in a sworn statement, and which is now offered into evidence as exhibit C-44."
Justice Cobb reviewed Dr. Wagner's statement. "Any objections, Mr. Silboy?"
"No, your Honour."
"Crown exhibit C-44 is admitted into evidence."
"Please read the statement to the jury, Dr. Creighton."
The psychiatrist cleared his throat. "'I, Janos Wagner, general practitioner of medicine in Belgrade, Yugoslavia, received my medical licence on August 1st, 1932. Igor Raznatovic was my patient from April 5, 1940 to September 14, 1951. He presented as a well-nourished male with an unremarkable medical history. At no time did he exhibit any manifestations of mental illness or bizarre behaviour while he was my patient.'"

"Thank you, Dr. Creighton." Angelo had one final question. "What was the accused's mental state on the day he raped complainant X?"

"He was of sound mind."

"That is all."

Olly stood up to begin cross-examination. "When did you conduct your psychiatric evaluation of Mr. Raznatovic?"

"During the last week of February."

"How can you determine Mr. Raznatovic's state of mind three weeks after the fact?"

"I have nearly thirty years of psychiatric experience and wrote thousands of cases in strict accordance with the *International Statistical Classification of Diseases and Related Health Problems Manual.*"

Olly silently ridiculed the wordy title. Strewth, no wonder shrinks are full of themselves. "Dr. Creighton, even with specialized training and experience such as yours, isn't it difficult for a psychiatrist to assess some mental disorders and the degree to which they are present?"

"Sometimes."

The Crown had conveniently sidestepped an important detail during their line of questioning -- the cause of deviancy. And if there was anything Olly could be sure about, it was that mothers and fathers were now being blamed for their children's behaviour. It certainly wouldn't hurt to draw sympathy from the jury and cut Igor a break if the insanity plea fails. He asked the witness, "What causes deviancy?"

Worlock leaned into Angelo and whispered, "Is this bad?"

"Silly-boy's fishing for sympathy. I doubt the jury will take the bait."

Dr. Creighton said, "Deviancy is caused by the emotional deprivation of parents and their failure to instill an appropriate set of standards and values in the growing child. Without proper guidance, the child doesn't learn to deal constructively with frustration, or have a conscience about his actions when his parents continually conduct themselves in a manner which adversely affects him."

"Why do you think Mr. Raznatovic is a deviant?"

"His father was a stern patriarchal figure who revolved his family's life around the Roman Catholic church to the point of obsession, making his only child attend confession every day to seek repentance. When the father was absent, the mother allowed her son unrestricted self-gratification. In other words, she let him do or have whatever he wanted. Then the father punished his son severely when he found out he was being disobeyed. The behaviour patterns exhibited by his parents created conflicting signals for the young boy."

"Does mental illness begin at an early age?"

"Not always."

"Is it possible a person may not show signs of mental illness until they are in their forties or fifties?"

"Yes."

"Is it also possible that Mr. Raznatovic could be one of those people who becomes mentally ill later in life?"

"I can't predict whether he'll become mentally ill in the future."

"I'm referring to the future that came and went on February 2nd, long after Mr. Raznatovic's physician in Yugoslavia last saw him."

"I already testified that I found Mr. Raznatovic to be of sound mind."

"So you said. How does the accused describe the way he felt when he punished the complainant?"

"He said he was in heaven."

"Why do you think he said that?"

"He was expressing feelings of pleasure."

Igor listened intently. He had tricked them all. They had no idea God spoke to him, and that's all that mattered. The Voice was safe.

"What is the general perception of God?"

"Objection. Irrelevant.

"Mr. Raznatovic used the word *heaven* to describe his feelings when he attacked the complainant," argued Olly. "Everyone knows that Heaven and God are like...um...," he wracked his brains for the right description, "...two peas in a pod."

Justice Cobb's centipede brows became quite animated. "Not the most appropriate metaphor, but I'll allow it. Please answer the question, Dr. Creighton."

Angelo wanted to laugh out loud at Silly-boy's catchy rhyme, *Heaven and God are like two peas in a pod.*

The witness said, "Most people believe God is an abstract manifestation of the ultimate being who looks human but has superhuman powers. Like a genie in the bottle, everything we wish for, He should just give it to us. Money, fame, power, worldly goods. Our saving grace are the souls who pray to God for guidance, wisdom, and courage to face their ills. We are forever seeking God. Seeking His help and blessings to validate His existence. We pray to Him to make things better and thank Him when things go well. Of course, we blame Him when things go wrong."

"Do most people believe God lives in heaven?"

"Yes."

"If the accused believes he has a special relationship with God, was he telling you he followed God's will on the day he raped the complainant?"

"Objection!" As a devout Roman Catholic, when it suited him, Angelo had been listening with interest. After all, wasn't God a crucial part of every non-heathen's life? Now, he drew the line. "Your Honour, the defence is encouraging the witness to assign a hidden meaning to an inconsequential phrase. Therefore, I must confess I have also expressed the belief I was in heaven, and most of those expressions took place in my bedroom." Angelo lifted his left hand to show the gold band on his ring finger. "It's okay, I'm married."

The courtroom broke out in titters which cut the oppressive air like a knife.

"Silence in the courtroom!" demanded Justice Cobb. "Mr. Murano, you are overruled and definitely out of order."

"Yes, your Honour."

Dr. Creighton replied to Olly's question, "Mr. Raznatovic did not tell me he was following God's will."

"Could he have implied it when he said he was in heaven?"

"I don't know. He did not elaborate."

"Did Mr. Raznatovic tell you he tried to kill complainant X with the pole?"

"No."

"With the pitchfork?"

"No."

"In fact, what did he say?"

"He said he wasn't trying to kill her."

"No further questions."

That wasn't too shabby, Silly-boy, but I can do better, thought Angelo. He said, "Redirect, your Honour."

"Proceed."

"Dr. Creighton, could Mr. Raznatovic have been manipulating you when he said he was not trying to kill the complainant?"

"Yes, manipulation is a prevalent symptom of a psychopath or sociopath."

"That's all." Angelo wanted the jury to question Igor's real motives.

Court adjourned for lunch.

Courtroom 2 at 1:05 p.m.

Helmut Jung was ready for the Crown prosecutor. His blond crewcut was cut very short which made him seem bald and his face rounder. He had tree stump legs, and his arms looked like they could rip apart his pale blue shirt and brown jacket if he flexed his muscles. Carting a carnival around Australia was hard physical labour which gave him a better workout than lifting weights.

Angelo said, "Please state your full name and profession."

"Helmut Gottfried Jung. The 'j' is pronounced like the 'y' in yes." It never ceased to amaze him how non-Europeans couldn't pronounce his one-syllable name properly. "I'm the owner of *Fun Land Carnival* which has been touring Australia for the last two years."

"Mr. Jung, please describe the events of last February 2nd which led you to Mr. Gibson's barn."

Helmut waited many months for this moment. He needed to help the little girl, and this was the only way he could think of doing it. "I was at the carnival inside Gibson's shearing shed making sure everything was running smoothly. All of a sudden, the mother rushes in shouting for her daughter...the complainant. After a quick search inside, me and four of my men, and a woman from the area, started looking outside. We checked the well beside the shearing shed, but didn't think she was down there. Then we walked over and checked the trucks. Nothing. So, we headed for the barn. If we didn't find her there, we were going to split up and search the whole farm."

"Continue, Mr. Jung."

"As we were walking towards the barn, I saw Smithy." Helmut pointed at Niel. "He stuck his head outside the barn window and was moving his head around, looking one way, then the other. When he turned in my direction, he noticed me. He jerked his head back inside the barn real quick. Then I heard loud voices coming from the barn."

"Did you hear what the voices were saying?"

"No."

"Please describe Mr. Smithy's reaction when he saw you."

"His eyes got wider and his jaw dropped."

"Did he say anything to you?"

"No, he disappeared real quick from the window."

"Then what happened?"

"I peered through a crack in the planks on the barn door, and I saw him." Helmut pointed his finger at Igor.

Justice Cobb interrupted, "For the record, the witness has identified the accused Igor Raznatovic. Please continue."

"I saw him with a pitchfork and a little girl. She was lying on the ground. I didn't like what I saw, so I told the woman who was with us to call the police. Then I got my men to help me break down the door, only it wouldn't budge. We kept heaving on it until we heard the crossbar sliding across from inside.

Raznatovic opened the door, and me and my men pushed it open the rest of the way." Helmut paused, not sure if he was supposed to say anything else.

"Did you see Mr. Raznatovic use the pitchfork in a way that made you think he was going to hurt the complainant?"

"Objection. Leading."

"Sustained. Please rephrase, Mr. Murano."

"Mr. Jung, what was Mr. Raznatovic doing with the pitchfork when you looked through the crack in the barn door?"

"He was holding it over the girl in a downward position."

"What happened after you and your men pushed open the barn door?"

"Raznatovic stood in front of us, smiling, with the pitchfork in his hand."

"Did he point the pitchfork at you?"

"No."

"How did you feel with him standing in front of you with the pitchfork?"

"I was ready for a fight, but he didn't make a move on me."

"Then what happened?"

"I used my work glove to take the pitchfork from him. You know, so I won't destroy fingerprint evidence."

"Thank you, Mr. Jung. Did Mr. Raznatovic put up a fight when you took the pitchfork?"

"No, he let go, just like that."

"What was his overall demeanor?"

"He was calm and kept smiling at us."

Angelo could feel a victory dance going off inside his head. Helmut's last statement should convince the jury that Igor was only interested in puncturing Marika to death with the bloody pitchfork after his failed pole bashing. Unless they went the wrong way and thought the pervert was crazy.

"What else did you see?"

"I saw blood all over the little girl and on the ground, and a large wet stain under her." Helmut pointed at Niel who was still grimacing and jerking the knot on his tie, making it tighter instead of loosening it. "He stood by doing nothing."

Justice Cobb interjected, "For the record, the witness has identified the accused Niel Smithy. Continue."

"What happened next?"

"The mother rushes in." Helmut shook his head sadly. "She was real quiet until she screamed."

"What happened after that?"

"The mother starts blaming herself for going home to look for her daughter instead of going to the barn. She yelled, 'I hate you, God.'"

"Then what happened?"

"I tore a piece from my shirt and gave it to the mother to use on her daughter's wounds. Then I told my men to take Raznatovic and Smithy outside to wait for the police. That's when Raznatovic shouted at the mother, 'Your daughter is a dirty little girl. She pulled her underpants down for lolly.'"

"What crossed your mind when he made that statement?"

"At first, I was shocked and confused, but I met people like him before, so I started wondering what game was he playing. I tell you though, the other people with me were saying maybe the girl brought it upon herself."

Come on, Silly-boy, give us a hearsay objection, thought Angelo. He was ready to argue that it's not hearsay if the witness is not trying to prove a fact but only saying such a statement was made by another person. Olly said nothing. He wasn't as dumb as Angelo thought he was.

The prosecutor had no more questions for Helmut Jung.

Olly stood up to cross-examine. "While you were outside the barn door peering through the crack, how far were you from complainant X as she lay on the ground?"

"About twenty feet."

"How wide was the crack in the barn door?"

"I'd say half an inch."

Olly picked up two pads of paper and held them up half an inch apart as he faced the jury. He leaned forward and squinted through the slit. "Are you absolutely certain you saw Mr. Raznatovic holding the pitchfork over the complainant? I'm standing roughly twenty feet from the jurors and have trouble seeing them through the narrow opening."

"Objection. Argumentative."

"Withdrawn, your Honour."

"The jury will disregard Mr. Silboy's last remarks."

"Did you see Mr. Raznatovic raise the pitchfork in the air?"

Helmut hesitated. After several seconds, he said, "No."

"Therefore, the pitchfork was not in striking position."

"Objection. It is a little premature for closing arguments," said Angelo.

Justice Cobb instructed, "Strike Mr. Silboy's statement. I direct the jury to ignore it."

"I'm finished with the witness."

The trial adjourned for the day. Tomorrow, witnesses from *Fun Land Carnival* were scheduled to take the stand. Marika was expected to testify the next day.

A Dinkum Ordinary Bloke
Worlock asked Angelo, "How's it going so far?"

"Silly-boy surprised me a couple of times. But as I see it, this is a case of good against evil. And good eventually triumphs over evil."

"Do all Roman Catholics view the sanctity of life as black and white as you do?"

Angelo chuckled. "Ecclesiastes. God shall bring every work into judgment, with every secret thing, whether it be good, or whether it be evil."

"If you say so." Worlock gave his friend a bemused look. "How can you be a God-fearing man who insults people?"

"You mean Silly-boy? When we were law students, he called me a wop one too many times. Insulted my Italian heritage every chance he got. Nobody does that to me and gets away with it." Angelo smiled impishly. "I go to confession once a week."

"When a person quotes from the Bible, he's either devoted or fanatical. What are you?"

"I'm not telling," said Angelo in a secretive tone. Then he laughed heartily. "Actually, I get my inspiration from cowboy movies."

"That's what I like about you, old boy. Just when I think I read you, you show me how illiterate I can be."

"Ah hah! You do like me. I wasn't sure." Angelo slapped Worlock on the back. "A dinkum ordinary bloke lies beneath this flash exterior." Then he turned serious. "The jurors have enough common sense not to acquit on the grounds of insanity unless it's obvious and extreme. By the end of the trial, they will know insanity can easily be feigned because I'm morse coding the message every chance I get."

"Ready for tomorrow?"

"I'm always ready." Hungry stomach gurgles punctuated Angelo's last sentence. "Let's get some grub."

Thursday, September 12 at 7:03 a.m.
1 Finch Street

Bloodshot eyes stared at Attila in the bathroom mirror. That's what a broken promise culminating in a night of rum binging will do. What a weak bastard he was. He looked terrible and couldn't let Marika see him like this. Grabbing a razor, he shaved and bathed before grabbing a cup of coffee. He gulped quickly at the burning sips of black fluid, wondering how he was going to be able to drive Marika to the courthouse.

"Marjorie will be here soon, Anna." He silently thanked their friend for agreeing to keep his wife out of the loop while the trial ran its course.

"I spoke to Sofia on the phone. She sounds nice." Hesitantly, Anna asked, "Are you and Marika going to be okay without me for ten days?"

"Of course. Now that I'm cooking, we'll eat well for a change." Attila hoped he would make Anna angry enough to jump into Marjorie's car and keep her that way so she won't come back early.

"You better be joking," huffed Anna.

"Sure am." Not, added Attila silently.

As he waited by the car, he watched Marika dragging her feet towards him. Her thick auburn hair was now cut short and hugging the nape of her neck. He had asked Anna to get her ready, not give her a haircut. Throughout most of the night as he watched over his little girl sleeping with her teddy bears, her hair was long and shiny.

Marika cried when her mother cut off her hair. She begged her not to do it, but Anna wouldn't listen. She looked like a boy now and was angry. She was glad her mother was going away for a few days. Her daddy would never cut her hair. He liked it long.

"Your hair looks nice." Attila told a little white lie as he patted his daughter's head. "I want you to listen carefully. You're going to be in a large room with people sitting on benches."

"Aren't I going to Sofia's house?"

"Tomorrow. But for today, you're going to spend a few minutes in a room with some people. I want you to walk up to the front, and sit down in the chair Mr. Murano wants you to sit in. All you have to do is what he tells you to do." Attila looked down at Marika's large red rimmed eyes, wanting desperately to take her anywhere but to the place waiting for them.

She looked at him with a sad expression. "What does he want me to do, Daddy?"

"You have to turn around and lift your blouse to show your back. He may ask you some other questions, and one other man might ask you questions too. If you don't know what they're talking about, tell them you don't know. And don't mention your name, okay?"

"Yes, Daddy. Why do I have to show my back?" Marika felt strange. Having to be in a room with people she didn't know scared her.

"Everyone wants to see your lovely back. After it's finished, I'm taking you to the You Yangs Mountains to look for koala bears."

Marika looked solemnly at her daddy. She didn't care about the You Yangs Mountains anymore. What he wanted her to do frightened her so much, all she could think about was the room full of strangers.

Courtroom 2 at 8:55 a.m.

Igor sat impassively beside Olly waiting for Marika's arrival. In contrast, Niel was a bundle of nerves, his left leg twitching uncontrollably as his stained fingers tapped the polished table. Igor looked at his old cobber with annoyance. He was thinking of kicking the doofart's chair over when no one was looking. Distractions were not welcome because he had waited too long to see the little girl who needed to be wiped out forever. Then the restless pain surging through his body every time he thought of her would finally leave him alone.

He kept his secret safe. Olly told him not to hide anything, but Igor couldn't risk angering the Voice by revealing its presence. If he did, the psychiatrists will drug him into a zombie state, maybe even subject him to horrifying electric shocks to make him a total vegetable. He was petrified of that, but no matter what happened to him, the Voice was invincible.

When they kept digging during their evaluations, he divulged his childhood to lead them away from the Voice. He did throw them a few small bones to insinuate his actions had something to do with God. The gullible psychiatrists lapped up every word.

Igor knew he wasn't insane and argued incessantly with Olly about saying he was. He relented after being warned of the harsh life in gaol if he was found guilty, especially for a child molester. He hated being demeaned in front of all these people. Why were they allowed to learn about his life and pass judgment on him? He knew they will soon be watching every breath Marika took. She was the one who was evil, not him. Thinking about her made him snarl out loud.

Olly said sternly, "I told you to maintain decorum."

Igor scowled at the lawyer. *Make up your mind, you stupid idiot. Do you want people to think I'm insane or not? And aren't you and that smarmy Murano fine examples of decorum.* It angered him to do what Olly told him to do.

Only the Voice could command him.

Why are Circus Clowns Scary?

Marika felt a wave of uncontrollable fear as she entered the unfamiliar building. The vast ceiling with its elaborate crystal chandelier and red-carpeted stairs overwhelmed her. It didn't help that people were whispering and turning their heads to look her way as she walked up the stairs. When she and her daddy reached the second floor, a group of reporters waiting at the landing went into action. Attila froze as the men rushed towards Marika, calling out questions and falling over each other to be heard. Luckily, the simultaneous verbal barrage made it difficult to understand what anyone was saying.

"Back up, fellas!" Worlock appeared out of nowhere, cordoning off the reporters with a lecture on courthouse etiquette. They were herded to the opposite end of the corridor while father and daughter sat together on the bench outside Courtroom 2.

Marika's heart was pounding and she wanted to run outside and hide in the car, but Attila held her hand tightly. She looked warily at the reporters hovering down the corridor. "Daddy, why are they staring at me?"

Attila shook his head. "You're mistaken." He hated lying, his gruffness surprising the little girl. The moment he dreaded had arrived when Angelo appeared in front of Marika like a stealthy ninja to take her hand and lead her into the courtroom.

Standing at the back with Worlock as previously arranged, Attila stared at Igor, wanting to poke out the pedophile's eyes before he had a chance to see Marika. Reluctantly taking his gaze off Igor, he searched the room thinking it looked more crammed than usual. Was extra seating added for today's main event? No, it was still the same number of spectators who were waiting with so much anticipation for the object of the trial that they had swollen into a school of puffer fish. Bloated bastards.

The sea of strange cold faces made Marika's stomach hurt. The big room with its dark walls created a depressing gloom, and the stern-faced man draped in black at the huge wooden bench made her big eyes grow bigger.

Sensing the little girl's fear, Angelo held her hand close to him to let her know she was not alone. When she looked up at him, he smiled at her, trying to create a sense of reassurance and keep her from noticing Igor. Glancing at Professor Laramy and Dr. Bowker seated in the front row, the prosecutor expected them to provide support if Marika needed it. In their professional opinion, the little girl most likely won't remember the rape today, but warned him it was still possible. They waited like everyone else, knowing that only thirteen feet separated the little girl from the man who did unspeakable things to her.

When Marika stepped into Igor's line of sight, he noticed her haircut. What was she trying to do? Look like a boy? All it did was enhance her delicate face and big eyes. He didn't like her new hair, sending her a silent message. You can't escape what I have in store for you, dirty little girl.

Angelo led Marika to the witness box and instructed her to sit down. The tipstaff brought over the Bible, but Justice Cobb curtly brushed him away with his hand. Just like her former friend, Marika would have no understanding of taking an oath. The judge was ready to test the little girl's intelligence and ability to be truthful. "Do you know what telling the truth means?"

Marika nodded, unable to speak to the black robed, wig-wearing man who was almost as scary as a circus clown.

"You have to say yes or no."

"Yes."

"Do you know what a lie is?"

"Yes, my teacher sent a boy to the corner for lying."

"Does that mean it's a good thing or a bad thing?"

"A bad thing."

"Why?"

"It's not nice to make up stories."

"Good. I want you to tell the truth in the courtroom. No lying."

Marika was afraid of the judge and nodded again. "Okay."

Justice Cobb was satisfied with Marika's demeanor. He said, "Proceed, Mr. Murano."

Angelo smiled again at the little girl. "How are you?" he asked casually.

"Fine," said Marika timidly.

"How old are you?"

"Five."

"Have you seen a courtroom before?"

"No."

"It looks big and strange, but it's actually a good place." Angelo spoke to Marika as if they were two friends sharing a secret. He decided it was now or never. "May I see your back?"

Marika hesitated as she looked at her daddy. When Attila nodded with encouragement, she got up. "Okay."

"Permission to approach the witness, your Honour."

"Proceed."

Angelo partially blocked Igor's view as the little girl turned around and started to move her blouse upwards. Suddenly, Marika felt the prosecutor's big hand clumsily pulling her blouse higher. She didn't like her bare back being exposed to strangers.

Justice Cobb motioned to the jurors to get up and walk past the witness box in a single line. Each of them glanced at the vivid red lines rising up from Marika's skirt band before silently returning to their seats.

Angelo observed each juror as he held onto the blouse. Although they appeared to be unmoved, he was good at reading body language. There was no reaction when they saw the photographs of Marika's scars. Seeing the wounds up close was a different story. They were touched by the sight of the small disfigured back. He let go of the blouse after the final juror walked by.

"I have no more questions."

Marika hurriedly pulled down her blouse, the hem settling loosely around her hips. She felt embarrassed and wanted to tuck it inside her skirt, but not in front of all those strangers. As she turned around to face the courtroom, she tried to avoid the sea of stern faces by focusing on her daddy way in the back.

It was Olly's turn. "Do you remember a fun fair near your old house?"

"Objection!" Angelo hurled himself out of his chair as he stood up. "Your Honour, may we approach the bench?" He walked towards the judge without waiting for permission.

"Don't let me stop you, Mr. Murano," said Justice Cobb sarcastically.

Angelo spoke heatedly, "Mr. Silboy is putting the witness in harm's way with this line of questioning."

Justice Cobb held up his hand. "Keep your voice down, the witness can hear you."

Olly argued, "Your Honour, the defence is trying to establish whether or not she has any memory of being attacked."

"I'm going to allow the question, but with it comes a warning. Be mindful of the witness's age and condition. Do I make myself clear, Mr. Silboy?"

"Yes, your Honour." Olly was never very good with little blighters and they sensed it. With a constipated grimace of a smile directed at Marika, he asked again, "Do you remember a fun fair near your old house?"

"No," said Marika nervously.

"Do you remember anything happening that you don't understand?"

"No."

"Tell me if you recognize anyone over there." Olly pointed at the defence table where Igor and Niel sat beside the legal aid solicitor.

Attila took a step forward, but Worlock sensed the move and put a hand on the father's shoulder.

Igor didn't care that everyone was looking his way. He had eyes for no one but Marika, and wanted her to remember everything when she saw him. Most of all, he wanted to see the incredible fear on her face again.

"Recog...?" Marika stumbled over the unfamiliar word.

"Have you seen any of those people before?"

Justice Cobb held his breath as he leaned forward in his chair to escape the incessant buzzing of a fly that became loud and intrusive. He made a mental note to tell the tipstaff to roll up his newspaper during recess and swat the fly into an early demise.

The reporters stopped writing in their notepads, sensing the heightened anticipation in the courtroom while the press outside hung around the doors as if they were receiving telepathic signals from their two colleagues. Everyone else sat on the edge of their seats waiting for the silent drum roll to finally stop.

It felt like an eternity before Marika turned her head in the direction of Olly's outstretched arm. She didn't recognize the legal aid solicitor. There was also no sign of recognition when she glanced at Niel who was avoiding her by staring at his hands with a silly smirk. When she looked at Igor, he sneaked her a sly grin. Nothing. As she turned to face Olly, she stopped and looked at Igor again, a shy smile forming on her lips. Apart from Mr. Murano and her daddy, the stranger sitting nearby was the only person in the room who seemed friendly.

Igor knew it. Marika was his for the taking.

Angelo blinked twice to make sure he wasn't imagining things. As soon as he realized Igor's ugly face was casting a spell over Marika, he distracted her by pushing his exhibit binder off the edge of the table so that it landed on the floor with a thud. The unbelievable gall of the pedophile. Igor had just tried to manipulate his victim in front of the whole courtroom. Luckily, Marika tilted her head away, so the jurors didn't see the smile.

"Have you ever seen any of those people before?" Olly reminded the little girl, pointing towards the defence table.

Say no, begged Attila.

"No."

Olly got his answer from Marika herself. She didn't remember being raped, just like the doctors said. If she did, her reaction to Igor would have been one of absolute terror. "That is all."

"Any further witnesses, Mr. Murano?" asked Justice Cobb.

Angelo stood up. "No, your Honour. The Crown rests its case."

Worlock released his hand from Attila's shoulder which propelled the father down the aisle like a wind-up toy airplane. He grabbed Marika and together they hurried out of the courtroom.

On Princes Highway, Attila rolled down his car window, hoping the fresh air would remove the stench that clung to him the last few days. "We're on our way to koala country." He was going to keep his promise.

"I want to go home, Daddy."

"What's the matter?" Did her testimony provoke horrible images that were now confusing her? Attila looked down at his daughter, her solemn tone depressing him. Maybe it was the strange experience of the morning which unnerved her. "Okay, let's go home."

Marika woke up screaming that night. Startled out of a troubled sleep, Attila stumbled into her room.

"Turn on the light! Turn on the light!" Marika jumped up and down on the bed flailing her arms.

Attila quickly flicked on the ceiling light. "What's the matter?"

"I saw a dark man in a hat! He had a pitchfork! And my chest was hurting and burning. I tried to find Mommy!"

Attila grabbed the hysterical child. "You were having a bad dream."

"I'm scared, daddy!"

Attila desperately tried to think of something to make his daughter forget her very real nightmare. "What's your favourite nursery rhyme?"

"Baa, baa, black sheep!" cried Marika.

Attila would do anything for her, even sing a silly nursery rhyme. "I don't know all the words, so you have to sing along with me, okay?"

Marika trembled as tears flowed down her cheeks. "Yes, Daddy."

When Attila began to sing, he sounded like a tenor, a really terrible one. His daughter joined in with her timid high-pitched voice. "Baa, baa, black sheep, have you any wool? Yes sir, yes sir, three bags full…"

"Meeowwwwww, meeowwwwww…"

The father and daughter duo stopped and looked at each other in surprise. A feral cat decided to sing along, either that or she was in heat. Attila was tempted to go outside and turn on the garden hose, but the caterwauling distracted Marika to the point where she even giggled.

"Daddy, don't you like cats?"

Attila didn't want to tell his daughter that he had an aversion towards hissing balls of fur. "I'm a dog lover with a soft spot for Hungarian vizslas — beautiful sporting dogs, very loyal." He encouraged her to keep singing while the feline crooned to the lonely tomcats prowling the streets of Norlane.

When they finished three verses, Attila held Marika in his arms until she fell asleep.

Tomorrow, he was going to flush out any lingering cats and board up the crawlspace.

Friday, September 13 at 8:45 a.m.
Courtroom 2

Angelo sat alone in a small breakout room beside Courtroom 2 going over questions for the defence psychiatrists testifying on Monday.

There was a knock on the door. Without looking up, he said, "Come in, Thomas."

"G'day, Angelo. Thought I'd find you here," said Olly. He sat down in a chair on the other side of the table.

"Silboy. What can I do for you?" Angelo knew his adversary was on a fishing expedition. Calling him by his first name was a dead giveaway.

"Igor wants to take the stand in his own defence, and if he does, his testimony could be interpreted in three ways, as I see it. He might come across as sane as you and me, or a sign above his head will flash manipulator, thanks to you. There's even a possibility he'll show his true insane colours." Olly put his hands on the table. "As I see it, one of us is going to lose if Igor testifies in front of the jury."

Angelo took a deep breath, tilted his head back and folded his hands behind his neck, a move which filled his lungs with fresh oxygen. "Cut the crap, Silboy." Olly was dangling Igor as bait, but Angelo could play along for the fun of it. "As I see it, according to your theory I'm ahead two to one. You don't want your client to take the stand and very likely make you look like a bloody fool, isn't that right?"

Olly envied the handsome young Italian who got the highest test scores in law school without trying. "I know what I'm talking about. Igor's insane." It was time to get rid of the clinical words. "He's a nutcase."

"As in macadamia?" joked Angelo.

Olly refused to be distracted by the prosecutor's eternal childishness. "I'd stake my career on it."

"But you won't."

Olly revealed his frustration. "It's clear as day. If you spent as much time with him as I have, you'd see it. One minute, he's your average Joe. The next, he's glaring at you in a way that speaks of the devil himself." He got up and took a few paces before he faced the wall and turned back. Might as well be candid. It may do some good with a bloke like Murano. "I have to unwind with a couple of lagers after I've gone a round with him."

Angelo almost felt sorry for Olly. The man was trying to prove he's not such a bad bloke. Maybe he wasn't, if one ignores his prejudice towards Italians. He probably had a faithful pigeon-toed dog he saved from the pound who wagged his tail and licked his master's face. But the man was his adversary, and it was a golden rule of Angelo's to never feel sorry for an opponent, especially a prick like Silly-boy. Still, having to look into the face of evil as often as he claims would unhinge anyone.

How do you defend the devil?

Angelo was ready to get down to business. He didn't want Raznatovic testifying either, and Olly had no idea he was being played like a fiddle. "Go on."

"What are the chances of the mother testifying?"

If you only knew, Silly-boy. Angelo pretended to do him a favour. "About as much chance as Igor testifying."

Olly was never going to let Igor testify. He just wanted to make sure Anna Paprika didn't either. People had soft spots for mothers, and he couldn't risk her blank mind turning the jury against his clients. He left Angelo alone, believing they had an unspoken understanding.

Morse Code Signals

Angelo sat in the empty courtroom drawing squiggles of man-o-war jellyfish on his notepad. His favourite juvenile pastime followed him from Naples secondary school where doodling pads were school textbooks or desktops. Mercifully, his red bow-tied Latin teacher and draculian headmaster with the hefty leather straps took different paths from him.

"Beaut flowers."

Worlock's strong voice startled Angelo. Without turning around, he said, "Beaut jellyfish, you sticky beak."

"Busybody, am I?" Worlock sat down beside the prosecutor. "I noticed Marika's reaction to Raznatovic."

"No worries, the jury didn't see it." Angelo changed the conversation. "I had a chat with the illustrious Silly-boy."

Worlock knew Angelo enjoyed shredding Olly on a personal level. When they attended law school at the same time, Angelo dismissed Olly as a second rate student who was bound to become a second-rate barrister. "Do tell."

Angelo pulled a long face. "He made a half-cocked threat about putting Razzy on the stand if Anna testifies. Little did the git know I'm not totally insensitive to her condition. As for Razzy, should he take the stand in his own defence? Depends. Would he have pulled off one of his manipulations which I believe he would have done, and would the jury see it for what it is, or would they believe what the perv wants them to believe? It could have gone either way."

"Is Creighton's testimony enough to put the insanity issue to rest?"

"He's one flaming good shrink. And don't forget, I'm nudging the jury to reach the right verdicts." Angelo tapped the table as if he was sending morse code signals.

Monday September 16 at 9:05 a.m.
Courtroom 2

The defence was ready to begin.

Dr. Goulding sat in the witness chair, dressed in brown, or dingo shit, as his wife liked to say when she was angry with him. He wondered if he should have put on his charcoal suit that he saved for weddings and funerals. A tall heavy set man like himself could look just as good as the slender Dr. Creighton. He was proud of his grey bottle brush moustache, but was also thinking he should have shaved it off this morning. He tried to give it a light trim yesterday, but snipped it back too far, making his wide lips the focal point of his otherwise bland face. He reminded himself to never go anywhere near a pair of scissors after getting wasted on lager.

Olly said to his expert witness, "Please tell the court your full name and profession."

"Dr. Arnold Bartholomew Goulding. I'm a licensed psychiatrist for the last thirty years, and I teach criminal psychology at Melbourne University since 1951."

Mr. Silboy asked, "Dr. Goulding, did you examine Mr. Raznatovic?"

"Yes, I did."

"On what date did you begin?"

"The fifth of February."

"Is there an advantage to examining the accused so soon after he attacked the complainant?"

"Yes, indeed. We obtain an accurate diagnosis of his state of mind."

"What was Mr. Raznatovic's state of mind on February 2nd?"

"He was suffering from a mental disorder. He still is."

"Please describe his mental disorder."

"Mr. Raznatovic suffers from delusions which are irresistible, overpowering impulses or urges. He's incapable of disobeying them."

"Are you sure about the diagnosis?"

"A careful item-by-item evaluation confirmed the criteria for such a diagnosis has been met."

Olly was feeling a modest high because the ball was in his court now. "Could you please explain the term *insanity* from a medical point of view?"

"It connotes a legal definition, therefore never used in a clinical diagnosis. However, it is a term that is still defined in the medical field as being a disease of the mind which renders the sufferer incapable of appreciating the nature and quality of an act, or knowing it is right or wrong. If the insane individual commits a crime, he lacks the state of mind to be held responsible."

"Thank you, Dr. Goulding. Did the accused tell you he raped complainant X?"

"Yes, however, he prefers to use the term *punish*."

"Does Mr. Raznatovic know what he did to the complainant was wrong?"

"No, he kept saying it was the right thing to do because God will be happy with him."

"Did you tell him there were consequences?"

"Yes."

"What did he say?"

"He said nothing."

"What else can you tell us about Mr. Raznatovic?"

"He believes he has a special relationship with God, and thinks he was doing God's will when he attacked the complainant."

"What is the prognosis for a man who has delusions like Mr. Raznatovic?"

"I treated similar patients who resumed normal lives after medical treatment."

"What does that mean for Mr. Raznatovic?"

"There's hope for him to lead a normal life too."

"Please describe his relationship with the complainant."

Angelo stood up. "Objection. Misleading the jury. The term relationship implies a bond exists between the complainant and the accused."

"Overruled. I'm sure the jury understands it was used in the broadest sense of the word."

Dr. Goulding said, "Something intangible about the little girl brought on the delusional state which controls Mr. Raznatovic. He talks about her as if she was his possession to do with as he pleases, and he believes he has God's permission. There's so much more to explore before we have the whole picture of his mental disorder. However, what's absolutely clear is his fixation towards the complainant."

"Did Mr. Raznatovic tell you that he intended to hurt her?"

"No, he did not."

"Did he tell you that he tried to kill her?" Shades of Pavlov and his dogs. The more Olly repeated the same question resulting in the same answer, the more the jury had to sit up and listen.

"He denied trying to kill her."

"In your opinion, what does Mr. Raznatovic need to get better?"

"He needs psychiatric treatment."

"Do you disagree with the Crown's psychiatrist that Mr. Raznatovic was of sound mind when he attacked the complainant?"

"Yes, I most certainly disagree."

"Why?"

"Mr. Raznatovic suffers from a disorder of the mind which urged him to commit criminal acts he had no control over. He did not know he was doing something wrong."

"Thank you, Dr. Goulding." Olly could now focus on his other client. "Did you perform an intelligence quotient test on Mr. Smithy?"

"Yes."

"What type of test?"

"The Stanford-Binet IQ test."

"Please describe it to the jury."

"The Stanford-Binet test was originally developed as a method of identifying intellectually stunted children for their placement in special education programs. It is a cognitive ability assessment used to measure intelligence quotient, or IQ for short. Five factors are measured -- fluid reasoning, knowledge, quantitative reasoning, visual-spatial processing, and working memory. Each of these factors is tested in two separate domains, verbal and nonverbal."

"What were the results of Mr. Smithy's IQ test?"

"He scored an IQ of 70 which is borderline intellectual intelligence."

"In comparison, what is the average IQ for most people?"

"Between 85-115."

"How does an IQ of 70 affect Mr. Smithy's cognitive function?"

"He had some difficulty with perceptual reasoning and problem-solving skills."

"What does perceptual reasoning mean?"

"It is a person's ability to visualize information."

"And what about problem-solving skills?"

"This refers to a person's ability to find solutions to problems."

"Did these deficiencies affect Mr. Smithy's behaviour on the day Mr. Raznatovic attacked the complainant?"

"They placed limitations on his ability to react appropriately, such as intervene or go for help."

"No further questions."

Justice Cobb said, "Cross-examine, Mr. Murano?"

"If it pleases the court, your Honour." Angelo went right for Dr. Goulding's jugular. "Mr. Raznatovic knew which of your buttons to push when you were making your evaluation, didn't he?"

"Objection. Argumentative."

"Sustained."

Angelo said, "How do you know if your evaluation of Mr. Raznatovic is reliable?"

"In the course of my lengthy psychiatric career, I have seen thousands of patients," Dr. Goulding said matter of factly. "I am a consummate professional."

"Let me elaborate further. Dr. Creighton testified that it is sometimes difficult to obtain the right diagnosis of a patient's mental condition. Would you agree with this part of his testimony?"

"Well, yes, I have to agree."

"Would you also agree it is possible for a manipulative patient to fool an experienced psychiatrist?"

Dr. Goulding answered reluctantly, "Yes, it's possible."

Angelo stopped there. Let the jury decide if Igor got the upper hand with the consummate professional.

He turned his attention to the second accused. All he needed to do now was convince the jurors that Niel was the rat that pulled the wool over the good doctor's eyes. He asked, "What is the IQ rating for mild mental retardation?"

"Between 55-69."

"What are the lower IQ's?"

"Moderate mental retardation between 40-54. Severe mental retardation 20-39, and profound below 20."

"With an IQ of 70, is Mr. Smithy any of the above?"

"No. But he's..."

"Yes or no."

Dr. Goulding didn't like being cut off. He grunted, "No."

"Does Mr. Smithy do his own shopping and cooking?"

"Yes."

"Did he go to school?"

"Yes."

"For how long?"

"He spent seven years in the public education system."

"Did he acquire any academic skills?"

"Yes, he did. However, his grades were below average."

"So were mine until secondary school."

"Objection! Irrelevant. Mr. Murano is not testifying."

"Remark withdrawn." The Crown prosecutor was satisfied he got his message across to the jury. If Smithy was retarded, then Angelo was Japanese. "No further questions."

Olly concluded the morning uneventfully with his other expert witness, psychiatrist Dr. Benjamin Hill.

Courtroom 2 at 2:00 p.m.

Riley Gibson was a bony man with huge flappy ears and the parched, wrinkled skin of a face exposed to many years of brutish Australian sun. His long chin moved to the right with a faint clicking sound when he stopped speaking, the result of a kick from a wild horse.

Olly said, "Mr. Gibson, what is your connection to Mr. Raznatovic and Mr. Smithy?"

"I own a farm that's been in my family since the turn of the century. Those two were employed as my farmhands." Click.

"How long did Mr. Raznatovic and Mr. Smithy work for you?"

"I reckon about five years. Niel came and went, but Igor hung around most of the time." Click.

"You would be referring to their itinerant status?"

"Yep, that's right." Click.

"In those five years, how well did you get to know them?"

"Niel's your average simple bloke. I never really knew what he did when he wasn't helpin' out on the farm, but I know he has family in the Outback. As for Igor, he was an all right bloke, s'long as you didn't cross him." Click.

"Please explain."

"When he wasn't pleased with somethin' he was quite the moody bugger." Click.

"Did you wonder about Mr. Raznatovic's mental health?"

"Objection. Calls for a conclusion." Angelo added, "And the witness is not a medical expert."

Olly argued, "Your Honour, Mr. Gibson is a respected member of the farming community in Bacchus Marsh, which makes him a reliable witness."

"Sustained. Please rephrase the question."

"Mr. Gibson, please describe Mr. Raznatovic's behaviour."

Riley tapped his right temple. "Well, I thought he wasn't all there, if you catch my drift. I can't put my finger on anythin' in particular, but he kinda gave me the willies." Click.

"No further questions."

Angelo stood up, ready for cross-examination. "Do you travel?"

"Objection. Irrelevant."

"I beg the court's indulgence. The reason for this line of questioning will become apparent."

"I'll allow it, if you get to the point quickly, Mr. Murano."

"Yes, your Honour." Angelo repeated his question. "Do you travel, Mr. Gibson?"

"I buy and sell horses. Goin' to Kiwi land to get me some more." Click.

"By Kiwi land, do you mean New Zealand?"

"Yep, that's right." Click.

"Prior to February 2nd, who looked after the farm while you were away on your trips?"

"Igor did." Click.

Angelo put on his best perplexed face as he looked at the jury, and then at Riley. "You just told us you thought Mr. Raznatovic wasn't all there, so why did you let him manage your livelihood?"

Riley Gibson fidgeted in his chair, the contradiction of his words tying up his tongue.

It was obvious to Angelo that the witness was having difficulty with the question. "Let me rephrase. Do you think Mr. Raznatovic was capable of running the farm in your absence?"

Riley Gibson fidgeted some more. His reputation took a hit for hiring a pervert foreigner. But Igor was not incompetent as far as he could tell. "Yep, he was capable, all right." Click.

"What do you know about Niel's character?" Another reminder that although the trial was mainly about Igor, it was also about Smithy.

"He's the kinda bloke who likes to please the person he's hangin' around with." Click.

"Did Mr. Smithy drive any vehicles on the farm?"

"Objection. Irrelevant."

"Your Honour, this speaks to Mr. Smithy's level of intelligence."

"Overruled. Mr. Gibson, answer the question."

"Yep, on occasion he's driven my tractor and pickup truck." Click.

"Is he a good driver?"

"Yep, he was all right." Click.

Angelo did what he needed to do. He conveyed to the jury that a disagreeable creep was rational enough to run a farm. As for Smithy, he was not as stupid as Silly-boy wants him to be. The prosecutor smiled benignly at the farmer. "No further questions."

Olly jumped up. "Redirect, your Honour."

"Proceed."

"Is your farm a complex operation?"

"Not anymore. Been windin' down business, got rid of the jumbucks years ago...y'know, sheep. All that's left is the horse tradin'. I have a cow and chickens, but that's 'cause my wife likes fresh milk and eggs on the table." Click.

"Who did the bookkeeping while Mr. Raznatovic minded the farm?"

"My wife." Click.

"That is all, your Honour." Olly wanted to show the jury that even a sicko like Igor can run Riley Gibson's farm.

Igor scribbled several notes to Olly, demanding to be put on the witness stand. Finally, the barrister stood up. "Your Honour, defence requests a brief recess."

Justice Cobb put down his pen, "Let's call it a day. Trial is adjourned until tomorrow at 9 a.m."

Lis*t*en *to Me*

Igor pounced on his barrister. "That wop Murano is tricky."

The ethnic slur reminded Olly of his competitive law school days, and wondered if he sounded as disparaging as Igor when he used to taunt the arrogant Angelo.

"What about the test?"

Sweet Jesus, not again. "The genetic testing to find an extra y chromosome in males?"

Igor reminded Olly, "You said it's used as evidence for insanity cases in America."

Olly sighed. How does a person reason with a man who has a few loose screws? "I already told you that Dr. Goulding suggested against it. Your past history doesn't lead to a predilection of a sexual disorder, and the odds are greatly against you having the xyy chromosome factor. Not only that, the test has to be done in America."

"But..."

Olly interrupted, "There hasn't been a case in an Australian court of law that used the test, so there's a great deal of controversy about reliability which means it will probably be ruled inadmissible as evidence."

Igor couldn't stand not being the master of his own destiny. "I want to take the stand," he demanded.

Here we go again. "Igor, sit down while I explain one more time why you don't fit the perception of an insane person. People expect a frothing mouth with rolling eyes and incoherent babbling."

"I want to prove Marika's a dirty little girl who deserved to be punished!" Igor spoke with a venom that made Olly wince.

"All you're going to succeed in doing is angering the jury. Normal decent people don't believe a child of such a tender age could understand the connotation of sex, let alone initiate it. You also beat her badly, inflicting awful wounds on her body. So, let me convince the jury that you were not in your right mind." Olly stopped to assess all there was to know about Igor. He said with a sense of urgency, "If there's anything you're keeping from me which will add weight to your plea of insanity, tell me now."

Igor didn't blink as he stared back. If he bared the Voice, he wouldn't be blamed for his attack on Marika. But at what price? The Voice would be revealed. It was his. He had something special that no one else had. No, he couldn't tell anyone else. He tried again, staring with an intensity that unnerved his barrister. "I want to take the stand."

The twitch over Olly's left eye started to rhumba. "I told you no."

Igor stood up and banged the table with his ham fist. "I say yes!"

"Sit down, Igor. It's in your best interest to be found insane, and the best way to create the illusion is if you stay silent. We're wasting time and energy on a useless exercise. Make this the last time."

"Get more psychiatrists."

"Two's enough."

"Why are you making out like I'm still insane?"

"You can't turn it on and off like a faucet. The jury is more likely to believe a pervasive insanity affected your judgment when you attacked that little girl."

"If the jury doesn't find me insane, then what?"

"Like I told you before, if the jury finds you sane, you did not have the intent to hurt or kill. This is permissible under the insanity plea."

Igor was the defence barrister's most difficult client to date. There were times when Olly wondered if he should be defending a pedophile rapist, but he had already invested too much time and effort. Besides, the publicity was great, a trade-off for taking the case pro bono. Murano thought he was a money-grubbing dirt bag, and he was all that. He had no regrets about his love affair with money.

The Barn

Worlock drove away from the courthouse. Deep in thought, he suddenly became aware of the back end of a tram as it squealed to a stop to let off passengers. Another inch and his car would have smacked into it. He could feel himself being pulled in a certain direction. As soon as he drove out of the tracks, he headed for Bacchus Marsh.

Riley Gibson's farm was still the same scrubby eyesore. Helmut Jung's traveling fun fair had skulked away with the knowledge it was the catalyst that brought Marika and Igor together. Maybe that's what Worlock sensed when he saw Helmut holding vigil by the barn door. Guilt. The same set of circumstances which placed Marika in Igor's evil clutches wouldn't have been set in motion if Helmut chose another place for his carnival. Was it possible another little girl existed who could have taken Marika's place? Worlock stroked his chin. Igor wanted her, and no one else. Of that he was sure, but what if Igor had even the remotest desire to attack other children, now that he tasted Marika's flesh? He must be locked away for a long time, and Worlock had to do what he could to help Angelo clinch the case.

The policeman was drawn to the barn rotting away in the middle of the barren ground surrounding it. He looked at the bare patch where Igor's shack used to stand. It had been bulldozed to the ground and used as firewood.

The rope that cordoned off the crime scene was still there. Worlock stepped over it with his long legs, eyeing the peeling planks which looked as if the three little pigs' nemesis could blow them down in one breath. Tightening the belt around his trench coat, he unlocked the padlock on the creaking barn door and went inside. The barn was stripped bare of all working tools because Gibson built a new barn on the other side of the main house.

The stench of old manure and molding hay assailed his nostrils, but there was another reeking smell of horror that took over as Worlock pushed aside the brittle hay in the middle of the floor to reveal old stains. He caught sight of a discarded Wrigley's chewing gum wrapper and a half eaten chocolate licorice bullet lying nearby. Neighbourhood urchins had managed to find their way into the barn even though all the access points were locked up. No doubt, they were eager to explore the infamous barn where a little girl who used to be a friend was brutally touched and made to bleed in pain.

His eyes kept going to the wall hooks where Riley Gibson's three whips used to hang, and to the floor imprint of the storage box which was no longer there. Why did Igor waste precious time going for the whip inside a locked box? If Igor chose one of the three others, he'd have enough time to use the pitchfork.

And Marika would be dead.

THE PAPRIKA DIARY, A LONELY SECRET

Tuesday September 17 at 9:15 a.m.
Courtroom 2

Niel sat down in the witness box trying to be inconspicuous by slouching down in the chair. He finally let go of his tie knot which he pushed and pulled since day one of the trial. His black hair was trimmed back after it was doused with disinfectant to kill a bad case of lice, but sections continued to kink in all directions. Igor had been the star of the trial. Now, the spectators were eager to hear from Niel.

Olly asked, "What were you doing in Mr. Gibson's barn on the morning of February 2nd?"

"I was helpin' Igor pitch hay an' muck out the stalls."

"What did you use to pitch hay?"

"The pitchfork." Niel had just provided an innocent reason for his fingerprints being on the pitchfork.

Olly walked over to the Crown's exhibit table and picked up exhibit C-38. "Do you mean this pitchfork?"

"Yeah, that's the one."

"What did Mr. Raznatovic talk about while you cleaned up the barn?"

"He was narked about the heat an' flies buzzin' around the shh...," Niel almost forgot Olly's warning to avoid cuss words.

"Around the what?"

"Manure."

Olly wondered if Niel was going to come through for him as he asked, "How did you react when you saw complainant X in the barn?"

Niel said, "I..I..I was surprised."

Don't stammer, you idiot, thought Olly. The jurors will think you're lying. I want them to think Igor acted impulsively. "Please describe what happened in the barn on February 2nd."

Niel was going into stress overload. He didn't want to talk about the rape, especially not in the courtroom where every word he said was being recorded. It was done. It was over. He glanced at Igor, but got no answer from him. Forgetting what Olly wanted him to say, Niel could only think of doing it his way, "Igor hit the kid over the head, then screws an' whips her."

Olly could feel the milk from his morning coffee curdling inside his stomach as he listened to hours of coaching being flushed down the crapper in a matter of ten seconds.

Angelo stood up. "Your Honour, please instruct the witness to use appropriate language."

"Mr. Smithy, the court will not tolerate gutter slang. Is that clear?" Justice Cobb said sternly.

Niel said sullenly, "Yeah."

"Yeah, what?"

"Yeah, your Honour."

Olly asked, "When did Mr. Raznatovic pick up the pitchfork?"

Niel knew what to say this time, "He got spooked when he heard the blokes outside the barn."

"You mean the search party?"

"Yeah."

Olly liked the brilliance of it all. Murano was implying the search party stopped Igor from killing Marika with the pitchfork, but a slight manipulation of the facts offered a more innocent motive. "When Igor attacked the complainant, what did you do?"

"Nothin'."

"Why didn't you stop him or go for help?"

"I was afraid of what Igor would do to me."

"Why?"

The loaded question which Niel was dreading. He was supposed to say he thought Igor was crazy, but what if Igor changed his mind and Niel said the wrong thing? Igor will crack his head open like a walnut if he ever got his hands on him. Niel glanced at his mate for a sign, but there was none.

Olly repeated the question, "Why?"

Niel said the first thing that popped into his head. "I was thinkin' he'd chuck a spaz."

"Queen's English, if you please."

"Like I was sayin', I thought Igor will get angry."

"What does Mr. Raznatovic do when he gets angry?"

"Yells an' swears."

"What else?"

Niel kept his mouth shut. He wanted to jump up and say he saved the kid's life by stalling Igor. Then the court would be more lenient with him, but he could also expect a life of living hell once Igor was free to roam Bacchus Marsh again. He'd rather spend a few more years behind bars.

Olly didn't like a witness who changed his story. Niel was supposed to mention the time that Igor went berserk and smashed his own furniture to pieces, all because Riley Gibson wouldn't let him go on a horse buying trip to Kiwi Land. "Your Honour, Mr. Smithy is being uncooperative. Request permission to treat him as a hostile witness."

"Motion granted," said Justice Cobb.

Olly stated, "Isn't it true that you saw Mr. Raznatovic tear his place apart?"

Niel said nothing.

"Mr. Smithy, answer the question," ordered the judge.

"Yeah." Niel shifted uncomfortably in his seat.

"Why did he do that?"

"Riley told him he couldn't go on a horse buyin' trip. So, he went back to his place an' trashed the table an' chairs."

"Was he behaving in a strange manner?"

"Yeah, his eyes was bulgin' out, an' he was swingin' his arms all over the place."

Olly sent a subliminal message to the jury...*bulging eyes like a crazy man*. The knot-pulling dipstick remembered what he was supposed to say.

"Did Mr. Raznatovic tell you he wanted to hurt the complainant?"

"Nah."

"Did he tell you that he wanted to kill her?"

Niel shook his head adamantly, "Nah." He thought silently, Igor didn't tell me. He told Marika.

So far so good. Olly turned around to look at the gallery and found himself staring at an attractive female. He twirled around as if he had just seen a ghost. "Does Mr. Raznatovic have a girlfriend?" Olly was sure he knew the answer. After all, never break the cardinal rule of asking a question without knowing the answer. Try not to, anyway.

Angelo was on the verge of objecting, but decided against it. He was curious about what Smithy would say.

Niel was surprised by the unrehearsed question. He looked at his mate's blank face and back at Olly. No help from either of them. "Nah."

"Does he like women?"

"I dunno."

"What does he say about them?"

"He told me they're the devil's helpers." The words slipped out of Niel's mouth before he realized what he was saying. He glanced nervously at Igor again.

Olly's hunch paid off. God, the devil, Marika. Connect the dots and a deeply disturbed person emerges. Now, if only the jury believed the testimony of a person who looks more like a dirty rat.

"Why does Mr. Raznatovic describe women as the devil's helpers?"

"Never said why."

"When did Mr. Raznatovic say women were the *devil's helpers*?"

"We was walkin' on the main street in Bacchus Marsh."

"Describe the women that Mr. Raznatovic said were the *devil's helpers*."

"Good lookin' sheilas with red lips an' big gazongas." Niel had no clue about all the new questions and was afraid to say that every female crossing Igor's path was in cahoots with the devil.

"You mean breasts?"

"Yeah, that's right."

Olly stopped. He broke the cardinal rule — never ask a question to which he didn't know the answer, several questions ago. "I'm finished."

Angelo stood up and opened his robe, placing his hands inside the pockets of his pants, the best way he knew to get comfortable during cross-examination of a slimy individual. "You wanted to rape the complainant real bad after your mate finished with her, didn't you?"

Olly jumped up. "Objection! Argumentative. Assumes fact not in evidence."

"Sustained."

It was Angelo's plan to unsettle the witness right from the start. "On the morning of February 2nd, did you notice Mr. Raznatovic leaving the barn?"

"Yeah."

"What time did he leave?"

"Dunno, I don't got a watch."

"How long was he gone?"

"Dunno."

"Can you give an estimate?"

"Nah."

Angelo persisted. "More than a couple of minutes?"

"Objection."

"Sustained. Mr. Murano, move on."

Niel frowned at Angelo who managed to get under his skin and crawl up and down like feasting ants. He began to scratch his face and neck.

Angelo watched the witness squirming with each scratch. *Was he falling apart already?* The defence had tried to skip through Niel's testimony. No problem. Angelo was going to squeeze the details out of the itchy accused. "What was Mr. Raznatovic doing when you first saw him with the complainant?"

"Dunno."

"May I remind you that you are under oath?"

As if I care, thought Niel. "He was lookin' out the barn window."

"How did the complainant end up on the barn floor?"

"Igor hit her on the head."

"With what?"

"The pole."

Angelo picked up the pole from the exhibit table. "Do you mean this pole?"

"Yeah, that one."

"The witness has identified Crown exhibit C-14. Then what happened?"

"Like I said, Igor…raped…," Niel bit his bottom lip to avoid blurting out Marika's name. He started over, "Igor raped the complainant."

"What happened to her underpants?" There was no doubt in Angelo's mind that Raznatovic was responsible.

"You mean after Igor pulled 'em off?"

Bingo. It was exactly what Angelo wanted to hear. "Are you saying Mr. Raznatovic's infamous one-liner is a lie?"

"What?"

"Let me spell it out for you. Mr. Raznatovic said the complainant pulled down her underpants for lolly. Was he lying?"

Niel glanced at Igor.

"Your Honour, please instruct the witness to stop looking at Mr. Raznatovic when I ask a question."

Justice Cobb said to the accused, "Keep your eyes on Mr. Murano during your testimony, unless I'm speaking to you."

"Yeah, your Honour."

Angelo repeated the question, "Did Mr. Raznatovic lie when he said the complainant pulled her underpants down for lolly?"

"I guess."

"Yes or no."

"Yeah," Niel said with resignation. Igor was going to be very angry with him.

Angelo had no problem reading Niel's dejected expression. *That's right, you should watch your back with your poor excuse for a friend.* He asked his next question, "Please describe what happened after Mr. Raznatovic raped the complainant."

"He went to a storage box with whips. Got one an' whipped her."

"Where was the storage box?"

"Inside the barn."

"What did Mr. Raznatovic do after he whipped the complainant?"

It was time to lie again. "Nothin' until he heard the blokes outside the barn an' picked up the pitchfork."

Angelo wanted to say, your ugly nose just sprouted ten feet, Pinocchio. Instead, he said, "Mr. Smithy, are you able to lift bales of hay?"

Finally, some respect from the poncy lawyer. Niel lapped up the words like a thirsty kitten attacking a bowl of cream. He was pleased when Angelo pronounced his first name properly, and it felt good when he called him mister to his face. "I can lift hay all day, if I have to." Niel's chest swelled with pride. "I look puny, but I got big muscles."

"Did Mr. Raznatovic lift as many bales as you?"

"Nah, his back ain't so good."

"If you're so strong, why were you afraid of him?"

"Dunno." Niel suddenly felt like a fuckwit.

"What's the real reason you stayed in the barn instead of going for help or coming to the complainant's rescue? Is it because you enjoyed watching Mr. Raznatovic rape and whip her back to shreds?"

Olly jumped up in anger. "Objection! Badgering the witness!"

"Withdrawn. No further questions." Angelo looked over and saw Thomas waving his hand like a school kid desperate for a bathroom break. "Request a recess, your Honour."

"Court will take an early lunch. Be back at half past one."

Courtroom 2 at 1:30 p.m.

Justice Cobb was not in a good mood. He had expected a quiet lunch with his regular order, a Myer's ham sandwich and a ripe juicy tomato from his greenhouse. Instead, he found himself back in the courtroom with the two barristers, and no jury. The Crown had a late witness and new evidence. After it was all said and done, the judge overruled Olly's objection and denied his requests for a curriculum vitae, time to research the new information, and obtain a rebuttal witness.

With the trial back in session, Justice Cobb asked, "Any more witnesses, Mr. Silboy?"

"No, your Honour. Defence rests."

The judge said, "Normally, I would not entertain disclosure of a witness at this late hour. In this case, however, I could find no nefarious intent to surprise the defence, and Mr. Murano assured me the subject matter of the witness's testimony is legally and factually relevant to his case. Therefore, as the court has the discretion to allow expert testimony where a party fails to give proper notice, I'm going to allow the Crown its late witness." He turned towards Angelo. "Mr. Murano, you may reopen your case."

"I owe you one," Angelo whispered to Worlock, the inspector still keeping him company at the prosecution table. He stood up and announced, "Crown recalls Inspector Worlock."

After Worlock sat in the witness box, Angelo handed new exhibits to him. He asked, "Do you recognize the photographs in your hands?"

"They were taken at the crime scene on February 2nd."

"Do you recognize the objects in the photographs?"

"Yes, I do."

"Please describe them to the jury."

"Three whips and a storage box that were kept inside Mr. Gibson's barn."

"Would you say they are fair and accurate photographs of what you saw on February 2nd?"

"Yes."

"Your Honour, Crown offers exhibits C-45 to C-48 into evidence."

"Mr. Silboy, any objections?"

"No, your Honour."

After the exhibits were admitted, Thomas was right on cue pushing a dolly cart with a large wooden box up the aisle. Angelo asked, "Inspector, do you recognize exhibit C-49, the object brought into the courtroom?"

"Yes, it's the same object in the photographs — the storage box for the whip, exhibit C-32.

Maybe it was all the coffee Angelo drank before returning to the courtroom because he found himself in a boisterous mood. "Your Honour! The Crown offers exhibit C-49 into evidence!"

Justice Cobb was used to his tipstaff's booming voice, but preferred his barristers to be more dignified. "Contrary to popular belief, I'm not a deaf old codger, Mr. Murano."

"Sorry, your Honour."

"Mr. Silboy?"

"I never thought you were a deaf old codger, your Honour."

Justice Cobb said tersely, "Why thank you, Mr. Silboy. Do you have any objections to the Crown's exhibit?"

Olly was embarrassed, and rightfully so. "No, your Honour."

"Crown exhibit C-49 is admitted into evidence."

Angelo asked, "How accessible were the three whips that hung over the box on the day of the crime?"

"They were readily accessible."

Angelo dismissed the witness. "The Crown recalls Niel Smithy."

The accused reluctantly got up and returned to the witness box.

"You are still under oath, Mr. Smithy."

"Yeah."

"In previous testimony, you said Mr. Raznatovic got the whip and assaulted the complainant with it. Can you recall how long it took him to walk over to the storage box and remove the whip?"

"Not long."

"Please translate 'not long' into seconds."

Niel mentally counted every step Igor took to obtain the whip. "I reckon twenty-five seconds."

"Your Honour, the amount of time Mr. Raznatovic took to retrieve the whip is of relevance to the Crown's case. Requesting permission to conduct a re-enactment with the witness stepping in for Mr. Raznatovic."

"Any objections, Mr. Silboy?"

"None, your Honouor."

"You may proceed, Mr. Murano."

Angelo picked up a stopwatch belonging to Worlock. "Permission to use this stopwatch, your Honour."

Justice Cobb waved Angelo to the bench.

When the prosecutor handed the stopwatch to the judge, he said, "You have to press the button at the side…"

"I know how to use a stopwatch, Mr. Murano." Justice Cobb checked the ticking hand against the courtroom clock and was satisfied. He handed the stopwatch back to the prosecutor with one word, "Bloviate."

Angelo shrugged his shoulders. "Your Honour?"

Justice Cobb kept the prosecutor guessing. "Your witness is waiting, Mr. Murano."

Angelo wasn't sure if Justice Cobb was trying to make a point, or just happened to like the sound of his obscure word. He returned to his table, and whispered to Thomas, "Find out what bloviate means."

Still wet behind the ears as a junior barrister, Thomas was happy as a quokka, the cutest grinning marsupial in Australia. To learn from the great Angelo Murano was indeed a privilege. He scribbled the obscure word on his notepad. "The Birdman strikes again, sir."

Angelo turned to Niel. "I want you to stand the same distance from the storage box as Mr. Raznatovic did on the day of the crime. When the tipstaff says go, you will proceed to the storage box and remove the whip."

Niel left the witness box and stood in the well in front of the judge's bench, watching the tipstaff with shifty eyes.

The tipstaff boomed, "Go!"

Niel scurried over to the box and unlocked it. After he opened the lid, he pulled out exhibit C-32 with a flourish.

Angelo said, "Stop the watch!" He took the whip from Niel and instructed him to return to the witness box. Turning to the tipstaff, he asked, "How long did it take the witness to remove the whip from the box?"

"Twenty-three seconds!"

"Thank you, tipstaff." Angelo was satisfied. Whether it was one second or twenty-three, Igor wasted valuable time, not because he was insane but because he was making calculated choices and taking a course of action. "You may step down, Mr. Smithy."

Angelo was ready for his late witness. "The Crown calls Enrico Modesto."

A swarthy skinned man, in his late forties, slick black hair and eyebrows, made his way down the aisle towards the witness box. His posture was a little too perfect giving the impression that he was leaning backwards as he walked.

Everyone was curious about the witness, watching him closely as he was sworn in.

Angelo winked imperceptibly at Worlock. The latter pulled a rabbit out of a hat, but couldn't logically explain how he did it. It was thanks to him that the late witness was about to give testimony. "Please state your full name and occupation."

"Enrico Juan Jose Xavier Modesto. I run a successful family business in my home city of Madrid manufacturing fine leather goods. I recently opened a shop here in Melbourne." Enrico spoke flawless English with a pleasant Spanish accent.

"Do you make whips?"

"Yes, we are the leading exporters in Spain. It is my specialty to make a well-balanced whip."

"How long have you been making whips?"

"Me personally, thirty years. Seventy-five for my family business."

Angelo showed exhibit C-32 to the witness. "Please describe this whip to the jury."

The witness asked, "May I test it?"

Justice Cobb remembered the pole incident. This time he knew what to expect with the element of surprise no longer a threat. "Since you're an expert on making whips, I assume you're an expert on using them and will put no one in harm's way?"

"You are correct, sir. I mean, your Honour."

"Carry on," said the judge.

"Your Honour, permission to approach the witness."

"Go ahead, Mr. Murano."

Angelo placed the whip in the witness's right hand.

Enrico stood up and walked to the front of the judicial bench. He placed his left hand elegantly on his left hip, moved his right arm backwards, and brought it forward quickly as he uncoiled the whip with a sharp flick of his wrist. Snap. The whip cracked the air with a mini-sonic boom, the static-charged energy surging across the room. The tip landed just shy of the jury box, causing the jurors to flinch.

"It is a most unusual bull whip made of kangaroo hide which I am reluctant to say is more durable than Spanish cow leather. It has a comfortable wrist band, a thong made of several braids attached to a single fall piece ten inches long, and a cracker tip. Balance is very good, but the whip is so new, it is stiff for lack of use. This means it is not easy to handle like a broken-in whip." His keen eye noted the twelve inch handle. "A very creative craftsman made this whip."

"Why do you say that?"

"The most distinguishing feature is the grip."

"By grip, you mean the handle?"

"Yes, that is right."

"Please tell the court why the grip is so special."

"The grip is called a pizzle, a term to describe a flogging instrument made from an animal's...how shall I say...penis. Can I say that word here?" The witness realized it was too late to ask permission. "It is not the whole penis which would be three feet long or more. Nevertheless, it is the penis of a very big bull."

Audible gasps interrupted the witness's testimony. Justice Cobb thought it was odd. The mention of human genitalia didn't spark the same reaction from the shocked audience. All he had to do was raise his hand and the courtroom was quiet again.

Angelo asked, "Would you say this whip is a male symbol of sexual domination and authority over the female?"

"Objection. Pure conjecture." Olly thought the prosecution went too far. "The witness is not an expert in matters of a sexual nature. And where is the evidence that shows Mr. Raznatovic was aware of the grip?"

"Sustained."

"Thank you, that is all, Mr. Modesto."

"Mr. Silboy, do you wish to cross-examine the witness?"

Now that Olly knew the grip was a bull's donger, he could see the resemblance. There was nothing else to say because a picture speaks a thousand words. "No, your Honour."

Angelo anticipated the defence's grounds for objection. "The Crown recalls Riley Gibson."

The farmer walked through the courtroom doors and sat down in the witness box.

Angelo said, "You are under oath, Mr. Gibson." He held up exhibit C-32. "Do you recognize this whip?"

"Yep, it's mine." Click.

"Do you know what the grip is made of?"

The witness briefly looked down at his shoes, then back at Angelo. They'll find out anyway if they question the person he bought it from. "Yep." Click.

"Well, what is the grip?"

Riley Gibson scratched his head nervously. "A bull's whatsit." Click.

"Could you be more specific?"

The embarrassed farmer said, "A bull's penis." Click.

"Did Mr. Raznatovic know what it was?"

Riley Gibson looked at his former employee, deciding the man was in no position to hurt him for a long time. "Yep. Told him never to use it, just leave it locked up in the storage box. If anyone was goin' to use it, it was me." Click.

Angelo was thinking perhaps Gibson had some kind of fetish, but held his tongue. The good farmer was not on trial. "What was the accused's reaction when you first showed him the whip and told him the grip was the penis of a bull?"

"He kept strokin' it up and down with his hands. Made me kinda uncomfortable." Click.

Uh-huh. Angelo thought, bet you wanted to shove it up your arse for a bit of jolly, Mr. Kinky Farmer. He hid the disgust from his face as a most unpleasant image of Gibson and the pizzle popped into his head. He hoped it wasn't going to hang around like one of those catchy but very annoying tunes. "No further questions."

"Mr. Silboy, do you wish to cross-examine the witness?"

"No, your Honour."

Justice Cobb asked, "Mr. Murano?"

"The Crown rests its case."

Attila was certain he saw Igor sniggering. Without hesitation, he rushed towards the railing.

Everyone gasped as pandemonium reigned in the courtroom. Some half stood, not knowing what to do next, while others sat in their seats as if they were watching their tellies.

Worlock was caught by surprise. He had expected something to happen earlier, but he was still fast enough. He jumped up and stood in front of Igor like a brick wall, knowing the poor father wanted to beat his daughter's rapist into a bloody revolting mess. If Attila hurdled the railing and wrapped his hands around the latter's neck, Worlock wouldn't be able to pry them loose, even though he can remove beer bottle caps with his bare fingers.

Attila stopped short of the railing. Worlock's imposing presence could not be ignored. Besides, he was blocking Igor's ugly body.

The inspector said quietly, "You don't want a mistrial, do you? And if you become a vigilante, you won't be any good to Marika in gaol."

Attila turned around and walked out of the courtroom.

Wednesday, September 18 at 9:00 a.m.
Courtroom 2

The moment Angelo waited for was finally here. He knew what the matador faced in his moment of truth. Exhilaration tinged with a healthy fear of death. Perhaps he will fail and his blood will end up staining the ground. He had gone over his closing argument every night he lay in bed since the trial began. To present the pertinent facts he dished out during the trial in bits and pieces, to get guilty verdicts from a group who were ill at ease, maybe repulsed by the little girl's presence, even though she was the victim. It was up to him to make them feel sorry for her, and convince the jury that Raznatovic was a sane fiend.

As he stood before the packed courtroom in his full regalia of robe, jacket, jabot, round-toed black shoes, and tie-wig, he made a silent vow. This one's for you, Marika. He didn't need to read his argument. The words were lining up all by themselves like excited children waiting for an amusement park ride.

"Your Honour." Angelo nodded respectfully to Justice Cobb while drawing attention to his wig with a subtle hand gesture. He was not immune to his wife's persuasive female charms which convinced him to wear the roadkill for closing arguments.

He looked earnestly at the jurors, drawing them to his baby blue eyes, his favourite technique to bond with the jury. "Members of the jury, you will soon have very important decisions to make about Igor Raznatovic and Niel Smithy. But first, I have the very important final task of delivering the Crown's irrefutable evidence to you. Evidence which proves each element of each charge beyond a reasonable doubt. Assault. Rape. Attempted murder.

Mr. Raznatovic attacked the complainant in a number of sadistic ways. He bashed her on the head because it was her blood and tissue and his fingerprints on the pole. It was her blood and his fingerprints on the whip and the pitchfork. It was her blood draining out on the barn floor. And it was her blood on Mr. Raznatovic's genitals, fingers, and coveralls.

The evidence proves he violently raped and whipped her, and held a pitchfork over her body. It proves he bashed the complainant on the head so hard, he cracked her skull, leaving a permanent depression. He hit her too hard to stun her. All he had to do was push the little girl down if he only wanted her on the ground. There can be no other logical reason for bashing complainant X with the pole except he wanted to kill and defile her with impunity. But he miscalculated the force it took to strike a mortal wound.

Make no mistake, Mr. Raznatovic was taking a course of action that was going to get the job done in the end.

Dr. Creighton is the only psychiatrist who made the right diagnosis about Mr. Raznatovic. As a well-respected medical expert, he could not find any evidence to prove the accused was plagued by mental problems. There are no prior medical or police records to substantiate an insanity claim because they don't exist. And why is that? Because the accused is a sane man. You're supposed to think he was crazy. Why? Because Mr. Smithy says he saw him trash his place like a man out of control. Sounds like a temper tantrum to me.

The defence also wants you to believe Mr. Raznatovic was insane because he used the term 'devil's helpers' to describe women who wear red lipstick and are generously endowed. It would set a dangerous precedent to label someone insane because of derogatory comments made towards women.

What's really wrong with Mr. Raznatovic? Dr. Creighton testified the accused is a psychopath or sociopath, one with an introverted personality who possessed the capability of running Riley Gibson's farm during his employer's absence.

Mr. Raznatovic admitted he lured this small innocent child with a hint of lolly, something all children love to eat. But there was no lolly. He walked her towards the barn before dragging her the rest of the way. A manipulating pedophile in a hurry to attack his helpless victim. He was rational from the moment he spotted the pretty little girl who lived in a house near the barn where she was brutalized within an inch of her precious life.

The barn that was supposed to be her place of death.

If Mr. Raznatovic didn't know that what he was about to do was wrong, he would have attacked her right there at the well regardless of who saw him. He didn't do that because he was busy weighing his choices and making sure the area was deserted before he struck. Once he dragged the defenceless child inside the barn, he broke her skull, raped her savagely, and inflicted more pain with a whip that held special significance for him, a whip that gave him an extra boost of sexual power. The whip. Evidence of the accused's methodical intentions.

He tortured the complainant with the whip because of what its handle grip represents, the penis of one of the strongest animals in the animal kingdom — a bull. He went to a great deal of trouble to get that whip. He took the time to walk over to the storage box. Took the time to unlock it and remove the whip. All of which speak to making choices and taking a deliberate course of action. He knew what he had done was wrong, knew the consequences, but didn't care. All he cared about was satisfying his evil hunger.

The pitchfork. You must decide whose testimony is credible -- Mr. Helmut Jung's, a decent hardworking individual who saw Mr. Raznatovic holding the pitchfork over the complainant's battered body, or Mr. Smithy's, the accused's accomplice who claims Mr. Raznatovic only picked it up when he heard the search party. Ask yourself, did Mr. Raznatovic attack the people who came through the barn door? The indisputable evidence says no. He opened the door because he was not afraid of the search party. The pitchfork was meant for complainant X, and no one else."

Angelo pointed an accusing finger at Igor. "That man was getting ready to strike a fatal wound through her tiny chest. He was making choices and taking a course of action while he plotted the death of the little girl which gave the search party time to intervene. Caught in the act, otherwise the complainant would be dead. And this would be a murder trial.

Dr. Creighton's testimony says the accused is a manipulator. Besides the fact that Mr. Raznatovic lured the complainant with the promise of lolly, what better example can I give you than this one. 'She pulled her underpants down for lolly', so shouted the child rapist. In fact, the evidence proves it was Mr. Raznatovic who pulled off the complainant's panties after he whacked her over the head. Only a manipulator has the audacity to pass blame to an innocent child. He says things which produce the results he wants, and what he wants is for you to send him to a mental institution for treatment. One step away from freedom if you don't find him guilty.

Does he deserve leniency? I'll tell you what Mr. Raznatovic deserves — society's loathing for what the cowardly excuse of a human being did to one of its innocent children. The complainant fell into a coma and lost her memory of the vile assault. It was such a shock to her system that she developed amnesia to block out the memory of that horrible day, but it doesn't end there for her. One day, the memory may return to haunt her, and her parents must live with the possibility, day in and day out.

Some barristers may try to impress you with legalese like *actus non facit reum nisi mens sit rea*. Not me. I would simply tell you that an act does not make a person guilty unless their mind is also guilty. And the Crown's evidence proves Mr. Raznatovic's culpability beyond any reasonable doubt, both in behaviour and in mind. It is up to you to decide his guilt at the time he preyed on complainant X because you are the sole judges on the credibility of the evidence. You must make the world a safer place for her by doing the right thing. Find Mr. Raznatovic guilty of all charges."

Angelo felt like he was standing on top of Mt. Everest, and if he wasted even a second he might as well jump off into oblivion. He barely paused before directing the jury to the second accused. "Niel Smithy watched his mate Igor rape, assault, and attempt to murder complainant X. He is a very strong man who could have rescued the complainant if he wanted to. He also could have gone for help if he was afraid of Mr. Raznatovic, but he was the cobber, the partner in crime. He was the lookout who watched and enjoyed the whole despicable scene.

An IQ of 70 cannot be applied to both mild mental retardation and borderline intellectual intelligence which Mr. Silboy wants you to do. The two are distinct categories as explained by the defence's own expert witness. So, let me clear up any doubt you may have. An IQ of 70 applies to borderline intellectual intelligence...period. Mr. Smithy may not be an Einstein, but he does all right in the big bad world. He cooks, shops, even drives a tractor and a pick-up truck. He went to school for several years, and also had a job. Not everyone's ideal, but hey, it's a living.

Mr. Smithy crossed a threshold level of blameworthiness. Although his role is that of an aider and abettor, don't make the mistake of discounting his actions on February 2nd. He reached an agreement with his co-accused to commit crimes against the complainant by doing nothing to save her. He encouraged Mr. Raznatovic by making sure the coast was clear. He stuck his head out the barn window and searched the area like a good lookout would do. When he saw the search party, he jumped back inside to warn Mr. Raznatovic. He did not shout for help because he was an aider and abettor. Find Mr. Smithy guilty as principal offender in the second degree to rape, assault, and attempted murder."

Angelo was finished.

Olly was ready to fight the good fight, but following a smooth guy like Murano was going to be a tall order. He wasn't an eloquent speaker, whether he read from a script or off-the-cuff. However, his client was insane and he had to believe the jury will see the truth for what it really is. "The evidence does not lie. Mr. Raznatovic raped and beat the complainant on that fateful Saturday. But you heard the testimonies of two expert psychiatrists, Dr. Goulding and Dr. Hill, who have more than fifty years' combined psychiatric experience. Half a century. They evaluated Mr. Raznatovic independently of each other, and both reached the same conclusion. He is mentally infirm and suffers from an overpowering delusion. That delusion was in full active mode on the day that Mr. Raznatovic crossed paths with the complainant. Mr. Raznatovic believes he has a special relationship with God, that he was doing God's will when he attacked the complainant. This belief of his is a false fixation, making it impossible to appreciate the wrongness of his acts. He believes that there are women who are the devil's helpers. Do not make the mistake of taking it out of context, like the Crown prosecutor did. It ties in with the other insanity evidence which corroborates his delusional disorder.

The Crown suggests Mr. Raznatovic was too sane to be insane. It's just a theory. I see a pattern of severe mental disease, and so must you. Yes, Riley Gibson let him look after the farm. He was a hardworking farmer with a wife who looked after the financial affairs in his absence. He always made sure there was very little that could go wrong when he wasn't around. So, even though he thought Mr. Raznatovic was not all there, he let him look after the farm because there wasn't much to look after. I'll tell you another thing. Mr. Raznatovic trashing his place because he couldn't go on a trip with the boss was much more than a temper tantrum. His behaviour speaks to a derangement of the mind.

People attending the fun fair were inside the shearing shed enjoying the activities, all except the complainant who stood vigil at the well, waiting for mum to take her home. Her world collided with Mr. Raznatovic that morning, simply because he stood outside the barn. It was his job to be there.

You heard the Crown's version of the events. Now, I'll tell you what happened. The accused suffered an involuntary impulse to grab the complainant because she was inside his territory, his domain. That's all. A sick impulse driven by insanity. Once the complainant was inside the barn, Mr. Raznatovic hit her over the head. He only wanted to stun her to make it easier to commit further violence. You saw the pole. It's too long and unwieldy to use as a murder weapon.

The Crown claims Mr. Raznatovic was making rational choices and taking a course of action when he wasted precious time procuring a whip from inside a locked box, just because it held special significance for him. By wasting precious time, he put himself in considerable jeopardy of being caught. Why? Because he didn't realize that what he was doing was wrong. Anyone in their right mind would have disappeared quickly to avoid being captured, but not Mr. Raznatovic. He remained at the crime scene while the search party tried to break down the barn door. He was the one who opened the door to let those people inside, and they testified he was smiling at them. These are not the acts of a sane man.

Now, let me put the contentious pitchfork to rest by using the Crown's own argument. You have to decide which evidence is credible — the testimony of Mr. Smithy who was inside the barn watching the crimes unfold right in front of him, or Mr. Jung testifying to what he thinks he saw after catching a glimpse from the other side of a barn door which was several feet away from the complainant.

I want you to put aside the charges against Mr. Smithy for a moment, and focus on the fact that he testified under oath. His low IQ doesn't impede him from telling the court what happened, and he clearly stated that Mr. Raznatovic was not trying to kill the complainant with the pitchfork. Mr. Smithy saw the accused picking it up when he heard the search party outside, an obvious attempt to defend himself against them. But he didn't need to use the pitchfork because no one attacked him. If that isn't enough, Mr. Raznatovic has stated several times he was not attempting to murder the complainant.

If you're still not sure about Mr. Smithy's testimony or Mr. Raznatovic's statement, the medical evidence should convince you they told the truth. There were no wounds on the complainant's body made by the pitchfork. She's still alive which is substantive proof that Mr. Raznatovic wasn't interested in killing her because in actual fact, he did have enough time to use the pitchfork. It only takes a couple of seconds to kill with a pitchfork according to Inspector Worlock. Therefore, if Mr. Raznatovic didn't want to kill the complainant with the pitchfork, it stands to reason he didn't want to kill her with the pole.

The defence wants you to understand, for the sake of consistency, that Mr. Raznatovic pleaded not guilty by reason of insanity to all three charges. But he did not intend to hurt or kill the complainant, and you cannot convict him of assault, rape, and attempted murder if intent cannot be proved beyond a reasonable doubt. The testimonies of Dr. Goulding and Dr. Hill satisfy the legal burden of proving insanity on a balance of probabilities. Mr. Raznatovic was mentally sick and not aware that what he was doing was wrong when he attacked the complainant on that fateful day.

Rex versus Porter 1933. In his citation, the distinguished Chief Justice Dixon said it is perfectly useless for the law to attempt, by way of threatening punishment, to deter people from committing crimes if their mental condition prevents them from being influenced by the possibility or probability of further punishment, if they cannot understand what they are doing."

Olly looked at each juror, silently urging them to make the right decision. "Mr. Raznatovic's fate is in your hands. We ask you to render a fair verdict of not guilty by reason of insanity.

What of Niel Smithy charged with being a principal in the second degree? He's certainly not a learned man, but someone who's mentally equipped to muck out horse stalls and bale hay. The Stanford-Binet test for mild retardation is between 55-69. Despite the Crown's argument, they cannot change the fact that Mr. Smithy's IQ of 70 is right at the borderline of mild retardation. You heard the expert testimony from Dr. Goulding. Mr. Smithy lacks appropriate problem-solving skills which affected his judgment on February 2nd.

This is a man who knows something sick festers inside his friend's mind and it scares the living daylights out of him. If Mr. Smithy tried to intervene while the complainant was being attacked, he himself could have been the next target. That is why he did not ask for help when he saw the search party approaching the barn. He would have been no match regardless of the fact he may have been physically stronger. And what does the Crown base their argument on? Mr. Smithy can bale hay all day long and Igor can't."

Olly put his notes down and looked at the jury with all the sincerity he could muster. "Baling hay all day long is not an indicator of strength when it comes to a sparring match between two men. Mr. Smithy is a simpleton trapped by Mr. Raznatovic's delusions. You have not heard any substantial evidence that Mr. Smithy intended to harm the complainant. He lacks the cognitive function to understand what he was witnessing and what he should have done to save her. I ask you to find him not guilty of aiding and abetting."

The Summation

Justice Cobb addressed the jury, "My role as judge is to decide issues of law which makes it my duty and responsibility to instruct you on what the laws of this state require. It is your duty to decide issues of fact based on the evidence you find credible and apply the facts to the law. The principle of fundamental justice is that an accused is innocent until proven guilty. An accused is also presumed sane unless proved otherwise."

Justice Cobb rubbed his hands together for his favourite subject of English law. "The question of insanity during the commission of an offence is determined by applying the M'Naghten Rule, a law named after a Scotsman, Daniel M'Naghten. In 1843, he tried to kill England's Prime Minister because he thought the man wanted to kill him. But he killed the prime minister's secretary by mistake. At his trial, he was described as a person with morbid delusions and found not guilty by reason of insanity. The contentious verdict caused such a public hue and cry that British Parliament introduced the M'Naghten Rule, a test for criminal insanity. An accused can only use insanity as a defence if, at the time of committing the act, he was labouring under such a defect of reason from a disease of the mind, as not to know the nature and quality of the act he was doing, or if he did know it, he didn't know what he was doing was wrong.

The term wrong has created a conundrum in legal circles by defining a perpetrator's actions as being against the law, or against commonly held moral principles. Like many of my learned colleagues, I'm convinced the M'Naghten Rule has established the concept of morality, and not legality, to be applied to a perpetrator's conduct."

Privy to Justice Cobb's idiosyncracies, the tipstaff knew he was going to drain the swamp of everything there was to know about the term wrong. The tipstaff gave a warning cough as if he was clearing his throat, "Ahem."

Justice Cobb frowned at the interruption, but knew what it meant — enough already about the five letter word which inspires heated debates amongst judges. He reluctantly changed the direction of his summation.

"The charges of assault — the intentionally harmful touching of another person causing serious physical injury, rape — forced vaginal penetration. Wounding with attempt to commit murder — a person must have deliberately or recklessly, with extreme disregard for human life, cause injury in an attempt to kill someone.

You must ask yourself, did the Crown prove their case against Mr. Raznatovic beyond a reasonable doubt? Here is where you walk a slippery slope. If you decide the Crown proved the physical and mental elements of a charge, you must step back and consider if Mr. Raznatovic was insane when he committed the criminal acts. Because it is possible to wilfully carry out a criminal act, and be incapable of understanding the nature of the act or distinguishing between right and wrong.

It is up to you to decide if the defence proved insanity within a reasonable doubt. Because if you do, you must find the accused not guilty by reason of insanity.

However, if the Crown proved a charge, but the defence did not prove insanity, you must find Mr. Raznatovic guilty. If the Crown did not prove a charge, you must acquit him.

This brings us to Mr. Smithy who is charged with being a principal in the second degree. The law recognizes that two or more individuals can act jointly to commit the same crime. Mere presence at the scene of the crime doesn't necessarily make an accused criminally liable unless that person solicited, insisted, encouraged or intentionally aided the other to engage in such conduct. The person charged with being an aider and abettor must also possess the state of mind required to commit the offence.

If the Crown proved a charge, you must find Mr. Smithy guilty. If the Crown did not prove a charge, you must find him not guilty.

Please continue to listen as I clarify the role of expert witnesses who gave opinions about technical matters which you may consider when deciding this case. They are qualified to give an opinion because of their training, education, experience. You can give their opinion as much or as little weight as you think it deserves. Consider the expert's knowledge and the rest of the evidence, including the testimony of the other witnesses when you decide on the reliability of his opinion. And let me be clear about this. You are to review all the witness testimonies with equal care.

You may ask me anything, but don't ask me how to measure *beyond or within a reasonable doubt*. The court tends to discourage judges like me from defining these terms to a jury. You should understand the terms on your own. However, do not make the mistake of applying a percentage scale. Disagreement will invariably arise amongst yourselves which results in a misunderstanding of the standard of proof.

And now a gentle reminder about dictionaries. Do not ask for one because you won't get it. If I find out you sneaked a dictionary into deliberations, you will be cited for juror misconduct and the defence can seek a mistrial."

That was about as gentle as a cricket bat to the head, thought Angelo.

Justice Cobb could see the jury reacting in surprise. "I have my reasons. Dictionaries can be misinterpreted as they don't purport to include every legal implication of a particular word. Use common sense to guide you in the right direction when you make your decisions."

After reviewing the Crimes Act, he concluded his summation. "Listen respectfully to each other's views and reach a unanimous agreement because that is what's required to acquit or convict the accused. No matter how convincing the Crown and defence were, remember what I told you in pre-trial instructions...anything the barristers say is not evidence, including their closing arguments. You must base your conclusions solely on the evidence lawfully admitted that you believe to be true, so that you can make a reliable judgment. Deliberate the facts without sympathy or bias towards the Crown or the defence, and reach your verdicts within the parameters of the law as determined by the presiding judge...yours truly."

Friday, September 20 at 11:00 a.m.
Courtroom 2

"Has the jury reached a decision, Mr. Foreman?"
"We have, your Honour."
Without expression, Justice Cobb read the verdict before handing it to his tipstaff. "Will the accused please rise?"
Igor and Niel stood up and waited.

Attila sat beside Worlock, both of them anxious to hear the verdict. Angelo remained at the prosecution table with Thomas, his normally steady heart banging inside his chest as if it were a netball dribbling down centre court during a game between Flinders and Hovel, his law school teams. He remembered all the cases he prosecuted, but couldn't recall a time when he felt this much concern about a verdict. Guilty was the only word he wanted to hear, and he had to stop himself from tearing the sheet out of the foreman's hand.

The tipstaff bellowed to the foreman, "How do you find the accused, Mr. Raznatovic, on the first count of assault?"

"Guilty."

"On the second count of rape?"

"Guilty."

"On the third count of wounding with attempt to commit murder?"

"Not guilty."

Angelo watched a conviction of attempted murder grow wings and fly out the window. *Fuck it*. He was very tempted to fling his wig across the courtroom.

Justice Cobb noticed the spectators were finally behaving like a model courtroom. Not a sound, just the way he liked it.

Attila said nothing. He knew deep down that Igor would escape the attempted murder charge. His heart wanted to hear guilty, but forever the realistic pessimist, his head knew better.

Igor was relieved he won't be humiliated by anymore psychiatrists. Most important of all, the Voice would remain his secret. He turned his thoughts to the day he will meet Marika again, and drew comfort from it.

The tipstaff asked the foreman, "How do you find Mr. Smithy on the first count of assault, principal in the second degree?"

"Guilty."

"On the second count of rape, principal in the second degree?"

"Guilty."

The writing was on the wall.

"On the third count of wounding with attempt to commit murder, principal in the second degree?"

"Not guilty."

Handsome Son of a Bitch

After the prisoners were remanded back into custody, Justice Cobb headed for his chambers to begin the sentencing phase. The courtroom emptied quickly, leaving behind the two barristers, Attila, and Worlock.

As a Crown prosecutor, Angelo was not happy with the outcome. But it wasn't all bad. One of the worst degenerates he ever prosecuted was still going to gaol for at least twenty years, less the time spent in custody. And although Niel was found guilty of the same charges, he guessed the latter's sentence at no more than fifteen years. He shook off the disappointment by giving Attila a smile and a thumbs up sign. Then, as hard as it was to do, he turned and looked at Olly. No handshake. There was too much animosity between the adversaries. Instead, they acknowledged each other with a forced nod, fully aware they were dissatisfied with the verdicts for different reasons.

A deflated Olly couldn't resist a parting shot, "You know what you're missing?"

"Two peas in a pod?" Angelo couldn't resist making fun of Olly's ridiculous metaphor, *Heaven and God are like two peas in a pod.*

The defence barrister said nothing.

Angelo stuck his tongue in the space where his whopper of a wisdom tooth used to be. "How about my back molar?"

Olly ignored the prosecutor's childish attempt at levity. "You're missing a physical flaw to temper that vanity of yours."

"Did you just call me a handsome son of a bitch?"

"You're full of shit, Murano."

"You got a deformity and you're taking it out on me. Why don't you clomp back to the stables?"

That was the straw that broke the camel's back. Olly stepped forward and swung an angry punch at Angelo, but the latter ducked, causing Olly to lose his balance.

It wasn't a courtroom scene that Angelo ever really envisioned between himself and Silly-boy. But it was happening right now as he grabbed his adversary to prevent him from crashing to the floor. At the same time, he had to balance himself to stay upright because the grunting defence barrister was trying to push him down.

Worlock stepped up and hooked his right hand inside the collar of Olly's shirt, yanking the man backwards. It was an impressive move which easily separated the two barristers.

A red-faced Olly shook off Worlock's strong arms. In a defiant voice, he dared the policeman, "Are you going to arrest me for assault?"

"I only saw you swatting at a pesky fly." Worlock turned towards Angelo with a warning glance. "Isn't that right, Mr. Murano?"

The Crown prosecutor gave his mate an amused look. He'd never been compared to the lowly insect before. To get in character, he clenched his teeth together and said, "Bzzz."

Olly shook his head in disgust and marched out of the courtroom.

"What was that?" Worlock was almost afraid to ask.

"A pesky fly saying yes."

"That's what I thought."

Angelo took off his lopsided wig and combed his fingers through his hair. He smiled apologetically at Attila who had been watching the melodrama with disbelief. "Mr. Silboy gets quite emotional at the end of a trial. He'll be fine." The prosecutor turned easily to the matter at hand. "Raznatovic is going to gaol for a long time."

Attila preferred the good old days when a criminal like Igor would have been put to death. Now that a prison sentence was a sure thing, it gave him a tenuous sense of closure, something he didn't think he'd feel so soon. He was ready to go home and never talk about the trial again. "It's over, Angelo."

"Not quite. The defence always appeals when a verdict goes against them." Angelo placed a consoling hand on Attila's back. "The sentence is still going to be substantial, however, in this case I know it hardly seems enough for what Raznatovic did to your daughter. We must look at it as a victory though. A degenerate like him is a prime target for the other gaol birds, and every day he spends behind bars will feel like an eternity."

Expect the Unexpected

Justice Cobb delivered a surprising blow to the Crown. Igor was sentenced to fifteen years less seven months at H.M. Prison Pentridge, the largest maximum security gaol in Victoria. Niel ended up at Ballarat Gaol for ten years minus the time spent in custody.

Justice Cobb sat in his chambers wondering what Lady Justice would say to him if she could speak. He should have imposed the maximum sentences, but with the power to exercise broad discretion, he couldn't ignore the defence's insanity evidence. It wasn't enough to negate the charges, but for sentencing it was sufficient to invoke mitigating circumstances. Having a cousin who was mad as a hatter, the judge instinctively knew when a person's perceptions were skewed by mental sickness, and Raznatovic definitely fit the bill. As for Smithy, he was a man with borderline intelligence who testified against his mate.

A Consoling Lager

Worlock and Angelo sat in their favourite bar finishing a pint of lager without saying a word. Then they had another. Finally, Worlock said, "What did I tell you? Judges are sooks. Wimps. Cobb should have slapped Razzy with twenty for the rape and four for the beating."

Angelo wiped the froth from his lips. "It's Razzy now, is it? Took you long enough to emulate me, Oscar."

"Smart-arse, you know that's my grandfather's moniker." Worlock zoomed a bowl of peanuts at Angelo whose reflexes were dulled by the alcohol, but he still managed to catch the speeding object before it fell off the table. "What about an appeal?"

"And risk a retrial with a new jury finding Razzy insane? Justice will be better served in gaol."

Worlock was going to run harder tomorrow morning to purge his system of the toxic disappointment he felt for the Paprika family. "Besides, I got the feeling Attila wants this all to go away, so his family can get on with life."

"Four out of six guilty verdicts ain't bad."

Worlock knew his mate was lying. Nothing but a clean sweep would have been acceptable in this case.

Angelo teased the policeman, "Do you bloviate?"

"I don't think that's any of your business, mate."

"Which means you don't know," said Angelo confidently.

"You're right," conceded Worlock. "The judge at it again?"

"Listen and learn. Bloviate...to speak with verbosity."

"I'm not the one who could ever be accused of that."

"I have no idea what you mean," said Angelo. He reached out and tipped Worlock's empty glass over. It began to roll ominously towards the policeman.

Worlock grabbed the glass and stood it upright. "You're just a big kid wearing a grown-up body."

"You found out my secret," said Angelo with a wink. Then he frowned. "Silly-boy tried to punch my lights out."

"What do you expect when you compare his feet to the hooves of a horse?"

"He's got a grudge against anyone who can wear penny loafers. Besides, he started it by saying I'm full of shit."

"You went too far."

"Crikey, it's not my fault he's got gimpy feet." Angelo suddenly realized he was a little too uninhibited, even for him. "You're my best mate. Are we good here?"

Worlock nodded. "Yeah, we're good. I don't pay attention to half the things you say when you're pissed from anger or alcohol."

"Glad to hear it. You okay with what happened between us a few years ago?"

"How many times do I have to tell you Sofia wasn't the one for me."

"Why wasn't she the one?"

Sofia was the woman that Worlock wanted until she fell in love with his best friend. At first, he wanted to beat the shit out of Angelo, and refused to speak to him for a whole year. But he began to miss his best mate, and one day, words of wisdom filled his stubborn head as he ran along the beach.

Sofia didn't love you the way you were meant to be loved. The woman of your dreams will show up one day, so Angelo did you a favour. Rein in your ego and be the person I think you are, or continue to wallow in self-pity and jealousy. Forgiveness is highly underrated.

Worlock replied, "Because she chose you." He blew the head off his third pint, causing a layer of suds to land squarely on Angelo's face.

"Now, who's the big kid?" The prosecutor wiped the froth off with his hand and noisily licked his fingers. He wasn't the type to waste a good lager.

Where Bad Men Go

Pentridge Prison's high bluestone brick walls dominated the surrounding area with the commanding presence of a fortress. Black crosses were etched into the two lopsided tower turrets flanking the security gate, a sign from the Voice that Igor was meant to be coming here.

Noisy neighbourhood boys played with a tennis ball along the perimeter as the prison van drove up to the gate. The driver suddenly blasted a loud horn to announce the arrival of a new inmate to invisible sentry guards. Sitting on a cold metal bench, Igor peered out of a small vent dividing the front compartment from the back of the van. For the first time since he was convicted, he felt a strong sense of foreboding as the gate slowly rolled upwards. He sent urgent messages to the Voice, but there was only silence greeting him.

As the driver drove into the prison yard, he said, "Rise and shine, Razzmatazz. Your new mates want to give you a warm welcome."

"Raznatovic," grumbled Igor.

"That's what I said." The driver's laughter was interrupted by a flying object hitting the top of the van. Thunk. He said angrily, "Hoodlum kids keep throwing balls stuck with knives over the wall. There better not be anything sticking out of the ball this time or I'll throw 'em into a cell."

Clowns Get Around

"Strip down, Raznatovic, and don't make me tell you again," ordered a blue uniformed warder.

A naked Igor was marched to a cold shower in a damp, ammonia-smelling stall where a bucket of disinfectant was tossed at him.

After a scrub down with a sharp-bristle brush, a still naked Igor followed the warder to a door.

Igor growled, "Give me some clothes."

"You're new here, so I'm going to cut you some slack. The next time you challenge me, I'll beat you to a bloody pulp and have the warden's blessing. Got that?"

"God is on my side."

"Not if you're a pedophile."

"You can't frighten me."

"We'll see how you feel in a few minutes." The warder opened a door and pushed Igor into a gloomy corridor lined with silent gaolers hiding their faces with creepy clown masks. "See the clothes and shoes on that table down at the end? Go get 'em. But first, say g'day to the boys who want to give you an honorary reception."

"You are trying to humiliate me."

"I've got news for you. Pentridge has a tradition for new prisoners, and today...you're it."

Igor reluctantly took a step forward when he felt a horrific sting across his back. He yelled out in pain, and turned to see a cotton corded cat o'nine tails swishing into the air as it was tossed to a gaoler further down the line. Igor steeled himself for three more floggings, numerous butt-kicks and punches in the head. He stumbled several times, but made it to the end of the corridor.

The warder said perfunctorily, "Get dressed."

Igor cringed in pain, his arms wrapped around his head a little too late.

"Don't be a sniveling sheila. The boys barely broke your skin."

The honorary reception was one of many degrading rituals designed to reform Pentridge inmates by breaking their spirit.

Welcome to Hell

Igor was escorted through a labyrinth of bleak concrete tunnel-like corridors, the stench of human badness, suffering, and fear threatening him at every turn. On the way to his cell in maximum security H Division, he noticed all the cells were open and empty. Each cell had a door made of heavy wood and metal rivets, and had a built-in trap door for meal trays. A peep hole above the trap door allowed warders to check on the inmates during lockdown.

An annoying loud bell rang as Igor waited for the warder to finish a cursory check of his cell. He stood at the entrance hurting from head to toe while the dregs of society filed back to their cells.

A tough looking convict stopped outside the cell next to Igor's, scowling at his new neighbour. He rolled up his sleeve, flexing a muscular bicep to make his tattooed anchor twitch. "Welcome to Hell Division," the convict said in a menacing tone.

Igor looked at the man as if he were cow dung on the bottom of his shoe. Although he wanted to collapse right there on the cold concrete floor, he wasn't going to give these goons the satisfaction of knowing they can break him so easily.

His cell contained a narrow steel bed frame bolted to the floor, a thin lumpy mattress, and a pillow covered with a folded grey blanket. He was revolted by a wooden stool with a hole and a reeking bucket for his toilet. To make matters worse, he was expected to march his piss and shit-filled bucket to a sewer hole in the yard.

"I want a cell with a proper toilet," he demanded.

The warder replied, "You'll get what we give you. And to keep you fit as a fiddle, you'll be breaking rocks starting tomorrow."

Igor remembered the black crosses. This hell hole was where he was supposed to be. So, as hard as it was going to be, all he had to do was count the days and behave himself. He looked down at his grey prison jacket, heavy denim pants, his clunky black prison shoes. He missed his fedora.

High risk offenders in H Division ate breakfast, lunch, and dinner in their cells, so there was no mingling during meal breaks. Encounters with the other inmates took place during prison chores, at the rock pile, and in the exercise yard where he was subjected to taunting by the other inmates. It was during his weekly shower where he worried the most about being attacked with a razor blade hidden in a bar of soap. He was warned numerous times about slashings being a common occurrence.

On the fifth day of prison life, Igor was assigned laundry duty one day a week. He was escorted to a steamy cavernous room with exposed water pipes running along the ceiling and walls. Large tumbling machines whirred and clanked noisily. Several prisoners busy with their chores barely glanced at him.

Igor was ordered to empty bins of dirty clothing and bedding.

"I don't do laundry," he said with arrogance.

The warder felt no sympathy for the new prisoner. "You do now."

Igor stood wearily beside a large concrete tub cursing the filthy garments that had to be scrubbed before shoving them into the washing machines. His wounded back and arms hurt from breaking rocks for three days. His head still hurt from being used as a punching bag.

The afternoon laundry shift was almost over but when he looked around, the warders on duty had mysteriously disappeared.

A strong pair of hands swung Igor around in the opposite direction, grabbing the front of his shirt. "Glad to make your acquaintance, Eye-gor. I understand you're a famous pervert who likes small cracks. That makes you a rock spider, don't it?"

Igor stared at the very broad chest of Pete, a six foot six inch blond musclebound man, better known to the prison population as The Great White, in honour of the feared shark patrolling Australian waters. He said with annoyance, "My name is Ee-gor."

"Eye-gor, Ee-gor. I don't see no difference."

"Get your hands off me. Let me go." Igor struggled to remove Pete's huge sinewy hands from his shirt.

Pete smacked Igor's hands away as if he were admonishing a naughty child. "Is that what the little girl begged you to do? If I was you, I'd be pissin' my grundies because we may be the only blokes who feel revenge is the right justice for the kid." He grabbed and brutally twisted a hunk of Igor's oily black hair, pulling him to the middle of the dank noisy room before letting him go.

A small crowd of previously bored but now excited men dropped whatever they were doing, and made a tight circle around the two figures. Finally, some fun and games.

"I don't like rock spiders," Pete whispered sinisterly in Igor's ear.

Igor began to sweat profusely from fear.

Pete pressed his pickle nose into Igor's fleshy snout before pushing him away. "You're worse than a dog, an' I don't mean the kind that goes woof." He barked like a chihuahua which made the men laugh hysterically. "I'm talkin' about screw informers. Did you know crims were flogged fifty to a hundred times in the good ol' days? I hear you got a taste of your own medicine." Pete banged his chest to show he was the boss. "This old lag don't have to get no one's permission because I am the law here!"

Igor opened his mouth, but couldn't think of anything to say to the gigantic brute who kept circling him.

The Great White smiled broadly as he pulled Igor's mouth wide open. "Ugly yellow teeth...I got a better idea." Peering inside, he said, "Look at that crooked mess, an' lookee here...a couple of great whoppin' holes. I never met a foreigner with a decent set of choppers." The smile faded from a face ruined by a life of crime. "Want somethin' for the pain?"

One of the inmates handed Pete a long rusty metal instrument.

"Pliers? That should do somethin' all right."

The crowd welcomed the diversion, laughing at Pete's sadistic sense of humour. He was the greatest heavy Pentridge Prison had the pleasure of incarcerating. His massive size and long criminal record matched by an equally long sentence were held in high esteem by his fellow prisoners.

Not a word was spoken as two men held down Igor's flailing arms. Pete clamped the rusty pliers onto a molar. "This little piggy went to market." He twisted, and yanked, and twisted without mercy.

Igor moaned and squirmed, struggling desperately to free himself.

Pete coaxed the tooth, "Come on, little bugger." The tooth finally obliged and Pete flung it across the room. He yelled victoriously, "Bonzer!"

Igor screamed like a hyena, the tumbling machines and rotating jumbo dryers drowning out the noise.

Four more crude extractions were punctuated by hearty bonzers.

Blood dripped down Igor's chin, saturating his white sweat-stained shirt.

"Shut his gob."

A dirty rag was shoved into Igor's bleeding mouth.

"I plan to be a dentist when I grow up," announced Pete. "Think I'll make a good one, Eye-gor?" He knew he wasn't going to get answer. After all, what could his victim say with a mouth full of rag? Pete nodded to the two men to let go of his patient.

Dropping to the chipped concrete floor, Igor groaned in muffled agony.

"Do you like coke, Eye-gor?" Pete produced a bottle of coca-cola, caressing the hourglass shape with a hand. "Reminds me of a full-figured sheila. I get horny just lookin' at it." Pete snapped his giant fingers at the crowd that was hanging off his every word. "Lose his pants an' hold him down."

The Aussie with the twitching anchor tattoo stepped forward, ripping off Igor's pants and underwear with a shank hidden inside his shoe.

Pete took stock of Igor's thick legs covered in matted black hair. "You're very ugly an' smell of horse crotch. I wouldn't dare do the naughty with you, nor my mates here who'll stick their doodle into just about any manly freckle. We'll have to get satisfaction another way."

A writhing Igor was turned over onto his stomach, and one of the men standing nearby came over and sat on top of him. Two others pulled his legs apart.

"I used to pour coke on my rusty car battery; cleaned it up real nice. Should do wonders for your sewer system," smirked Pete.

Laughter did not return to the crowd caught up in a feverish pitch of perverted lust. Pete slipped on a rubber glove, pried off the cap, shoved the bottle into Igor's tight anus, twisting and pushing as far as it will go. Igor screamed into the dirty rag as if he was being skinned alive. As soon as Pete pulled the bottle out, blood mixed with feces and coke gushed forth like an avalanche. He threw the weapon and glove into a metal dustbin which caused the sound of breaking glass. Stepping back to survey his handiwork, his calm voice belied the violent act he had just committed. "You don't seem very enthusiastic. What with all that squirmin' an' moanin', I thought it'd be right up your alley."

The satiated crowd laughed raucously, for the innuendo in Pete's jokes never ceased to be a source of fun in such a miserable place.

An inmate assigned as a lookout rushed into the laundry room. "Warders!"

"They were supposed to hang around F Block playin' bingo with the sheilas. As for you..." Pete knelt down beside the prostrate body, grabbed a hunk of hair, twisting it into a knot. It was the only way he could hold onto the slippery mess. He pulled Igor's head up. "Name names an' I'll cut off your tally whacker. Then I'll make you eat it."

Igor's head hit the floor with a thwack as Pete shoved him back down. The Great White pretended to be disappointed. "I guess Eye-gor would've preferred a thirst-quenching Fanta."

September 23, 1957 at 5:20 p.m.
1 Finch Street

Marika ran to the front door when she heard a car pull up to the driveway. "Daddy! Daddy! Mommy's back!"

"Hello, dear," Anna breezed into the house to give Marika a big hug. "I missed you."

"I missed you too." Marika wasn't angry with her mother anymore.

"I had a wonderful time with Marjorie. We saw many nice things on our way to Sydney, and they will be your bedtime stories."

"I can't wait, Mommy. Sofia is going to have a baby, and she made me pasghetti and meatballs!"

Anna chuckled, "It's called spa--ghetti. But I like the way you say it better." She hugged Marika again.

"Mommy, how did the baby get inside Sofia's tummy?"

"Later, dear." Sex was the last thing Anna wanted to talk about with her little daughter. She hurriedly changed the subject. "Did you have a nice time with Sofia?"

"Yes, Mommy. She taught me Italian, and we went for walks and had ice cream."

"What Italian did you learn?"

"Bella means beautiful. Bambino means baby."

"Very good. Now listen, I want you to go and wash your hands and face. Marjorie's getting some treats from the car. She'll be having supper with us." She sniffed the air. "Something nice is cooking in the kitchen."

Attila was stirring a big pot of bubbling porkolt when Anna found him in the kitchen. She said warmly, "I'm glad you made me go. The scenery was breathtaking, and I met Magdi, Marjorie's other Hungarian friend."

"Who are you and what have you done with my grumpy wife?"

Anna quipped, "You should have me back to my old self in no time."

After supper, Attila walked Marjorie to her car. "How was Anna during the trip?"

"She was rather uptight the first day, then she started to unwind with the weather being so pleasant and sunny. I'm not exaggerating when I tell you the coastal drive to Sydney is absolutely magical. There were many fabulous beaches and most of them deserted, crystal blue lagoons, rocky coves and cliffs, islands with boat rides, and national parks filled with birds and all sorts of wildlife. We even saw a hump back whale in the Tasman Sea."

"You're a good friend to Anna."

After Marjorie departed, Marika brushed her teeth and went to her bedroom, waiting excitedly for her mother.

Anna dropped by the living room where Attila was bent in front of the television rotating the channel tuner. The telly was a great relaxer before his nightly studying.

Anna said, "Marika told me you boarded up the crawlspace."

"Fornicating felines make a terrible racket."

Shaking her head in dismay, Anna said, "You're either turning the hose on them or taking away their shelter."

"Not anymore," Attila said smugly. He returned to his chair and smiled innocently at Anna, "Do you want to watch I've Got a Secret ?"

A Parade of Penguins

Marika curled up under her blanket waiting for Anna to begin the first story about her trip.

With a smile, Anna ran a finger gently along her daughter's nose. "We drove down the coast just like my finger is making its way down your nosey."

Marika giggled. "Where did you go, Mommy?"

"Marjorie and I went across the ocean on a bridge to Phillip Island."

The little girl's eyes grew bigger.

"When the sun set, we sat down on the beach with a flashlight." Pause. "And waited." Pause again. The suspense was building for her daughter.

Marika asked excitedly, "For what, Mommy?"

Anna's eyes grew bigger too. In a dramatic voice, she said, "Penguins!"

Marika repeated in awe, "Penguins!"

"A parade of cute little penguins marched out of the sea in their dark blue and white coats."

"What do they do in the sea?"

"Fish for food and swim around with each other. At night, they return to their nests on the island. And guess what? I held a fuzzy baby penguin in my hand."

Marika couldn't get enough of the penguins. "Did he bite?"

"No, dear. They're so friendly, they will come right up to you before they go to their nests."

"Tell me more!"

"We'll get Daddy to take us there, okay?"

"Yes, Mommy."

"That's all for now, sweetheart. Time to go to sleep." Anna could have said more. That the harmless little penguins were being killed off by dogs and foxes. Not the way to end a nice bedtime story.

The following night

Anna tucked the blanket around Marika and sat down on the bed beside her. "Ready to hear more about Phillip Island?"

"Yes, Mommy!"

"The next day we saw koala bears."

"I love them!"

"I know you do. There were lots of them sitting in the trees with their babies. The mommy koala bears were hugging their children to protect them from danger." Without warning, a stream of tears ran down Anna's face. "Sorry, Marika, I don't feel well." She hurried out of the bedroom.

Marika jumped out of bed and ran to her father who was watching television. "Daddy! Mommy's crying!"

Attila sighed. Once Anna learned how to cry, she couldn't stop. Now it was back to the uneasy way things were before the road trip.

January 1958

Upside Down Sharks
Marika's days were spent in fear of the night.

Falling asleep was the key that unlocked a door to the sinister land of creepy crawly nightmares. Faceless swirling entities waited for the little girl to shut her eyes, preparing her for the man in the black hat, the one that wanted to hurt her over and over again.

When Marika lost her appetite, her weight dropped until she was on the verge of emaciation, her ribs protruding from her chest.

Anna dismissed her daughter's screams as the product of an overactive imagination. Her weight loss, a problem she will get over. It was just as well because Anna was far too busy writing a novel, this time a science fiction novel about flying saucers, an unexpected and drastic departure from her mystery romances.

It was summer that came to the rescue of a little girl desperately needing a helping hand. She spent weekends with her father at the Shell Club for employees, playing billiards and table tennis. Although Marika was too young to play well, she had a fit of giggles whenever she sent the occasional ping pong ball over the net, knowing that her dad was going to jump like a kangaroo to catch her wild balls.

As much fun as the Shell Club was, the best time they had was at Anglesea, the little girl's favourite beach. Every time Attila waded into the ocean carrying Marika, he would toss her into the air and catch her at the last minute.

Marika would shriek, "Daddy, the sharks will bite me if you drop me in the water!"

"I don't see any sharks, little one."

"They could be swimming upside down so we can't see their fins!"

The hot sun, the sea, the freedom they offered, always put Attila in a good mood. Sharing all of it with his cute daughter was an added bonus. "I guess it's okay if they nibble on your father's toes?"

"You're strong, Daddy! You can kick them in their noses!"

The cleansing sea air aroused a healthy appetite for newspaper-wrapped fish and chips, and American hotdogs, plump, juicy, delicious, smothered in ketchup, purchased from a shack beside the sandy beach.

Whenever they showed up early, it was just them and a bunch of loyal seagulls waiting patiently for falling food crumbs. There was nothing better than a day at the beach.

February 1958

The Bully
Igor's appeal was dismissed.

Attila grabbed Marika in a big hug, dancing like a silly man holding onto her hands until she couldn't stop giggling, even when the gyrations were over. Soon after, the little girl's headaches and nightmares mysteriously stopped, the reporters continued to leave her alone, and she started grade one at Norlane State School. Miss Grady noticed her painfully thin pupil didn't play with the other children during recess. Instead, she would cling like a sticky spider web to the chain link fence surrounding the school yard. The teacher decided it was her duty to do something about it. She ordered Marika's classmates to include her in their games. At first, they were reluctant to engage with the weird scrawny girl, but once they dragged her into their circle of fun, her defences melted. They discovered a nice kid who leapfrogged over posts mounted in the school yard and swung backwards hands-free with her stick legs wrapped around the playground's horizontal bar.

The same personality which made friends also attracted the school bully, a tough tank of a girl with short choppy white hair, brown freckles on her nose, pouting lips that looked like they were ready to burst open. People called her Sandra, but Marika knew her as the bully.

The bully tormented the meek waif with the funny rhyming name, kicking and shoving her to the ground, and hiding behind corners to trip her. When she wasn't physically abusive, she was stealing Marika's school supplies or stuffing her desk ink well with blotting paper.

As soon as the bullying threatened to become a regular part of their daughter's life, Attila and Anna complained to the headmaster who spoke to the bully's parents. They refused to admit their daughter was a prepubescent thug, creating a circle of accusations and denials.

No one understood how sad and vulnerable Marika was feeling, but at least her daddy tried to make her feel better. She would ride her little red bike around the garden, eagerly waiting for him.

When Attila came home from work, they would sit on the back porch sharing a Mars bar. A taste explosion of chocolate, caramel, and nougat.

Who Wrote the Oxford Dictionary?

The bully made it her priority to torment her victim as often as possible.

One day, she confronted Marika in the school yard after school. In a smug voice, she said, "My parents said you were raped."

Marika didn't wait to hear anything else. She ran all the way home. Huffing and puffing, she found her mother cooking in the kitchen. "The bully says...I was...raped. What does it mean?"

Anna was taken aback. *What do little girls talk about these days?* "You must have misunderstood her."

"No, I didn't. What is rape?"

Rape was not a subject that Anna was willing to discuss with her young daughter. "There's no such word. Maybe she said you were raised. You know, by your parents."

Marika knew what she heard. Her mother was wrong. She went to the living room and picked up the Oxford dictionary. "Rape -- carry off by force. Violate chastity of; ravish; act of raping. Rape -- plant used as food for sheep. Plant with oil-yielding seed. She flicked through the pages. Chastity —chasteness. More flicking of pages. Ravish — carry off by force. Commit rape upon. Enrapture. Fill with delight."

Marika scratched her head. "None of it makes any sense."

Attila sprang into action as soon as he heard the bully's latest abuse against his child. One phone call sent two of Worlock's biggest, toughest looking policemen to the bully's home.

The freckle-nosed tank stopped terrorizing Marika, but the damage was done.

A Great Hiding Place

Marika became belligerent and stubborn at home, her temperamental behaviour creating trouble for her mother. Battles were fought in the kitchen because she refused to eat meals which didn't taste or look aesthetically pleasing to her.

"Eat those eggs!" Anna shouted in frustration one Saturday morning. She had just finished making the fourth batch of fried eggs for her daughter.

"They're too runny, and you broke the yolks on the other ones!"

The shouting traveled down the corridor into Attila's bedroom where he was trying to sleep after a long night of studying. He stroked his hair in annoyance, wondering whether he should investigate or wait until the commotion stopped.

"Eat those eggs now!"

Hauling himself out of bed, Attila walked into the kitchen where his eyes went from wife to daughter to four plates of eggs. He was never allowed to leave the table without finishing all the food on his plate when he was a little boy. "Marika, eat those eggs your mother made for you."

"No!"

Marika's lack of obedience didn't sit well with a groggy Attila. He pulled her off the kitchen chair and smacked her on the rump.

Her eyes opened wide in disbelief, prompting huge tears to trickle down her cheeks. She turned and ran from the room.

That was the first time Attila ever raised his hand against his daughter, and it would be the last. Whatever he had seen in her eyes, it was more than the suffering from a smack on the backside. When he entered her bedroom, Marika was nowhere. He peered under the bed and behind the curtains, positive she had charged into her sanctuary. He looked at the small wardrobe. There was just enough space below the hanging clothes for a child to hide. Pulling open the door, he found a pair of big eyes blinking at him from behind a hanging dress. Holding out his hand, he said, "I won't smack you again."

Marika didn't budge.

Attila tried to pull her out by her wrists, but she had wedged herself in by planting long slender feet and hands on either side of the wardrobe. She clenched her jaw, straining to keep her hands on the flimsy walls which caused them to bulge outwards. Stymied, Attila let go to avoid bruising a young girl determined to stay put. He left the bedroom.

Crouching inside her hiding place, Marika could hear the family car pulling away from the house.

A few minutes later, the car was back with Attila rustling a small paper bag. Sticking his head inside the wardrobe, he said, "Do you prefer a Mars bar or a Cadbury Flake?"

Marika looked at her daddy's sad face. He sounded gentle and kind, not like before.

"A Mars bar."

CHAPTER 10

A Pirouette

Tuesday, February 12, 1963 at 12:10 p.m.
Norlane, Geelong

Scrumptious fried smells from sizzling fish, chips, and battered potatoes clogged the fish and chip shop opposite Norlane State School.

Marika was there with with her best friend, Raelene, a young girl who recently moved with her parents into 3 Finch Street, the house next door to the Paprikas. The chubby girl had an explosion of red curls, freckles all over her body, and loved eating packages of butter like other kids scarfed down lolly. The friends were both ten years old and in the same Grade 5 class.

Raelene said impatiently, "Marika, hurry up and order something. I want to play hopscotch afterwards."

Marika loved the crispy battered potatoes which looked like spinning disks. She asked for sixpence worth.

The new owner, a wiry man with a narrow face and high forehead, put down his exceptionally long pair of tongs, and swiftly wrapped up four greasy pieces in newspaper. As he placed the neat package into the hand reaching over his counter, he lingered over the thin girl's name. "Are you from Bacchus Marsh?"

"No."

"Are you sure? I'm from there, and your name sounds familiar."

Marika said nothing else.

The girls returned to the school yard where they sat on a bench enjoying their greasy fried lunch.

Raelene said for no good reason at all, "Nothing strange ever happens to me. Has anything strange ever happened to you?"

"Funny you should ask me that," said Marika. "I was walking home yesterday, and when I got to the top of my street, something really daft happened."

"What?"

"Don't laugh." Marika looked earnestly at Raelene, wondering if she said too much already. She didn't want to lose a best friend, but the need to confide was overwhelming. Hesitantly, she said, "I felt myself falling forward, but I wasn't really falling. I was floating above the pavement, and it was a few seconds before I ended up flat on my stomach."

Raelene looked at Marika as if she was pulling her leg. "Are you kidding? No one can do what you just described."

Marika began to doubt herself. Was she crazy? And yet something told her she will always remember the incredible feeling of gliding like a bird, real or not. She quickly changed the conversation. "Do you want to go to the city with me and my parents on Saturday? I'm going to Purdy's to buy some swapping cards."

"I can't. I have to go to church with my family."

That Evening after Supper

"Daddy, are we from Bacchus Marsh? The fish and chip man wants to know."

Attila dropped the newspaper on his lap and looked cautiously at his daughter. It was bound to happen. "He mistook you for someone else."

"Why don't we go to church, like Raelene and her family?"

"We think religion begins at home." Attila hoped the answer will satisfy his daughter because he didn't want to tell her about the robotic communists who wouldn't let Hungarians go to church or practice their religion, that his faith began to erode with every horror he experienced during the war. If there was a God, He wouldn't have let people suffer the way they did. He wouldn't have let Marika suffer.

The next day, the two girls were back at the fish and chip shop for lunch. Marika noticed a dark green car parked outside, and as she opened the shop door, a big man got out. He followed her inside and stood imposingly against the wall, but didn't order anything. As soon as she approached the counter, the owner handed his tongs with an embarrassed grin to a female assistant and disappeared into the backroom.

The following day when the two girls returned for another greasy meal, the same big man was sitting in his green car. When the girls glanced at him, he quickly produced a newspaper.

Marika nudged Raelene. "That man's back again. He must like the fish and chips."

"I don't see any food." Raelene looked at her friend as if she was stupid. "He's looking at you out of the corner of his eye. Wanna bet he's a spy or a bad man?"

Her friend's wild imagination encouraged Marika's curiosity, and that evening, she told her father about the big man in the dark green car.

Attila sighed. *This girl sees everything.* "I'm sure it's nothing."

The following day, the big man in the dark green car was gone. Marika and Raelene never saw him again.

The Smiths

Elizabeth and Harold Smith were a reserved English couple who lived on Melbourne Road at the corner of Finch Street, their house flanking the west side of the Paprika home. They had a seventeen year old son, Colin, who was finishing up the last year of grammar school. Elizabeth and Harold ignored the Paprikas like they ignored most of their neighbours. Except for the occasional g'day and other harmless pleasantries, the Smiths preferred to keep to themselves. That way they could avoid those nasty neighbour spats.

On a sunny spring afternoon, Elizabeth's groggy eyes focused on the alarm clock. It was three thirty, not yet time for the alarm to go off. So, what woke her up?

The sound of metal sliding rhythmically across the sidewalk outside her bedroom window jarred her ears. Darned kids. Trouble had a way of finding the Smiths despite their best efforts to avoid the neighbours. Elizabeth moved to the window, pushing it all the way up. She leaned out, looking for the roller skating culprit. There she was, turning around at the corner and skating back towards her. Elizabeth noted the tall thin figure, her large luminescent eyes and short cropped hair framing her delicate face. It was the girl next door.

"Young lady, I don't want you roller skating up and down the sidewalk outside my house. Your noise disturbs me. Do I make myself clear?" Elizabeth spoke curtly with an upper class English accent.

Marika stopped dead in her tracks, frightened by the mean-looking woman who had an oval face with stunning grey eyes and straight black hair tied in a bun. Marika raced away in her brand new roller skates, back to the safety of her house.

Although Elizabeth was pleased with the results, she was rather surprised at the frightened reaction. "My goodness, maybe I was too severe. I must be quite a horrid sight when I'm woken so rudely from my afternoon nap."

Sweet Red Stuff Jogs a Memory

Over the next two months, Elizabeth noticed the girl roller skating in the opposite direction of her house. She must be the only child in Geelong who didn't have to be warned again. Elizabeth thought often about the skinny girl with the sad face, the strange child who didn't act like others her age.

Today was Sunday, and every Sunday Elizabeth prepared roast beef, Yorkshire pudding, and whatever vegetables beckoned her from the back patch. She picked up her brown wicker basket and strolled to the bottom of the garden skirted by a high wood fence. Moving gingerly through rows of snap peas, corn, and carrots, she contemplated picking some of each. "You all deserve to be on the dining table this evening, so a hodge podge it will be."

"Marika! Lunch is ready!"

Elizabeth looked towards the high wood fence where the voice was coming from. "Marika," repeated Elizabeth. "Pretty name, certainly not a common one. And the mother speaks with a heavy European accent." As she bent down to pull up a carrot, she repeated the girl's name which seemed familiar, but she didn't know why.

It came to her at the supper table. That was the name of the poor girl who was raped in Bacchus Marsh. While she was having her hair done, she had learned the name from her hairdresser who was dating a policeman, but she couldn't remember the family name. It was on the tip of her tongue like an ulcerated taste bud. Looks like there was going to be no enjoyment of supper until she remembered.

A very tall young man, all legs and arms, bounded into the kitchen. His smoky grey eyes and black hair were his mother's. "Hi Mom, Dad. Sorry I'm late." Colin knew his mother didn't like it when he was tardy. He bent down to kiss her on the cheek before grabbing a glass jar of red powder from the cupboard.

Elizabeth absentmindedly watched Colin sprinkle the sweet smoky spice over his potatoes. All of a sudden, her memory was jogged. She smacked the table with an open hand. "Paprika!"

"Yes, Mom. If you behave yourself, I'll put some on your potatoes..." Colin shook the jar with a wild glint in his eye, "...and you can shout at the top of your lungs..."

"Paprika!" exclaimed Harold who was Elizabeth's husband. He and his son had a good old laugh after that.

In spite of Elizabeth's newfound knowledge, she couldn't help but smile at the sight of her boys cracking up at her expense. "I think the child who lives next door is the child who was attacked by that filthy degenerate in Bacchus Marsh."

Harold's boyish face and red hair reminded Elizabeth she was married to a much younger man. It never used to bother her, but now that she was forty-nine, she could see the difference. As far as she could tell though, Harold still loved her as much as he did on the day he proposed. He was such a love.

"Are you sure, honey? As you say, it's been a long time," offered Harold.

"She's about the same age. I just need to know her last name."

"What would Miss Marple do?" Harold teased Elizabeth. She was a big Agatha Christie fan.

Elizabeth pursed her red lips. "Are you implying I'm as old as Miss Marple?"

Harold knew his wife's age was a sensitive subject, and tried to deflect the hurricane coming his way. "I had to choose between Miss Marple or Hercule Poirot, and I don't think your moustache is long enough to compete with Poirot's." Sometimes brutal humour eased any tension between the couple.

Elizabeth wondered if her husband noticed the coarse black hair sullying her upper lip, or was he trying to be a wicked type of funny? She aimed a carrot at him, but finally conceded, "You think you know me so well, don't you? One day, you'll be in for a surprise." She smiled like a goof.

"I can't wait, my lover-ly."

Colin groaned as he shoveled down his food. "Please, not while I'm eating."

A Covert Operation

The next day, Elizabeth waited outside for the postman. "Hurry up, man. You're always on time, except today when I want you to be."

The object of her impatience walked by, shoving mail into the tin postbox perched on a pole behind the black wrought iron gate of 1 Finch Street.

Being a huge Cliff Richard fan, Elizabeth whistled an off-key rendition of her favourite song, *A Summer Holiday*, as she loitered on the sidewalk giving the postman time to disappear down the street. Her hands shook with anticipation. "You are quite the pitiful moggy," she derided herself. A quick scan of the area told her no one was watching, or not that she could see. She released the postbox's cheap latch, and pulled open the lid. The name Paprika peered at her from the top envelope.

Elizabeth went home deep in thought.

That evening, she said to her husband, "No wonder the child was frightened of me. I have to make amends, so I'm going to invite her for a visit."

"I thought you hated other people's children," said Harold.

Elizabeth raised a delicately plucked eyebrow, and corrected her husband, "Not hate, dear, just dislike intensely. This girl is different and all because of such an ugly tragedy."

The next day, Elizabeth approached Marika as she played hopscotch on the sidewalk. She said pleasantly, "Hello, how are you?"

Marika peeked nervously over her shoulder, but the mean lady didn't look so mean anymore. She sounded like the Queen speaking to her subjects on television, and her regal beauty reminded the young girl of Margot Fonteyn, the famous English ballerina. She sort of looked like Audrey Hepburn too.

"I was born in England," said Marika timidly.

Elizabeth was elated. "Then we should be friends. I don't mind if you skate past my home, except from three to four in the afternoon during my beauty sleep. Would you like to meet Mr. Royal? He loves to have his tummy rubbed."

Marika was intrigued. "Who is Mr. Royal?"

Elizabeth opened her gate and pointed to a large fluffy grey cat lying on his back with four stubby limbs sticking up in the air. "Mr. Royal is an avid sun worshipper."

"Can I pet him?"

"Yes, but only if you call me Auntie Betty."

Ostrich Legs and Caterpillar Arms

Harold had a good chuckle that night as Elizabeth recounted her meeting with Marika. "Would you pass the salt, Auntie Betty?" he teased.

"No one is allowed to call me that, except Marika. Or you'll be sorry, Uncle Harry."

Her husband surrendered with an apologetic bow of his head. "Has she said anything about what happened to her?"

"Not a word. It's obvious the poor child doesn't remember."

Attila and Anna encouraged Marika's new friendship because they could see a spark in their daughter's solemn face every time she visited Auntie Betty.

One day, Marika showed up at Elizabeth's home with an uneven homemade haircut. "My mom likes short hair and won't let me grow mine. She says my hair hangs like string when it gets too long, but I feel ugly if it's short." Marika was so miserable, she was on the verge of tears. "The kids at school tell me I look like a boy, that I'm skinny and have ostrich legs with caterpillar arms."

"The time will come when you'll fill out very nicely, and with your height and exquisite face, you're going to look like a model. You wait and see. And don't worry about your short hair because in a few years you'll be able to wear it the way you want. Your mother will change, and so will you."

"How long is your hair?"

Elizabeth got up and pulled the pins out of her bun. As the last one was removed, jet black hair cascaded down to her waist. Ingesting two teaspoons of blackstrap molasses daily along with a good soak in the heated syrupy liquid kept the grey away.

Marika gasped with envy. "You have such long shiny hair."

"I'm going to share a secret with you. No one else is privy to this." Elizabeth noticed the confusion on Marika's face. "What I mean is that no one else has ever seen what I'm about to show you, not even my husband." She walked into the middle of her elegant sitting room, moved aside the coffee table, and rolled up the area rug. Then she took off her shoes. "I do this when I'm all alone. It makes me feel giddy and happy."

Elizabeth stood up on the balls of her stocking feet and executed a perfect pirouette, thanks to many years of childhood ballet lessons. As she gracefully twirled around and around, her long hair twirled after her. It was a mesmerizing scene. Finally, Elizabeth stopped and her hair fell back into place.

To think that Auntie Betty had never shared her secret with anyone else made Marika feel special. The magical moment was over, but she would remember it forever.

CHAPTER 11

Hide a Family

Tuesday, April 2, 1963 at 11:17 a.m.
Norlane, Geelong

The powers-that-be decided Niel was eligible for parole. He was pleased as punch, except there was no way in hell that he would report to a parole officer. He liked his plan better...hightail it to Coober Pedy where his relatives live and get lost in a cave.

"The screws won't never find me in the Outback."

But first, he wanted to prove to Igor he wasn't a doofart anymore. He was going to locate Marika for his dangerous cobber to make up for snitching on him. At the same time, he'll have some fun with her because his gaol mates didn't let him forget the reason he ended up behind bars. Rubbing his right leg, he remembered the day a metal pipe was wielded with a mighty swing to hit its mark. He walked with a permanent limp because the bone in his leg cracked to smithereens.

From the days of the trial, Niel remembered Marika's father worked at the Shell Refinery. He drove to Corio Bay and waited at a discreet distance in a car borrowed from an old mate. For the next two days, he waited nervously at the same spot until he recognized the tall blond figure walking towards the parking lot. He followed the grey Morris Oxford to Finch Street with a promise to return very soon.

On Friday, Marika came home early from school because a boy in her class sharpened his pencil to an invisible point and jammed it into her left thigh while she was reading Brer Rabbit and the Briar Patch. She wanted to scream from the sharp pain, but nothing happened. All she could do was sit at her desk and whimper like a sick puppy until the teacher told her to go home. She spent the afternoon flying back and forth on her royal blue painted swing wishing she could have stuck her pencil into the boy's flesh.

"Hey there, it's Marika, ain't it?" A scratchy voice at the front gate called out to the girl on the swing.

Marika looked over to find a scruffy haired, rat-faced man carrying a dirty grey duffle bag over his right shoulder. "How do you know my name?"

"You was this high when we met." Niel stuck his nicotine-stained hand out at knee level.

Marika got off the swing, slowly approaching the gate where Niel waited anxiously on the other side. "You know me?"

"That's what I'm sayin', ain't I? You're practically all growed up. Must be ten years old now." He said crudely, "Got any hair at the top of your legs yet?" He had to act fast. "Wanna go on a picnic with me up the street to a park? I got a lotta grub." He remembered the girl liked lolly. "An' licorice." Patting his duffle bag, he parted his lips in a smile that was a dentist's nightmare.

Marika jumped in fright when she saw the black teeth. Repulsed by his sinister dirtiness, she backed away, even though she was separated from him by the closed gate.

"Come on, what d'ya say?" Niel stiffened as he glanced towards the house.

"Marika! Go inside now!" Anna rushed from the back porch with a long kitchen broom in her hand. "Call your father and tell him to get the police!"

Marika ran inside the house. She poked a trembling finger into the holes on the telephone and dialed her daddy's office number, but a busy signal blared into her ear. Dropping the phone, she rushed into her bedroom and shut herself inside the wardrobe, desperately hoping the man won't hurt Mommy and then come after her.

Intense fear flooded Anna as she glared at the nasty looking man. She aimed the stick end of the broom from a safe distance to prevent him from grabbing it. "The police will be here any minute!"

Niel's face turned very ugly with the urge to throttle the woman in front of him. He reached for the gate, fumbling with the awkward latch.

Suddenly, he spotted a young couple walking down the street towards him. He said angrily, "I suffered because of your bitch of a daughter. So did Igor. He was swashed real bad in gaol, an' when he gets out he's goin' to pay you a visit."

Niel hurriedly limped up the street and around the corner of Melbourne Road to his waiting car.

The Next Day

Worlock could find no trace of Niel after scouring Geelong, and so far, the state troopers hadn't located him in the countryside. "Smithy was paroled ahead of schedule, and no one thought it important to let me know. He's probably headed for Coober Pedy in South Australia where unsavoury relatives live in caves."

"What are they, a bunch of animals?" said Attila.

"If I told you they gnaw on human bones, I wouldn't be far off the mark." The inspector winked at Attila to show he was joking. Sort of. "Actually, the main reason for living in caves is to beat the summer heat."

"Can you catch him?"

Worlock sighed. "Finding a shifty criminal who grew up in the Outback presents a challenge."

"I'm not scared of Smithy, but if he got this close to Marika, what's going to happen when Raznatovic is released from gaol?"

"If he behaves himself, he'll be paroled in four years."

The two men were sipping coffee as they sat at a rickety card table in the Paprika kitchen.

Attila said bitterly, "I wanted to talk to Anna about Smithy, have it out with her, but she began to pound the keys of her typewriter. It sounded like she was bashing the shit out of it."

Worlock nodded his head sympathetically. "It must be difficult carrying the burden all by yourself. She still doesn't remember?"

Attila shrugged his shoulders. "I don't know. If she doesn't, I can't risk her having a nervous breakdown by telling her what happened to Marika."

"Understandable."

With the threat of the nightmare starting all over again, Attila finally made up his mind. "Our life's become a waiting game. The only thing in my control is where we live."

"Where are you going?"

"Canada." Attila was going to break his promise about never again sailing on a boat, but it was made before his daughter's life was at stake.

"I hear Canada is a great country."

"It's about as far away as we can get from Raznatovic without having to go to the North Pole."

"I don't blame you, he's a crafty evil man. I could try my best to stoop to his level and think one step ahead of him, but even if I moved in with your family and watched over Marika like a hawk, there's no guarantee I will always be able to protect her."

Attila pondered the stark words. He was doing the right thing by taking his daughter far away.

Worlock realized he might never see the Paprikas again. "Here's my home address and phone number." He jotted in his notebook and tore the sheet off for Attila. "Keep in touch, won't you?"

Attila held out his hand to give the inspector a healthy handshake. "You've been a really decent chap." Worlock was the one constant in his messed up life.

"Do you need some help with expenses?"

"That's very kind of you, but Anna offered her inheritance."

Breaking the News

Marika didn't want to believe her mother. Moving to the other side of the world was beyond her scope of thinking. Sad expressions flickered across her face as she thought of her home, her country, her friends. She thought of Raelene and how they were inseparable, making it that much harder to give up a promising friendship.

"Everyone has a summer cottage, and there's snow in the winter. You'll love Canada with its green forests and blue lakes," offered Anna.

The dam was ready to burst. "No, I won't!" Marika ran to her room to release the flood of tears. She sobbed into her pillow as she cuddled her teddy bears. "My parents didn't even bother to ask me what I think about leaving Australia, a crazy girl who wonders if she can fly."

Attila's Way

Attila borrowed two bicycles from the Coopers and coerced Anna into riding around Norlane with him. Unfortunately, his wife rode two-wheelers like she drove automobiles, but that didn't stop Attila. He wanted to remember every last inch of the place he fondly called home for the last several years. And what better way than riding a bike. He plunked a protesting Anna on his handlebar and away they went, just the two of them enjoying the speed of Attila's pumping legs, with Anna shrieking in between giggles like a lovestruck teenager.

June 10, 1963

The Big Day

Anna tried to convince her daughter that it was time to let go of her teddy bears. Their fur was worn, Teddy was missing his red bow tie and stringy hair, but to throw them away was unthinkable to Marika. It was bad enough that she had to leave behind her beloved red tricycle. After nestling the bears into her bag of clothes, she had to say goodbye to her best friend.

Marika sat forlornly on Raelene's porch feeling lonely already. "I'm going to miss you."

Raelene twirled a lock of curly red hair around her forefinger. "Me too. My mom says she wishes we could move to Canada."

"Can I write to you? We can be pen pals and visit each other."

"Okay."

It was time to say goodbye to one more person. Marika's special grown up friend.

Elizabeth handed over a gift and gave the sad face a kiss and a hug. "I will miss you, Marika. Don't forget, you are going to be a beautiful young lady. I know this with absolute certainty."

The gift was a small white jewelry box. When Marika lifted the lid, Elizabeth's floral scented perfume floated up to her nose as a tiny pink ballerina twirled around to the tinkling of chime music. She watched in wonder, remembering their secret. "Thank you, Auntie Betty." Big tears from the girl's eyes plopped onto the black and white checkerboard linoleum. She gave Elizabeth one last hug and ran out the back door.

Standing in front of the yellow stucco bungalow which held most of her life, she said with overwhelming sadness, "Goodbye."

CHAPTER 12

Home Sweet Canada

Friday, July 5, 1963 at 10:20 p.m.
Vancouver, Canada

From the railing of the S.S. Oriana, the Paprikas watched darkness settle over Vancouver. Haloed lights dotted the city's magnificent skyline of tall buildings and mountains as they waited to begin their new life in Canada.

Anna knew her family was where they were supposed to be. Beside her, Attila was silently saying goodbye to the best job he ever had, but he didn't miss it enough to want to go back. He also had no regrets about what he did with a box of matches on their last day in Australia.

Marika looked at her mom and dad with great despair. Being eleven years old and acutely homesick, she was faithful to Australia because it was her home, not this country which snowed in winter.

One Month Later
Thorncliffe Park, Toronto

Attila and his family took a train eastward to the province of Ontario after unsuccessful attempts to find employment in Vancouver. They moved to

Thorncliffe Park, a former racetrack for thoroughbred horses transformed into a new community for baby boomers, one of Toronto's first high-rise communities. There was something different about it. Low-rise apartment buildings were built inside a semi-circular configuration of high-rise buildings lining the outer edge. The taller apartments had spectacular views of the Don Valley, a city paradise of trails, trees, and picnic benches.

Somebody must have had a sense of humour or an interesting way of remembering the former racetrack — the architectural design created a horseshoe-shaped community. Within the horseshoe was a parkette, a public school, a library. At the open end of the horseshoe was an indoor shopping mall, Thorncliffe Plaza, one of the first of its kind in Canada.

With very little money left, the Paprikas' apartment was bare except for cheap beds, one dresser with a drawer for each of them, a coffee table, a sofa, and an armchair. Blankets covered the windows for privacy. A long narrow hallway connected an extra large L-shaped living/dining room and galley kitchen to three bedrooms and one and a half bathrooms. Anna was pleased to have a proper refrigerator, the freezer compartment already needing to be defrosted. As for Marika, she enjoyed living fifteen floors above the ground because of the balcony, spending many nights watching the bountiful stars in the sky.

When they realized two incomes were needed to support their modest lifestyle, the population of civil servants increased by two. Anna became a clerk for OHSIP, the Ontario Health Services Insurance Plan, and Attila joined the Department of National Revenue as a federal tax auditor. His Australian accounting courses weren't recognized in Canada which meant he'd have to start all over if he wanted a degree. Like bloody hell, he thought. He'll make do as an auditor until he had enough tax experience to advance to unit head, his ultimate goal.

Marika fought hard to remain loyal to Geelong, visiting it in her nightly dreams, writing letters to Raelene. She promised to hate Canada forever and begged her parents every day to put her on a ship back to Australia. In spite of her animosity, she had no trouble making friends quickly because the kids at school genuinely welcomed the shy Aussie girl with the funny name.

The family had barely settled in when Attila bought a used Pontiac Skylark, taking them on many trips to discover Ontario. Two of their favourite spots turned out to be Algonquin Park, a wildlife sanctuary with vast lands covered in trees and thousands of islands, and the immensely popular Niagara Falls, the majestic aura of its powerful rushing waters reaching out to enthralled visitors as they leaned against dangerously low railings for the perfect snapshot. There was something invigorating about the air that surrounded the cascading waters, leaving people with a good feeling.

Two years later, the Paprikas' apartment was full of furniture and nice curtains. Marika had friends and stopped whining for Geelong. The crazy girl who thinks she can fly had fallen in love with Canada.

CHAPTER 13

An Unexpected Trip

Saturday, July 9, 1966
Toronto, Canada

Marika gazed into the full length mirror leaning against her bedroom wall. She said happily to her blossoming image, "Auntie Betty was right, I'm starting to fill out."

She was all of fourteen, but already stood five feet nine inches. Long in limbs, slender in body, beautiful in face, her thick auburn hair was worn long and straight. The tiny black mole under her left eye drew people to her big eyes. And like all budding teenagers, she was more self-absorbed with what she didn't like.

Anna caught her daughter poking and pulling at her hair.

"What's wrong? I can hear you complaining from the kitchen."

"Stupid cowlick dominates my whole face." Marika licked it down with spit-covered fingers.

"It enhances your face," Anna corrected her daughter's negative attitude. *She's so much like her father.* "Yesterday it was the itty bitty bump on the bridge of your lovely nose. Tomorrow it will be your mole."

"The bump is grotesquely huge. I want a nose job."

"You want a doctor to break your nose with a hammer?" Anna was horrified at the thought.

"You're just trying to scare me out of it."

Anna waved a dismissive hand in the air. There was no point talking to Marika when she was engrossed in herself. She returned to the kitchen to make a pot of csipetke, the family's favourite pinched dumplings which would pair up perfectly with some leftover chicken paprikash.

Marika trotted on her mother's heels seeking reassurance there was no similarity between her nose and Jimmy Durante's schnozzola.

Attila looked up from his living room armchair positioned part way into the dining room and right beside the kitchen entrance. He put the tv guide down and said, "The Paprika nose has been in my family for generations. Boring families pass down junk like jewelry, antiques, land, houses, whereas the interesting Paprikas pass down a bump on the nose. Be proud and wear it well."

"You're kidding, right?" Marika walked up to her dad and stared at him until she caught a twinkle in his eye.

"Yes, I am, except for, be proud and wear it well."

"Yuck!" Marika let him know she totally disagreed. Disgust registered on her face as she decided to tackle her cowlick again.

Although Anna was busy scraping the csipetke from a tablespoon into boiling salted water, she felt unappreciated, and couldn't keep the hurt from her voice, "I went to a lot of trouble to make the cowlick for you. When you were a little girl, I used to twirl a lock of your hair until it stood up by itself."

"You're responsible for this freaking tuft!" Marika shrieked incredulously. "Mom, I will never speak to you again!"

Anna was shocked at her daughter's hostile reaction. "Is that any way to talk to me?"

"Apologize to your mother," Attila chided Marika.

Marika ran to the bathroom just in time see the cowlick spring back to life. She had better get used to the kink because it was going nowhere. "Mom! Come here!" she shouted as if her clothes were on fire.

When Anna found her daughter fussing with her cowlick, she scolded her, "You should only scream like that if there's an emergency. Do you want me to have a heart attack?"

Marika said forlornly, "Sorry for the drama queen thing. I hate being a teenager."

All was forgiven with the apology. "Come here, pet." Anna put a consoling arm around her daughter. "Do you know I used to do things to make myself more beautiful? Women are like that, especially the younger ones."

"Is being shy around guys part of growing up? Bess is my age, but she doesn't have any trouble with them."

"When you look into the mirror, you don't see your best friend, do you?" Anna pinched her daughter's pale cheeks to make them pink. This time Marika was too slow to escape her mother's annoying attempts to rearrange her face. "The boys are even more shy than you because of your beauty. Teenage males don't like rejection, so they wait for you to make the first move." Anna tried to make her daughter feel better. "It will change."

"A guy will say hi, and I say hi back. Then stupid things happen to me like soggy armpits and stammering. So, what do I do? I leave very quickly and usually trip while I'm at it." She added morosely, "I'm surprised I haven't farted in front of a guy."

"Don't be vulgar, dear." Anna led Marika back to the kitchen. "Make yourself useful and take care of the csipetke. We don't want them to be overcooked." After watching her daughter strain the steaming dumplings through a colander, she offered, "I'll let you in on a little secret, darling. Women are better than men."

"I heard that, Anna," said an offended Attila.

"You shouldn't listen to other people's conversations."

"Then other people should not be having conversations in front of husbands."

Whenever Attila passed blame back onto Anna, it always exasperated her. But she decided to ignore him because she had a story to tell her daughter, right after she finished tossing the dumplings in a light drizzle of corn oil to keep them from sticking together.

Once Anna was ready, she said, "You've got to let the power of imagination make you strong."

"What?"

"Remember the Hungarian butcher who defied a Soviet tank?"

"Not again," groaned Marika.

Anna was not dissuaded. "The story contains a valuable lesson."

"It's only valuable if a Soviet tank gets in my way."

"Maybe this time you will listen, and get it." Anna wagged her finger at Marika. "During the war, a homeless man made his bed by the side of the road..."

"What road?" Marika interrupted her mother.

"For God's sake, what does it matter what road? And don't think I'm so stupid that I have no idea you're being sarcastic. Now be quiet." Anna started again, "The homeless man needed to quell his relentless demons with alcohol."

"Amen," said Attila in the vapid tone of a preacher.

Anna left the kitchen to confront her husband who was reclining comfortably in the armchair, his feet resting on a footstool. When he looked up, she gave him a dirty look.

An anxious Marika could see the signs of a potentially nasty argument -- Anna's insulting remark about men, the dirty look, Attila telling Anna it was her fault that he was listening to her private conversation with Marika. To distract her parents, the limber girl dived onto the sofa. It was a rather cheap piece of furniture with skinny wooden legs and noisy springs that squeaked and boinged loudly. "Okay, Mom. I'm listening." She pretended to sound enthusiastic.

"Do you have to launch yourself into the sofa like a torpedo? You'll break it one day." Now that Anna had simmered down, she resumed her story which was meant to inspire listeners with its message, not provoke snide remarks from unappreciative husbands and children. "As I was saying before I was so rudely interrupted, a homeless man slept beside the road. He drank anything with alcohol including bottles of lavender cologne, and one day while he lay beside the road in a drunken stupor, his left foot became pinned under a Soviet artillery tank that had stopped to survey the area. Sixteen tons of metal caused him to emit a scream that would shatter plexiglass."

Attila corrected his wife, "Industrial strength glass."

"Do you want to tell the story, Mr. Know-It-All?"

Attila picked up the tv guide again. He was thinking he should turn on the television and drown out his wife's ridiculous tale.

"The bone-chilling cry caught the attention of a butcher down the road. Stepping outside the butcher shop with fresh sausage links in his hands, he hurried towards the unholy noise as a crowd of children and old women converged on the scene. He knew he had to act quickly, but being of medium height and build, he was not an unusually strong man. Nevertheless, with sausage links now wrapped around his average neck like a fat pink pearl necklace, he grabbed the bottom of the belted wheel. He imagined himself lifting the tank, and with incredible determination, he heaved it a good six inches off the road which gave the old women an opportunity to pull the homeless man out of harm's way. The butcher let go of the tank, and the women who had seen just about everything during the war were very impressed with him." Anna sighed with satisfaction. The story kept getting better and better, aging like a fine wine.

Marika said facetiously, "But all the red-faced butcher could think about was what to say to the Soviet rearing his hideous head from the tank. Let's hope he likes sausages."

She and her dad began to hoot with laughter.

Anna twisted her mouth mockingly. "Very funny, young lady. What's not to like about a story which boasts of the Hungarian spirit?"

"Newsflash, Mom. It's so fake!"

"Go ahead, be like your father. I choose to believe."

Attila said proudly, "Like father, like daughter."

"Oh, shut up!" shouted Anna.

Marika switched to another subject quickly. "Can we change our last name to something that makes us sound cool, so kids will stop making fun?"

"No, for the thousandth time."

Marika changed the subject again. "Mom, I want to go swimming at the Donview Club next door, so I bought a bikini with my allowance." She scrunched up her face, hoping her mother won't object to the revealing costume.

"You can't be that shy if you're willing to wear a skimpy bathing suit. It doesn't show half your breasts and bum, does it?"

"No, Mom. I'll show you." Marika bounced out of the living room.

She stood in front of her bedroom mirror checking the graceful lines of red and black swirls decorating her modest bikini. As she twisted around to get a rear view, she noticed pale marks on the lower part of an otherwise unblemished back. She moved close to the mirror, still twisted in an awkward position. Counting four pale pink lines as thick as the fattest worms covering the sidewalk after a heavy rainfall, she wondered what they were.

Anna walked into Marika's bedroom. "That's a lovely figure in a nice bikini, so you have nothing to worry about."

"Mom, what are these strange marks?"

Anna visually inspected her daughter's back. "They're stretch marks. Stop worrying so much because you can hardly see them."

"Don't you have to be fat and lose weight to get stretch marks?"

"Maybe you have a skin condition."

Marika gave her mother a doubtful look. "They do kind of look like stretch marks, but they're so uneven and slanted."

"You're making a mountain out of a mole hill."

Wednesday, September 28, 1966
Leaside High School

Marika stood in the gymnasium self-consciously wearing her school's totally unflattering blue bloomers which poofed out at the hips like a mule carrying a stuffed saddle. Her gym teacher Mrs. Lakefield was waiting for Bill Underwood, the creator of Defendo, a defence technique so simple to use that even eighty year old women could ward off burly thugs. And yet it was respected enough to earn him invitations to train police officers around the country.

When Marika saw Bess joking around with classmates, she felt left out. Her best friend was three inches shorter than her, and being a serious female jock, she was very strong and muscular. Her size six feet made Marika's niner's look positively huge. What attracted the guys were Bess's long sunny blonde hair, baby blue eyes, and cute snub nose.

A laughing Bess joined Marika. "Hey, somebody's grandfather just walked in wearing black ballet slippers."

"That must be Bill Underwood. Stop laughing."

"Lighten up." Bess playfully pulled on a strand of Marika's hair who in turn yanked roughly on her best friend's hair. The latter yelped.

Mrs. Lakefield settled a cold look on Marika. The teacher was used to her star athlete horsing around, but Marika should know better than to respond. It only encouraged Bess Taylor to be a rebellious spirit instead of reaching her potential to dominate high school sports.

Marika looked away dejectedly, feeling the heat of embarrassment crawling all over her face and scalp. She hated any kind of attention.

The school guest stood in the middle of the gymnasium holding his giant belly in a ho-ho-ho Santa Claus grip. When he introduced himself, he spoke with a soft lisp as if his dentures didn't fit properly. "Hi kids. I'm Bill Underwood, and I do look like somebody's grandfather."

Marika expected Mrs. Lakefield to lecture Bess, but the teacher joined the group laughter. She muttered, "Teacher's pet."

Bill Underwood announced, "If I can get a two hundred and ninety pound man to go down on his knees and beg for mercy by bending his thumb back, so can you."

By the end of the demonstration, Marika knew how to bend digits, twist limbs, and toss people with minimum effort, and yet have her pretend assailant literally crawling on the floor in submission. The technique was so easy that she practised on her parents for several weeks until they finally begged her to stop.

"This is neat stuff," Marika said with admiration.

Victoria, Australia
Monday, January 2, 1967 at 10:00 a.m.

Father Donovan
Igor marked off his last day in Pentridge, drawing a black cross on the calendar hanging on the bare cell wall. He hated the stinking rectangular closet

of a room that was home for the last nine years and four months, and was glad to be paroled a month early. He didn't want to be late for his and Marika's tenth anniversary. As he glanced around the cell, he remembered the day he was attacked by Pete. It took a long time to recover from the surgery for his ripped innards. He received a few more bashings for being a pervert. When he didn't hand over his tobacco rations fast enough, that was cause for a punch in the stomach or the face, leaving him with a broken nose and another lost tooth.

He never had to break another rock again even though the hard labour kept him strong. Hands resting on his head, he touched the bald spot baring his scalp. He needed his hat. Then he would find Marika, her home address etched into his memory after a prison visit from one of Niel's felonious mates, a peace offering for having to rat him out at the trial.

As Igor walked the corridor to freedom, the warder couldn't resist a parting shot. "Hey Iggy, Father Donovan is waiting for his new altar boy."

Igor was sick and tired of people insulting his name. "It's Igor, you idiot," he said in a surly tone. No need to think twice about offending a uniform now.

The warder slammed the door behind Pentridge's least popular resident.

Igor breathed in a lungful of fresh air piggybacking a brisk breeze. It was good to rejoin the world.

Father Donovan bestowed a holy smile on the released prisoner as he watched him fill his chest with oxygen. The priest was a jovial rotund figure with a bald head and no eyebrows, but any resemblance to a bowling ball was purely coincidental. As he approached Igor, his long sleeved black cassock flapped against his legs, and although it was made of lightweight cotton, its black weave drew the sun's rays; a sweaty inconvenience he was willing to endure for his devotion to the church. He adjusted his detachable white collar to stop it from chafing his neck.

Producing a weak smile, Igor cupped his hands and meekly held them out. After all, he needed to keep on fooling the priest. "Bless me, Father."

During gaol visits, Father Donovan noticed the Bible clutched in Igor's hands, and believed the prisoner when he tearfully expressed remorse for the pain he caused his little victim. The Father made the sign of the cross and warmly said, "Blessed art thou, and it shall be well with thee."

Igor was using the good Father for two things; a sanctuary and a job. Both would come in handy when he finished off Marika. His instant respectability will confuse the police who may suspect him, but won't be able to prove it, especially if they can't find a body, or him, if he decided to disappear.

At first, he wanted Niel to grab Marika and bring her to him, but that would have meant hunting down a doofart noodling for opals in Coober Pedy. And the only way to get there was to trudge through a blistering Outback crawling with Murris and grubworms. He was going to have to get Marika himself.

Having a priest in his pocket provided the parolee with a small rent-free house and the use of a second-hand car, both donated to the church by Father Donovan's parishioners. The house was located in an isolated area above a gorge in the Pink Cliffs Reserve of Heathcote, a former gold rush town with colourful pink clay soil exposed through years of mining.

The hub of the 1800's gold craze was the northwest city of Bendigo which was a half hour drive from Heathcote. And although much of the green landscape of Bendigo and the surrounding towns were stripped down by the early miners, there were still breathtaking views of mountains overlooking rocky gorges and valleys of evergreen, gum and eucalyptus trees, winding rivers and creeks. If one wanted more fun and excitement than Heathcote and Bendigo could offer, a pleasant drive southwards would find the capital city of Melbourne.

Igor's life got even better when he was offered a modest salary to tend the grounds of Father Donovan's church, the Sacred Heart Cathedral in Bendigo, a breathtaking example of Gothic revival architecture with marble floors and a magnificent carved timber ceiling.

What parole officer wouldn't be impressed with all that?

Thursday, February 2, 1967 at 1:15 p.m.

God is on My Side
It had been harder to wait out the past two months than it was during all the years spent in gaol. Father Donovan was away on church business for the next ten days. As Igor didn't have to see his parole officer for another week, there was nothing stopping him from going after Marika.

He stared at his face in the bathroom mirror. It was marked by deep folds, a twisted broken nose, his cheeks and lips sunken because of six missing teeth. He refused to wear his uncomfortable bridge, but now he put it into his mouth. A toothless man would attract more attention. He put on his only suit, attempting to smooth away the black wrinkles with his hands before putting on his beloved fedora. He stroked the brim, remembering the day he was reunited with his hat.

"I am handsome again." Igor admired his reflection in the mirror. He was ready. "I'm coming for you, Marika."

Walking over to a dresser in his bedroom, Igor pulled out a flat custom-made oak case and opened the lid to reveal seven long depressions fanned out across the width of soft black velvet. One of the depressions was already filled with an object, an exquisite knife of infinite beauty which would inflict much damage if it slid in and out of tender young flesh. He tied a rope around the knife handle and pinned it to the inside of his jacket before getting in the car and driving in a southward direction towards Geelong. Two hours later, he was parked outside Norlane Grammar School after preliminary research confirmed the school's close proximity to Finch Street. As a teenager, Marika must be enrolled there for the new school year.

His arrival was timed for afternoon dismissal. In a matter of minutes, girls and boys in dark grey school uniforms piled out of the doors to go home. Igor waited as if he were someone's father searching the groups of chattering kids, but there was no sign of Marika. He knew what she looked like because he dreamed about her all the time, watching her grow up right inside his head. Her reddish brown hair was long and straight, and he could never forget those big eyes and the mole.

Half an hour later, the last of the student stragglers were gone. He was now alone, wondering what happened to Marika. The janitor was busy sweeping the steps, so the brick building must be empty.

Igor drove slowly towards Finch Street hoping to find her walking home, but there was no one resembling her. He parked the car outside 1 Finch Street, scanning the neighbourhood as he cautiously approached the wrought iron gate, the same spot that Niel degraded with his putrid presence. He took a calculated risk, but at this time of day, no car in the driveway, Attila was at work. The mother he could handle if she showed up.

"Excuse me, are you looking for someone?" A young female standing on the sidewalk interrupted Igor's three minute silence.

Twirling around in surprise, he looked into the unfriendly eyes of a petite blonde-haired woman with black roots, holding a gurgling baby. Disappointment registered on his face because it wasn't Marika or her mother. His body was taut and ready to pounce, but now he forced himself to relax. He pointed at the yellow stucco bungalow. "I'm an old friend of the Paprikas who live here," he said in his thick Yugoslavian accent.

"They don't live here. I do."

Igor couldn't believe his ears.

The woman didn't feel comfortable with the foreign stranger standing at her gate dressed inappropriately in black from head to toe like a deranged vampire on such a hot summer day. Her voice took on a defensive tone, "Would you like to speak to my husband? He's in the house."

Igor tried to digest the unwelcome news.

"Are you looking for the Paprikas?"

Igor turned to see a young girl with short curly red hair and a face drenched in freckles walking towards him. She was dressed in the grey uniform of Norlane Grammar School. "They moved to Canada. Did you say you're a friend of theirs?"

Canada. Igor could hardly contain himself. *Relax, don't mess it up. I've come this far because God is on my side.* He smiled broadly, and was glad he was wearing his bridge. "We are old friends. I'm from Hungary too, as you can probably tell from my accent." *Stupid Australians can't tell the difference between a Yugoslav or a Hungarian.* "Do you have their address in Canada?" He clutched at the hardness of the knife hiding inside his jacket, giving it a quick downward stroke to soothe his addled mind.

Raelene looked at the stranger, wondering what to do. Igor kept smiling until she finally said, "I'll give it to you." She tore a piece of paper from her school book and wrote down Marika's new address.

Igor grabbed the paper without saying a word. This unexpected turn of events was going to make him late for their anniversary.

CHAPTER 14

Obsession

Saturday, February 4, 1967 at 9:05 a.m.
Toronto, Canada

    Igor arrived in Canada with time to spare. He just had to remember his return to Australia was going to reduce his cushion by tacking on an extra day when he crossed back over the international date line. He grumbled at the stewardess who wished him a pleasant stay in Toronto. At first, he was furious that Marika dared to move away from him. She was supposed to be waiting for him to take her, but the more he thought about the change in his plan, the more he preferred it. Here in Toronto, thousands of miles away from the copper Worlock, he could finish his mission and be safely back in Heathcote. No one would be the wiser. If fingers started pointing at him, he could be conveniently lost in the Outback, just like Niel. Even if he was caught, he didn't care. Marika would be dead and he'd be at peace.
    He drove his rented car out of Toronto International Airport. Checking into the nearby Regal Constellation Hotel, the first thing he did was pick up the phone book. Running his finger along the page, he stopped half way down at the single listing for Paprika. Sure enough, they were living at the address the freckle-

faced Aussie kid gave him. Making no attempt to hide from him, they must think he's no longer a threat to their precious daughter.

As he dialed the phone number, he chuckled at the parents' stupidity. Then he checked his watch. It was lunch hour on a Saturday, so the object of his mission had to be eating lunch. "Pick up the phone, Marika." After so many years, he desperately needed to hear her voice. His impatient fingers stretched the black spiral telephone cord.

"Hello?"

The young female voice spoke softly into Igor's ear which caused his heart to palpitate. He closed his eyes and envisioned Marika in all her glory.

"Hello?" When Marika still got no reply, she hung up the phone. At first, she thought it was Bess because they had a date to play mini-golf on the lower level of Thorncliffe Plaza. Maybe it was a guy from school who wanted to hear her voice. She felt a twinge of sadness. That was all any guy will get from her.

When the apartment buzzer sounded forty minutes later, she spoke into the intercom, "Okay, Bess." She threw on her green elephant-wale corduroy car coat, pulled on her black knee high boots, and was nearly out the front door when the intercom buzzed again. She pushed the button. "What is it?"

"Is this Marika?" A young crackly male voice spoke with hesitation. "It's Jeff. Someone wants you to come down."

It was a kid who lived in her building. "Who does?"

"A friend."

"A girl?"

"No."

"So, a boy."

"Kind of."

What does that mean? Marika's stomach fluttered with butterflies. What if it was Travis Loner, the Leaside football player she admired from afar? He seemed to be very interested in her. Should she go without waiting for Bess? Marika made a quick decision. "I'm coming down." She ran to her bedroom closet, pulling out her favourite pair of bell bottom jeans and a stringy crocheted top. Then she realized it would take too long to change, and decided to make do with her white blouse, navy blue mini-skirt, and heavy black tights. She couldn't keep Travis waiting.

She ran to the bathroom mirror to comb her hair before rushing out of the apartment, shouting happily, "See you later, Dad!"

Marika took the elevator down to the lobby, and walked nervously outside to the front of the building. *You can do it, scaredy cat. Just smile, say hi, and whatever you do, don't run away this time.*

A couple of days ago, a heavy snowfall was plowed to the edge of the street and sidewalks, leaving white hills near the Paprikas' twenty storey apartment building. A cold snap was putting a deep chill in the air which made Marika shiver as she stepped outside. She buttoned up her car coat, watching a middle-aged man in a black coat and hat walking towards her.

Igor stopped in front of Marika, hiding his tumultuous emotions with a serene smile. She looked exactly like she did in his dreams. Heat rose from his torso, filling his head until it pounded in monotonous rhythm. He wanted to take her hand and go back to his waiting car. A memory from yesteryear when she put her tiny hand in his, and they went to the barn to begin their journey together.

Kids were playing in the snow banks under the watchful eyes of a couple of parents, so he had to make her come with him willingly, just like he did ten years ago. She must still like lolly, or maybe something else nice and sweet.

"Hello, Marika. My name is Igor Raznatovic." His hot breath puffed out in clouds which blew into her face to join the air coming out of her nose. He wasn't worried because he knew she wouldn't recognize his name.

Marika listened respectfully to the man's velvet accent while looking every which way for Travis. She said in a disappointed voice, "Hello."

"I'm an old family friend."

"You know my mom and dad?"

"I knew you as a little girl."

"I'll tell my dad you're here." Marika was curious. She thought the only visitor her father was expecting today was Willy Winston, his best friend. It was their poker and television sports day.

Igor jumped slightly. *Don't do that, you dirty girl.* "I'll see him later. Right now, I'd like to talk to you." He smiled again, fully aware it produced a hypnotic effect when he wanted it to. "I know you because we had a special relationship."

Marika didn't remember the stranger, not even his crooked nose seemed familiar. "My parents never mentioned you. How do you say your last name again?"

"Raznatovic."

"Razan...towing. Sorry, I can't say it."

"I live in Australia and that's where I met you." To reduce any anxiety Marika might be feeling towards him, Igor said, "And your parents." He stomped his new black shoes on the ground. "I forgot how cold it gets in the northern hemisphere, so I'm not wearing warm boots like you." He pointed towards the teenager's legs.

The mention of her old home lowered Marika's guard. "Are you from Geelong?"

"Bacchus Marsh." Igor's black eyes darted nervously to the lobby door, afraid of Attila pouncing on him and blowing his plans to kingdom come.

"I don't remember Bacchus Marsh. Why don't you go up and see my dad?" Marika motioned towards the lobby.

"No!" Igor immediately apologized, "I'm sorry, it's just that I'm so happy to see you again." He needed to ask the same burning question from a long time ago. "Do you go to church every Sunday?"

Marika frowned at the peculiar question. "Not really."

Igor struggled to hide his immense displeasure. "I remember how much you like lolly. I'll buy some for you, or do you like ice cream?" He started to move towards his maroon rental car parked at the curb. "Would you like to go to the Regal Constellation Hotel? It has all kinds of ice cream, and then you can show me the city."

Ice cream in winter? What a nerd. "No, thank you." Marika had no intention of going with the strange man.

Igor was losing her. He said with urgency, "The chocolate ice cream is delicious. Is chocolate your favourite? How about vanilla or strawberry?"

Marika shook her head and backed away from the stranger as he tried to entice her with his outstretched arm.

Igor was beyond desperate and surveyed the area again. The parents had left with their children, leaving one playing down by the end of the building. He moved quickly towards Marika, his eyes locked onto her as if she were a target on a radar screen. One more step and he could drag her to the car.

"Marika, you were supposed to wait for my call. Ready to go?"

Igor stopped as if a freight train hit him. He was so preoccupied with Marika that he didn't notice anyone approaching from behind. A tough looking girl with long blonde hair wearing a purple coat and the same kind of boots as Marika's appeared out of nowhere. She had a voice to match her strong body which made him think she won't be afraid to get physical and scream if he touched Marika.

"Hi, Bess." Marika turned to look back at Igor. "It was nice meeting you, but I have to go now. Bye." She waved at him as she walked with Bess to the sidewalk, busy now with people getting off the Thorncliffe bus.

Igor burned with disappointment. He had lost his opportunity to nab Marika.

Bess cautiously watched the man in the black coat and hat. "He's looking at you in a real gross way. Who is he?"

"Kind of strange, isn't he? Says he's an old friend of my parents. I told him to go upstairs, but he just kept talking to me."

"Check him out. He looks like he wants to do something really horrible to you."

Marika shoved her best friend in the shoulder. "Don't be silly, Bess." She glanced sideways to find Igor glaring at her as he walked towards the maroon car. Bess was right. He looked like he hated her, but that's ridiculous; a minute ago he oozed nice. Nothing made sense right now, except maybe he's angry that she didn't want to share ice cream with him. She lifted her hand to wave goodbye again, hoping to placate him, but Igor continued to project a real ugly, sinister face.

"Let's go. Forget about the weirdo."

Marika felt bad about making the stranger angry. "I don't like hurting his feelings. Do you think I'm crazy?"

"Yes. Now let's go have some fun, crazy girl."

A Name from the Past

When Marika returned home two hours later, there was no sign of the stranger or his car. As she walked down the hall towards her apartment, she heard her dad laughing loudly. The stranger must have parked his car in the visitor's area at the back and gone up to visit her dad.

She found Attila sitting alone in the living room watching the family's new black and white Admiral television set. "What are you laughing at?"

"My hero."

"That would be Bugs Bunny." Marika sat down on the couch to watch the rabbit having fun at Daffy Duck's expense. "I met an old friend of yours and mom's outside. Told him to come up and see you."

Attila was paying more attention to the cartoon than to what his daughter was saying. If he had to make a choice between his hero or his cigarettes, it would be a close one. "Mmm."

"Dad!"

"Who was it?"

"He said his name was Igor Raz...Raz..." Marika stuttered over the last name becoming a vague memory already.

A dreaded name from the past caused Attila's heart to explode like a water bomb inside his chest. He had to force himself to remain outwardly calm. "I don't know anyone by the name of Igor Raz Raz."

"No, Dad, just one Raz and something on the end of it. He knew my name and mentioned Australia."

"Doesn't ring a bell." Attila was being honest this time because the psycho rapist's name was actually ringing every bloody emergency alarm in the northern hemisphere, and it was all happening inside his head. His daughter had no idea what he was thinking and he wanted to keep it that way. He asked as pleasantly as he could, "Is he still here?"

"I didn't see him downstairs."

"What did he seem like?"

"He kind of talked to me like I was a little girl."

"Did he say anything else?" Attila lit a cigarette while he paced the living room floor, his trembling kneecaps making it difficult to walk.

"He wanted me to go to the Regal Constellation Hotel for ice cream. I think I hurt his feelings because he acted strange when I wouldn't go with him."

Yeah, I bet, thought Attila. "It's just one of those unexplainable encounters like a case of mistaken identity. Don't worry about it." He silently cursed himself for not protecting his daughter better.

Marika shrugged her shoulders. "Okay, Dad. You seem tense."

"I'm missing the Bugs Bunny show."

Marika giggled as she went into her bedroom. She closed the door, and turned on her portable record player. Time for some Rubber Soul. Every single song on the album was a masterpiece of poetry, harmony and rhythm.

As soon as the usual cacophony of Beatles music blared from his daughter's room, Attila turned off the television. He picked up the phone to call Worlock, then put the receiver down. What could the man do from Australia? As the inspector once said, even if he moved in with the Paprikas, he couldn't guarantee Marika will be protected from an evil like Raznatovic. Calling the local police would bring clumsy cops to his home asking unwanted questions. He won't be able to keep the secret from her anymore. Horrible memories rushed back to haunt him, making the familiar sick feeling churn his stomach.

The intercom buzzed, and Attila froze. *The bastard's back. Calm down and answer the intercom. Pretend to be Marika.* The intercom was a piece of junk, so he could pull it off.

"Yes, hello?" Attila spoke in a soft falsetto voice, his heart thumping madly, causing pressure to build up in his chest until he could hardly take a decent breath.

"Anna? Marika? It's Willy."

Attila reverted to his normal voice. "Oh, it's you." He forgot his best friend was coming over for the afternoon. The pressure in his chest eased off slightly as he let go of the intercom button.

The intercom buzzed again. Attila said, "Yes?"

"Tone down the enthusiasm, my bredda." Willy liked to throw in a bit of Jamaican patois once in a while. "I can't play poker with you if you don't open the door. Is there some sort of password to get in?"

"Sorry, Willy." Attila unlocked the lobby door.

There was no time to waste. He quickly picked up the phone and dialed the operator. "I want the number and address for the Regal Constellation Hotel." Within thirty seconds, he was speaking to the hotel's front desk. "Do you have a guest named Igor Raznatovic?"

"Yes, sir. He went up to his room a short while ago. I'll connect you."

"No! I just want to know if he's staying there." Attila put the phone down, thinking the bastard was arrogant enough to register in his own name. *At least he's not hanging around Thorncliffe Park.*

There was a knock on the front door. When Attila opened it, a big black man with golden honey skin and crinkled light brown hair greeted him with a nudge on the shoulder. "Hey, man, what's up with the girly voice? Something wrong with your high tech intercom?" His famous horsey laugh filled the apartment as he tapped the cheap metal box beside the front door.

The two men became instant friends at work because Attila liked the friendly Jamaican who was as big a soccer fan as he was. Willy enjoyed the Hungarian's sarcastic sense of humour and intelligence.

It was hard not to be affected by Willy's hilarious neighing, but today was different. There would be no teasing today because Attila could only think about Igor. He said, "An emergency has come up, so I have to leave for awhile. Anna should be home shortly and Marika's in her room." He gave a tense smile. "Willy, you'll be doing me a big favour if you stick around to make sure she stays home. Don't allow anyone else into the apartment, besides Anna. Okay?"

Willy was perplexed, wanting to ask what all the mystery was about, but he knew his best friend well enough to know that now was not a good time. He merely said, "Sure, my bredda. Is there anything I can do to help with the emergency?"

"You're doing that by babysitting Marika. There's beer in the fridge and pretzels on the table. Oh yeah, and sloppy Joes on the stove." Attila rushed out of the apartment before Willy could say anything else.

The Hunt is On

Attila drove to the Regal Constellation Hotel in his blue Buick Skylark praying furiously that Igor was still there. Many years had passed and the urge to kill him had died down, but if he saw the beast again, he knew the flames could be fanned just by looking at his grotesque face. He was going to beat Igor into a coma. Afterwards, he would decide whether to finish the job or call the police. He didn't want to go to gaol because of Igor, but if it meant Marika will finally be safe, he had no choice.

Forty-five minutes later, Attila was running through the lobby of the hotel. He breathlessly asked the desk clerk for Igor's room number.

"I'm sorry, sir. Mr. Raznatovic checked out."

"Damn it!" Attila banged the desk in frustration. "Did he say where he was going?"

The surprised clerk said, "No, sir."

Attila ran over to the nearest pay phone.

Anna picked up the ringing phone. "Hello?"

"When did you get back?" Without waiting for a response, Attila rattled off, "Is Marika still in her room? And is Willy there?"

"Yes, they're both here. Do you want to speak to Willy?"

"No, just give him more food and beer. I don't want you or Marika to leave the apartment until I get back. Under no circumstances. Is that understood?"

"Why?"

"For God's sake, Anna, do as I ask, and tell Willy he has to wait for me." He hung up the phone.

Attila's thinking cap went into overdrive. Igor attempted to kidnap Marika and failed. What would the bastard do now? Try again? Go shopping for souvenirs? Don't be a fool. The only souvenir he wants is his daughter. Surely, Igor realized Marika would have told him about their meeting. The pervert was so desperate he even gave away the name of his hotel.

Attila called other hotels without any luck. He finally sat down in the lobby hoping a miracle will return Igor to him. He should call the police, but it was his duty to keep Marika's secret from her.

"Sir," the desk clerk called out to Attila. "The doorman said Mr. Raznatovic took a taxi to the airport."

Attila hurried over to the desk. "Is he sure?"

"Oh, yes. The gentleman's not easy to forget."

A Madman at the Airport

Attila sped along Highway 401 as if he were being chased by a posse of cops. At Toronto International Airport, he screeched to a halt, stopping the car over a white dividing line. He jumped out, looked at his sloppy parking, and jumped back in. Swearing at himself, he re-parked the car with no time to spare. He'll just have to run that much faster as he dashed through the terminal like a madman checking the boards for Australia-bound planes. A Qantas flight was getting ready to leave from Gate 22 which meant more running down interminably long corridors and bumping into people and luggage.

At Gate 22, he tried to board the plane.

A stewardess stopped him. "Sorry, sir, you're too late. The plane is taxiing down the runway."

Already out of breath, Attila rushed to the observation deck to watch the Qantas plane move slowly past him. He occasionally swam with Marika at the Donview Club or rode a bike around Thorncliffe Park, but it wasn't enough exercise to offset seven years of a mostly sedentary lifestyle full of steak and potatoes, liquor, cigarettes, rich desserts. They had taken a toll on his physical stamina, his chest groaning in pain from the exertion as he peered into each tiny window looking for Igor. Suddenly, he spotted a familiar profile wearing a black hat. He watched helplessly as the plane headed into the sky. The child molester spends ten years in gaol for what he did to Marika. What does he do as soon as he gets out? He flies all the way to Canada to rape her again, and kill her this time. But he's unsuccessful, so he flies all the way back to Australia. Igor was even more evil and erratic than Attila thought, and now, he'll have to come up with an explanation for his lunatic behaviour by the time he got home.

He fretted until he was beyond miserable. The right thing to do was report the attempted kidnapping of his daughter to the Toronto police, but he knew enough of the law to know that since the felony happened here, they'd bring Igor back to Canada. Then there was no way to keep Marika's past from her. He couldn't even tell Worlock because the man would take Igor into custody when he landed on Australian turf and have him extradited to Canada. It was pure agony all the way home as Attila waged an internal battle.

By the time he arrived at Thorncliffe Park, he decided not to involve the police. He was going to hire a private detective agency to monitor all Toronto-bound airlines originating from Australia. If Igor ever showed up again in Canada, he would be ready for the evil bastard.

Putting a Spin on Failure

Igor sat alone in a window seat, his piercing black eyes boring a hole into the back of the seat ahead of him. Coming face to face with his obsession had driven him into a silent frenzy. He was so close, he almost had Marika, but that friend of hers ruined everything. Too bad he slipped up and told Marika the name of his hotel.

What did the Voice have to say to him?

Marika is a big girl now. It's not easy to get a big girl to go with you anywhere, especially if you talk to her like she was a little girl.

"Go to hell!" shouted Igor.

Startled passengers turned to stare at the man wearing a black fedora. A pretty stewardess appeared at his side. "Is everything all right, sir?"

"Go away."

The stewardess hurried down the aisle to warn the rest of the crew about the rude passenger.

Igor, I will disappear if you ever talk to me like that again.

"Sorry," muttered Igor.

What did you expect? There's a world of difference between a four year old and a fourteen year old. Just like there's a world of difference between a fourteen year old and a twenty-four year old.

"What are you saying?"

On February 2, 1977, Marika will be twenty-four years old. Twenty years after you started your mission, she will be ready to come to you. All you have to do is wait, and when the time is right, I will tell you how to bring her to you.

Igor wanted to believe the Voice. "This was not a trick?"

No, you were getting reacquainted before the final meeting. She's worth waiting for, isn't she?

"Yes."

Marika has to come to you without protest, like she did in 1957. You missed your tenth anniversary because it wasn't meant to be now.

"She will come to me?"

Yes, Igor.

"Ten more years. What do I do in the meantime?"

Count the days and live your life. The next ten years will go by very quickly. Be comforted by the fact that Marika will be in her absolute prime when you complete your mission.

"What if she has a boyfriend or a husband?" Igor didn't want any other man touching his Marika.

She will be alone.

"Won't her father have me arrested when I land in Australia?"

Forget about it. He'll do anything to keep you a secret from his precious daughter.

November 1967

A Physician Gets the Wrong Idea

Marika settled into a cinema seat beside Bess to watch the anticipated premiere of Wait Until Dark. Marika watched Audrey Hepburn move daintily across the big screen, fondly remembering Auntie Betty twirl around as if she would never stop, her glorious black hair twirling after her.

The packed audience gasped in shock, moaning every time the killer moved in on blind Audrey. Bess clung to the arms of her seat, gasping louder than anyone else which was a surprising reaction for a tough jock. Marika opened her mouth many times, but couldn't shriek even when the headlights of a screeching car lit up the entire audience.

As the two girls walked home, Bess asked, "Didn't you like the movie?"

"I loved it. I've seen every movie Audrey Hepburn ever made."

"You were so quiet, I thought you were bored."

Marika shook her head. "I can't scream. Whenever I go on the roller coaster, I must be the only person who has no voice. I'm pathetic." As soon as she finished speaking, she buckled down to the ground.

Bess grabbed her friend's arm. "What's the matter?"

"I'm feeling really sharp pain," moaned Marika. She was doubled over from a strong cramp in her lower abdomen. Bess waited until her friend felt better before continuing on their way home.

By the next day, the pain was back. Anna was worried it might be a sign of appendicitis, so she took her daughter to see the family doctor. When they reached the lobby, Marika asked her mother to wait there, insisting she was old enough to see the doctor by herself.

Dr. James was a rectangular faced man who wore bouffant grey hair and the very common black plastic rimmed glasses. In the examination room, he palpated Marika's abdomen, deciding she probably had a cyst on her right ovary. He told her he was going to examine her internally.

Marika cringed. She never had an internal examination before, and almost bolted from the room. Instead, she lay frozen like a creamsicle. He's the doctor, so she let him open her legs and poke a gloved finger inside her. She squirmed with embarrassment as the doctor began to mutter.

"I shouldn't be surprised with what young girls do today. But I'm very surprised at you, Marika." The doctor's face turned beet red with indignation, and without warning he shoved a cold instrument into her vagina, oblivious to his youthful patient's alarmed reaction. The torturous instrument and the lecture that came with it made Marika cry tears of pain and humiliation. She couldn't understand what was wrong, but for some reason the doctor was very angry and disappointed with her. He was making her feel as if she did something terrible, ignoring the tears streaking her face while he poked more deeply. When he was finished, he left the inconsolable girl crying on the table.

A few minutes later, the receptionist walked into the room trying to cajole a weeping Marika into getting dressed. She said frostily, "Other patients want to see Dr. James."

Marika ran out of the office after getting dressed.

Anna found herself chasing her daughter through the lobby. She shouted, "Please stop, dear! I can't keep up with you and your long legs!" When the hysterical teenager slowed down, Anna finally caught up with her.

It took Marika nearly ten minutes to tell her mother what happened.

Anna was furious. "Wait here," she ordered. Leaving Australia behind brought back some of her spunk.

Marika watched in horror as her mother marched down the corridor and into the doctor's office. *Oh God, Mom's going to make a scene.*

Anna stomped past the receptionist.

"Dr. James is with another patient. You can't go in there, Mrs. Paprika!"

Anna headed for the examination room and threw open the door to find the physician getting ready to stick his finger into an elderly man's rectum. "You work fast, doctor. First my fourteen year old daughter's vagina, and now this man's ass."

"Mrs. Paprika..." the receptionist tried to pull her out of the room.

Anna turned around and pushed the irritating woman away.

The doctor began to make indignant noises that sounded like a series of splutters. "Excuse me, what do you think..."

"I'll tell you what I think! How dare you give my daughter an internal examination!" Anna shouted at Dr. James before he could finish his sentence. "You have no right to touch a fourteen year old girl just because you think she has a cyst." The respectful relationship between doctor and patient was severed, and she showed no mercy. "Any excuse to get a look at my daughter's private parts. You're disgusting and I'm going to report you to the medical association!" Anna stormed out of the examination room.

Dr. James shouted after her, "You're daughter's been having sex! Ask her about that!"

Blame the Horse
Anna followed Marika into her bedroom and closed the door. "Are you having sex with boys?"

Marika couldn't believe her ears. She expected her mother to comfort her, not attack her. She started crying again. "Mom, how can you ask me such a thing? I can't even go near a guy without turning into jello."

Anna wanted to believe her daughter. "You mustn't tell your father what that bum doctor did to you today because he would kill him. We're never going back to Dr. James."

"He was shouting loud enough for the whole building to hear I've been having sex, which I haven't!" Marika said in a worried tone, "Is he implying my hymen is gone?"

Anna was very uncomfortable talking to her daughter about sex and intimate body parts. She muttered, "It happens to some girls who go horseback riding."

"I've never been on a horse in my life!"

"Maybe you were born without one." Anna added, "That's all I want to say."

"Oh, great...born deformed. I feel like shit, and you don't want to talk about it anymore."

"Marika! Apologize for swearing."

"Why is it okay for adults to swear, but not teenagers? Never mind, there's no logical answer to that one. You win. I don't want to talk about it anymore either because after all this crap, the pain is gone. And that's good because I don't ever want to see a doctor again."

The Spring of 1968

An Ordinary Day with the Paprikas

While hippies were busy engaging in free love, flower power, and bringing peace to the world, shy sixteen year old Marika sat on the sidelines intimidating the boys at school with her beauty, ensuring she was still dateless.

In the meantime, Anna kept Marika on her toes. She appeared at her daughter's open bedroom door with an announcement. "I decided to invent something."

Marika put her school book down and said, "What do you mean, Mom?"

"I have a great idea." Anna's voice tinkled with excitement.

Uh-oh. What is it this time? wondered Marika. "Aren't you busy writing? Any luck with the outer space story?"

Anna's happy face took a turn for the worse. "I've come to the conclusion it's easier to become the first female prime minister than it is to get published. Agents are such snobs. It's who you know, not what you've done. You have my blessing to be anything you want to be, except a book agent. They pledge allegiance to the almighty publisher in the sky by promising to discriminate against talented writers, ignore their phone calls and letters, or deign to accept a few measly manuscript pages, so they can practise hoop shots into the waste basket."

Marika stifled a giggle. "Hoop shots? Mom, you're too funny."

"Can you come up with anything better?"

"It requires me to think like you."

"You're being sarcastic."

"Mom, you are unique, and I say that with love. Did you get another rejection?"

Anna didn't have to answer. Her face said it all. "I'm not going to stop. One day, I'll be famous. In the meantime, I have an idea."

"What?"

"Something that would appeal to menstruating women. I never thought I'd prefer to have periods again over taking hormone pills made from horse pee."

"Mom, please! Are you trying to embarrass me?"

"Stop being so sensitive and listen. I think those sanitary belts you have to wear are awful. You have three choices -- white, clumsy, and boring. That's it. Obviously they were designed by a man who doesn't have to wear the stupid things."

By now, Marika's eyes had glazed over.

Attila walked by and stopped to ask, "What are you girls talking about?"

"Sanitary belts," said Anna.

"I think I hear the kettle boiling." Attila disappeared quickly.

Anna turned back to face Marika who was staring at the ceiling. "As I was saying, what if we fancied them up with pretty colours or cute little designs?" Anna was once again brimming over with enthusiasm.

"We?"

"You're the artist in the family."

"You mean my sporadic sketchings?"

"Of course."

"Great idea, Mom."

"Thank you, dear."

Marika knew the *great idea* would go away, like all the other off-the-wall ideas her mother came up with. And she was thankful because this latest one was a doozy.

CHAPTER 15

Spread Those Wings

Saturday, May 29, 1971
Toronto, Canada

Marika smiled at her parents from the podium as she collected her high school diploma. She was proud of the way they looked for their age. Anna's short wavy hair was still black, thanks to umpteen bottles of hair dye. She had to fight to keep her waist, but maintained a figure worth showing off. A new addition to her wardrobe was a pair of peach framed prescription eye glasses which she wore for reading and watching television.

The cumbersome days of straightening her legs were over. Not because she magically shifted the bones in her legs and repositioned her knees. She just didn't care what they looked like anymore.

Attila developed a slight stoop, but his hair was still blond with a touch of garish, dubious thanks to Grecian Formula. He relinquished his dependence on Brylcreem, leaving his hair to do what it wanted which wasn't much because he kept it trimmed very short. Giving up sports several years ago meant his body was no longer toned to perfection, but he had inherited a slim body which was in good shape except for a modest paunch above the belt.

Marika thought it was too depressing to think about her parents' fashion sense which decidedly became middle-aged frump with the emphasis on nylon and polyester. Her mother showed off her hourglass figure with tailored clothes worn by women her age, while her dad had a wardrobe of pale blue and spotless white dress shirts and uninspiring work suits for the office. For leisure wear, he preferred short-sleeved jersey shirts in dismal monochromes of grey, olive green, dark blue. Completing the casual attire was a pair of dark brown or grey pants topped with a short zippered medium grey jacket — a walking ad for all that was uncool about polyester.

He scoffed at a male world gone crazy for men's platform shoes, chunky chained medallions, bell bottoms, impossibly tight t-shirts and dress shirts, and sideburns that looked like baby beavers... without the tails. Same as his wife, he wore prescription glasses except his were framed in the ubiquitous black plastic.

Attila smiled lovingly at his graduating daughter. She was very much like other young women, wearing skirts ranging from mini to maxi, loose peasant blouses, ponchos, embroidered headbands and neck chokers, primping her eyes with heavy mascara, two different shades of liner, and clunking around in heavy platform shoes. The most ridiculous apparel was her collection of low-cut bell bottom pants that cleaned the floor as she walked. After all, she was only nineteen.

Although her taste in clothes and makeup were not to his liking, she had a good head on her shoulders. Raznatovic must be an aging cripple by now. It was time to stop worrying about Marika's safety and terminate the services of the private detective.

Friday, September 1, 1972

Life Goes On
Anna tested the faltering communist regime by visiting her family in Hungary. As it was still too dangerous to put her daughter at risk, she ended up going alone. Attila had a very good reason for not taking a chance, opting to stay home with Marika.

Sadly, Margit died unexpectedly from a liver ailment on the day that Anna arrived in Eger. Her death was less than a week after her brother Sandor suffered a fatal heart attack. It was to be a joyous summer reunion, but instead she attended two funerals.

Eight bittersweet weeks were spent getting to know an older Horka who had become a responsible adult with a doting spouse and a teenage son. He was the proud curator of an artifacts museum which gave him the opportunity to continue carving his wood sculptures. Anna would have been thrilled to have him immigrate to Canada when the time was right. She asked him, but he said he loved Hungary too much to leave.

Upon her return to Canada, Marika broke the news that she was moving to her own apartment. "You and Dad don't need to support me anymore because I've got a job as a secretary at an insurance company."

"What about university?"

"I'm not sure what I want to do. I'll decide when I turn twenty-five and get my inheritance from Grammy Porridge."

"You're almost twenty years old. You have a job and you're moving out, so throw away your teddy bears."

Marika looked up from a cardboard box filled with her belongings. She pouted her lips, "No, I can't. They've been with me since forever." She picked up Teddy and tweaked his ears.

"They're old stuffed toys full of germs. Material stuffed with more material."

"That's pretty cold coming from the woman who used to read them bedtime stories and style their fur. Dad wouldn't say that." Sometimes, Marika couldn't understand her mother at all.

"He said things that hurt me."

A crease appeared across Marika's forehead. "People don't mean what they say in the heat of an argument."

"Yes, they do."

"Okay, what did Dad say that hurt you?"

Anna sighed. Her daughter was such a sensitive person. She wondered if Marika could cope with living by herself. And she wondered if she can condense so many years into a few minutes to explain how she and Attila drifted apart until indifference replaced the passion and closeness they once shared. Isn't that what happens to all couples who've been together so long? Anna shook her head. Too depressing. "If you want the bears, keep them."

Late that night, Anna found Marika standing on the balcony staring up at the stars. "You come out here often. What's the matter?"

"I can't put my finger on it, but I feel different from everyone. It bugs me that I have so much trouble with guys."

"So what? You're young."

"I didn't have a single date in high school. Five years. Must be a record of some kind."

"Men aren't interesting until they get older. Your turn will come because you're a beautiful woman, just don't be so shy."

"That's so easy to say. All I want to do is hide when I'm out there." Marika waved her hand in the air, indicating she meant the whole wide world. "Crowds make me panic."

"Do you want me to read your palm?"

Marika wrinkled her nose, thoroughly confused with her mother's train of thought. "How's that going to help me?"

"It's fun, and maybe I can tell you when you're going to meet the love of your life."

Marika rolled her eyes in exasperation. "No, thanks. I don't want to get my hopes up and it doesn't come true. So, when did you learn palmistry?"

"I borrowed a book from the library after watching the Amazing Kreskin."

"That makes perfect sense." Marika was being facetious, but her mom failed to notice.

Anna felt sorry for her daughter. Beautiful and gentle, and yet she couldn't enjoy life at all, not like Anna...or Kati. "Darling, have you ever seen a photo of your father's sister?"

"No, he doesn't talk about Aunt Kati."

"She was probably the most beautiful woman in Eger, and my best friend." Anna pulled Marika into the living room and told her to wait on the couch. Within a few minutes, she was back with an old eight by ten black and white photograph. "I don't know why I never showed it to you before. Probably because it upsets your dad to see Kati's photo." Anna sighed. "I envied her."

"Why?"

"She was beautiful, strong, and didn't have to run away from Hungary to find herself. I, on the other hand, didn't stop running until I was far away from the country I loved. I didn't have enough faith in myself as a Hungarian, not enough faith in my fellow countrymen that we can rise above all that happened during the war." Anna paused to wipe away a few tears of regret. "I was too impatient and indignant to wait any longer."

"Are you feeling sorry you didn't publish anything once you left Hungary?"

Anna walked over to the large window overlooking the Don Valley Parkway, her eyes following car headlights as they skittered along the winding road. "I thought once I escaped Hungary, I could pick up where I left off. Being so angry with the communists, I didn't realize something very important."

"Which was what?"

"That I needed Hungary. It was the country I was born in which gave me my drive and ambition. I did better there, even with communism. At least my articles and books were still being published. I just had to be careful I didn't write anything provocative." She took a breath to steady herself because the memories were still painful. "When I went home to Eger recently, I felt so much stronger there than I do here. Anyway, I'm still trying, but being a mother does change priorities for many women."

"Is that your way of saying I'm important to you?"

"Yes, dear." Anna sat down beside Marika and patted her knee. "Look at Kati. You are her exact image, only your hair and eyes are a different colour. Find her in you, or life will be difficult."

"May I keep this photo?"

"Oh my goodness! I totally forgot." Anna left the room. A few minutes later, she returned with a small packet of wrinkled tissue and handed it to her daughter.

Marika peeled back the tissue to reveal Mama Paprika's necklace.

"It belonged to your paternal grandmother. Kati wanted you to have it."

Marika held the delicate chain up to the light before clasping it around her neck. She stroked the gold cross lying against her skin.

"It looks beautiful on you."

"I love it." Wearing something that Kati wanted her to have, made Marika feel close to her. She looked at the photo again. They were so much alike they could have been twins.

Monday, September 4, 1972

Popcorn Time

"Is the popcorn ready?" Attila turned on the television and sat down in his favourite armchair.

"In a minute, I'm melting the butter," said Marika from the kitchen.

Attila could hear the annoying sound of Anna's new Olympia typewriter coming from the bedroom. He shouted, "Hurry up, Anna! You'll miss Mark Spitz!"

"Okay, I'm coming!" Anna reluctantly stopped typing and walked down the hall to the living room. She promptly sat down on the sofa, and said, "What's the big deal? He's not Canadian or Hungarian."

"If you paid more attention to the Munich Olympics, you would realize he's going for his seventh gold medal. He's a fucking miracle."

Anna could swear her husband was trying to annoy her. "The miracle you hoped to be?"

"Don't ruin this for me, Anna. I don't want to miss any of the Olympic highlights."

"And you're not ruining this for me?"

A worried Marika rushed into the living room with two bowls of popcorn. "Here, Dad, this one's for you. Lots of salt and butter." She handed over a bowl, hoping to distract him. "Just the way you like it."

The smell of hot buttered popcorn was too good to resist. Attila popped a big fluffy kernel in his mouth.

Sitting down on the sofa, Marika gave the second bowl to her mother. "Has the swimming event started?"

Attila said, "The commentators are still yapping." Then he said proudly, "Guess who trained Spitz to become an Olympic swimmer."

"You," said Anna jokingly.

With a tinge of sarcasm, Attila said, "Remember when I said I was going to the horse races or bike riding? I was secretly flying back and forth in a private jet to train Spitz in California."

Anna said, "Don't be silly, you can't fly to California and back in just a few hours."

Attila looked at his wife in disbelief. "You still don't understand my sense of humour after all these years. I was trying to be as ridiculous as you."

"You're terrible," Anna said in a hurt tone.

"I'm just being honest."

Marika jumped up to distract her parents again. "I know, I know! A Hungarian, but which one?"

Attila decided to ignore Anna and smiled at his daughter. "Clever girl. Ervin Zador was Spitz's trainer."

Anna said bitterly, "Oh yes, the one who had his face bashed in by a Soviet at the Melbourne Olympics."

In a snippy tone, Attila said, "Eloquent as always, Anna. It was a historical moment you made me miss at the water polo match you didn't want to watch."

"Okay, Smarty Pants. You can cheer Mark Spitz on without me. Heaven forbid I should make you miss any other historical moments at the Olympics!" Anna got up and marched back to the bedroom.

"Dad, that was mean." Marika followed her mother, leaving Attila alone in the living room.

He shrugged his shoulders. "All I said was the truth." Then he shouted at the two women like a petulant child, "Am I supposed to watch Spitz by myself?"

Tuesday, September 5, 1972

Shocking News
"This is terrible."

Anna walked into the living room the next morning to find Attila glued to the television. "Don't tell me you were up all night. What's the matter? Is Mark Spitz stuck with a measly six gold medals?" She was still in a grotty mood from last night, but when Attila didn't react in the expected manner, she said, "Well, what's so terrible?"

"Palestinian terrorists are holding the Israeli athletes hostage at the Olympics."

"Oh no!"

"It's not going to end well. Terrorists are unpredictable bastards."

CHAPTER 16

The Stained Carpet

Friday, March 21, 1975 at 5:20 p.m.
Toronto, Canada

Attila sat in his armchair with a dinner tray on his lap. He had just polished off his favourite meal, a thick juicy steak with fried onions and mushrooms, and was taking a bite of leftover cake from Marika's twenty-third birthday when he felt a severe constricting pain in his chest. He thought it was heartburn and took a couple of Rolaids. The pain didn't go away. It got worse. As he stood up to go to his bedroom, he collapsed in a heap on the living room floor, knocking down the lamp beside his armchair.

Anna rushed down the hallway to investigate the crashing noise, and found her husband lying unconscious. She shook him as she shouted desperately, "Attila! Wake up!" She watched his chest, but his breath was so shallow she thought she was imagining it. As she reached for the phone, her heart was racing, and her skin prickled with the horrible thought that Attila was dying.

Miss Doofus
Marika stretched her arms out and yawned. It was well past her quitting time, and she was the only one left in the office. The same old mind patter occupied

her thoughts. Why does she put up with such a yuck job? She managed to save enough money to go to university if she got a student loan, but being mired in routine was the safest way of getting through the days.

You are boring, Miss Doofus.

Her telephone rang. "Hi, Mom." The only person who could possibly be calling her at work this late would be her mother.

"How did you know it was me?" Anna's voice shook with worry. "Your dad had a heart attack and was taken to Central Hospital."

Too upset to drive her car, Marika sat in a taxi staring at the people walking along the streets lit by neon store lights, feeling like an alien from another planet. As she thought about her father, she had to fight back the tears. Not yet, not until she knew his condition.

She found her mother sitting pensively in a hospital waiting room, staring at the wall in front of her. "How's Dad?"

"I'm so glad to see you, darling. Dr. Mayer says your father suffered a mild heart attack, whatever that means." She took her daughter's hand and said, "He'll be happy to see you."

A week later, Attila was handed a prescription for a beta blocker and nitroglycerin, and told to go home. Dr. Mayer looked like a wise old owl with blinking eyes and pudgy cheeks. He was such an astute surgeon that Attila guessed he was of Hungarian descent. To his utter dismay, the doctor turned out to be from Romania.

In a soft accented voice, the unassuming doctor gave his patient a warning. "Smoking stresses your heart. You're lucky it wasn't more serious, and you have your athletic days to thank for that."

Anna brought her husband home from the hospital in a taxi. As they approached their apartment, he stopped. A pained expression on his face caused Anna's skin to prickle again. She was frightened he was having another heart attack. "What's the matter, are you sick? I'll call an ambulance!" She hurriedly unlocked the door.

Attila grimaced as he pointed down at the stained patch of carpet outside their apartment door. "Look at it."

Anna was torn between rushing to the phone to save her husband's life, or stopping to chat about the hallway carpet. She said the first thing that popped into her head. "I cleaned it."

"I told you to leave the carpet alone. You don't know how to clean anything properly." Attila shook his head in disgust. "It looks like garbage was rubbed into it which makes me sick just looking at the mess. What's the matter with you?"

Anna recoiled. The time was long gone when she avoided arguments with Attila because it was beneath her. "What's the matter with me?" She yelled, "What's the matter with you! Your body's still warm from lying in a hospital bed after suffering a heart attack. You're alive, but no glad to be home! All you care about is a fucking piece of carpet!" She stormed into the apartment, throwing Attila's overnight bag against the nearest wall. "I should be given a medal for putting up with you and your fastidiousness. And your snoring! Even with separate bedrooms, it still drives me crazy!"

Attila stood forlornly in the corridor like a chastised school boy. Anna really let him have it this time.

Marika was in the kitchen hoping to greet her father with a delicious home cooked meal when the unmistakable sounds of an argument interrupted her good intentions. She groaned, "Here we go again."

It was a regular occurrence for her parents to blow up at each other once a week, and over the silliest of things.

Two Days Later

Attila likes Rubbing Alcohol
Marika paid another home visit, hoping to find a peaceful household this time. As she entered the front door, she could smell rubbing alcohol and cigarettes.

It couldn't be her mother because she gave up cigarettes many years ago, and never returned to the filthy habit. She said to her dad, "Dr. Mayer doesn't want you smoking."

Attila was sitting in his armchair reading the newspaper. "If I want to smoke, I'll smoke. I enjoy it. Despite what Dr. Mayer says, it has nothing to do with my heart. Doctors can be wrong, you know. How many times have they steered patients into their graves with botched surgeries and killer prescriptions?"

Marika groaned. "You know Dr. Mayer isn't wrong. You think he's right up there with the perfect porkolt. And you're impossible. Watching tv, drinking, and smoking all the time doesn't seem healthy."

"That's exactly what I want to do when I come home after a hard day's work as an underpaid unit head dealing with lazy incompetent employees, crooks, deadbeats, and plain old bastards screwing the income tax department." He added, "And mark my words, if the bastards are ripping us off, they're also cheating the Old Age Security pension department. I have a contact there who confided in me that millions of taxpayers' hard-earned dollars are being flushed down the toilet every year because of client fraud and bad business practices.

Geriatric cheats are the worst, hiding behind their wrinkles and false teeth." Attila snorted with disgust. Then he looked at his daughter's bored face and realized she was too young to care about income tax and pension cheaters. He peered over the top of his glasses. "As a taxpayer, you should be concerned about what happens to your money."

Marika said nothing. She detested politics, especially after her dad warned her about arrogant bungling politicians.

Attila suddenly remembered a physical activity that he did every weekend. "You're forgetting about my betting trips to Ladbrokes and Greenwood race track."

Marika wondered if her dad was trying to be funny or serious.

"Do you remember when I chauffeured you as a teenager to Eaton's department store, so you can spend the allowance I gave you?"

He was trying to make a point which was a good memory for Marika. "I always started my shopping with a vanilla ice cream waffle. It was so darn delicious, but we're getting off topic." She flung her arms out in front of her. In a frustrated tone, she said, "Driving is not exercise. Why don't you go swimming again? You're a dolphin in water and your crawl is hypnotic to watch, or how about riding a bike? Why did you stop? Why don't you stop smoking instead? Mom did."

The energy of a young adult can be overwhelming, but Attila loved his daughter. "I'm not your mother."

"Why do you guys fight so much? Why don't you take Mom out to a restaurant or a movie?"

"All this from smoking a cigarette? Darling, I suggest to your mother that we go to the Goulash Pot, but she wants a fancier restaurant with music and dancing. That's not my thing, and going to the movies is out of the question. I always end up with a slob beside me who can't stop coughing. On the other side, there's a peasant who doesn't use deodorant, and behind me is someone with restless leg syndrome. In front of me is an oversized head blocking my view, and two aisles away is someone with a big yapping mouth." Attila patted the sidearm of his chair, so Marika came over and sat down.

He continued, "When your mother is not a slave to her typewriter, I take her to the race track. She likes watching the horses and sometimes even wins a few bucks. We also sunbathe together in the back of the building."

"Do you hold each other's hands while you're getting a tan?"

"Don't be stupid, Marika."

The unmistakable smell of rubbing alcohol was even stronger now. Marika sniffed the top of her father's head. "Why do you use stinky rubbing alcohol on your hair?"

"It kills the germs which weaken the roots, and that's the reason I still have a full head of hair. I clean everything with rubbing alcohol."

"I bet Mom doesn't want to be near you when you smell gross."

"Your mother and I are old married people. As long as it's not body odour, we don't care what we smell like to each other."

Marika felt sorry for her parents. She was a romantic, and wished they were happier with each other. Why can't people who are lifelong companions remember what it was like to be alone, searching for that special someone? She bent down and kissed her father's cheek. "Want to play a game of chess?"

Attila grinned toothily at his daughter, "Only if you finally let me win." The only other person who could beat him at chess was Kati.

CHAPTER 17

Vanilla - Who Knew?

Late November 1976
Toronto, Canada

    Marika was pen pals with Wendy Williams, a secretary at her company's branch office in London, England. When Marika was invited for a visit, she accepted without hesitation. Wendy was a woman with loads of confidence, her engaging personality bubbling through the telephone during their overseas chats. A person that Marika definitely wanted to meet.
    Marika was now wearing makeup that gave her a more natural look, but her hair was still long and loose with soft bangs. Checking her bedroom closet, she wondered what people would think if she wore her favourite bell bottoms, a fashion that was going out of style. She decided to take her slightly flared blue jeans, a couple of turtlenecks, and a classy black dress to London.
    The best way to prepare for a trip was to make a list. Seconds after she sat down on the couch with a pen and pad, there was a knock on her apartment door.
    Anna stood in the hallway with a large casserole dish. "Your dad made porkolt and I made the csipetke." She placed the casserole dish on the kitchen counter before joining her daughter in the living room. Marika was smiling so

broadly, Anna couldn't help but notice. "Darling, you should smile like that more often. It looks so much better than that constant frown of yours. You're already getting wrinkles at the top of your nose." She came over to rub her daughter's forehead as if her thumb was a wrinkle eraser.

Marika jerked her head backwards. "Mom, stop it! I hate it when you do that. I want to tell you some good news." She usually preferred being close to home, but this time she looked forward to going overseas.

"What is it?"

"I'm going to London in December. Ten days. I'll be staying with Wendy at her Kensington-Chelsea flat."

"I see Prince Charles isn't married yet."

Marika sighed. Her mother's mind was a puzzling thing. "What are you suggesting? That I hang out at Buckingham Palace and offer myself as a wife? I believe he prefers blondes."

"If you happen to meet him, be nice."

"I'll take a crash course on how to talk from the back of my throat, so I can fit in with the Royals." Marika laughed at the silliness of their conversation. "Do you want anything from London?"

"Underwear from Marks and Spencer."

Monday, December 6, 1976
London, England

Five Hundred Varieties of Cheese
The plane landed at Heathrow Airport on a drizzly afternoon.

After breezing through customs as a British subject, Marika looked around the terminal noticing every sensible arm carried an umbrella. "I forgot something, didn't I?"

Standing in the congested arrivals lounge, she waited for a bouncy woman with very short, straight, dirty blonde hair and huge round tortoise shell glasses. That was the description Wendy shared with Marika, who in turn described herself as a tall stick with long auburn hair. The descriptions must have been adequate because they simultaneously spotted each other.

"Marika!"

"Wendy!"

The two young women hugged as if they knew each other forever. When Marika pulled out a cheap Kodak camera from her carry-on bag, she snapped several photos of Wendy making funny faces.

In an upper class English accent, Wendy said, "You are absolutely beautiful, Marika. I just saw a man walk into a postcard stand because he couldn't take his eyes off you. From the way you described yourself, I was expecting a skeleton who starved on a Biafran diet. I stocked my kitchen with scads of food to shovel into you." She dug into a large green vinyl shopping bag emblazoned with the gold letters of Harrods. "I telepathically knew you wouldn't have a brolly. Am I right?" Wendy grinned as she held out a black umbrella.

Marika laughed. "Yes, you are. Is the weather always like this in December?" She followed Wendy outside to her custom lime green Volkswagen beetle.

"Just about, I'm afraid. By the end of the month, the rain will turn into the white stuff."

Wendy lived in a roomy second floor flat of a large Victorian terrace house filled with bric-a-brac she collected from flea markets. Once Marika settled down, she had a good night's sleep. The following day, Wendy took her down to the London office, whirling her guest through many handshakes and hellos.

Marika gushed afterwards, "The people are so nice, and I dig all the different British accents."

Next stop was Harrods where they included a browse-through of the cheese section at the famous department store.

Wendy said, "I love my cheese, and Harrods claims to sell over five hundred varieties. When I was young and foolish, I started counting...and counting. Boredom set in at two hundred." She looked over to her right. "Blimey, this has been going on a lot lately."

A conga line of Arab women, possessions of Arab sheikhs rolling in oil money, glided down the aisle in flowing black robes covering them from head to toe. All anyone ever saw of these mysterious women were their black kohl-rimmed eyes.

After Harrods, it was a breathless pace of one sight after another. Marble Arch, Piccadilly Circus, Buckingham Palace, Westminster Cathedral, Hyde Park, St. Mary Abbots Hospital, Kensington Palace, the Tower of London, and Marks and Spencer for her mom's underwear order. Pubs were part of their daily itinerary which gave Wendy the opportunity to order a large Guinness for her guest.

"Why do you insist I drink this stuff?" The bitter brown liquid didn't appeal to Marika.

"I'm glad you're too polite to refuse because it's good for you. Your skin is a deathly shade of pale and a Guinness will fatten your blood."

"You should talk. You're even paler than me. This ale makes me feel giddy, but you're right about one thing. I'm too polite to refuse."

"Right you are. Now drink up, there's more to see."

With four more days to go, Wendy took her Canadian visitor to lunch at Cranks, London's famous health food shop which opened its door during the mod revolution of the sixties. Sitting at a round white iron table, Wendy asked, "Do you mind if I have a fag?"

Marika was too nice to say it bothered her and that smoking in an organic vegetarian restaurant was counterproductive. She said instead, "Do you know you're the first smoker who asked me if I mind?"

Wendy nonchalantly waved her hand in the air. "I know some people can't handle the smell. So, what is it?"

"No, it's okay."

"Don't let that polite streak of yours become a defect." Wendy pointed at her friend's bowl. "Is it good?"

"I really like the oregano flavour of this buckwheat and potato soup."

"Or-egg-unno? Where are you from?"

Marika wasn't sure if Wendy was teasing her, and she could feel her face turning red from the attention of other diners.

Wendy leaned forward. "It's ori-gah-no." Noticing Marika's burning cheeks, she smiled broadly, "I'm pulling your leg. Being such snobs, we British love to elongate as many of our words as possible." When she saw Marika gazing at a good-looking guy with long brown locks sitting at another table, she asked, "Do you have a boyfriend?"

Marika hesitated. She didn't want Wendy to think she was a loser in the guy department. "There's no one in my life right now."

"I can't imagine you without a boyfriend for long."

"How about you?"

"Just broke up with an Irish bloke. He treated me nice, but there was no spark, you know what I mean?"

"More like two friends?"

"You could say that." Wendy looked out the window at the grey sky. "It's supposed to be cold and sunny tomorrow. A good day to show you the countryside."

The next morning they woke up to brilliant sunshine.

"Hallelujah!" Wendy pranced around her drawing room, happy the weather forecast was right. "Come here, Marika, I bought you something." She held up a red tartan kilt with pleats.

Marika's big eyes lit up as she put it on. "The kilt is gorgeous. My mom will especially love it because she says I wear too much black."

"You have to put the pin in like this." Wendy adjusted a giant gold pin which held the kilt together in the front. "I would kill to have your slim hips."

"And I'd kill to have big breasts like yours."

"Sagging knockers like mine? Bollocks." Wendy eyed the plaid figure like a designer scrutinizing a model on a catwalk. "Do you have a cardigan to go with the skirt? Perhaps a black one, since you like that colour so much."

"How about a fuzzy white angora turtleneck?"

Wendy stuck a finger in her mouth and pretended to gag as she rummaged through her closet. "Are you trying to gross me out?" She pulled out a hug-fitting black cashmere pullover with a provocative v-neckline. She threw it at Marika.

Marika tried to refuse the pullover. "No, I can't. You've been so generous."

Wendy persisted. "I love you already, but you do tire me. You're just as important as the next person. Try to remember that, okay?"

England is Such Fun

After touring Windsor Castle, Cambridge, and Hampton Court in three days, they returned to Wendy's apartment for afternoon tea and biscuits.

A still energetic Marika said, "Do you know, I haven't been on a double decker bus yet. I've got to do that before I go home tomorrow."

Wendy joked, "You mean I took you all over the city and countryside, watching you take tons of photos, when all I had to do was stick you on a bus to make your visit fun?"

Marika played along. "Yup." She quickly changed her clothes, putting on the black cashmere pullover and red tartan kilt with the big gold pin. She borrowed a pair of Wendy's sleek back suede boots and a double-breasted pea jacket of the same colour.

When the women went outside, Wendy stopped beside her car parked on the street. She stared at a white spot on the lime green bonnet.

Marika said, "Bird droppings bother you?"

"A couple of months ago, I thought a neighbour's parrot was using my car as a toilet." Wendy pointed up at the window of a house on the opposite side of the street. "The bird sat on the ledge watching me, and I would tease it with a few parrot jokes. You know, 'polly want a cracker' shtick. Then I'd find suspicious white crud on my windshield or other parts of the car. I was right royally pissed, but it was no use complaining to the owner, a dotty ninety year old dear. So, one morning at sunrise, I hid behind a bush with a fire extinguisher, just to scare the bird." She paused, then said, "Ask me what I saw."

"What did you see?"

"A bloke who lived nearby stopped at my car, took out his stiff willy, and wanked all over my Beetle."

Marika shrieked in disgust. "Gross! What did you do?"

"I kicked him up his bloody arse, and when he turned towards me with his shocked face, I sprayed him. When he started running, I ran after him spraying all the way. The foamy beast scurried back to his cave. The coppers treated it like a joke, but they must have frightened him because I haven't seen the bleeter since." Wendy stared at the spot on her bonnet. "Just regular doody. Let's go."

The friends rode Kensington High Street on the upper deck of Number 49. It was fun looking down on everything, and Marika started giggling. She felt as if she were on an amusement ride as the driver whipped dangerously around tight corners. They got off at one of Wendy's favourite shopping places, Kensington Flea Market. Two floors were crammed with stalls plying tie-dyed garments, see-through lacy blouses, round-toed leather and suede boots, jewelry, trinkets for every room in the house.

Wendy said, "Go Christmas shopping."

Marika thought it was a great idea. She bought her mother a pale sea green silk scarf which was trimmed in burgundy. But shopping for her dad wasn't going to be so easy. At a stall of tie-dyed apparel, she finally picked out a gaudy buttoned shirt in his two favourite colours of black and gold. She giggled as she imagined him thanking her sweetly while he choked inside. She couldn't wait to gross him out.

A very old woman with opaque eyes sat at a cheap plastic table in the next stall. The tiny booth was bare except for the table, a narrow shelf with a dented aluminum kettle, chipped cups and saucers, and a box.

Marika whispered to Wendy, "What does she do?"

"She reads tea leaves, palms, that kind of thing. It'll cost you a couple of quid."

On a whim, Marika sat down in front of the woman while Wendy wandered around the nearby stalls.

The old woman transfixed her milky eyes on a spot in the middle of Marika's forehead. "Such sadness in one so young. I've met you before."

Marika didn't recognize the woman sitting in front of her. "When?"

"You were a wee baby."

Wee baby indeed. Marika wondered if she was senile.

The old woman pushed aside the kettle and cups with a bony wrinkled hand. "I don't need these for you." She got up gingerly and tottered over on unsteady legs to the box. She pulled out a withered black stick. "I give this to people with your problem. An hour before you go to bed, put this into a pot of milk or water, simmer it on the stove and place the pot by your bed. The aroma will fill your room while you sleep."

Marika wrinkled her nose as she reluctantly picked up the stick. "What is it?"

"Vanilla pods are not poisonous, dearie."

"Oh." Marika laughed with embarrassment, imagining the stick to be all kinds of vulgar things, but not a harmless cooking essence.

"It's an ancient remedy, and one of the catalysts to reawaken your childhood."

"What?" Marika was intrigued, and wanted to know more.

"You can't move forward until you go backward to clear up the cobwebs."

"Pardon?" Marika was now intrigued and confused at the same time.

The old woman ignored the question. "The second catalyst will arrive soon. No money from you, dearie...good luck and God bless you." She bent her head downwards to dismiss Marika.

Wendy came over when she noticed the old woman had stopped talking. "What did she say?"

"She wants me to sleep with a vanilla pod to make my cobwebs go away."

Wendy said incredulously, "Absolute rubbish!" Then she thought about it for a moment. "I shouldn't be so judgmental. Maybe she knows something we don't."

"I think you're right on the money about the rubbish part."

Wendy rubbed her throat. "I'm getting a sore throat from all our cavorting. Let's nip into Barker's up the street for some lozenges."

As soon as the two women entered the pharmacy section of the department store, they separated. While Wendy waited in line to pay for her Vicks cough drops, Marika checked out a nearby shelf. Suddenly, she began to laugh in amazement.

When Wendy finished paying for her purchase, she walked up to her laughing friend. "What's so funny?"

"Look!" Marika's finger pointed at a display of sanitary belts.

Wendy said mockingly, "How old are you really, silly twit?"

Marika lightly smacked her friend on the arm. "Check out those brilliant colours, and the ones with pretty scalloped edging. Do you know my mother once tried to sell me on the most ridiculous idea she ever had, that women needed sexy sanitary belts. I thought she was poco loco, but you know I've never seen anything like them back in Canada."

"Your mom's a visionary! Want to buy one to show her?"

"No way. It'll just remind the visionary of what could have been."

When they returned to the street to wait for a bus, Wendy said, "I've got to get you home because you need a good night's sleep for the flight tomorrow." She chucked Marika under the chin. "You're a good egg. I'm going to miss you."

"Same here. You're one of a kind."

"I'll take that as a compliment." Wendy slid her huge glasses down to the tip of her nose.

Marika giggled as she watched her friend slowly slide her glasses back up. They were the same age, but Wendy was more like a confident older sister who sauntered through life's hiccoughs.

They snapped up the last two remaining seats on the lower deck of Number 49 for their return trip without checking the upper floor. That's where the smokers went, a place to avoid as far as Marika was concerned.

"You really hate cigarette smoke, don't you?" said Wendy.

The bus stopped briefly to let on a young Indian man wearing black corduroy pants and an unbuttoned red plaid flannel hunter jacket. He stood beside Marika who was taking up an aisle seat, and as the bus pulled away from the stop, he grabbed the overhead grip. The bus driver speeded up around a curve in the street, making the standing passengers lose their balance.

The Indian bumped into Marika's shoulder.

Wendy commented, "The driver must be related to the one who got us here."

"To answer your question, smoke from cigarettes didn't bother me that much until my father had a heart attack. His doctor thinks smoking caused it, and since I started living on my own, I find a huge difference in the quality of air when I visit my parents or go to work where people smoke like chimneys. I absolutely hate it now."

"Is your dad okay?"

"I think so." Marika became distracted when she realized the young Indian man kept banging into her left shoulder, even when the bus was idling. Her friend's voice faded into the background as she focused on the man rhythmically bumping against her. She looked up at his face and noticed his eyes were closed, his head pointed towards the ceiling as if he were lost in his own little world.

Marika whispered to Wendy, "What's with him?"

Wendy looked over, quickly summed up the situation and whispered back, "He's having sex with your shoulder, and I don't think he understands English because he'd be scurrying away right now."

Marika froze.

"I'll take care of him," said Wendy.

Scenes of being bullied in school filled Marika's head until she was fuming. No longer a gangly kid running to her parents or hiding in a closet, she placed a firm hand on Wendy's arm to stop her. She removed the giant gold safety pin from her kilt without moving her shoulder. Silently, she counted one-two-three before plunging the open pin straight into the man's engorged pecker.

The Indian screamed bloody murder in a foreign language, his eyes rolling back into his head as he jumped backwards into two startled passengers. They all fell on the floor in a heap with the Indian man jumping up like a jack-in-the-box. He rushed off the bus and down the street as if ghosts with big safety pins were chasing him. A busload of people quietly watched him fall down one more time before disappearing from sight.

"You think he would have the sense to pull the pin out," Wendy remarked casually.

Marika was too stunned by her own reaction to say anything. As the bus lurched around another bend, the jolt brought her back. "I'm sorry about the gold pin."

"Bloody hell, who'd have guessed when I bought the pin, it would end up in some bloke's thingamajig." Wendy leaned over and gave her friend a big kiss on the cheek. "Just when I decide you're a helpless woman, you do something wilder than I ever would have."

"Really?" Marika was flushed with excitement.

"You're just as gobsmacked as I am, aren't you?"

"Yes, even though I don't know what that means."

"You had no idea you could be a tough bitch," explained Wendy.

"London is an eye opener. You've got a bleeter who wanks on cars and a lech who wanks on double decker buses."

"You're quite hilarious too." Wendy laughed heartily. "There isn't a city in the world that doesn't have a bleeter and a lech."

The next day, the two women said their goodbyes at Heathrow on another drizzling day. They were lifelong friends now, and agreed that next time it would be Wendy's turn to come to Toronto.

CHAPTER 18

A Messenger

Sunday, December 12, 1976 at 1:30 p.m.
Heathcote, Australia

Igor was fifty-nine years old with a pot belly that now flopped over the waistband of his pants. He walked with a slight limp from an arthritic left knee, and his head was perched even more precariously forward on his grossly misaligned neck. Grey hair was sparse on top, and his attempt to rearrange it into a full head of hair was something for people to laugh at. The folds between his twisted nose and sunken cheeks emulated the face of a bloodhound. Loose eyelid skin hung over his black eyes like a canopy. Fat puffy lower lids hinted at failing kidneys.

For the last ten years, he meticulously marked off every day on his calendars with a black cross. With each cross bringing him closer to Marika, he could feel the excitement growing inside him as their twentieth anniversary drew achingly near. The Voice was right all along. Time flew by so quickly, he could barely believe a decade had passed since his aborted mission to Canada.

He cackled with delight. "Marika will come to me."

When Father Donovan died, he had completed his parole and remained as a tenant on the church's land, still attending to the grounds of Sacred Heart

Cathedral in Bendigo to get the money he needed to build his perfect knife collection. He walked over to his top dresser drawer, and took out a small wooden box. When he opened it, he gazed in awe at the dull coin resting on his favourite material of black velvet. It was the same twopence he used to lure Marika to the barn. Olly had returned not only his hat to him, but also the coin. To find the twopence still existed had pleased him very much, and now he began to polish the surface, restoring the shine of a newly minted copper coin.

Friday, December 24, 1976
Toronto, Canada

Let's Entertain the Neighbours
Anna was looking forward to tomorrow's annual Christmas Day festivities which included lots of presents under a fresh Christmas tree loaded with ornaments and colourful foil-wrapped chocolates, plenty of rum-laced cinnamon eggnog, more chocolates, and a plump, crispy-skinned chicken filled with a delicious sage bread stuffing taken to an inspirational level with ground beef, bacon, green peppers, onions, celery, and dried apricots. Her roasted paprika potatoes, homemade gravy, cranberry jelly, and brussel sprouts would complete the special meal. Even Attila had to admit his wife's cooking had improved so much over the years that she made a fantastic Christmas supper.

After Anna finished checking her list of things to do in the kitchen, she went to her dresser mirror and checked her hair. She had a trim, colour, and set that morning, and began to loosen the black curls with a brush.

Crash.

Still brushing her hair, Anna followed the direction of the noise which came from the living room. "What was that bang?"

Attila had just returned home loaded with grocery bags that he placed on the dining room table. He pointed towards the empty wall above the sofa. "The painting fell off the hook." Since his wife was going to unpack the bags to make sure he got everything she wanted, he took a piece of sliced ham from the fridge and ate it all up as he sat down in his armchair.

"That's odd, the hook is still in the wall," said Anna. She peered behind the sofa at the fallen Portuguese sunset. "Oh no."

Should he, or shouldn't he? After an interminable pause, Attila decided he should because Anna was going to tell him anyway. "What do you mean by oh no?"

"A picture which falls down for no apparent reason means death in the family."

Attila peered over the top of his glasses. "Where do you get these bad omens from?"

"My family, when I was growing up."

Although Attila wanted badly to respond to that, he pressed his lips together, and began to scan the tv guide. He didn't feel like arguing today.

Anna rummaged through the grocery bags. She pulled out two boxes of chocolates and waved them in the air with a disapproving look. "These are milk chocolates. I wanted dark."

"I couldn't find any."

"Did Black Magic suddenly drop off the face of the Earth?"

Anna sounded a tad unpleasant. Attila had a bad feeling their weekly blow-up was about to rock the apartment, and tried to avoid a nasty scene by burying his face in the tv guide which was way smaller than his head. He took a toothpick from his shirt pocket and began to pick at the spaces between his teeth.

Anna marched up to him and yanked the tv guide from his hands.

Attila groaned, "Come on, Anna, I've seen you eat milk chocolates. Anyway, I was distracted by a dirty two dollar bill the cashier at the previous store gave me for change. I can't stand it when I hand over a crisp clean note and get back something that looks like a dog's breakfast."

Anna felt the hurt of being overlooked again. "Shut up about you and your obsession with dirty money! Like I haven't heard it before, ad nauseum. Let's get back to me." She tossed the tv guide on the floor. When she saw the toothpick sticking out of her husband's lips, she pulled it out of his mouth and poked it into the armchair rest. "You're always buying milk chocolate. Do you ever ask me what I want? No!"

Attila didn't want to be drawn into the tedium of another stupid argument but as always, all their stupid arguments were like powerful magnets drawing them together in mortal verbal combat. "Dark chocolate is too bitter. How can you eat that stuff?"

"Now the truth comes out. You're insulting dark chocolate because I happen to like it! Which means you're insulting me!" She slammed her brush down on the dining room table, and headed towards the bedroom after grabbing her winter coat. "I'm leaving!"

"Leaving what? The room...the apartment...me?"

"All three!" Anna threw her manuscript and a bottle of Tippex on top of her typewriter, and zipped up the case. Then she shoved her Marks and Spencer undies, polyester nightie, and toothbrush into her coat pocket.

Attila was waiting at the front door with another toothpick in his mouth. "Heaven forbid you should complain about my manners, so allow me." He opened the door and bowed as Anna stormed past him. "Merry Christmas," he said with enough sarcasm to annoy his wife even more.

Anna turned around in the corridor and said with an ugly smile, "Merry Christmas, asshole."

"Surely a famous Hungarian author can do better than that," Attila goaded her.

Anna's voice shook with anger, "Merry Christmas, you selfish, conceited, big nosed...fat head!"

"That's more like it."

"You asked for it!"

"Most wives leave with a suitcase, not a portable typewriter."

"Shut up!"

"How do you plan to get to Marika's place? Stick out your thumb, or wait at the bus stop foaming with anger?"

"Wait at the bus stop fooming with anger!"

"Foaming." Attila corrected Anna's pronunciation.

"Get lost!"

"What do you want from me? So, I didn't get the chocolates you wanted. I've cut back on drinking!" Attila's voice was getting louder, and the two of them ended up having a shouting match down the corridor as Anna marched towards the elevators.

"Big deal, one less drink a year! And I fail to see what my chocolates have to do with it!"

"I cut my drinking in half because you nagged me incessantly about my poor saturated liver!" Every time they had a doozy argument, he was very tempted to accuse Anna of causing their daughter's rape, and he wanted to see the tears in her eyes when he told her that he didn't escape Hungary to be with her. He did it to save himself from the Soviets. But he always managed to stop himself before it was too late to do irreparable damage.

"Now who's hurting what!"

"Speaking in riddles again, Anna!"

"You're hurting your lungs with all your smoking!"

"You're nuts!"

"So are you!"

The tears began to pour down Anna's face as she stormed into the waiting elevator. "And you forgot our last three anniversaries!" she shouted at Attila as the elevator door closed.

A Shoulder to Lean On

Marika opened her front door to find a glum mother holding on to her typewriter.

"Hello, dear. I left your father."

"It's Christmas Eve, mom."

"Chocolates."

"What?"

"We had an argument about chocolates."

"That's horrible!" said Marika, as she tried tried to stifle a giggle.

Anna sat down on the sofa, wiping away the tears rolling down her cheeks. "Dear, it's more than that. This has been building up for years. You know how much I wanted to have a house. I'm sick of apartments. Getting stuck in the elevator, and walking up and down fifteen flights of stairs when the power goes out. Battles with noisy neighbours. I want a garden, a vegetable patch. Your father shows me the balcony pots. I look at this wonderful custom-built house on Bessborough Drive in Leaside...fifty thousand dollars. The bank says no. Can you imagine? We both have government jobs and the smug loan officer says no. So, I say to your father, let's try other banks. Your father says one is enough. Besides, he's afraid of what will happen if he loses his job, or has to mow the lawn with his bad heart.

What about the house near Mount Pleasant Cemetery? Such a lovely little bungalow. Twenty-five thousand dollars. In front of the real estate agent, your father says in an offended voice, 'I'd rather be on welfare than live in a house with such small rooms'. I could have hit him, I'm so fed up.

Then there are times when your father is almost tolerable before he starts wallowing about the decay of society." Anna imitated Attila's deep voice, "People are a bunch of bastards, especially the politicians. Crime will get worse because the Liberals are bringing in unsavoury immigrants, and mark my words, there'll be more wars because people are...a bunch of bastards."

Marika was impressed with the near perfect imitation.

Anna wasn't finished. "I don't need to remind you about the stupid toilet paper."

Marika almost burst out laughing. From chocolate to wars to politicians to toilet paper. Only her mother could make such a diverse speech in less than three minutes. "The problem worked itself out, didn't it?"

"Barely. Can you imagine two grown people who survived a world war, a daring escape through a minefield, moving all around the world, losing loved ones..." Anna's voice trailed away before regaining momentum, "...only to reach the point where we were ready to strangle each other with paper you wipe your bum with."

"All because Dad wanted the toilet roll put on the holder so the paper feeds under, while you wanted it to feed over."

Anna snorted, "Every time he used the bathroom, he flipped the roll the way he wanted it. Then I'd come in and change it back."

"I remember. With my mediator skills, you guys eventually agreed that whoever finishes the last roll can put the new one on the way they want to, and it had to stay that way. Right?"

Anna grumbled something in Hungarian.

"How can anyone argue about chocolates?"

"Your father only thinks of himself. I like dark chocolate and he prefers milk. So, what colour is our sofa?"

What did the sofa have to do with chocolates? Marika was perplexed. Her mother often did that to her. "It's dark blue with some beige."

Anna slapped her knee. "There, you see! I like light colours and he likes dark colours. We had such a row in the Bad Boy furniture store, but because I'm big enough to give in, we ended up with a sofa that's dark and ugly!"

Marika touched her left palm with her right finger. "Let me see if I got this straight. You like dark chocolates, light colours, and toilet paper that feeds over."

Anna nodded curtly.

Marika then touched her right palm with her left finger. "Dad likes milk chocolates, dark colours, and toilet paper that feeds under."

"You have a solution?"

"I'll make you a cup of Sanka and show you my vacation photos again."

"Not all three hundred?"

Later that Day

A Way to Anna's Heart

A special delivery arrived at Marika's front door. She handed the very heavy, long white box of flowers to Anna.

Anna handed it back. "I didn't know you were seeing anyone."

"I'm not. I think this is for you, Mom." Marika returned the box to her.

"It's too heavy for flowers. Your father probably sent a note attached to a brick, thanking me that he now has the toilet paper to himself."

"Just open it, or I will."

Reluctantly, Anna lifted the lid which prompted a cascade of tears.

A curious Marika peeked inside to find the box crammed with dark chocolate marzipan, her mother's favourite sweets.

Anna dabbed her tears. "I have a confession to make. The chocolate argument was blown out of proportion."

"No, really?"

"Let me finish, dear. I overreacted because I got the latest rejection letter from a publisher this morning."

"They're idiots."

Anna sighed. "I never used to let it bother me, always being optimistic someone will finally see how good my manuscript is."

"No longer an optimist?"

"Just for today. I'll be fine tomorrow."

Marika tapped the white box. "Dad was never one to say I love you, but I think this is definitely his way of saying it." She pecked her mother on the cheek. "Get your typewriter and I'll drive you home."

"Yes, dear. We're going to have a wonderful Christmas."

Friday, December 31, 1976
Heathcote, Australia

Another Spelling Bee
"I want the phone number and address for Attila Paprika."

"How do you spell the last name, sir?" asked the overseas telephone operator.

"P-a-p-r-i-k-a."

Igor wasn't sure what kind of response he would get. After the aborted mission to Canada, he discovered the family's phone number was no longer in service, and wanted to write a letter to them. The Voice told him to wait, and he ended up waiting a decade.

"There's a Toronto listing for the name of M. Paprika."

M for Marika. She must have her own place, and didn't bother to hide it which means she still doesn't remember what happened in 1957. Igor was going to change that very soon. He wrote the address and phone number on a slip of paper, then picked up the glinting twopence with a snigger. "You can't escape me, Marika." The coin was wrapped up in white tissue paper and tucked carefully inside a waiting envelope with Igor's name and address written in the upper left hand corner.

"Go fetch Marika."

Saturday, January 1, 1977 at 6:07 p.m.
Toronto, Canada

This Male Appendage is a Turn-On
Marika stopped under the street light to check the address on the New Year's Day invitation card. She glanced at the thirty storey building in front of her. This was the place. She hurried into the warmth of the lobby, looking forward to spending the evening with three close friends from work who weren't able to get together for New Year's Eve. By the time she reached her friend Chrissy's apartment, she was sweating from the heat. She unbuttoned her winter coat before knocking on the door.

Chrissy greeted her last guest with a cheery smile. She was a happy thirty-two year old with greyish blue eyes that were always heavily outlined with her favourite slate grey eyeliner. She wore her light brown hair long and straight, same as most of the women her age. Her passion was historical romance novels and right now she couldn't get enough of Barbara Cartland, the English author who published a record-breaking twenty novels last year.

She admired Marika's auburn hair, pretty pink lips, and long-fringed black eyelashes. "You look beautiful as always. Are you wearing an angora sweater with your black cords?"

Marika looked down at her fuzzy white turtleneck which felt soft and cuddly. "Yes, do you like it?" She held out a large foil covered dish, and said, "I brought homemade lasagna."

"What, no goulash?" joked Chrissy. When she saw her guest's crestfallen face, she quickly placated her, "Just kidding, lasagna's my favourite."

A relieved Marika smiled at two young women seated on large green paisley covered cushions thrown on the floor in a living room filled with tropical plants and statues of owls. For some unknown reason Chrissy thought the hooting bird was completely adorable.

One of the young women was Heather, a twenty-three year old political activist who declared war against the Canadian government for condoning inhumane seal hunts. When she wasn't working, writing petitions, or attending protests with a small group of dedicated university students, she was fostering homeless pugs, her favourite breed of dog. Her face was free of makeup because she didn't need it, and her beautiful almond shaped eyes suggested an Asian heritage even though she was Caucasian. Extra long cocoa brown hair was ironed every day to make it super straight, and those Cyd Charisse's legs of hers proved she was a hot babe.

The second guest was studious Eileen who was the same age as Marika. She possessed the sweet-looking face of a teenager. Her thick hair, the colour reminiscent of melted caramels, was worn in a perky shoulder-length bob. She was an avid cook who collected and tested recipes. Gourmet was her favourite food magazine, and for tonight she made a delicious lemon creme brulee for dessert.

After sitting at the dining table eating a melange of Italian, Chinese, French, and North American comfort food, the women each grabbed a big paisley cushion and plopped down on the carpet. Chrissy disappeared into the kitchen, the sound of popping permeating the living room three minutes later. She called out, "I hope everyone likes butter because I used half a pound of the stuff!" The women moaned and laughed together.

The apartment was filled with giggles as four friends got to know each other in a way they never could have at the office. After an immature popcorn throwing fight, filling up on juicy office gossip, and grooving to pop music, talk became intimate when the music turned romantic. Red Italian wine mellowed out the evening.

What was a female get-together without dissecting the male species?

"You know where I go to boost my spirits? The horse races." Chrissy swilled her glass of wine.

"Like to gamble? Win more than you lose, eh?" said Eileen.

"Oh sure, I make the odd bet, so it won't look like I'm soliciting. But you know, if you've got boobs, large or small, every second guy looks at you like you're related to Northern Dancer. It's such an ego booster."

All the girls laughed uproariously.

"I'm not kidding. From the jockey taking my parking fee at the entrance who wants to go out to dinner with me, to the old buzzard who keeps dropping his smelly stogie out of his mouth whenever I walk by, it's great! I love the attention."

Heather plumped her pillow and leaned against it. "Have you ever gone out with one of those guys?"

Chrissy shook her head vehemently. "Heck no, I wouldn't be caught dead with them. They're all check-plaid, cigar-chomping, hawk-spitting animals."

Eileen and Heather picked up the same cushion and threw it at Chrissy who managed to kick it into Marika's face.

All the women, except Marika, found it easy to divulge their innermost feelings about the opposite sex. Eileen piped up, "Heather, what do you like most in a man?"

Heather put on a serious face and said solemnly, "His butt." She rounded her hands in the air as if she were feeling a guy's ass right in front of her friends.

The women laughed again.

Heather said, "What about you, Marika?"

Marika shook her head. She was already embarrassed as she listened to the conversation. And now that keen attention was directed her way, she wanted to leave the room. "I can't do this."

Suddenly, three paisley cushions were placed on top of her, not to suffocate, but just enough to force her into joining the conversation.

Marika shrieked at the women's craziness.

Chrissy shouted, "Is that the muffled sound of someone crying uncle?"

Marika's response could barely be heard through the cushions. "Okay! I give up. But you're all going to be disappointed." The cushions were gone and she sat up, pulling tousled hair off her face. "What I like in a man is a thick, well developed..." she paused, becoming shy again. Will they think she's strange?

The insatiable lusting women could only picture one male appendage fitting her description, and leaned forward in unison. With bated breath, they panted, "Yes, yes?"

"...forearm."

The women fell back on their cushions, at first confused. Then they began to laugh, thinking Marika was teasing them.

"I'm really talking about forearms here. To me, they signify a man who's strong, works hard, and cares for his body. When he puts his arms around you, it must feel protective and loving, so very sexy."

Her friends loved Marika's explanation and nodded in agreement.

Chrissy said, "I don't think any of us can top that. And now that the subject of men has been exhausted, Heather, how are the protests going?"

"Good. I figure if even one person signs our petitions, it's a success."

"The one person being you?" said Chrissy cheekily.

"Funny girl. There's ten of us who stick together, and we decided to have a striptease protest. We're going to wear layers of clothes and each time five people sign the petition, we peel off an item of clothing. So, who wants to join the group for a worthy cause?"

Eileen asked, "Any men in your group, Heather?" The possibility of seeing naked men in the flesh was a great incentive.

"Four. Eileen?"

"I'm there!"

"Chrissy?"

"Hell, yes!"

"Marika?"

Silence.

"Marika?"

Marika cringed. Take off her clothes in front of strangers? Hell, no! "I'll sign the petition."

All three women shouted, "Party pooper!"

Marika said hesitantly, "You'll get arrested for indecent exposure."

Heather shook her head. "It will mostly be university students who have a code of honour. No snitching. What do you say, Marika?"

"I'll think about it."

Heather grabbed a paisley cushion. "Pillows, girls!"

Chrissy, Heather, and Eileen whacked the party pooper silly and then turned on each other with howls of laughter until their youthful energy was spent.

It was time for Heather and Eileen to go home. At the door, Heather said, "Mark your calendars for the Ides of March because I expect all of you to show off your butt-naked bodies at the protest! That includes you, Marika!"

Dream on, thought Marika, as she waved goodbye to her two friends.

Chrissy sat down on the floor picking popcorn out of her guest's hair. "I'm glad you stayed behind, so we can talk. Something bothers you, eh?" She was sincere and wanted to help.

More wine relaxed Marika enough that she unburdened her woes. "I sometimes wonder if I'm crazy, and then I read in a travel book that Hungary has the highest suicide rate. It seems that Hungarians possess the inclination to doom. To confuse things even more, the previous section claims they're hospitable, friendly, and generous, even with strangers. They're fuzzy warm, and go out of their way to make you feel good. So, it's such a contradiction to discover underneath all the wonderful stuff, they're planning to hang themselves. Apparently, it's the way they like to go, if you know what I mean. Maybe that's my problem. I suffer from the Hungarian malady of inclination to doom. Or is it gloom?"

Chrissy listened to the strangest conversation she had heard in quite a while. "I think gloom and doom go together like salt and pepper. Do you think about committing suicide?"

Marika bolted upright. "Good Lord, no!"

"Then I think it's safe to say you don't suffer from this inclination, okay?"

"Okay," said Marika doubtfully.

Chrissy patted her friend's arm. "Tell me what's really going on with you."

"I know Mom loves me, and I try talking to her, but there's a wall between us. She says I'm too sensitive which I'm so sick of hearing, and this stupid need of mine to please everyone means ignoring what I want." Marika gave a thumbs-down sign. "I'm a fake."

Chrissy nodded. "You have a heart of gold, but want to stop sucking up to every Tom, Dick, and Harry."

Marika squinted one eye. "You're not being lewd, are you?"

Chrissy laughed out loud. "I'll rephrase. You want to be honest about your feelings with other people."

Marika's eyes lit up. Her friend understood what she was trying to say. "That's it exactly. I'm afraid to do anything that will take me in a new direction. That's why I'm still slogging away at the office as a secretary which is a fine job if you like it, but it's not for me. There's money in the bank to kick-start a university degree, and I won't do anything about it."

"I understand all you're saying, but you haven't mentioned your number one problem." Chrissy looked earnestly at Marika. "Men."

Marika looked down at her cushion, tracing a green paisley print with her finger. "How did you know?"

"I see the forlorn way you look at the guys in the office."

"Didn't know I was so obvious."

"You may never guess, but I banged my head against that wall many times." Chrissy pointed at one of the kitchen walls. "Do you know I only had five dates in high school, and never understood why all of my friends were so lucky they dated all the time. I thought I was good looking. Anyway, I was twenty-one when a sixty year old man asked me out. Being so desperate, I jumped at the chance. That's when I realized I needed professional help."

"A psychiatrist?" Marika was leery. She heard stories about psychiatrists from her dad. None of them were good.

"It took two years, but I finally came to terms with the fact that I needed to like myself more. I started to have nice relationships with nice men. Not just crazy people need a psychiatrist. People like you and me benefit very much, but you have to find the right one. There's a whole bunch who should skydive without parachutes." Chrissy smiled kindly at her friend. "Let me know because I can recommend a great shrink."

Marika smiled back. It was comforting to know there was someone else who used to have a problem dating men. Maybe there was hope after all, but she didn't think she could ever see a psychiatrist.

CHAPTER 19

It Is What It Is

Wednesday, January 5, 1977 at 7:00 a.m.
Heathcote, Australia

Igor slashed a large cross on his wall calendar. It was time to perfect his plan. A breeze sneaked through his open living room window, but it was too weak to cool the summer heat already oppressive so early in the day. He sweated through his brown-soiled singlet which was once pristine white when it left the store shelf. As he passed by the window, the local blue-winged kookaburra sitting in a nearby gum tree started laughing. Igor snarled, "Used to be a rooster. Now it's a damned burra." He took off his shoe and threw it out the window high up into the air to hit the bird. It missed.

He stopped in front of his bedroom dresser and opened the oak case to reveal powerful extensions of his deranged mind. He tenderly stroked seven knife blades with a finger, each one chosen because of their unique design, but for all their uniqueness, they shared two things. They had the power to inflict terrible pain and stop life.

Which will be the chosen one? Igor picked up the first knife that he took to Finch Street a long time ago. It was nicknamed the buccaneer because of its gracefully curved nine inch blade ending in a point that was invisible to the naked eye. The D-guard fighting grip allowed him to hold on with all his strength. With it, he could slay a tiger. The handle was pure craftmanship. Someone had slaved away for a long time inlaying it with strip metal shaped into four leaf clovers. The overall length of fifteen inches made it rather awkward to conceal, but it still had a chance. After all, it was one of the chosen seven.

He picked up the second knife which he called the tiger shark because of its jaunty lines. It was another nine inch blade, but different from the buccaneer with its custom smelted carbon steel and reinforced tip. Perfect for pointing, slicing, and chopping. The double stitched heavy duty leather scabbard made for a comfortable grip, especially if he wanted to do a lot of slicing and chopping. Being a total of fourteen inches, it too was on the long side, but had just as much of a chance as his first knife. For it was also one of the chosen seven.

Igor thrust the third knife into the air. He liked its name, the saboteur. It was hand ground from stainless steel, and possessed a razor sharp edge that was bead blasted to a combat finish. A bonus was the black linen handle, black being his favourite colour. The overall length was only seven inches, making it more compact than the first two. It was a knife that could be well hidden.

The fourth was not very practical, but it was his whaling knife which packed a sharp punch with its durable blade. What intrigued him the most was the handle made from a scrimshawed whale tooth. The knife possessed fine balance for its size and weight, so it felt lighter than it really was. It was big and strong, and he knew it won't let him down if he chose it.

He picked up the fifth knife, his folding dirk which was small and neat, and fit very nicely in his hand. Handsomely slim with a single edged blade, it lacked a barrier guard to separate the blade from the handle. The fluted ivory and nickel silver handle was embossed with a mother-of-pearl push button in which a small ruby glinted. It was the kind of knife that was used to end a tough fight.

The dagger, his sixth knife, was hand forged, hammer packed, and tempered to produce a Damascus blade with a hard cutting edge. The back of the blade and tang were soft to provide maximum strength. All this spoke of skilled craftsmanship which he could appreciate in such a deadly instrument. The ivory handle offered a touch of elegance, and if one held the knife up to the light, it revealed an undulating pattern of curves up and down the blade. The dagger was on the long side with its eight inch blade and four inch handle, but it was one of the chosen seven.

Igor sighed with pleasure as he held up the last of his seven knives. Mokume stiletto was his most expensive knife, and well worth every penny. Expensive because the work involved in creating the wood-grain metal employed an ancient Japanese technique. The bolster was absolutely stunning with its combination of gold, copper, silver, brass swirling intricacy. The slender six inch blade reminded him of a miniature sword as he twisted, poked, and prodded at the delectably invisible form of Marika.

He couldn't decide which knife to use. Dancing around the floor in front of a wall mirror in his living room, he practised over and over with all of his precious knives.

Thrusting, jabbing, and pulling back very slowly.

Tuesday, January 4, 1977 at 5:00 p.m.
Toronto, Canada

Taking the First Step
Marika punched at the keys of the typewriter as she tried to decipher her supervisor's chicken-scratches that he had the audacity to call handwriting. It was time to go home, but she started thinking about her intimate conversation with Chrissy. If she ever went to see a psychiatrist, she would have to hide it from her father.

Chrissy stopped in front of Marika's desk. "Are you ready?"

Marika hesitated before nodding her head.

Two days later, she walked up to a renovated three-storey house in mid-town Toronto, and paused to read the simple bronze plaque, Dr. Jonas Madoc. Then she went inside and sat down in the waiting room, flicking through a dog-eared women's fashion magazine without looking at it.

The receptionist stood up and stuck her head out of the glass partition. "You can go in now."

Dr. Madoc stood up to greet his new patient.

Marika almost bolted from the office because the psychiatrist was drop-dead gorgeous. He had to be at least six feet tall with sexy dark brown eyes framed by sombre glasses. She loved his espresso-coloured hair which was wavy and a little on the long side.

Marika's imagination began to run amok. Thank goodness Dr. Madoc wasn't a regular physician who would tell her to take off her clothes. Having to undress for him would be more traumatic than jumping in front of a speeding truck. He was a breath of fresh air for the kooks occupying his black leather sofa. Female kooks that is, or a guy who was only interested in other men. Chrissy said he came highly recommended. Were his looks the secret of his success? The man doesn't need to open his mouth at all. Just drink his face and feel a cure coming on.

Shut up! Shut up! Marika forced herself to stop the mind patter which kept her awake many nights. She hadn't even spoken to him yet, for crying out loud. Maybe he's obnoxious and condescending. Oh God, he's smiling. What a great smile.

"Please sit over here, Miss Paprika." Dr. Madoc pointed towards the sofa before he sat down in a red upholstered armchair.

A million scattered thoughts bounced inside Marika's skull. Chrissy, I'm going to kill you. How can I tell him I'm scared of men? I should have gone to a female psychiatrist. Are there any? Smarten up, you milquetoast rabbit.

It took all of her willpower to keep her hands down by her sides instead of wrapped around her throbbing head. She wasn't enjoying the moment and squirmed as if she was sitting on rocks.

Dr. Madoc observed his patient closely. She probably didn't realize he could sense a multitude of expressions flickering behind her delicate fine-boned face. "If it's okay with you, I'd like to call you by your first name, and perhaps this visit can help us get comfortable with each other."

Fine by me, thought Marika. She tried not to get trapped by those amazing brown eyes, but she kept wandering back to them. Yes, she was not imagining it. He really is gorgeous and should be a…"movie star."

"Did you say movie star?" asked Dr. Madoc.

Marika was shocked she had spoken out loud. She quickly said, "No, I said you start." She looked away, feeling embarrassed about her slip of the tongue and the little white lie to cover it up.

Dr. Madoc insisted his new patient lead the way, so they discussed topics like the weather, good restaurants, bad restaurants, good movies, bad movies. The psychiatrist didn't mind because trivial stuff usually paved the way to everyone's sore spot. At the end of the allotted hour, he held the door open for her. "Please talk to my secretary about your next appointment, okay?"

Marika nodded and left.

The psychiatrist closed the door and sat down at his desk, going over the brief notes he made during the last sixty minutes. His newest patient was so physically beautiful, he almost lost his professional detachment. He knew of colleagues who felt strong attractions to their patients, but he thought it could never happen to him. He had always prided himself on his ability to maintain a strict doctor-patient relationship, until he met Marika.

She acted as if everything was fine, but her big hazel eyes kept imploring him to help her. He was so drawn to her, he could feel himself being pulled into her world. Dr. Madoc hoped the beautiful woman with the rhyming name would return.

"I'll never be able to look at a jar of paprika the same way again."

Tuesday, January 11, 1977 at 2:05 p.m.

Building Self-Esteem

The following week, Marika sat on the black leather sofa for a second session with Dr. Madoc. She babbled inanely again because she didn't think she could reveal intimate facts about herself. Carefully avoiding the psychiatrist's analyzing eyes, she searched for a neutral object. On the wall behind his desk were five framed diplomas. What more did she need as proof of his credentials? Turning back to look at him, she realized that here in this office, he was a skilled professional. She was the patient and he was the doctor, and it was time to get to the point or it will take forever.

"I'm a shy person especially around men. In fact, I'm so shy I panic when they come too close." There, she said it.

Dr. Madoc thought Marika's white angora turtleneck sweater and red tartan kilt coupled with her hair pulled back into a messy ponytail made her look like an insecure teenager. "Why do you react that way around men?"

"I don't know."

"Okay, you know what your problem is. That's good. As to the whys, we'll explore your life together to see if we can figure this out. Don't you like men?"

Marika stammered, "I...I...I'm a normal person. I'd like to have a relationship with a man. In my mind, it's so easy, but in real life it petrifies me."

"You mean sex?"

"No!" Marika looked mortified as she glanced at the diplomas again. "Yes, that's part of it, but just being close to a man petrifies me."

"Is it because the closeness could lead to sex?"

Marika thought about it. He was probably right. "Yes."

Dr. Madoc was surprised with her candor. He expected it to take many more hours to get to the root of her problem. It was obvious she desperately wanted help. "I noticed that when you referred to yourself you were neutral about your gender. How do you feel as a woman?"

"Um, well, um, I have the body of a woman, I guess, but I don't really feel much of one."

"Why?"

"I don't know."

"Do you think you can't sexually fulfill a man or yourself?"

Marika couldn't believe she was talking about sex with a hunky guy. She glanced over at the diplomas again and nodded shyly. "There are other things which bother me too, like mucking around in a job I don't like. It feels safe doing the same old thing because I'm scared of the uncertainty." Marika tapped her chest with a hand. "And I think I'm too nice."

Dr. Madoc smiled at her. "Would you like to end the session now, or continue?"

Marika loved the way he smiled. "Continue."

"Why?"

It was getting easier to talk to Dr. Madoc, although he did have an annoying habit of asking why. Isn't he supposed to tell her? "Because I think you can help me." His intelligent face intrigued her, and he lifted her spirits by just being there.

"I want you to do an exercise to build self-confidence as a woman. When you go home tonight, practise saying this sentence in as many different ways as you can think of...*I love being a woman*."

"Pardon?"

"Watch yourself in a mirror and say out loud...*I love being a woman*. It's called positive reinforcement. Eventually, you can trick the mind into believing what you say, even if you don't believe it at first. To keep the repetition interesting, you can try different ways. For instance, you can say it in a happy way, and then sad. Go for angry, seductive, strong. Keep doing this exercise every day, and pay attention to your feelings because we'll talk about them later. And if you're ready, during the next session we'll explore your early years."

"Okay, but I had a normal childhood." Marika flashed her first smile, making Dr. Madoc want to reach out and touch her.

What should he do? He had to fight to keep his perspective from the moment he set eyes on her. He really should send her to another psychiatrist, but he didn't want to lose her. And besides, she was showing more faith in him with every passing minute they were together. There was a world of pain behind those eyes, and what he wanted to do more than anything was to pick her up in his arms and tell her she'll be all right, that he will make the pain go away.

Bum Struts

Marika tossed her heavy winter coat on the hall bench and threw her boots on the floor. There was something gratifying about dumping her stuff at the front door, as if she was unloading the day's crap. Her dad would not be of the same opinion. She giggled as she imagined him chiding her while he picked up her coat and boots and put them neatly inside the closet.

She stepped into the living room to admire her newly acquired print collection of two landscapes painted by Tom Thomson, a famous Canadian artist who inspired other artists known as the dynamic Group of Seven. Like everyone else, she was fascinated by Thomson and the mystery surrounding his death at the age of thirty-nine after his body was found in a lake. The official cause of drowning had fueled many rumours of suicide and murder, but even without all the speculation, Marika thought there was a haunting quality about his paintings as he masterfully captured Canadian scenery with every stroke of his brush.

Reluctantly turning away from her prints, it was time to start Dr. Madoc's exercise, so she went to her bedroom. There wasn't much space after it was cluttered with house plants, something she had in common with Chrissy. She had to skirt around a couple of towering dieffenbachias to get to her bed. As usual, the oil-filled radiators were releasing so much heat she had to crack open the window.

Standing nervously in front of her full length mirror, she watched her own eyes looking back at her. Then she made sure the curtains were fully closed and peeked under the double bed at a pair of fluffy pink slippers waiting for her feet. Nobody hiding there. She returned to the mirror, put on a smile and said out loud, "I love being a woman." Nothing.

Broadening her smile to ludicrous proportions, Marika laughed as she said, "I love being a woman." That felt rather interesting. When she saw her two teddy bears sitting on the corner dresser, she laughed at herself. "Silly, aren't I?" All of a sudden, she frowned like a child whose puppy was missing. "I love being a woman," she said sadly, but didn't like the emotion she was far too familiar with.

What next? Squeezing her eyes into slits of fury, she jutted her lips outrageously. "I love being a woman!" She wasn't sure how she felt, but if anyone were listening they'd have gotten the message loud and clear.

Now, for the strong woman. She imagined being a female president of the largest corporation in Canada. Settling into her limousine, the confident executive took off a shoe and poked the back of her male chauffeur's cap with a stiletto heel. "I love being a woman, and don't you forget it." She smiled. A ridiculous skit, but the best feeling so far.

The next one needed a very creative imagination because *sexually seductive* was unnatural to her. So, do it like Marilyn Monroe with breathiness and bum struts. Too embarrassing. Who else was sexy? Greta Garbo. She had an attractive way of tilting her head backwards to laugh. Marika took a deep breath, made contact with herself in the mirror, and pulled off her white sweater. How can anyone be sexy in a lumpy turtleneck? She stood in the middle of the bedroom in her red pleated kilt and delicate white camisole beginning to feel more the part of a seductress. She tilted her head like Greta, but it still wasn't enough. She needed to show some leg. Her kilt inched up her slender thighs, and as it reached higher and higher, she began to tremble violently. Alarmed at her reaction, she looked at her face and saw sheer terror. Feeling sick to her stomach, she let go of the kilt.

Wednesday, January 26, 1977 at 6:20 p.m.

Destiny Calls

Marika finally got around to cleaning out the suitcase that had gone to London with her. She came across the vanilla pod wedged into a side pocket. Picking up the pod, she twirled it in her hand, and was just about to flick it into the garbage can when she remembered the senile old woman's words. Something mystical about them made her hold onto the wrinkled black stick as if it was a magic wand. Feeling somewhat foolish, she decided to simmer the pod in a pot of water. By the time she was ready for bed, the pot was sitting on her nightstand. As Marika nestled under the covers, a tasty aroma filled the bedroom, and she promptly fell asleep.

When she woke up the next morning, it took her a minute to remember the cold vanilla water a foot away from her head. She frowned with the knowledge that she didn't feel any different. Old women with bony wrinkled hands should definitely be avoided. But her opaque eyes kept haunting Marika all day.

"Okay, let's go backwards to clear up those darned cobwebs." She decided to give the vanilla pod one more chance to do its thing. The cloying scent of vanilla was much stronger that night, the pod having released most of its essence in boiling water instead of the previous night's gentle simmer. As she slept, she began to dream about the black shadow of a man in dark blue coveralls wearing a hat. He held something in his hand, but she couldn't make out what it was. As she tried to see more clearly, he stood in blackness waiting for her, and then it was over.

Marika woke up remembering the dream, and it stayed with her. *Is this what the old woman meant? No, it couldn't be.* The dream was so vague she finally put it out of her mind after a satisfying dinner of spaghetti and meatballs.

The phone rang.

It was Anna. "Hello, dear. Your dad and I are having our annual belated New Year's party tomorrow night. There'll be friends, food, music, and you're invited...as usual."

"Okay, I'll be there...as usual," said Marika. She hung up the phone, thinking now was a good time to go through the backlog of mail waiting at the other end of her dining table. She really should buy a desk. The bills were pushed aside. They can continue to wait. It was the envelope with the Australian postmark which piqued her curiosity. Could it be from her old friend Raelene, even though they lost touch many years ago? She read the handwritten name and address in the left hand corner. The name seemed familiar. Expecting to find a letter, Marika found tissue paper instead. "That's strange." Even more strange, it was wrapped around an Australian twopence. She held the coin up to the light to get a better look.

"Holy cow...1957. I turned five that year." She wondered if it was a valuable old coin, and read the name and address on the envelope again. "Igor Razna...tovic, 4 Mundy Side Road, Heathcote, Victoria, Australia." The name was definitely familiar. Placing the coin, envelope, and tissue paper on her nightstand, she made a mental note to ask her parents if they knew someone called Igor Raznatovic.

While she slept that night, her soft facial features became taut. An ominous feeling invaded her subconscious, tearing and pulling apart her restful pose. She tossed and turned, pushing the covers around with restless legs. It was black everywhere, and as she continued to sleep, she was held captive in a suffocating embrace. A deep smooth voice with a heavy European accent spoke to her. It was offering her a shiny twopence. The coin was in someone's hand which moved sinisterly towards her, and as it drew closer, the hand stretched into an arm, and then a shoulder. A body began to form, and finally a head. The shadowy figure was enveloped in a protective mist. Marika kept straining to see who was standing in front of her, but she had no control over the apparition. She waited in frustration until a wind roared past her, dissipating the haze covering the figure like a grey shield. A hard face glared at her with piercing eyes as black as the hat he wore. Eyes that didn't smile while the soothing velvety voice droned on.

There's lolly for you.

Marika floated forward, mesmerized by the voice and the glittering twopence winking at her from the man's outstretched hand. She had to have it. As she followed him, she became disconnected from her body, and was now up in the air looking down at the scene playing before her. She watched the man drag a little girl with auburn hair into a barn. The barn door slammed shut, and the man fell on top of her. Marika watched helplessly as the child tried to scream. Suddenly, she was the little girl gasping for air, the man crushing her with his large body. Unbearable pain zig-zagged through her like a bolt of lightning, and now she was the one trying to scream. But nothing came out.

After an eternity, the man got up, and stood in front of Marika with a long whip. She was paralyzed, her attempts to get up and run away completely futile. In desperation, she flapped her arms as if they were wings, trying to will herself to fly away before the man hurt her anymore. But she couldn't fly. She lay helplessly on the hard ground while the man whipped her over and over again. And all she could think about was where was her mommy.

Marika thrashed around in bed, still asleep, still tormented as her head exploded into a nightmare of horrifying dimensions. She continued to lie on the hard ground while the man pressed a pitchfork into her chest. The velvet voice was now rasping at her. *Time for you to die. This is God's way of punishing dirty, dirty little girls.* As the tines of the pitchfork pierced Marika's body, the man looked up. He was distracted by the sound of shrill rings floating into the barn. He glared in the direction the intrusive sound was coming from.

With the man's attention momentarily diverted, Marika strained to escape the trance-like nightmare. It took all her subconscious energy before she was able to wake up, sweating with inconsolable fear.

Her telephone was ringing. She reached out and grabbed the receiver. "Who is it?" Her voice shook as she blurted out the question.

There was no answer. Click.

Marika hung up the phone and fell backwards. She was exhausted. A strong breeze was blowing through the open bedroom window, creating a chill. She flicked on the bedside lamp which bathed the room in comforting light. After a few deep breaths, she got out of bed to rinse her face with cold water. Looking into the bathroom mirror, she saw the same fear etched into her face when she tried to act seductively a couple of nights ago. But something was niggling at her. What was it?

She pulled off her nightgown and ran to the full length mirror in her bedroom. As she turned to look at her body, she noted the four pale marks across her lower back. How many times did the man whip her? She counted them. "Slash one, slash two, slash three, slash four." Those weren't stretch marks. They were very old scars.

Marika trembled violently, trying to deny what was now so obvious. She shook her head, crying, "No, no, no!" Feeling faint, she sat on the edge of the bed staring blankly at her naked mirror image, goose bumps covering her skin. Her eyes widened with the cruel truth that hid in the shadows of her mind all these years, creating chaos in her life. She was an untouchable. A distant object like one of those Ming vases put on display in a proper gloomy museum, but never to be touched because it could break into a million pieces.

Glancing desperately at her two teddy bears resting on the dresser, she cried, "Is that why I can't bear to be near a man?"

Old fragments seemingly unrelated came together like a jigsaw puzzle to form a sordid picture. A kaleidoscope of past events flashed by, and Marika remembered them all. The woman in the shop calling her a dirty little girl, the fish and chip man asking her about Bacchus Marsh, the big stranger in the dark green car who must have been a policeman, the scruffy man with the rotting black teeth, the internal examination revealing a shocking revelation, seeing the scars for the first time when she tried on her bikini. The next memory rapidly unfolded before her. An old family friend who wanted to buy her ice cream. She picked up the envelope on her nightstand and read the name again. "Igor Raznatovic."

It was him.

She ran into the bathroom feeling the violent urge to retch, but nothing came out. Somehow, she managed to grab her teddy bears, crawl back into bed and roll into a fetal position, pulling the blanket over their heads. She hugged her bears desperately, trying to release the hurt from her body and soul as she began to sing in a little girl voice, "Baa, baa, black sheep..."

Saturday, January 29, 1977 at 7:33 p.m.

Party Night

Anna looked lovely in a burgundy polyester cocktail dress which hugged her curvy figure and fell just below her knees. It was not a colour that she would normally wear, but everything else about the new apparel, the simple slinky design and scooped neckline, were perfect for tonight's accessories. The pale sea green silk scarf with the burgundy border that Marika got for her in London was wrapped around her throat, the tapered ends trailing seductively down her back. She wore a pair of white high heel shoes dyed dark burgundy to match her dress. The stunning smoky topaz from Ceylon that cost only two English pounds was now set in a pendant on a long gold chain, taking centre stage above her generous cleavage. Missing from the ensemble was her peach framed glasses which she wore more often nowadays, but would have certainly ruined her glamorous look.

Attila stood beside the dining room table feeling outrageously fetching in a brand new pair of charcoal polyester pants and the black and gold tie-dyed shirt that Marika bought for him. At first, he nearly choked on his cigarette when he opened the Christmas gift. Anna and Marika had laughed their heads off while they sipped on their eggnog, but he decided to have the last laugh tonight. The gaudy shirt made him the centre of attention at his party, just the way he liked it. He slipped on his black framed glasses to get a better look at the six guests as they grazed on assorted cheese cubes and crackers, green olives, pickles, liverwurst pate, Hungarian salami, cocktail sausages.

Willy, and his wife Retinella, who was big, coffee brown, and Jamaican like her husband, happily munched on several cocktail sausages and olives.

The second couple were John and Shirley Ryan. John was a tall lanky middle-aged man with a long hangdog face and conservatively cut light brown hair receding at the forehead. His bossy wife, an attractive woman who was almost as tall as her husband, had a va-va-voom hourglass body, and wore her dyed blonde hair in a teased bouffant. While his wife nursed a gin and tonic, John was busy devouring crackers smothered with liverwurst pate, salami, and pickles. Attila met his friend several years ago at the tax department after he emigrated from England with Shirley. The couple had a British sense of humour which Attila enjoyed immensely; all three couldn't get enough of Peter Sellers and Monty Python.

The last couple invited to the party were Anna's friends, Canadian-born Rita and Tom Bishop. Rita was a slim plain woman in her mid-forties who had black hair like Anna, only hers was still natural which she wore straight and long. Tonight, she made the effort to doll herself up, and looked surprisingly pretty with mascara, pale blue eyeshadow, red lips, and a push-up bra under her black cocktail dress. She worked in the same clerical unit as Anna, both of them commiserating over the confusing office politics of a government department. Her husband Tom, a manager at Imperial Oil, was a fit good-looking man with deep blue eyes, a ready smile, and shaggy blond hair that tested his company's grooming policy. He was a sports junkie, his major passion being hockey, whether he was watching a game or wielding a stick himself, it didn't matter as long as he was doing one or the other. He had just finished playing a game with some buddies before coming to the party, and was satisfying his hungry appetite with a generous helping of all the hor d'oeuvres, while Rita nibbled on cheese and crackers.

The host kept warning his guests to leave room for the main course. When he disappeared into the kitchen, it wasn't long before he returned to the dining room table holding onto an elegant white soup tureen. With a corny, "Ta-da!", he lifted the lid to release the delicious steaming aroma of porkolt. The guests moaned with pleasure as they breathed in the smoky paprika-infused meat. Attila wasted no time ladling the rich stew onto matching white porcelain plates, and Anna plunked down spoonfuls of csipetke and pickled cucumber salad before handing out the food. Everyone, including Shirley the imbiber and Rita the nibbler, enjoyed the Hungarian meal so much, they went back for seconds.

As if the appetizers and main course weren't enough, the side hutch in the dining room was overflowing with desserts of dobostorta, cheese strudel, rum balls, poppyseed and walnut baiglis, and rum scented chestnut puree topped with real whipped cream.

Once the guests were incredibly stuffed with food, it was time to groove to the sounds of Attila's favourite musical group Abba and indulge heavily in alcohol and cigarettes. Anna believed the right people made for a good party, but her husband believed the honour went to booze. When she complained that he was overdoing it, Attila said matter-of-factly, "You can take the rottenest bastard in the world, fill him with booze, and he'll turn out to be quite nice."

"Like you?" Anna smiled wickedly.

"Hah, hah, Alice. You're a real riot. Bang zoom...to the moon." Attila did his best to make Ralph Kramden of *The Honeymooners* proud.

"Why didn't we invite any Hungarians?"

"I don't like mixing with them because we all become the life of the party. Former ping pong champions want to be the centre of attention." He smirked at Anna.

Anna smirked back at him, but she wasn't sure if he was pulling her leg or not. She listened with one eyebrow raised as Attila dominated a monologue on the virtues of Hungary. The three couples enjoyed their captivating host, his mellow voice holding only a hint of an old Hungarian accent, unlike Anna's which stayed the same over the years.

"As I was saying, it wasn't that Pauling character who discovered the power of Vitamin C. It was Nobel prize winning Albert Szent-Gyorgi. He also found a cancer cure in the 1950's by applying the theory of quantum mechanics, but the greedy pharmaceutical companies conspired to keep it a secret from the public. And so my friends, do you know his nationality?" Attila stuck out his chin and puckered his lips, distorting his face into a caricature of himself.

Anna rolled her eyes while the guests laughed and shouted in unison, "Hungarian!"

Attila nodded his head with a silly grin. "Good old Laszlo Biro invented the ballpoint pen. Edward Teller invented the hydrogen bomb, and Leo Szilgard paved the way for the nuclear bomb. All Hungarian!" Attila stopped to take a sip of rum and coke.

Anna wanted their guests to know she wasn't proud of Teller and Szilgard's accomplishments. She said, "Attila..."

"Shush, I'm not finished. Which country in Europe developed the first subway system and has the oldest zoo in the world?" He held up his hands like a conductor leading a symphony orchestra.

Anna reluctantly admitted her husband was sort of fun tonight. She threw her hands in the air and decided to play along.

Everyone shouted, "Hungary!"

As soon as *Dancing Queen* filled the living room, Attila traipsed playfully around the living room, shaking his butt like a 5.7 earthquake tremor as he topped up drinks. Back in his armchair, he wailed, "Ouch, I think I pulled my gluteus maximus." Howls of merriment greeted Attila, and he said jokingly, "Anna, why did you make me shake my ass at our guests? You little minx."

More laughter filled the living room as Anna said indignantly, "Oh, shut up."

Attila resumed his game. "Which country won fifty-three gold medals, seventeen silver, and thirty-four bronze at the 1952 Helsinki Olympics?"

The guests were very impressed with the tally of medals. They bellowed and cheered, "Hungary!"

Attila touched his chest, "You warm the cockles of this Magyar's heart with your adoration."

Everyone burst out laughing again.

"Hungary boasted an Olympic water polo player. His name was..."

Anna interrupted her husband, "Yes, yes, Ervin Zador. Mark Spitz. Move on to the next one." The last time she and Attila argued about Zador was five years ago, and she didn't want to get into another heated argument in front of friends.

Attila's jaw dropped in mock surprise. "I better do what the wife wants." He pouted his lips, pretending to drag out the next Hungarian prodigy. "So many to choose from. Let me think. Let me think. I have it! Hungary boasted a world champion soccer team in the fifties and a famous soccer player by the name of Ferenc Puskas. He was short and stocky, and one could say overweight — no one's idea of a great athlete. Anyway, in the internationals, he played eighty-four games and scored a record eighty-three goals. When he played in the Hungarian and Spanish leagues, he scored five hundred and fourteen goals out of five hundred and twenty-nine matches."

Tom said with admiration, "I'm feeling the love for those crazy Hungarian athletes!"

As if he were Puskas, Attila acknowledged the praise with a bow. "We beat England at Wembley Stadium on November 25, 1953. The final score was six to three, the first home loss suffered by the British. Puskas scored two of our goals. At first, the fans couldn't believe what they saw. Through the dead silence, you could hear a fart fifteen rows away. We developed a unique ground-play which totally confused the Brits because they liked to keep the ball up in the air. Even when we used air passes, they were still beaten at their own game. But you know, the home fans were a class act. Our team went into the stadium the bad guys. By the end of the game, the stadium of a hundred thousand erupted into thunderous applause and cheers. Months later, the newspapers were still writing articles of praise about the Magic Magyars."

Attila reached for a bowl on the coffee table. "Nuts anyone?" He threw a brazil nut high into the air, catching the falling object in his open mouth. The guests clapped. When he finished chewing, he said, "Where was I? Oh yes. No such thing as soccer hooliganism back then. The youth of today should be kicked up their backsides. Final exams in high school over here are a joke. In Hungary, the exams were given orally by a panel of examiners. Bloodsucking torturers, to be exact." Attila tapped the side of his head where the smart part of a person's brain was supposed to be. "We knew what had to be done to make it through the cerebral test."

"Take drugs?" offered John.

Attila feigned a disgusted look at his English friend. "Just before exams, we sat in a bathtub filled with ice for at least thirty minutes. It was so invigorating it gave us nerves of ice, and I do mean literally."

The guests shivered in jest.

Willy asked, "What about Hungarian gypsies?" He already knew what his host would say, and a very cheeky smile formed on his lips.

Attila was not happy anymore. "There are no Hungarian gypsies. The thieving bastards come from Romania."

The other guests gave Willy a sour look. The best way to spoil Attila's fun party was to talk about gypsies.

It didn't take long for the host to perk up again. The booze, cigarettes, food, and great friends made it difficult to stay annoyed. "It took an absolute genius to invent the Rubik's cube. Yes, I see you are all mouthing the H word which can only mean one thing. You have learned how to play the game!" Attila leaned back in his comfy chair. "So you see, my friends, if the Reds left Hungary alone, imagine what we could have achieved. Even with the Soviet bastards, we managed to survive far better than any other communist country." Attila popped another brazil nut in his mouth.

Shirley, who was tipsy by now, said with a wink, "Do you know Zsa Zsa Gabor?"

Attila spat out the nut, causing it to sail through the air like a miniature football. When it hit the living room curtain, he jumped up. "Who needs another drink?"

Cold and Wet

Marika dragged herself out of the security of her bed. She moved catatonically into the bathroom as if she were walking underwater. Her naked trembling form stood in the bathtub allowing cold water to rain down and startle her out of a stupor. The internal pain was so persistent that all she wanted to do was vomit into the toilet to get rid of it, but still nothing came out. Dripping wet, she pulled and tugged at her jeans and white t-shirt.

She had to see her parents.

Say Something

Anna opened her front door and found Marika standing there in a pair of sneakers, jeans, and a damp white t-shirt. "Where's your coat and boots, and why didn't you use your key?"

"I need to speak to you alone." Marika avoided the party in the living room and headed down the long hall towards her mother's bedroom.

Anna closed her bedroom door, clucking like a mother hen, "You look like a popsicle. I'll get something to warm you up." She opened her closet and pulled out an ivory cardigan which she tried to put around Marika's shoulders, but the latter tossed it on the bed.

Anna began to reproach her daughter, "Couldn't you have worn something nice? Even your black dress would have been better than jeans and a t-shirt." She reached her hand out to push Marika's bangs sideways. "You look much better when your hair is off your face."

"Mom, stop it." Marika agonized about how to start. "You've been keeping a secret from me."

"A secret from you? Darling, the only thing I haven't told you about isn't really a secret. I thought it might upset your delicate nature."

Marika felt the hackles rising up and down her spine. Might upset her delicate nature? She said angrily, "I have a right to know."

Anna sat on the edge of her bed. "Certainly, dear, if that's what you want. I don't know how you found out, but you and I are descendants of that dreadful Count Dracula."

"What?" Marika was stunned as well as confused.

"Not the Dracula with the cape and fangs, but the other one who really existed -- Count Vlad, the Impaler. The man Bram Stoker used for his Dracula character. You know, the Transylvanian who skewered people on stakes back in the fifteenth century. My distant cousin who lives in Burlington told me. We like to call her the Countess because she's rather lah-di-dah, but in a nice way...eccentric too."

"Oh, my God! Right now, I wouldn't care if Dad were the Impaler!"

"What's wrong with you?"

It was very typical of her mother to babble on about irrelevant topics. Marika took a deep breath to get back on track. "I didn't come here to discuss our illustrious lineage. There's something else, and you're keeping it from me."

Gales of laughter coming from the living room interrupted the uncomfortable silence.

"Dear, you must have the flu. Why don't you go home and get some rest?"

Marika's voice cracked. "Mom!" The vision of her nightmare came back, causing her words to tumble out in a rush, "I know I was raped by a man named Igor Raznatovic."

Anna looked at her daughter as if she had slapped her in the face. How could her own flesh and blood upset her while she was hostessing the Paprika annual party? "Why are you behaving like this? Are you on drugs?"

If only Marika could scream. "No! I know you don't want to admit it to me because it was your fault, wasn't it? I remember every horrible detail!"

Anna jumped up in outrage. "How dare you say such a vile thing to me! Get out now!"

"Not until you talk to me! Please." Marika was now down on the floor, begging with her hands that tugged at Anna's dress. She was desperate, almost more than on the terrible day when she begged her mother to rescue her from a horrible, evil man. "Don't shut me out. Please, Mom, please. I don't blame you. I love you." The need to hear an admission from her mother was so overpowering that Marika began to cry when she knew she wasn't getting anywhere.

Anna stood in the middle of her bedroom while Marika remained on her knees begging for help. She thought she was going to faint, but instead she stood there in her elegant attire as a tidal wave rushed towards her. She was drowning, but fighting at the same time to hold back the monstrous wave which brought back every single wretched detail that she kept hidden so well. She could no longer hide her daughter's rape, the memory of it returning on the day she saw Niel lurking at the front gate of 1 Finch Street so many years ago.

"Mom, say something!" Marika was wracked with sobs.

What should Anna do? She didn't want Marika to know the truth because it could destroy her life. Besides, it was her fault, just as Marika said. She was a careless mother, and could never admit it to her daughter, not to anyone. Never. "You're upsetting me very much with this rubbish talk of rape, and these accusations of blame are killing me." Anna's eyes streamed with tears. "You're crazy and belong in a mental institution." She would rather be a despicable coward and say that to her desperate daughter than tell her the truth.

Her mother's denial stunned Marika with its cruelty. "I used to think I was crazy! And now I know why! I can see it in your eyes! You know, and you won't help me!" She ran from the bedroom and out of the apartment, angrily slamming the front door behind her.

Anna blindly followed the fleeing figure to the front door. With tears pouring down her face, she sat on the floor peeking out of the mailbox slot, helplessly watching her daughter run down the corridor and disappear into an elevator. "I'm so sorry, my kislany, my child," she whispered apologetically.

"What the hell is going on?" said Attila as he stopped behind his wife. "Was that Marika?"

Anna said nothing.

"We have guests, for crying out loud. Couldn't you have chosen a better time to argue with Marika?" Attila pulled Anna up and escorted her back to the bedroom. "What happened?"

Unable to face her husband, Anna stood by the window staring into the night.

Her strange behaviour reminded Attila of the day she stood at a hospital window and he hoped the sun would blind her. No...not that, anything but what he was thinking. He shook his wife, just like he did a long time ago.

His wife cried again.

Attila had his answer. Marika remembered the rape.

Anna couldn't keep her secret anymore. It was time to tell Attila that her memory came back a long time ago, that she let him carry the burden by himself because she didn't want to admit she was guilty. "Attila, I need to tell you something."

"For God's sake, not now!" Attila rushed out the front door chasing after Marika while the bloody memories chased after him. Struggling to hold back the old pain, he waited impatiently for the elevator to reach the lobby. Then he ran out of the building's back entrance towards the visitor's parking area. If he was fast enough, he could stop his daughter. When he saw her car roaring out into the street, he cursed himself, "Hurry up, you stupid bastard! This will teach you for not looking after yourself!" He waved his arms, desperately trying to get her attention as she disappeared around a blind curve.

"Marika!" shouted Attila.

He ran out into the road, but his efforts were stymied by the cloak of the night. He stopped and leaned forward, hands on his thighs to catch his breath. Angina pain began to constrict his chest, and a shaky hand reached for the nitroglycerin in his pants pocket.

Suddenly, a car hit him from behind with a terrible bang. He was thrown into the air, coming to rest on a yellow stained snow bank by the side of the road. His black framed glasses flew off his face and sailed through the air to land beside him while the nitroglycerin container rolled down the street. The car that tossed him across the road like a rag doll screeched to a halt.

With eyes half closed, Attila watched people rushing over and touching him. Someone from the small crowd put a big coat over him saying help was on the way. He didn't know what all the fuss was about because he felt fine. In fact, he felt better than he had in years. As he got up to show them, a wailing ambulance stopped beside the crowd. He saw Willy and the rest of his guests running up to a body lying on the road. When he looked down to see who it was, he saw himself. He wanted to be shocked, but he felt so darn good.

An ambulance attendant kneeled over Attila to check for a pulse before pumping his chest. Everyone silently watched him perform lifesaving CPR, hoping with each breath and compression that the injured man will breathe again.

Next Day

The Blame Game
Marika picked up the ringing phone. "Hello?"
"Where have you been?" Anna's voice was very cold.
"I sat in my car all night, down by Ashbridges Bay."
"You killed your father."
Marika thought her mother was being horribly mean again by trying to punish her even more, for daring to demand the truth. "Stop it, Mom. If you mean Dad is upset about our fight last night..."
"He's dead."
A heart-wrenching, anguished cry from the other end of the phone penetrated Marika to the core of her being. Before she could say anything, her mother hung up.

Sunday Afternoon, January 30, 1977

Please Don't be Dead, Daddy
Willy told Marika the funeral was going to be held on Wednesday, but she couldn't wait. She watched the solemn funeral director open Attila's casket and quietly leave the room.

Feeling as black as the clothes she wore, Marika drew closer to the casket as if she were floating towards it. This is what a psychedelic trip must feel like. She forced herself to look inside. A waxen Attila seemed peaceful in final rest. Camouflaged by makeup, his facial injuries were barely noticeable. Tear drops cascaded down on him as she said, "You were a kind and gentle father." She bent over to kiss him on his cold cheek, wishing with all her heart he would open his eyes and smile at her with the resurrection of his life.

She placed a half eaten Mars Bar beside Attila, in honour of the special days that father and daughter spent on the back porch of their Geelong house sharing the chocolate treat.

"I love you, Daddy."

Marika held her father's hand. She knew he had been waiting for her. Now, she was going to wait with him until his spirit was ready to say goodbye to her.

A shaft of light broke through the stained glass mural above the casket, showering Attila with flecks of dancing colours. Marika watched the sunlight slowly move away, taking her father's spirit with it.

She stood on the top step outside the funeral home, the vision of the lonely casket containing her beloved father forever etched into her memory. Sometimes, it only takes one experience to change a person forever. She changed for the second time in her life. Everything that used to matter became insignificant -- her apartment, her job, her life. She turned to look at the darkening sky, a crazy rage burning her eyes. An evil man living at the bottom of the world had just awakened the scary blob inside her.

Marika could only think of one thing. Kill Igor Raznatovic.

CHAPTER 20

Beneath the Kookaburra

Monday, January 31, 1977 at noon
Toronto, Canada

Marika finished packing her carry-on bag. She shoved some clothes and toiletries that she didn't need into a small suitcase. A long-distance traveler without the expected set of luggage would look suspicious. She walked up to her nightstand, her hand hovering over the telephone for what seemed like an eternity. Finally, she pulled it away. Trying to reach her mother the last two days proved to be impossible because Anna wouldn't speak to her. Riddled with guilt over her father's death, she couldn't endure a physical confrontation in the midst of psyching herself up for a murder, so she stayed away from her parents' apartment. It was going to be emotionally painful to miss the funeral, but she was glad to have spent one final time alone with her dad.

In case she didn't come back home, a letter was dropped in the mailbox outside her building. She returned to her apartment and picked up a photograph of her parents and kissed it. Then she looked at the photo of Kati's beautiful face, running her fingers down the frame. Perhaps, she will soon be meeting the woman she looked like.

Remembering the travel agent's advice, Marika put on a pair of beige cotton khaki pants with side pockets and comfy running shoes before slipping on a loose short sleeved, rust-coloured blouse made of thin cotton. Although not the coolest clothes in her closet, they satisfied the need to protect her body from Igor's probing eyes, as well as being able to outmaneuver or outrun him.

During the taxi ride to Toronto International Airport, she glumly thought about how she bought a hand gun that morning, but left it at home. The clerk told her to buy one now because in a few months it was going to be mandatory to undergo a criminal background check. She wasn't sure if she could enter Australia unobtrusively with a gun, and tried to hide it in her carry-on bag, and then her suitcase. But even the most casual customs inspection would have found it. Her winter coat pockets were too small, and when she tried to hide it in her pants pocket, the butt stuck out like a sore thumb. She could throw on a jacket, but one wrong move would reveal the gun. She imagined the clunky metal piece falling into the plane's toilet bowl or in the aisle where everybody would see it. There would be probing questions she couldn't answer without implicating herself in a plot to kill an Australian citizen. Her stomach ached with the troubling fact that she was going to arrive in Australia without a weapon.

During the long uneventful flight with a brief stopover in Fiji, there was time to think about the possible scenario waiting for her. From her recollection of Igor, he must be at least sixty now; an old man who was most likely riddled with arthritis and failing eyesight. How much strength could an old man like that have? He wouldn't be able to catch a nimble young woman with long legs. Still, he was cunning, that she knew from the special reminder he sent her. It meant he was desperate to see her again. To apologize? Hardly. He's been waiting all these years to finish the job he started.

Wednesday, February 2, 1977 at 8:50 a.m.
Melbourne, Australia

Kangaroo Tails
As the plane dipped to give a panoramic view of Australia, Marika remembered the unique qualities which separated the country from the rest of the world. The place was inhabited with a hundred species of venomous snakes, seventy species of sharks roaming the coastal waters, kangaroos, koalas, dingos, platypus, and so many more unusual creatures. Then there was the kookaburra, a bird with a call that sounded like human laughter, making nicknames like the *laughing jackass* and the *ha ha pigeon* a suitable fit.

The hot barren centre of Australia was inhospitable, but to the aborigines it was a comfortable home. Marika peered down at the continent as a long buried homesickness threatened to ruin her plans. Before it got worse, she quickly shut down the emotions that would only get in the way of what she came to do.

When she stepped onto the airport tarmac, her skin sizzled like eggs on hot asphalt in response to the forty degree celsius heat. She took off her watch and gazed at it fondly. It was a Christmas present from her dad. The slim leather wristband will do nicely, so she quickly pulled her hair up into a ponytail and tied it with the watch.

All she wanted to do now was pick up her rental car and find a gun shop. A hand gun for a tourist will arouse suspicions, but maybe a hunting rifle present for her pretend Aussie boyfriend will go unchallenged. As she walked past the duty free shop, she saw a large white straw brimmed hat in the window, and decided to buy it. While standing at the cashier's counter, a display of souvenir letter openers caught her eye. The handle formed the body of a kangaroo with the tail resembling a long knife blade, and the pointy part looked sharp enough to give her an idea. If she could get close enough to Igor, the letter knife plunged deftly into his heart would end his life. Then if she had the bad luck to be caught, she could say she was defending herself with the souvenir, and get away with self-defence. After paying for the letter knife, she padded it with kleenex and slipped it into the right hand pocket of her khakis.

Marika frowned. Fat lot of good a letter knife would do to protect her from the gun Igor was going to use on her. As soon as she thought it, she dismissed the image of a gun. It wasn't his style.

The pleasant navy blue suited woman at the Hertz rental car booth handed Marika the keys to a white Honda Civic and a map of Melbourne. The clerk's familiar laid back Aussie drawl reminded her of how this place was her special home for many years.

"Driving is all on the left side of the road, same as in England and Japan. Be very careful at intersections where the 'give way to the right' rule applies. And watch out for the trams in Melbourne because you can only overtake them on the inside. Stop behind when passengers get on or off. As for speed limits, it is sixty kilometres per hour in built-up areas, and a hundred on the open highway."

Marika forced a weak smile. *Act casual. Say something like a regular tourist.* "When did Australia convert to the metric system?"

"I think it was in 1970, so we're about a hundred years behind the Europeans."

"Canada converted a few years ago, and I'm still trying to get used to it."

"What brings you to Australia?"

Don't you know? It must be written all over my face. I came back to murder a pedophile rapist. Marika scrutinized the smiling clerk's expression. She doesn't suspect a thing. "I used to live here."

"Oh, this is a sentimental journey."

"Something like that."

The clerk's smile became bigger and whiter. "Enjoy your stay in Australia."

Stick Shift - No Way

Marika tossed her straw hat, carry-on bag, suitcase, and winter coat into the booth of the Civic before she realized the car was equipped with a manual transmission. Damn, there was no way she would be able to drive with a stick shift, and rushed back inside.

She was ready to have a total meltdown at the Hertz rental booth by hurling disgusting swear words and pounding on the pleasant clerk's desk. How dare the perky woman with the fake smile not have the car she ordered. But she didn't come all this way to fall apart over the wrong automobile. She pulled herself together and calmly said, "I'm sorry, but I asked for a car with an automatic transmission."

"There's only one car available at the moment, and it has a manual drive. We should have an automatic later today if you'd like to wait?"

Marika scanned the area for Hertz's competitor without any luck. Where the hell was Avis when a desperate person needed them? She said with disappointment, "It's okay, I can't wait that long. Thank you very much."

Really, Marika? Thank you very much, no less. She wanted to slam herself into a wall and kick her own ass. Even with her dear father dead, her mother hating her, Igor waiting to kill her, she waiting to kill him -- and a manual transmission -- she never forgets to be polite.

She couldn't risk asking the fake smiler for directions to Heathcote, so she grabbed several maps on the way out, hoping one will provide clear directions to her destination. Huddled inside the Civic, she mapped a route that would get her to Heathcote in ninety minutes. Once she was finished, she folded the map and placed it on the seat beside her. Then she stared at the stick shift like it was her enemy. She was nineteen when she took a few lessons and discovered she hated manual transmissions, but she knew what to do...in theory. In real life, she had stopped traffic every five minutes. Changing gears was all about following the capital letter H and timing the clutch to keep the gears from grinding or stalling the car. If that wasn't enough of a challenge, she would have to use her less dominant left hand because the wheel was located on the right side of the car, a confusing situation for her brain. To make matters worse, she would also be driving on the wrong side of the road.

"The stick shift is in neutral. Now what?" It wasn't easy remembering information filed away under *S for Stupid*, but she was pretty sure she had to depress the clutch and turn the ignition. The engine roared to life.

"Thank you, God," she said with relief.

The heat of the day and a bad case of nerves turned her armpits into a soggy mess, so she turned on the air conditioner. What happened next was a blur -- stick shift in first gear, brake pedal to the floor, and emergency brake disengaged. Then she took her foot off the brake, moved it over to the gas pedal, and began to accelerate slowly as she eased up on the clutch.

"I'd be well on my way to Heathcote if I were driving a normal car," she said bitterly.

Momentarily distracted, she released the clutch too late and the car shot forward, but at least it moved in the right direction. Ugh. The vents were pumping hot air. No time to ditch the sucky car, so she rolled down the power windows.

"Oh shit, red light approaching fast." The car began to shake as Marika hit the brake pedal. The engine promptly died in the middle of the busy road. She sweated profusely as she put the stick shift into neutral and restarted the engine.

"Get off the road, you lousy female driver!" shouted an impatient bozo in the car behind her.

Marika stuck her head out of the window and angrily shouted back, "Male chauvinist pig!" When she looked back, the bozo gave her the finger. Any other day, she would have reacted to the rude gesture, but unwanted attention was the last thing she needed. "It's too late now." The male chauvinist pig would be only too happy to identify her in a police lineup after her mug and Igor's dead body were splashed across the front page of the newspapers.

"Calm down or jeopardize everything."

The ultimatum was enough to turn things around because the Civic decided to behave. The young woman was back in business as she drove onto Melbourne-Lancefield Road, following the signs that would eventually lead her to Northern Highway.

Clank, clank, clank.

"What the hell is that?" moaned Marika. As far as she could tell, the noise was coming from inside the car, not the engine. And that's all she cared about since there was no turning back.

She ached from a sleepless plane trip which had dragged on twenty hours longer than she wanted it to, but stopping at a hotel was out of the question.

When she reached Northern Highway, she pulled over at the first cheap restaurant; a strong cup of iced coffee topped with a scoop of vanilla ice cream was exactly what she needed. Feeling more alert, she wasted no time getting back on the road.

Pushing the Civic beyond the speed limit created a buzz that made her feel invincible. She needed it after the degrading experience with the stick shift. Wind blew through the car windows, whipping her ponytail into frenzied flight. It was just her and the land, and she could forget what lay ahead as she blended with the surroundings. Turning her head to look out the side window, she watched a kangaroo hopping along the barren land, but the cute marsupial disappeared too quickly. Reluctantly, her foot eased off the gas pedal. An encounter with the Aussie police and a speeding ticket were not on her agenda.

It was time to check her route. When she opened the map, a gust of strong wind surged through the open windows, blowing it to the rear seat behind her. With one hand on the steering wheel, she pulled her seat into a reclining position, and twisted her body as she stretched her right arm backwards. She groaned as she inched her fingers closer. Finally, she grabbed the corner of the map, put it back on the seat beside her, and plunked her shoulder bag on top as a paperweight.

She forced herself to look at the countryside which was parched brown in areas, but moments of relief were provided by tree clusters and tufts of green grass sprouting from the earth like porcupine quills. Giant birds which looked like turkeys dawdled along the ground with their black feathers and red heads, and furry koala bears decorated the eucalyptus and gum trees as if they were Christmas ornaments. There was even a thriving cornfield, the silky husks swaying gently in the wind. Spotting distant mountains, she wondered if they were the Great Dividing Range. Whatever name they went by, they were a sight for sore eyes. Vibrant healthy evergreen trees nestled along faraway hilly slopes fed by water from underground reservoirs. When she looked to her immediate right, she saw a dense forest with a creek flowing alongside the highway.

She was in the middle of a desert oasis.

Rendezvous with a Child Rapist

Marika sensed an evil presence as she breathed the stifling air in Heathcote. This was the small town where two people were going to journey back to the past and settle a score. She remembered that Heathcote was a former mining town from the gold rush days, and allowed herself a brief glance at the quaint merchant shops where the miners used to buy their staples or do business at the local bank and post office.

But this was not a sightseeing tour, so she kept driving.

It was eleven o'clock in the scorching sun. The heat was already searing the delicate flesh inside Marika's nostrils with every breath she took. Thankfully, her elevated heartbeat was steady enough with the help of adrenalin pumping through her veins. Gripping the steering wheel tightly, she clenched her jaw as she watched the road ahead.

Without warning, a leaning sign post appeared, and she slowed down to read the name. Mundy Side Road. She hesitated before taking the road. It was more of a narrow trail lined with sporadic trees, but amazingly, they turned into a picturesque canopy of leafy branches where trees on either side formed an arch. She wasn't sure if surreal was the right word, but driving under the canopy was an astonishing experience. Then it abruptly ended, and it was better this way. She came to commit murder, not enjoy nature.

Where were the neighbours? All she saw were koala bears watching her suspiciously from their tree branches. And just when she thought there was no one else to worry about, she passed two simple dwellings on either side of the road. Then one more. They all had hot tin roofs and acres of property at their disposal, but none of them belonged to Igor.

There was a light bend in the road up ahead, and she slowed down to read the number 4 sign on a rusted mail box. The smart thing to do was hide the car, so she turned off the road and drove behind some large bushes. Fetching her straw hat from the booth, she began treading softly over the brown earth to Igor's place.

Nestled amongst the eucalyptus and gum trees was a rundown wood-framed bungalow with blistering grey painted planks and a green tiled roof. The striped awning over the front porch and broken shutters on the windows showed former pride of ownership. Now the house had all the appeal of a shack. A rickety wooden picket fence with peeling white paint bordered the front of the property beside the dirt road, and a long gravel path led up to the front door. To the left of the house, a decaying wagon was tilted on its side with two large spoked wheels separated from the frame and lying forlornly beside it. Nearby was a big pile of chopped wood, a source of fuel which must be waiting for the upcoming winter. Behind the house were tall trees and a thick growth of bush followed by a wide clearing.

Marika hid behind a tree trunk at the outer edge of the neglected property, nervously watching the house for signs of movement. She took a few deep breaths to still her racing heart, but it didn't work. "Where's the angry, deranged woman who's going to kill Igor? And why am I doing this?" she asked herself. Because he'll never leave you alone until you take control, was her inner reply.

The memory of her dad's loving presence filled her with courage, and when she took another deep breath, this time it helped. The straw hat was tilted forward on her head to shade her eyes from the glaring sun as she slipped through a gap in the fence. It was a struggle to make her legs walk up the gravel path leading to the house, all the while expecting Igor to come out and shoot her. But something kept telling her that he didn't have a gun. With trembling knees, she climbed up the first wooden step of the porch which creaked under her foot.

She stopped as heart pounding terror paralyzed her.

Inside the House

Igor growled, "What's that noise? If those drunken ratshit Abos have come back looking for grog, I'll stick 'em." He peered through a slit in the living room curtain to find a tall feminine figure standing in the shadow of the porch awning.

She's here, said the Voice.

Igor grabbed his pristine hat and put it on his head. It was the only item of apparel that he kept in mint condition. "We have company." He opened the door, intently watching the statue-like figure with a face partially hidden by a large white hat.

Marika felt the sweat trickle down her arms as globules of perspiration broke out on her upper lip. She tilted her head upwards to get a good look. Her rapist looked the same, only now he was older, uglier, had less hair. His eyes were even more black; his nose still crooked, but it wasn't always like that, not the first time she and him crossed paths.

He stood on the porch in his damn black hat and dirty blue coveralls with a two-day old stubble coating his sunken cheeks and chin.

Were they the same hat and coveralls?

She could feel revulsion washing over her, and scolded herself. She didn't come this far to cry like a baby. Struggling to keep her composure, she took off the wide brimmed hat and flung it behind her like a frisbee. *Take a real good look at my face, Igor.*

From the hot thin air, she summoned up his words from a long time ago. "I'm an old family friend." Remembering her father as he lay in his coffin gave her the courage to speak in a strong clear voice.

Igor didn't like the female visitor mocking him. The Voice said it was Marika, but he needed to be sure. He scrutinized the reddish brown hair with its wispy bangs, the big eyes, and the mole. Maybe it wasn't a mole. The black spot underneath the woman's left eye could be a small fly gorging on moist flesh. He stared, but the spot didn't move. A fly would have been crawling by now and smacked away by an irritated hand. It was definitely a mole.

Igor tucked his right hand inside his pocket, absentmindedly stroking his crotch. He crooned, "Marika."

The young woman was worried about what Igor had inside his pocket, knowing each will soon reveal their choice of weapon.

Igor slowly took out his hand, relishing the power he had over his visitor. He was empty-handed.

Marika displayed not a single emotion while the pedophile dictated the moment.

Igor could see she was older and stronger looking. So different from the stupid little girl he remembered. Did she enter his domain by herself? He scanned the distance for signs of other people.

"I came alone."

Igor believed her, and his smug look returned. She was a stupid little girl then, and she's a stupid big girl now. Not much difference. "Have you been going to church every Sunday?" He threw his number one question at her in a strange lisp, scowling because he knew the answer.

Marika wondered if he wore loose dentures before recognizing the thing which commanded his mind and actions all those years ago in a dilapidated barn, and still pulling his strings. She ignored the question because there was not a chance in hell that she would give him any satisfaction. She could almost hear his stomach gurgling up bubbling molten lava. When will it boil over?

High up, perched on a branch, the resident blue-winged kookaburra looked down at the two figures staring at each other in motionless time. The scene below was boring, so he turned his feathered head to the sky.

Igor broke the silence. "Come inside and see my special collection of beautiful works of art that I have been polishing for you." He motioned the young woman to follow him in a game of cat and mouse. Spider and fly. Molester and victim.

Marika thought it was odd that Igor never acquired a drawl, even after all the years he spent in Australia. And while she was thinking, the adrenalin stampeded through her body, making it easier to speak with defiance. "Go inside and I'm gone. I don't want to see your special collection."

Igor felt the cruel insult. You may not want to see my special collection, but you're going to feel it, he thought to himself. He had to get his hands on her. Did she carry a weapon, a gun? No. He knew she didn't have a gun.

Marika again wondered if he had a weapon hiding inside his baggy coveralls. She stared at him from the bottom step, even though she wanted to look away. Something had to be done to stop his black eyes from immobilizing her, so she stuck her hand into her blouse pocket and when she pulled it out, she flicked something at him.

Igor ducked, but realized it was a small object which fell harmlessly at his feet. He looked down at the shiny twopence glinting at him and realized his messenger had come back home.

Marika seized the moment by heading towards the clearing which led to a cliff covered in swirling shades of pink clay. Looking back at Igor with loathing, she said, "Pink is not your colour."

CHAPTER 21

In and Out

Tuesday, February 1, 1977 at 8:00 p.m.
Toronto, Canada

Celestial Chimes

Anna stared at her haggard, lifeless face in the bathroom mirror, going back to the night of the party. She was having such a good time until Marika blew her away. She remembered pacing in her bedroom while the solemn guests said goodbye. They didn't want to intrude during a family crisis. Pacing even more furiously, she tried to lose the pain by out-walking it, but it had no trouble keeping up with her. She remembered when their friends returned through the unlocked front door and stood in her bedroom with looks of utter grief. She stared at them in surprise as Tom and John fought back tears, and the women cried unabashedly. But it was Willy who surprised her the most. He sobbed the loudest as he held out Attila's black framed glasses.

Anna watched six friends gaze helplessly at each other, none of them wanting to start first. She asked in a confused manner, "Why isn't my husband with his glasses?"

Retinella and Rita wrapped their arms around her while Willy pulled himself together. It was his duty as Attila's best friend to break the tragic news. In a heavy sob-laden voice, he said, "I'm sorry, Anna. A car ran over Attila and he's...he's gone."

Anna remembered collapsing into the women's arms as they tried to provide comfort and at the same time prevent her from rushing out of the apartment. It was six friends who helped her get through the night. Because of them, she hung on by a thread, and because of that, she couldn't see Marika. Because she hated her daughter, and the thread would break and she'd go insane.

That was a few days ago.

Tonight, it was remotely possible that she could face the reality of what happened. She prayed a lot to God, her faith restored with the passing of time. Why? She asked Him so many times.

The turning point came yesterday as she lay in a steaming hot bath trying to evaporate the gnawing hopeless feeling of guilt. The desire to end the pain by dying was uppermost in her mind when her swollen eyes looked down into the water. Staring into the clear hot liquid, she aimlessly watched an unusually long Grecian blond hair drifting in the tub. It began to rise upwards, one end crossing over the other to form a hollow balloon with two tails spinning like the blades of a fan in its effort to reach the surface. Finally, the wild gyrations were over when the strand reached the spot where water met air. She continued to watch as the hair unknotted itself on the calm surface and floated peacefully towards her. She placed her hand underneath until Attila's hair lay gently on her skin. As she lifted it, she felt a cool breeze, and when she gazed upwards, her husband's face was smiling at her, saying, *I love you. I've always loved you.*

She blinked and the apparition was gone. "I love you too! Don't leave me alone!" cried Anna. Attila's confession rang true like celestial chimes.

He loved her after all.

As she looked in the mirror remembering the special moment from yesterday, she knew she had to see Marika and say she was sorry for all the pain she caused. She dialed her daughter's number, but the phone kept ringing. Taking a taxi to Marika's apartment, she let herself in with a spare key and wandered into the bedroom. When she noticed dust covering the dieffenbachia leaves, she began to wipe them down with a damp face towel.

As she looked around, she noticed a crumpled airmail envelope and tissue paper on the nightstand. Absentmindedly, she picked up the envelope and read Igor's name and address handprinted in the upper left hand corner. She recognized the name all too well which sent her into panic mode as she frantically searched the bedroom closet to discover a carry-on bag and a small suitcase were missing. She should know because she gave the luggage set to her daughter as a birthday present last year.

"Marika's gone after him!"

Anna dizzily circled the room. "He'll kill her! What should I do?" Her mind desperately tried to find a solution, but it drew a blank. Then she did the only thing she could think of. She began to pray, and the answer came to her. She had to get back to her apartment.

When Anna reached home, she ran to a desk tucked away in a corner beside the balcony door, and began to toss papers into the air during her search for the family address book. Once she located it, she hurriedly flicked through the pages until she found what she was looking for. She grabbed the phone and dialed the operator.

"I need to make a long distance call to Australia...and hurry! It's a matter of life and death!"

Wednesday, February 2, 1977 at 11:27 a.m.
Sunbury, Greater Melbourne, Australia

A Day Off - Aussie Style

Worlock sat in his back garden lapping up the sun and an ice cold lager. He had taken the day off to reminisce about a little girl and the terrible crime that occurred two decades ago. Going down memory lane to a time that caused him many sleepless nights was something he needed to do. He remembered innocent little Marika, her bleeding body curled up in a fetal position, the two scrubby men who stood in front of him as if they were at a tea party. The trial, the verdicts, the disappointing sentences flashed before him until he had enough.

Although his short light brown hair was sprinkled with grey, the years were kind to him. Still handsome and healthy, his daily running kept him nicely toned, but the woman of his dreams remained elusive. He began to fast forward to April, the month of his fifty-fifth birthday which meant a plethora of gifts from his men, the sillier the better. They had the utmost respect for him and his unblemished police record. The respect was mutual and he would have no hesitation in laying down his life for them.

He looked over a side hedge at Miss Dankworth's house, the twin to his twenty-five year old red brick bungalow. His neighbour was a British spinster who didn't appreciate the fact that humour existed on the planet called Earth. He wondered what she would do if she saw him relaxing in nothing but his loose boxer shorts, an early birthday gift from one of his men who had moved back to England. He thought the underwear was rather funny with koala bears sipping lager on a white and green background of eucalyptus leaves. It's not as if he was parading himself in one of those tight European budgie smugglers. Skimpy, clingy polyester bathers or undergarments were not his style. Give him cotton boxers any day.

He admired his purple and yellow pansies growing in partial shade alongside the house. Magical seeds must have been inside the packets he bought from the nursery because they turned out to be hardy little flowers holding up to the hot weather. Then he looked down at his grass which was another story. It needed mowing and a drink of water, and his bushes were begging for a trim. They can wait.

When the phone started ringing, Worlock wondered whether he should pick it up.

Tuesday, February 1, 1977 at 9:27 p.m.
Toronto, Canada

A Bad Connection
Five rings, six rings, seven...
"Oh God, where is he?" cried Anna. "He must be at work." Nine rings. She kept praying and pacing the living room, stretching the telephone cord to its limit. Suddenly, she yelled, "Pick up the phone!"
"Hello?"
Anna's despair turned into hope. "Is this Inspector Worlock?"
"Chief Superintendent Worlock. Who is this, and where are you calling from? I can hardly hear you."
Anna shouted into the phone, "Anna Paprika! I'm calling from Toronto, Canada! We exchange Christmas cards every year!"
"Why, of course. How are you, Anna? And how's Attila and Marika?"
"There's no time for chit chat! Marika has gone after Igor Raznatovic! I found his name and address on an envelope, and her luggage is missing!" Anna's voice cracked with worry, "She's in Australia, so you've got to do something!"
"When did she leave Canada?"
"I'm not sure!" Anna's words lashed out at Worlock, desperately wanting to give the man what he needed to know, but failing miserably.
"Where's Igor?"
Anna pulled the crumpled envelope out of her bag and gave him the address in a shaking voice.
Worlock knew the place from post-Pentridge days. He often wondered if Anna would remember the rape, and from the frantic sound of her voice, he finally got his answer. "Where's Attila? Don't tell me he's gone after Marika?"

"He...he died a few days ago!" Anna began to cry into the phone before she forced herself to stop. She focused on her baby who could be tangling with a fiend at this very moment.

Worlock was momentarily lost for words. Attila was dead and Marika was in Australia looking for Igor, if she hadn't found him already. "I'm so sorry, Anna. I've got to move on this right away. Give me your phone number."

Anna shouted, "Have you got a pen and paper?"

"Go ahead." After Worlock wrote down the number, he hung up the telephone. His detective skills began to push Attila's death out of his mind because he couldn't do anything for the poor man. He had to concentrate on Marika.

The telephone operator connected him to Igor's phone, but it kept ringing. He slammed the receiver down and picked it up again. Should he call the state troopers? What if Marika managed to kill Igor? No, he had to do this alone. He slammed the receiver down again. Goodbye spotless record. After slipping on his trench coat and running shoes, he grabbed his gun and headed for his Holden, a souped-up performance car which bravely stood up to fifteen scorching summers. It had more grunt than the best sports vehicle around, and the dark grey and black paint shone like new.

Bugger. He would have to take a slow main road that linked to Northern Highway, but he wasn't going to let an inconvenience like an hour's drive get in his way. A mobile siren was placed on the car roof, and as the powerful engine turned over like a formula-one race car, he looked into the rearview mirror and said, "Find Marika before anything happens."

A lead foot and his beloved Holden will get him to Heathcote in half the normal time.

Let it All Hang Out

Marika planted her feet in the middle of the clearing with her back to the gorge, watching Igor limp towards her.

Twenty-five feet away, he stopped following the slender beauty. The woman was in his territory once again. *She thinks she's looking at a doddering old weakling, otherwise she wouldn't be here.* He said, "You have come to see me because you finally remembered our special relationship." Without any provocation, the bad memories of his incarceration flickered across his face, turning it splotchy red with anger. He snarled, "For such a puny little girl, you caused me a lot of pain."

Caused him a lot of pain? Marika wanted to hit him, and almost stepped over the invisible safety line she had drawn between herself and Igor.

"Want to hit me? You'd enjoy that."

Igor seemed to know what she was thinking, making her feel as if she was standing behind an x-ray machine exposing her to the bone.

"You were a dirty girl back then, and you're a dirty girl now with no respect for the Lord. Tell me you have suffered for your wickedness."

Marika looked at Igor more closely, and saw saliva drooling from his lips. The more he spoke, the worse his lisp became. It was obvious that his twisted mind took away the innocence of a happy child and forever marred life's memories for a mother and father. She found herself wondering if it would have been better if Igor killed her that day so long ago. Then she blinked away the image of her youthful death as she again locked onto his unrelenting glare. Remembering her dead father continued to give her the courage to stare back into the eyes of evil. Igor didn't look frail. It seemed he was not the weak old man she hoped to find.

Who's going to die today?

Buzzing flies kept circling and landing on Marika as if she were an airport runway. She fought back the overwhelming urge to swat at them because she didn't want Igor to think she was preparing to move in on him. He might do something first if he became irritated by her physical discomfort, and she couldn't let that happen. She stood still while the flies tormented her. At least they were less of a nuisance than their Canadian cousins, the notorious black flies which were twice the size and avaricious flesh eaters to boot. If one got sucked up her nose or smacked into her eyes, only then would she crush the gross little insect. Curiously though, not one fly landed on Igor.

Perhaps it was the long flight from Canada, the merciless heat or the flies, or all of it. Whatever it was, Marika felt the restrictive walls crumbling. "You sick old man! Fucking bastard!" She spat the string of words at Igor and braced herself. She had just given him the opportunity to go bananas and grab her by the throat or knock her to the ground.

Igor swayed back and forth like a willow in the wind, but he didn't move from his spot. His black eyes blazed evil hatred, making Marika feel the same fear she felt when he destroyed her childhood. "I'm going to punish you in the name of the Lord. Do you know what Igor stands for? Hero! I am a hero in God's eyes! I would have killed you if that stupid Niel didn't interrupt me. The pitchfork was less than an inch from skewering your chest while you blubbered like a baby."

Marika began to tremble with anger.

"Mommy, Mommy!" Igor mocked Marika with her four year old cries for help. "You pissed all over the floor...so very dirty." Remembering how close he came to killing her, Igor hopped with excitement. "I ripped you to shreds! And I squeezed your chest until you couldn't breathe!" He was sweating from his forehead, rivulets running down from below his black hat. The bulge in his pants throbbed noticeably.

The angry young woman saw the throbbing and her mind snapped. Civilization with its binding rules began to fall into a vortex. She advanced rapidly with the overpowering feeling she could pulverize the pedophile's head with her fists.

Igor watched every step the young woman took until she was ten feet away. He slowly stuck his hand into his right hand pocket and when he pulled it out, the sharp blade of his dirk flicked open with a swish as he pressed the ruby embedded in the handle.

Marika jumped back as if she had burned her hand on a hot stove. It was remarkable that both of them chose knives, except hers looked like a kangaroo tail. Too bad she didn't have time to ponder about the strange coincidence. And now that she was close enough, she could smell the odour of skunk emanating from the man's pores. Maybe that was why the flies avoided him.

Igor touched the tip of his knife before pointing its deadly beauty at the woman standing in front of him. "I'm going to punish you for the beatings I suffered in gaol!"

Marika wondered if a desperate man possessed the strength of several men because the figure standing in front of her looked like a mythical centaur, half man, half beast, his spewing mouth exuding an animalistic strength as he tried to intimidate her. But she refused to let the monster make her cry, and forced herself to relive the horrible images of her past until she was consumed with the same crazy rage she felt on the steps of the funeral home. This putrefaction of a mutant human was never going to hurt her or anyone else again. She reached into her right pocket, but all she found was the kleenex padding and a heavy cat's eye boulder marble.

A cat's eye boulder marble?

She held the big, clear glass globe with its red vane centre, remembering how she spotted it in her apartment elevator on the way to the airport. Absentmindedly, she put it in her pants pocket for a reason not apparent to her at the time. She panicked. The letter knife must have slipped right out of the kleenex, and now the momentum to hurl herself at her molester was slipping away. The only thing left to do was pray furiously.

Help me, God!

"Have you let any other man introduce his ruler to you?" asked Igor. But he knew the answer. "No, you haven't. You've been waiting for me because you were born to be punished by me, and no one else. I, and I alone pass judgment on you, Marika Paprika." He pointed an accusing finger at her as he said with self-righteousness, "Of the woman came the beginning of sin. Ecclesiastes Chapter 25, Verse 24."

That did it. Marika felt the last crumb of civilization disappear down the vortex which eddied around her struggling form. And sweet stupid Marika went with it. Wildness flooded her body once more, producing a raw scream of pure hatred as she lunged forward, flinging the marble with ferocity. It hit Igor on the left cheek, cracking the bone and causing him to yell out in pain. But he recovered quickly.

Marika continued to scream like a banshee warning of impending death, a scream which had been building up all these years and could finally be released.

The kookaburra looked down to find the source of the penetrating noise. The glint of the knife in the ugly animal's hand caught the bird's attention. This looks more interesting now, and he watched quietly as the two figures began to duel under the hot sun.

Funny how the mind works. Ten years ago, a little old man in black ballet slippers spent an afternoon teaching Marika simple defence moves which she practised for several weeks afterwards. She remembered her favourite one as she rushed towards Igor like a shrieking harpy, and automatically reached out to grab his free left hand.

Igor was slow to respond because of the distracting scream that wouldn't stop. An attempt to stab her in the heart missed its mark as she bent forward, swerving sideways, and he ended up nicking her left shoulder.

Marika didn't feel the pain as her left hand continued to hold Igor's in a vice-like grip. Her scream intensified as she quickly wrapped the fingers of her right hand under and around his left wrist. With the strength of a woman fighting for her life, she used her right hand to brutally twist his trapped hand in a one hundred and eighty degree turn which had his whole body flipping over in an arc. He landed with a heavy thud on the ground, kicking up a cloud of brown dust. Then his hat fell off and the dirk flew out of his hand to slide under nearby bushes. Marika stopped screaming as she turned in the direction of the knife. She took a step forward right on top of the wobbly boulder marble, and stumbled over. All she could do was crash to the ground, the impact knocking the wind out of her.

Igor grabbed his hat, put it back on, then lunged at the fallen woman by wrapping his sausage fingers around her neck. His old back injury began to hurt, but it didn't stop him. He snarled, baring his teeth to reveal a black space where his front teeth should be. More drool dribbled from the black space and down his chin as he slobbered, "I got you now, Marika!"

He pressed his fingers so deeply into the young woman's flesh that she couldn't pry them loose with her fingers. He bellowed, "Breaking rocks for ten years changes a man's body, and I've been chopping wood to keep me strong!" He squeezed harder. "Bet you didn't think this old man would have the arms of a gorilla!"

Dragging Marika to the edge of the cliff where the brown earth gave way to salmon pink clay, he squeezed and choked her neck with the energy of someone who had waited an eternity to do it.

The Afterlife
Attila could smell his sister's seductive Chanel No. 5. *Kati, is that you?*
Here I am, brother.
Attila turned in the direction of the flowing voice and saw his beautiful sister. He felt the blissful joy of being with her again. *You haven't changed, and this place feels like a wonderful dream. It's definitely better than hanging around Thorncliffe trying to get Anna's attention. She was a fearless woman and I envied her. Wish I told her she was amazing before it was too late. What a bastard I was...am I still a bastard?*
Your favourite word doesn't belong here.
I wanted to hurt Anna many times during a heated argument, that she was responsible for Marika's rape, and then I wanted to devastate her with my secret that the only reason I escaped Hungary was to save my sorry ass.
I have a little secret of my own, dear brother. And Anna was going to tell you about hers.
It sounds like everyone has a secret. What were you and Anna hiding from me?
You'll know soon.
A truth hit Attila like a ray of sunshine. *I used to think reincarnation and karma was all mumbo jumbo bullshit.*
Everything becomes crystal clear over here.
Attila was eager to shake off the earthly horrors he left behind. *What people do to each other are crimes worthy of soul purgatory.* He smiled at his beautiful sister. *Look at me, not only am I running off at the mouth, I'm also getting all spiritual.* As he telepathically spoke to Kati, he became connected to all living creatures on Earth without even realizing it. *I don't mean to alarm you...*
Nothing alarms me.
How do I say it?
You see a kaleidoscope of heartbreaking images.
I think I'm having a nightmare.
Tell me about it.

Cats are screeching at the top of their lungs, and Chinese bastards are throwing dogs against brick walls to break their legs. I've never seen a cat cry tears, but I'm seeing it now.

Little brother, what you think is only a nightmare is a vision of the future, and it is your special assignment. Many lost souls will cross over soon, and you are going to be one of their guardians.

Don't I get a chance to meet God?

You will. First, I have to tell you about your vision. A group of Chinese activists are going to try and rescue the animals you saw from the unspeakable cruelty of being boiled or skinned alive for their fur and flesh, but a fire that's supposed to be a distraction will burn out of control. Those poor creatures will die from smoke inhalation.

The lost souls are the activists?

The animals are the lost souls. Fur farms are an abomination.

Why me?

You know what it's like to feel helpless and afraid, and God knows that you love dogs, but you need to find room in your heart for all animals.

You mean cats...I haven't been nice to them.

Kati was the epitome of patience. *God created an ideal companion to ease a human's loneliness. It's not a well known fact that cats have healing gifts.*

Then why does God turn a blind eye to the cruelty? Attila had a perplexed look on his face. *Is it all to do with karma?*

It's a little more complicated. For now, all you need to know is that humans on Earth are there to learn, but their ego is the worst of all parasites. They easily forget their spiritual connection to the same magnificent source.

The more you say, the more I see.

That was very profound, little brother.

Is God a person?

Kati laughed heartily. It was the same question she asked when she crossed over. *All your questions will be answered at the right time.* She pointed in the distance to a magnificent structure of a building that sparkled like a waterfall of diamonds. *Before you take your assignment, you will visit your former life, so brace yourself because it won't be easy. And when you're finished, Mama and Papa have a welcome home party for you. All your friends will be there too.*

Attila felt such a yearning to enter the sparkling building because it would lead him to his parents and friends. But he didn't care to see the life he left because he wasn't proud of the way he lived. *I still feel confused.*

When your transformation is complete, your confusion will be a thing of the past.

You're thinking about Marika.

That's good, you can pick up my thoughts already.
She's in danger, isn't she?
I'm going to try and help her.
How are you going to do that?
All I know is that I have to offer Marika a choice. She has a certain amount of free will, so either of two things are going to happen. She changes her destiny or the bigger plan won't let her. Follow me if you want, but remember this is home and we are coming back.

The Cross

Marika lay helpless on the hot ground, her struggling hands slipping away from Igor as she lost the strength to remove his deadly grip. A black fog rolled ominously towards her as she stared at the damned black hat and contorted face with the bruised lump under the left eye.

Igor felt such elation when he looked at the red face, and as he watched, numerous tiny blood vessels burst, filling the whites of Marika's eyes with blood. This was power! He looked down at her left shoulder, noticing the large stain. More blood. And as he looked, he saw the cross hanging from a chain around her neck.

Dirty little girl has no right to wear the cross!

Marika didn't care what her killer was thinking. She floated far away. It was a glorious feeling, and she always knew she could glide through the air. Below her was a field of sunshine carpeted with beautiful flowers of every imaginable colour. She reached down to pick her favourite purple pansy with the yellow centre at the same time the pressure eased up on her neck.

Her eyes fluttered open to see the black fog part in the middle. *Oh no, back to this shithole.* Two shapes materialized in front of her, and as she watched, they took on the forms of Attila and Kati. They must be a sign of imminent death, and they were communicating in a way that was befitting a scene from *The Twilight Zone*.

Do you want to live, Marika?

As heavenly as it felt to float around picking pansies all day, Marika couldn't let Igor defile her body ever again. Without hesitation, she projected a deafening, *Yes, I do!*

As Igor ripped the chain from her neck with his right hand, she reached up and knocked the hat off his head with a mighty backwards swipe.

Startled, Igor dropped the necklace and let go of the delicate neck with his remaining hand in a futile attempt to grab his hat before it fell over the edge of the cliff.

He yelled in rage, "My hat!"

Marika let the oxygen rush into her starved lungs. She never thought she would be so grateful to swallow burning dusty air. Her body was flooded with strength as she crooked her right leg under Igor's body, grabbed the front of his coveralls and pushed upwards to heave him over her prostrate form.

Her second favourite Bill Underwood maneuver.

Igor sailed into oblivion. "It wasn't supposed to be like this!" he screamed at the Voice which ultimately deceived him.

Marika covered her ears as Igor's body smashed with bone-breaking thuds into the jutting rocks on the way down. He came to rest on top of his hat a hundred feet below.

"Until death do us part, gorilla arms." Marika squeezed the words out of her damaged vocal cords.

A Frustrated Copper

Worlock hit the steering wheel with his hands as he drove along Northern Highway like a bat out of hell. Deep down he knew he was too late. He turned off the road, taking a shortcut as he tore through the bush to get to Igor's place.

Stranger Things Happen

Marika's mysterious spurt of energy disappeared after she threw Igor into the gorge. She lay on the ground coughing in spasms until her throat seized up. After a couple of minutes, her laboured breathing became a little easier. She rolled over and crawled towards the edge of the cliff. It was a very long way down. No one could survive such a fall unless they were Igor whose strength didn't belong to an ordinary human being. What if he was right now slithering up the cliff like a lizard after its prey? She frantically scanned the bottom until she found him. There was no sign of life, so either he was paralyzed or dead. Hungry black-breasted buzzards circled the blue sky, but they must have known the flesh below wasn't fit for consumption and flew higher.

Blood dripped from the stinging stab wound as she sat up slowly. Her energy was coming back while her brain started processing confusing messages. One of them was very clear...get the hell out of there. Struggling to her feet, she slowly made her way to the Civic after picking up her straw hat. As soon as she opened the driver's door, she saw the metal tail of her kangaroo letter knife wedged in the gulley between the metal frame and seat. It must have fallen out when she twisted herself into a pretzel to retrieve the map, the noisy clanking inside the car masking the sound of metal hitting against metal.

Marika summoned up a whisper, "Screw you, letter knife. I didn't need you after all."

In Omnia Paratus

The Holden pulled up to 4 Mundy Side Road. So far, there was no sign of anything unusual. Worlock took out his gun and walked stealthily towards the house, scanning the door and the windows. When he looked down at the ground, he saw a spot of blood which sent him into a heightened state of alert. He moved quickly to the front porch, and hunched over in a defensive position with his gun cocked, trying to see through the open door. That's when he noticed the twopence. He bent down and squinted at the year. 1957. He wanted to pick up the coin, just in case Marika touched it, but it was unconscionable to contaminate a potential crime scene if she was the victim. As he approached the door, he could feel his adrenalin pumping out of control. A balancing mantra was called for, and in a whisper, he chanted, "In omnia paratus, in omnia paratus, in omnia paratus." His nervous system calmed down right away which enabled his police training to take over again. With no time to waste, he stepped inside the house and moved cautiously through the squalid rooms.

It was too bloody quiet. "Igor! Marika!" Nothing. Worlock spotted the open box of knives, and noticed one was missing. He ran outside to the back of the house, visually sweeping the area for clues. There were signs of a fierce struggle which disturbed the pink clay soil near the edge of the cliff. Then he saw the bloodied knife lying under a bush with blood stains on the ground nearby.

Whose blood was it?

The danger was over and Worlock put away his gun. When he began to move forward, he stepped on the boulder marble partially covered by loose soil. It was the last thing he expected to find at a crime scene. Buzzards circling high in the sky caught his attention as he arrived at the cliff's edge. His eyes weren't as good as they used to be, but they were good enough to see the body of a man at the bottom of the gorge. He climbed carefully down the slippery terrain to find Igor staring into the sky, eyes wide open.

That's funny. No hat. He always thought the pervert would die wearing it.

The memories flooded his brain a second time that day. A bleeding little girl being loaded into the ambulance. Anna acting like the living dead. Attila's heart wrenching tears. Watching a nervous but brave Marika baring her back to a courtroom full of ogling strangers. The day he learned the barn mysteriously burned down on the day that the Paprikas left Australia, and knew Attila was responsible.

The son of a bitch was finally dead. "You were garbage, Raznatovic, and you deserved to die like this." Worlock rifled through Igor's pockets, but they were empty. There was no doubt in his mind that Marika fought for her life, and since there were no knife wounds on the battered body, the blood on the cliff and in front of the house belonged to her.

He stood at the bottom of the cliff groaning quietly during his ascent. It had been a hell of a lot easier going down, and although he was a great runner, he wasn't a great climber. He sat down on the ground to remove a pebble from his shoe. That's when he noticed slender shoe prints and more blood spots leading towards the dirt road. He checked Igor's car before walking to the edge of the property, his eyes glued to the ground, and found what he was looking for, the faint tire marks of another vehicle which was smaller than his Holden. He looked both ways, but Marika was long gone.

Worlock returned to the cliff where he crouched down, staring intently at Marika's blood. It must be a superficial wound because she managed to leave the area, or it was more serious than he thought and she was in distress somewhere. He had no choice; it was time to bring in the state troopers. All of a sudden, a thin sliver of gold caught his eye. He reached out to pick it up, and discovered a delicate necklace which could only belong to Marika.

The resident kookaburra broke his silence with a trilling laugh.

Worlock jumped at the sound of a crazed man laughing until he realized where it was coming from.

"You saw it all, didn't you?" The policeman hunched down with the necklace in his hand as he looked up at the hysterical bird. "I sure could use some help."

Time for a Breather

Marika drove several kilometres along the highway before she realized she didn't remember getting that far. She glanced into the rearview mirror, and was horrified to see two blood-filled eyes staring back at her. She nearly rammed a car ahead of her, and veered onto the dirt shoulder to avoid a collision. The Civic careened out of control until it stopped in the cornfield that she passed on the way to Igor's place. She was glad the other car kept going.

The bleeding from her wounded shoulder had slowed down, but not before her blouse was saturated. Reaching up to gently stroke her injured throat, she realized her necklace was gone. In her hurry to escape from Igor's place, she had forgotten all about it.

Was that really her back at the gorge? She couldn't believe what she had done, and the way she felt was what a madwoman must feel like. She tried to laugh, but could only produce a hoarse panting sound. *If only someone could see the neurotic woman with red eyes hyperventilating in a cornfield.*

Oh my, I just called myself a woman. Dr. Madoc would be proud of me.

A Bittersweet Reunion

Worlock walked quickly to the front of the house when he heard the sound of a small car pulling up. A breathtakingly beautiful young woman covered in pink and brown dust, her auburn hair tied up in a scraggly ponytail, approached him cautiously in a faltering gait. If the fierce look on her bruised face meant anything, then she was hell-bent on stabbing him with a letter knife.

His tough heart melted as he watched a grown-up Marika, defiant and strong, struggle to stay upright. *Jesus.* He couldn't see the whites of her eyes for all the blood. The wound on her shoulder left a dried blood trail down her sunburned arm, and the deep angry red welts covering her throat looked serious. All he wanted to do was rush her to the nearest hospital.

"Hello, Marika. I don't know if you remember me, but my name is Matt Worlock." He smiled reassuringly. "I'm an old family friend, and we send each other Christmas cards, so you can put the knife down."

When Marika saw the black and grey car in front of Igor's house, she knew that she was taking a chance, but after what she went through, nothing was going to stop her from retrieving her priceless necklace. Now, she backed away with renewed fear from the strange man wearing boxer shorts and a trench coat. She thought about what he said. Her mom and dad did exchange Christmas cards with Matt Worlock, so the man standing in front of her was saying the right things. But was it really him after all these years. A respectable lawman wearing underpants in public? And saying he was an old family friend were the twisted words of Igor. It was all so confusing, that she just wanted to lie down and close her sore eyes.

"I won't hurt you, I'm a police officer." Worlock looked down apologetically at his underwear. "My badge is with my pants...and my pants are at home." He knew that he wasn't getting anywhere from the leery look on Marika's face. As he tried to think of something to placate her, he focused on her red eyes, and it came to him. "I gave you a little red tricycle when you moved to Finch Street."

Marika stopped moving backwards. Only the real Matt Worlock would know what they shared. Her mouth quivered as tears welled up in her eyes, making them sting like crazy. In a barely audible voice, she said, "Hi."

Worlock nodded with relief, knowing he had finally gained her trust. He walked up to her and took the letter knife, admiring its resemblance to a kangaroo before placing it inside his coat pocket. When he noticed a lady's slim watch hanging from her messed-up ponytail, he gently pulled it out and handed it to her as her hair cascaded below her shoulders.

"I believe this is what you came back for." Worlock gave her the necklace. "I'm afraid the clasp is broken."

They both heard distant sirens at the same time.

"State troopers are on their way. In the meantime, you need an ambulance."

"No, I hate them," rasped Marika.

Worlock swept the startled young woman up in his strong arms and walked towards the Holden. "I'm taking you to the hospital." He glanced at the nearby Civic with curiosity. "Is that a corn husk sticking out of the bonnet?"

Marika gave him a sheepish grin as she twirled the necklace around her finger to make a chain ring. She deflected his question with her own. "Are you wearing beer-guzzling koala bears?"

Worlock smiled back, thinking there was nothing ordinary about this beautiful young woman.

A Great Big Favour

Marika spent the last three days in hospital. Although her blood-filled eyes and bruised vocal cords needed a couple of weeks to heal, the welts on her throat were already fading into a yellow brown. She decided that she was a quick healer because her wounded shoulder felt better, so she discarded the sling the doctors made her wear.

Worlock walked into her private room with his hands behind his back, and couldn't help but notice an arrangement of gorgeous red roses beside Marika's hospital bed.

"What have you got there?" asked a curious Marika.

The policeman thought his gift paled in comparison to the three dozen perfect roses. He reluctantly produced a small bouquet of purple and yellow pansies from his garden, all because he had a hunch she would enjoy the delicate flowers. "I hope you like them."

Marika smiled happily as she took the bouquet and stroked the velvet petals. "These pansies are my favourite flowers."

Worlock strained to catch every word. It reminded him of another hospital room a long time ago with a slip of a girl brutally violated by the beast who now lay in a morgue. "I brought you something else." He reached into his coat pocket and pulled out Marika's necklace. "You gave this to me for safekeeping before you were admitted to the hospital, so I took the liberty of getting the clasp repaired."

"Thank you so much." A grateful Marika held out her hand.

"Allow me," said Worlock with a twinkle in his eye. As he leaned towards the young woman to place the cross around her neck, he could smell the harsh antibacterial soap she used in the shower that morning, and yet, with his face close to hers, her beautiful lips almost touching his, it was the most sensually intimate moment he had in a very long time. Carrying her in his arms didn't count because he was doing his duty as a policeman. But from now on, he supposed that just looking at her would leave him panting for more. *Okay, big boy, back off and give the lady room to breathe.* He got up and changed the subject. "A little bit of finagling and the media won't get wind of what happened until you're back in Canada."

"What about the police who questioned me?"

"Lucky for you, I've got some pull in that department." The evidence pointed to a clear-cut case of self-defence which meant tedious paperwork at various department levels. Worlock had to go over the Crown prosecutor's head, a South African control freak who ordered Marika not to leave the country until he said she could. An overseas phone call to an Italian bloke, a smart-ass judge on the Supreme Court, magically made the order disappear. "Not sure how much you remember of the trial and the prosecuting barrister, Angelo Murano. He sends his best wishes for a speedy recovery."

"I kind of remember him and his wife, Sofia. The red roses are from them."

"They're in Italy for their daughter's wedding, otherwise they would have come to see you." Worlock chuckled. "Angelo spared no expense -- a villa for the nuptials, a full orchestra, a famous Italian chef catering the food. And as best man, I'm supposed to be flying out the day after tomorrow."

"It sounds incredible. He must love his daughter a lot." Tears filled Marika's eyes. If she ever managed to fall in love, her dad will never walk her down the aisle.

"You can come with me or wait until they get back next week."

"I can't. My mother must be very worried about me."

"The doctor wants you to spend another day in the hospital."

Marika shook her head. "I hate hospitals more than ambulances." She stuck her tongue out to show the man she meant it, but the childish gesture only made him smile. "Did you call my mom?"

"I did, and she sends her love. So, if you hate hospital food and aren't well enough to fly home just yet, can I interest you in a small bungalow with a fridge full of steak and kidney pies and Chiko rolls?"

"You're wonderful. Wish you lived in Canada." Marika admired Worlock's handsome face. He was the sexiest older man she had ever met. "When you were wearing those cute boxer shorts and nothing else but your trench coat, I couldn't help but notice you have some serious scars on your leg." And a very nice chest for a man your age.

Worlock raised his eyebrows. "I'm impressed. You'd make an excellent eye witness."

"Did you get them in a shootout with a desperate villain?" Marika persisted with a giggle. She hoped she didn't sound like a blushing teenager.

"Nothing as respectable as that."

"Why do you wear the trench coat in hot weather?" asked Marika. As soon as the words were out of her mouth, she felt embarrassed. "I'm sorry, it's none of my business."

Worlock wondered what he should say. He knew enough of women to know they usually want the truth. But he wasn't ready to share his secret, even with one as special in his life as Marika. Was it morally unethical to desire a woman who was a little child when terrible circumstances brought them together? "Go back to Canada. Live your life, and if you're still curious, make it your business to find out."

At first, Marika wasn't sure what Worlock meant, and then she wondered if he was flirting with her. She looked into his steel blue eyes which briefly turned a lovely shade of sapphire. *How does he do that, and what would a future encounter be like with the handsome, mysterious Worlock? This is weird, he's old enough to be your father, but he's nothing like Dad. Stop already!*

In a calm voice that revealed none of the thoughts jammed inside her head, she said, "I'm booked on a plane to Toronto which leaves in five hours."

The young woman's resilience earned the policeman's admiration. "How did you book a flight with your injured throat?"

Marika leaned forward and placed her hand on his.

Her touch confirmed what Worlock was feeling towards her. What was he supposed to do with the romantic emotions that were a long time coming? *Bury it, she's going home.*

"I have a great big favour to ask you," she said sweetly.

A Thrill from the Past

Marika stood outside 1 Finch Street in Geelong with memories of growing up in the yellow stucco bungalow flooding her with weepy emotions. Only the house was now a weird mint green, and the imposing bushes had disappeared. Both the Smiths and Raelene were long gone, so it was just her and Worlock that day.

She couldn't believe her eyes when she saw her old red tricycle lying in a rusted heap at the foot of the driveway. The family who moved in after them had inherited her tricycle, and must have left it for the next occupants. Tears flowed down her face as she closed her eyes, remembering the fun she used to have on her little red tricycle.

Worlock was pleasantly surprised. His gift to Marika still appeared to be in working order. He remembered the day he spotted the shiny new three-wheeler and knew he had to give it to a special little girl. "Do you want your tricycle as a keepsake?"

"It belongs here."

Reclaim Life Before It's Too Late

A puzzled Marika stood in the arrivals lounge at Melbourne Airport, wondering if her escort had lost his sense of direction. "I'm supposed to be leaving," she said.

Worlock seemed distracted as he looked around. Suddenly, he saw a seated figure waving at him frantically. Nice to know he was still recognizable after all these years. He pointed ahead. "Over there."

Marika followed his pointing arm, but didn't see anything of interest. A small group of travelers blocked her view as they walked by. She kept on looking and when they moved out of the way, she noticed a little woman sitting in a chair pushed up against the floor-to-ceiling windows showcasing the airport runway. Taking off a pair of dark glasses that she wore to hide her red eyes, she realized her mother was right in front of her.

"Mom." Marika wanted to shout, but her sore throat was having none of that.

Anna stood up as her daughter rushed towards her. "Your beautiful eyes! Can you forgive me?"

Marika noticed her mother had been crying behind her peach framed glasses. Wrapping her arms around Anna, she gently lifted the little woman off the floor. "Ouch." Her injured shoulder wasn't ready for a nice big hug. "Yes, I love you."

"I love you too."

When they sat down, Marika said, "Igor can't hurt us anymore."

"I'm sorry you had to go through this alone. You're stronger than I thought." Anna reached up to stroke her daughter's bangs off her forehead. This time she got no resistance.

"Stronger than I thought too. He hunted me like I was an animal, setting the bait to lure me to my death. I'm not sorry about causing his."

"I'd be worried if you did."

"He wouldn't have stopped until he had his way."

"You must have been a desert warrior in a past life."

"Maybe a killer because I was planning to turn him into a corpse."

"Shoosh, it's our little secret." Anna put her finger to her lips. "Does it hurt to talk?"

"Not so much now."

"Your father would be proud of you."

"It's my fault Dad died." For this, Marika felt very guilty, and her pain was reflected in her mother's eyes.

"No, it's mine." Anna wanted to make up for the horrible things she said to Marika. Besides, she was responsible for her husband's death. If she had the courage and humility to admit the truth to her begging daughter, Attila would be alive today.

Marika knew her mother was trying to ease her conscience, but she would never stop blaming herself. "You're wrong, I had a choice. I could have talked to Dad instead of running out the door which made him follow me."

"We need to look at your father's death in a different way." A perfect example popped into Anna's head. "He had nine lives and used them all up." She almost smiled at the idea of comparing Attila to a cat, something he would certainly ridicule.

"What do you mean?"

"As a young boy, he was deathly ill from whooping cough, diphtheria, and tuberculosis. But he survived them all and grew up into a decent athlete. Then there was the war. He was nabbed by the Hungarian Arrow Cross Party, a bunch of anti-semitic fascists who found him and some other men hiding in the trees. He was going to be executed for not joining the German Army because they didn't care he was a university student. His own countrymen ordered him to stand up against a wall to be shot when a high ranking officer, an Eger policeman, recognized him at the last moment. He pulled your dad out of harm's way and let him escape, but that wasn't the end.

As the Soviet army started advancing, young Hungarian males were rounded up like animals and tortured without mercy. Your father didn't want to suffer the same fate, so he and two student friends hid in the Austrian Alps where they nearly froze to death in the snow with only a blanket to keep them warm at night. When they ended up as prisoners of war, your father was riddled with lice, and since there was no food, he starved until he could only crawl on the ground. Luckily, a nice young soldier painting the army trucks took pity on your father. He sneaked him away to a cattle train and gave him a bag of food to build up his strength. Wish I knew the soldier's name."

"Wow."

"After your father got off the train, he was walking home along a stretch of road when a Soviet bomber started dropping bombs. He jumped into a ditch fully expecting to be blown to bits, but the bombs fell on either side of him."

"Why didn't he tell me?"

"The war holds awful memories, so it was better to forget."

Anna and Marika huddled together sharing their love for Attila, oblivious to the scores of noisy travelers bustling past them.

"You inherited something from him."

"A bump on the nose," said Marika. She smiled sadly, remembering her dad joking with her so many years ago.

"No, dear." Taking her daughter's right hand, Anna turned it palm upwards. "I often wondered how a person faced death so many times and walked away each time. I found the answer in palmistry." Anna drew a circle with her finger around the same fleshy mound on Marika's hand. "Your father's Mount of Venus had a perfect Star of Luck."

Marika gazed at the distinctive lines on her palm. Protection provided by the Star of Luck was far more plausible than getting help from two dead people.

Anna needed to tell her that she remembered the horrible rape a long time ago. As she looked around the busy terminal, she noticed Worlock holding a bunch of pansies and watching them from a discreet distance. She couldn't bring herself to say it. Now was not the right time to hurt her daughter all over again. Instead, she said, "Can you cope with everything that's happened?"

"I don't know yet. I need to talk about what happened to me until I'm blue in the face."

"We both need to turn blue."

Marika giggled hoarsely. "You're funny, Mom."

"Thank you, sweetheart. Know anyone who's a good listener?"

"As a matter of fact, I do."

"The handsome man over there?" Anna looked at Worlock again.

"He is very handsome, isn't he? And so nice, but he's old enough to be my father."

Anna shook her head slowly. "You have only one father, dear."

Tears stung Marika's eyes as she nodded in agreement. "There's something else I need to do."

"What?"

"Find Bess and tell her she saved my life."

"What are you talking about?"

"I'll tell you the whole story on the way home. It should distract me from the fact that a cigar-shaped tin can is flying us home." Marika kissed her mother on the cheek. "Do you want to visit our old home on Finch Street? We can book a later flight."

"I'd rather remember the house as it used to be."

"Yeah, it's different now."

Anna summoned up a little bit of enthusiasm and said, "Marjorie and her husband are coming to Toronto."

"It'll be nice to see the Coopers again. What about Edward?"

"He's in South Africa, or was it South America? Anyway, I called Marjorie and she wanted to come to the airport."

"We could wait."

"Call me selfish, but I need to be alone with you."

Marika looked at her mother's tired face. "You just got off the plane. Can you handle going back right away?"

"I'll need a couple of rum and cokes." Attila's favourite drink. Tears began to stream down Anna's face. "I miss that smoking, boozing, infuriating..." She paused to wipe the tears. "I miss my husband."

"And I miss my dad."

"We have a funeral to attend."

Marika dabbed her wet bloodshot eyes. "You waited for me?"

"Your father loved you very much." Anna draped an arm around her daughter's shoulder. "If you're not at his funeral, we'll regret it for the rest of our lives."

CPSIA information can be obtained
at www.ICGtesting.com
Printed in the USA
LVHW03s0518290618
582135LV00001B/2/P